GRAVEMINDER

ALSO BY MELISSA MARR

Wicked Lovely

Ink Exchange

Fragile Eternity

Radiant Shadows

Darkest Mercy

GRAVE

MINDER

Melissa Marr

WILLIAM MORROW
An Imprint of HarperCollinsPublishers

GRAVEMINDER. Copyright © 2011 by Melissa Marr. All rights reserved. Printed in the United States of America. No part of this book may be used or reproduced in any manner whatsoever without written permission except in the case of brief quotations embodied in critical articles and reviews. For information address HarperCollins Publishers, 10 East 53rd Street, New York, NY 10022.

HarperCollins books may be purchased for educational, business, or sales promotional use. For information please write: Special Markets Department, HarperCollins Publishers, 10 East 53rd Street, New York, NY 10022.

FIRST EDITION

Designed by Jamie Lynn Kerner

Library of Congress Cataloging-in-Publication Data

Marr, Melissa.
  Graveminder / Melissa Marr. — 1st ed.
    p. cm.
  ISBN 978-0-06-182687-0 (hardcover)
  ISBN 978-0-06-208381-4 (international edition)
  1. Dead—Fiction. 2. Grandmothers—Death—Fiction. 3. Granddaughters—Fiction. 4. Homecoming—Fiction. 5. Family secrets—Fiction. 6. Supernatural—Fiction. I. Title.
  PS3613.A76872G73 2011
  813'.6—dc22

                              2010037261

11 12 13 14 15   OV/RRD   10 9 8 7 6 5 4 3 2 1

*To Dr. Charles J. Marr, teacher and poet, uncle and inspiration,
thank you for years of conversation, letters, and encouragement
for my lit-love. I love you, Uncle C.*

ACKNOWLEDGMENTS

I AM GRATEFUL TO MY DYNAMIC PUBLISHERS, Lisa Gallagher (yes, the bar is named for you) for acquiring the book and Liate Stehlik for support along the way; to my lovely agents, Merrilee Heifetz and Sally Wilcox, for crazy enthusiasm when I was drowning in doubt; and to my editors, Jennifer Brehl for early insights (especially on Charlie's attire and the tavern) and Kate Nintzel for kick-ass editorial notes, unflagging energy, and an amazing attitude.

I couldn't have written this book without the aid of "Undertaker Todd" (W. Todd Harra), who answered my incessant questions about the "dismal trade," let me read his collection of mortuary stories, and read *Graveminder* to assure that I had the details and terminology right. Thank you for everything. (Note: Any craft-related errors are obviously mine. Todd did a great job educating me, but I'm sure I'm not always the best student.)

Along with Todd, I had a slew of great friends who read the text, listened to my rambling, and otherwise held my hand along the trip. Thank you to all of you, especially Jennifer Barnes, Mark Del Franco, Rachael Morgan, and Jeaniene Frost.

Thanks to Stephanie Kuehnert for "lending" your awesome hair barrettes to Amity.

Thanks, Mum and Dad, for helping with gun shopping for Alicia (in this and the short story) and for the usual unflagging faith. You really are the best parents a person could hope to have.

And, as always, the largest debt of gratitude is to my spouse, Loch, and our ridiculously patient children. Thank you for not sealing me in the office when I was in the crazier parts of the revisions. I'm sure that took serious effort some days.

PROLOGUE

MAYLENE PUT ONE HAND ATOP THE STONE for support; pulling herself up from the soil got harder every year. Her knees had been problem enough, but of late the arthritis had started settling in her hips. She brushed the soil from her hands and from her skirt and pulled a small bottle from her pocket. Carefully avoiding the green shoots of the tulip bulbs she'd planted, Maylene tilted the bottle over the earth.

"Here you go, dear," she whispered. "It's not the shine we used to sip, but it's what I have to share."

She stroked the top of the stone. No grass clippings had collected there; no spider silk stretched from the top. She was careful of the smallest detail.

"Do you remember those days? Back porch, sunshine, and mason jars"—she paused at the remembered sweetness—"we were so foolish then . . . thinking there was a big ol' world out there to conquer."

Pete, for his part, wasn't likely to reply: those who were properly buried and minded didn't speak.

She made the rest of her rounds through Sweet Rest Cemetery, stopping to clean debris from stones, pour a bit of drink onto the ground, and say her words. Sweet Rest was the last of the cemeteries on the week's schedule, but she didn't shortchange the residents.

For a small town, Claysville had a high number of graveyards and cemeteries. By law, everyone ever born within town limits had to be buried here; consequently, the town had more deceased residents than living ones. Maylene wondered sometimes what would happen if the living knew of the bargain the town founders had made, but every time she'd broached the topic with Charles, she'd been rebuffed. Some battles weren't ones she could win—no matter how much she wanted them.

Or how much damn sense they make.

She glanced at the darkening sky. It was past time to be back home. She did her duty well enough that there hadn't been visitors in almost a full decade, but she still went home by sundown. A lifetime of habit didn't wane even when it seemed like it should.

Or not.

Maylene had only just tucked her flask into her front dress pocket when she saw the girl. She was too thin, concave stomach showing under her ripped T-shirt. Her feet were bare, and her jeans had holes in the knees. A smudge of dirt outlined her left cheek like badly applied rouge. Eyeliner was smudged under her eyes like she'd fallen asleep with her makeup still on. The girl walked through the well-manicured cemetery, not staying on the paths, but crossing through the grass until she stood in front of one of the older family mausoleums beside Maylene.

"I wasn't expecting you," Maylene murmured.

The girl's arms jutted out at awkward angles, not quite hands-on-hips-belligerent but not relaxed either, as if they weren't all the way under the girl's control. "I came to find you."

"I didn't know. If I'd known . . ."

"It doesn't matter now." The girl's attention was unwavering. "This is where *you* are."

"It is, at that." Maylene busied herself gathering up her gardening shears and watering can. She'd finished with the scrub brushes and already piled up most of her supplies. The bottles clinked as she tossed the watering can into her wheelbarrow.

The girl looked sad. Her soil-dark eyes were clouded over by tears that she hadn't been able to shed. "I came to find you."

"I couldn't have known." Maylene reached out and plucked a leaf from the girl's hair.

"Doesn't matter." She lifted a dirty hand, fingernails flashing chipped red polish, but she didn't seem to know what to do with her outstretched fingers. Little-girl fears warred with teen bravado in her expression. Bravado won. "I'm here now."

"All right, then." Maylene walked down the path toward one of the gates. She pulled the old key from her handbag, twisted it in the lock, and pushed open the gate. It creaked just a bit. *Might want to mention that to Liam*, she reminded herself. *He never can remember without a nagging.*

"Do you have pizza?" The girl's voice was soft in the air. "And chocolate drink? I like those chocolate drinks."

"I'm sure I have something I can fix." Maylene heard her own voice quiver. She was getting too old for surprises. Finding the girl here—*in this state*—was a few steps past a surprise. She shouldn't be here. Her parents shouldn't have let her roam; someone should have contacted Maylene before it got to this point. There were laws in Claysville.

Laws kept in place for just this reason.

They stepped through the gate onto the sidewalk. Outside the boundaries of Sweet Rest, the world wasn't nearly so tidy. The sidewalk had cracked, and from within those gaps spindly weeds were sprouting.

"Step on a crack, break your mama's back," the girl whispered, and then stomped her bare foot on the broken cement. She smiled at Maylene and added, "The bigger the crack, the worse it'll hurt her."

"That part doesn't rhyme," Maylene pointed out.

"It doesn't, does it?" She tilted her head for a moment and then said, "The bigger the *break*, the worse the *ache*. That works."

She swung her arms loosely as they walked, out of time with their steps, out of normal rhythm. Her steps were steady, but the pattern was erratic. Her feet came down on the sidewalk with such force that the broken cement tore at her bare feet.

Silently, Maylene pushed her wheelbarrow down the sidewalk until they came to the end of her driveway. She stopped, and with one hand, she pulled her flask out of her pocket and emptied it; with the other hand, she reached inside the postbox. In the back—folded up, stamped, and addressed—was an envelope. Her fingers trembled, but Maylene sealed the flask inside the envelope, slipped it inside the box, and raised the red flag to signal the carrier to take away the package. If she didn't come back to retrieve it in the morning, it would go to Rebekkah. Maylene put her hand on the side of the battered box for a moment, wishing that she'd had the courage to tell Rebekkah the things she needed to know before now.

"I'm hungry, Miss Maylene," the girl urged.

"I'm sorry," Maylene whispered. "Let me get you something warm to eat. Let me—"

"It's okay. You're going to save me, Miss Maylene." The girl gave her a genuine look of happiness. "I know it. I knew that if I found you everything would be okay."

1

BYRON MONTGOMERY HADN'T BEEN INSIDE THE BARROW HOUSE IN YEARS. Once he'd gone there every day to meet his high school girlfriend, Ella, and her stepsister, Rebekkah. They'd both been gone for nearly a decade, and for the first time, he was grateful. Ella and Rebekkah's grandmother lay on the kitchen floor in a puddle of partially congealed blood. Her head was twisted at an odd angle, and her arm was torn. The blood on the floor seemed to have come mostly from that one wound. It looked like she had a handprint bruise on her upper arm, but it was hard to tell with the amount of blood around her.

"Are you okay?" Chris stepped in front of him, temporarily blocking the sight of Maylene's body. The sheriff wasn't an unnaturally large man, but like all of the McInneys, he had the sort of presence that commanded attention under any circumstances. The attitude and musculature that had once made Chris a sight to see in a good bar fight now made him the sort of sheriff that invited trust.

"What?" Byron forced himself to stare only at Chris, to avoid looking at Maylene's body.

"Are you going to be sick or something . . . because of the"—Chris gestured at the floor—"blood and all."

"No." Byron shook his head. A person couldn't be an undertaker and get squeamish at the sight—*or scent*—of death. He'd worked at funeral homes outside of Claysville for eight years before he'd given in to the insistent urge to come back home. Out there, he'd seen the results of violent deaths, of children's deaths, of lingering deaths. He'd mourned some of them, even though they were strangers to him, but he'd never been sick from it. He wasn't going to get sick now either, but it *was* harder to be distant when the dead was some-one he'd known.

"Evelyn went and got her clean clothes." Chris leaned against the kitchen counter, and Byron noted that the blood spray hadn't touched that side of the room.

"Did you already collect evidence or . . . ?" Byron halted before he'd finished the sentence. He didn't know what all needed to be done. He'd picked up more bodies than he could count, but never from a still-fresh crime scene. He wasn't a pathologist or in any way involved in forensic investigation. His job commenced afterward, not at the scene of homicide. At least, it had been like that elsewhere. Now that he was back home, things weren't what he was used to. The small town of Claysville was a different sort of place from the cities he'd roamed. He hadn't realized exactly *how* different it was until he'd gone away . . . or maybe until he'd come back.

"Did I collect evidence of *what*?" Chris glowered at him with a menace that would make a lot of folks cringe, but Byron remem-bered when the sheriff had been one of the guys—likely to go into Shelly's Stop 'n' Shop to grab them a twelve-pack when Byron wasn't quite old enough to buy it for himself.

"The crime." Byron gestured at the kitchen. Blood spatter had arced across Maylene's floor and cabinet fronts. A plate and two drinking glasses sat on the table, proof that there had been a second person at the table—or that Maylene had set out two glasses for her-self. *So she might have known her attacker.* A chair was knocked back-ward on the floor. *She'd struggled.* A loaf of bread, with several slices cut and lying beside it, sat on the counter cutting board. *She'd trusted her attacker.* The bread knife had been washed and was the lone item in a narrow wooden drying rack beside the sink. *Someone—the attacker?—had cleaned up.* As Byron tried to assign meaning to what he saw around him, he wondered if Chris simply didn't want to talk about the evidence. *Maybe he sees something I'm missing?*

The lab tech, whom Byron didn't know, stepped into the kitchen. He didn't step in the blood on the floor, but if he had, his shoes were already covered by booties. The absence of his kit seemed to indicate that the tech had already done what he needed in this room.

Or wasn't going to be doing anything.

"Here." The tech held out disposable coveralls and disposable latex gloves. "Figured you'd need help getting her out of here."

Once Byron had the coveralls and gloves on, he looked from the tech to Chris. The attempt at patience vanished; he needed to know. "Chris? That's *Maylene*, and . . . just tell me you've got something to . . . I don't know, narrow in on whoever did this or *something*."

"Drop it." Chris shook his head and pushed away from the counter. Unlike the tech, he was very careful where he stepped. He walked toward the doorway into Maylene's living room, putting himself farther from the body, and caught Byron's gaze. "Just do your job."

"Right." Byron squatted down, started to reach out, and then looked up. "Is it safe to touch her? I don't want to disturb anything if you still need to collect—"

"You can do whatever you need." Chris didn't look at Maylene as he spoke. "I can't get anything else done until you take her out of here, and it's not right her lying there like that. So . . . just do it. Take her out of here."

Byron unzipped the body bag. Then, with a silent apology to the woman he'd once expected to be part of his family, he and the tech gently moved her body into the bag. Leaving it still unzipped, Byron straightened and peeled off his now-bloody gloves.

Chris' gaze dropped to Maylene's body inside the still-open bag.

Silently, he grabbed the biohazard bag and shoved it at the tech. Then the sheriff squatted down and zipped the bag, hiding Maylene's corpse from sight. "Not right for her to be looking like that."

"And it's not right to contaminate the exterior of the pouch," Byron retorted as he dropped the gloves in the biohazard bag, removed the coveralls, and carefully put them in the bag, too.

Chris crouched down, closed his eyes, and whispered something. Then he stood. "Come on. You need to get her up out of here."

The look he spared for Byron was accusatory, and for a split moment, Byron wanted to snarl at him. It wasn't that Byron didn't feel for the dead. He *did*. He took care of them, treated them with more care than a lot of people knew in their lives, but he didn't stand and weep. He couldn't. Distance was as essential as the rest of an undertaker's tools; without it, the job was impossible.

Some deaths got to him more than others; Maylene's was one of them. She'd had an office at his family funeral home and a long-standing relationship with his father. She'd raised the only two women he'd ever loved. She was all but family—but that didn't mean he was going to grieve *here*.

Silently and carefully, Byron and Chris carried Maylene to the cot Byron had left outside the door, and then they put her in the waiting hearse.

Once the back of the hearse was closed, Chris took several breaths. Byron doubted that the sheriff had ever dealt with a murder investigation. Claysville, for all of its eccentricities, was the safest town Byron had ever known. Growing up, he hadn't realized how rare that was.

"Chris? I know some people I could call if you wanted to call in help."

The sheriff nodded, but he refused to look at Byron. "Tell your father that—" Chris' voice broke. He cleared his throat and continued, "Tell him that I'll call Cissy and the girls."

"I will," Byron assured him.

Chris took several steps away. He stopped outside the same side door where they'd exited, but he didn't look back as he said, "I suspect *someone* will need to tell Rebekkah. Cissy isn't likely to call her, and she'll be needing to come home now."

2

REBEKKAH HAD SPENT THE BETTER PART OF THE DAY OUT WALKING around the Gas Light District with a sketchpad. She didn't have any projects right now, but she wasn't feeling the inspiration to create anything on her own either. Some people worked well with daily discipline, but she'd always been more of a need-a-deadline or consumed-by-vision artist. Unfortunately, that meant that she had nowhere to direct the restless energy she'd been feeling, so she went wandering with a sketchpad and an old SLR. When neither sketching nor photography had helped, she'd come back to the apartment only to find more than a dozen missed calls from an unknown number—and no messages.

"Restless day and random calls. Hmm. What do you think, Cherub?" Rebekkah stared out the window as she ran a hand over her cat's back.

She'd only been in San Diego three months, but the itch was back. She had almost two months before Steven returned and reclaimed his apartment, but she was ready to take off now.

Today feels worse.

Nothing looked quite right, felt quite right. The bright blue California sky seemed pale; the cranberry bread she'd grabbed at the bakery across the street was flavorless. Her typical edginess didn't

usually result in blunted senses, but today everything seemed somehow dulled.

"Maybe I'm sick. What do you think?"

The tabby cat on the windowsill flicked her tail.

The downstairs buzzer sounded, and Rebekkah glanced down at
the street. The delivery driver was already headed back in his truck.

"Occasionally, it would be nice if deliveries were actually *delivered* rather than left behind to be trampled or wet or taken," Rebekkah grumbled as she went down the two flights of stairs to the
entryway.

Outside the front door on the step on the building was a brown
envelope addressed in Maylene's spidery handwriting. Rebekkah
picked it up—and just about dropped it as she felt the contours of
what was inside.

"No." She tore the package open. The top of the envelope fluttered to the ground, landing by a bird-of-paradise plant beside the
door. Her grandmother Maylene's silver flask was nestled inside
the thick envelope. A white handkerchief with delicate tatting was
wrapped around it.

"No," she repeated.

Rebekkah stumbled as she ran back up the stairs. She slammed
open the door to the apartment, grabbed her mobile, and called her
grandmother.

"Where are you?" Rebekkah whispered as the ringing on the
other end continued. "Answer the phone. Come on. Come on. Answer."

Over and over, she dialed both of Maylene's numbers, but there
was no answer at the house phone or the mobile phone that Rebekkah had insisted her grandmother carry.

Rebekkah clutched the flask in her hand. It hadn't ever been out
of Maylene's possession for as long as Rebekkah had known her.
When Maylene left the house, it was in her handbag. In the garden,

it was in one of the deep pockets of her apron. At home, it sat on the kitchen counter or the nightstand. And at every funeral Rebekkah had attended with her grandmother, the flask was there.

Rebekkah stepped into the darkened room. She'd known Ella was laid out, but the wake didn't officially start for another hour. She pulled the door shut as carefully as she could, trying to keep silent. She walked to the end of the room. Tears ran down her cheeks, dripped onto her dress.

"It's okay to cry, Beks."

Rebekkah looked around the darkened room; her gaze darted over chairs and flower arrangements until she found her grandmother sitting in a big chair along the side of the room. "Maylene . . . I didn't . . . I thought I was alone with"—she looked at Ella—"with . . . I thought she was the only one here."

"She's not here at all." Maylene didn't turn her attention to Rebekkah or come out of the chair. She stayed in the shadows staring at her blood-family, at Ella.

"She shouldn't have done it." Rebekkah hated Ella a bit just then. She couldn't tell anyone, but she did. Her suicide made everyone cry; it made everything wrong. Rebekkah's mother, Julia, had come unhinged—searching Rebekkah's room for drugs, reading her journal, clutching her too tight. Jimmy, her stepdad, had started drinking the day they found Ella, and as far as Rebekkah could see, he hadn't stopped yet.

Maylene's voice was a whisper in the dark: "Come here."

Rebekkah went over and let Maylene pull her into a rose-scented embrace. Maylene stroked her hair and whispered soft words in a language Rebekkah didn't know, and Rebekkah wept all the tears she'd been holding on to.

When she stopped, Maylene opened up her giant handbag and pulled out a silver flask that was etched with roses and vines that twisted into initials, A.B.

"Bitter medicine." Maylene tipped it back and swallowed. Then she held it out.

Rebekkah accepted the flask with a shaky snot-and-tear-wet hand. She took a small sip and coughed as a burn spread from her throat to her stomach.

"You're not blood, but you're mine the same as she was." Maylene stood up and took the flask back. "More so, now."

She held up the flask like she was making a toast and said, "From my lips to your ears, you old bastard." She squeezed Rebekkah's hand as she swallowed the whiskey. "She's been well loved and will be still."

Then she looked at Rebekkah and held the flask out.

Silently, Rebekkah took a second sip.

"If anything happens to me, you mind her grave and mine the first three months. Just like when you go with me, you take care of the graves." Maylene looked fierce. Her grip on Rebekkah's hand tightened. "Promise me."

"I promise." Rebekkah's heartbeat sped. "Are you sick?"

"No, but I'm an old lady." She let go of Rebekkah's hand and reached down to touch Ella. "I thought you and Ella Mae would . . ." Maylene shook her head. "I need you, Rebekkah."

Rebekkah shivered. "Okay."

"Three sips for safety. No more. No less." Maylene held out the silver flask for the third time. "Three on your lips at the burial. Three at the soil for three months. You hear?"

Rebekkah nodded and took her third sip of the stuff.

Maylene leaned down to kiss Ella's forehead. "You sleep now. You hear me?" she whispered. "Sleep well, baby girl, and stay where I put you."

Rebekkah was still clutching the phone when it rang. She looked at the readout: it was Maylene's area code, but not either of her numbers. "Maylene?"

A man said, "Rebekkah Barrow?"

"Yes."

"Rebekkah, I need you to sit down," he said. "Are you sitting?"

"Sure," she lied. Her palms were sweating. "Mr. Montgomery? Is this . . ." Her words faded.

"It is. I'm so sorry, Rebekkah. Maylene is—"

"No," Rebekkah interrupted. "No!"

She slid down the wall as the world slipped out of focus, collapsed to the floor as her fears were confirmed, closed her eyes as her chest filled with a pain she hadn't felt in a very long time.

"I'm so sorry." William's voice gentled even more. "We've been trying to call all day, but the number we had for you was wrong."

"We?" Rebekkah stopped herself before she asked about Byron; she could handle a crisis without him at her side. He hadn't been at her side for years, and she was just fine. *Liar.* Rebekkah felt the numbness, the need-to-cry-scream-choke grief that she couldn't touch yet. She heard the whispered questions she'd wondered when Ella died. *How could she not tell me? Why didn't she call? Why didn't she reach for me? Why wasn't I there?*

"Rebekkah?"

"I'm here. Sorry . . . I just . . ."

"I know." William paused, and then reminded her, "Maylene *must* be interred within the next thirty-six hours. You need to come home tonight. Now."

"I . . . she . . ." There weren't words, not truly. The Claysville tendency to adopt green burial procedures, those that relied on the lack of embalming, unsettled her. She didn't want her grandmother to return to the soil: she wanted her to be alive.

Maylene is dead.

Just like Ella.

Just like Jimmy.

Rebekkah clutched the phone tightly enough that the edges creased her hand. "No one called . . . the hospital. No one called me. I would've been there if they called."

"I'm calling now. You need to come home now," he said.

"I can't get there that quickly. The wake . . . I can't be there *today.*"

"The funeral is tomorrow. Catch a red-eye."

She thought about it, the things she'd need to do. *Get Cherub's carrier. Trash. Empty the trash. Water the ivy. Do I have anything respectable to wear?* There were a dozen things to do. *Focus on those. Focus on the tasks. Call the airline.*

"Thank you. For taking care of her, I mean. I'm glad . . . not glad"—she stopped herself. "Actually, I'd really rather you hadn't called, but that wouldn't make her alive, would it?"

"No," he said softly.

The enormity of Maylene's being gone felt too huge then, like stones in Rebekkah's lungs, making it hard to move, taking up the space where air should be. She closed her eyes again and asked, "Did she . . . was she sick long? I didn't know. I was there at Christmas, but she never said anything. She seemed fine. If I'd known . . . I . . . I would've been there. I didn't know until you called."

He paused a beat too long before replying. "Call the airline, Rebekkah. Book a flight home. Questions can wait till you get here."

3

WILLIAM SLID HIS PHONE ACROSS THE DESK, FARTHER OUT OF REACH. "She's on her way. You could've called her; you probably should have."

"No." Byron sat beside his father's desk and stared at the page of crossed-out numbers for Rebekkah. Some were in Maylene's handwriting; others were in Rebekkah's. She was even worse than he'd been. *That doesn't mean I need to go running to her side.* He wasn't going to be cruel to her—*couldn't*—but he wasn't going to chase after her hoping for another kick in the face.

"Julia won't come with her. Even for this, she won't return to Claysville." William looked directly at Byron. "Rebekkah will need you."

He met his father's gaze. "And despite everything, I'll be here. You know that, and so does Rebekkah."

William nodded. "You're a good man."

At that, Byron's gaze dropped. He didn't feel like a good man; he felt tired of trying to live a life without Rebekkah—and utterly unable to live a life with her. *Because she can't let go of the past.* Byron's desire to be there for Rebekkah warred with the memories of the last time they'd spoken. They'd stood in the street outside a bar in Chicago, and Rebekkah had made it very clear that she didn't want him in her life. *Never, B. Don't you get it? I'm* never *going to be that girl, not for you or anyone else,* she'd half sobbed, half shouted, *especially not for you.* He'd known when he woke the next morning she'd be gone again; she'd vanished while he slept enough times that he was always a little surprised if she was actually there in the morning.

William pushed away from his desk. Briefly he clasped Byron's shoulder, and then walked to the door.

Maybe it was only to avoid the topic Byron didn't want to think about, but it was still a truth they needed to address. Byron started, "Rebekkah only lived here for a few years, and she hasn't lived here for *nine* years." He paused and waited then until his father looked at him before finishing: "She'll have questions, too."

William didn't cow easily, though. He merely nodded and said, "I know. Rebekkah will be told what she needs to know *when* she needs to know it. Maylene was very clear in how to handle matters. She had everything in order."

"And Maylene's planning . . . is that all in her nonexistent file? I looked, you know. The woman had an office here, but there's no paperwork on her. No plot. No prepaid anything. Nothing." Byron kept his voice even, but the frustration he'd felt for years over the unanswered questions seemed ready to bubble over. "One of these days, you're going to have to stop keeping secrets if I'm ever to be a real partner in the funeral home."

"All you need to know today is that Maylene didn't need a file. The Barrow woman pays no fees, Byron. There are traditions in Claysville." William turned and walked away, his departing footsteps muffled by the soft gray carpet that lined the hallways.

"Right," Byron muttered. "Traditions."

That excuse had worn thin long before Byron left Claysville the day after graduation from high school, and it hadn't gotten any more palatable in the eight years since. If anything, the frustration of these answerless discussions grew more pressing. The traditions here were more than small-town peculiarities: there was something different about Claysville, and Byron was certain his father knew what it was.

Normal towns don't lure you back.

Most people never moved away. They were born, lived, and died in the town limits. Byron hadn't realized how securely he was rooted in Claysville until he'd gotten out—and instantly felt the need to come back. He'd thought it would lessen, but the need to return home grew worse rather than better over time. Five months ago—after eight years of resisting it and not being able to ever assuage the need—he'd given in.

During those years away, he'd tried to stay in small towns, telling himself that maybe he wasn't cut out for city living. Then he'd tell himself it was the *wrong* town, *wrong* city. He'd tried towns so small that they were specks of dust, and larger ones, and then more cities. He'd tried living in Nashville, in Chicago, in Portland, in Phoenix, in Miami. He'd lied to himself, blaming each move on the weather, on the pollution, on the wrong culture or the wrong relationship or the wrong funeral home. *On everything but the truth.* In eight years, he'd lived in thirteen places—although, admittedly, a few of them were only for a couple of months—and he couldn't stop thinking the next move should be home every single time. The moment he crossed over the town line, every bit of wanderlust he'd been unable to sate dissipated; the vise that had tightened across his chest little by little over the years had suddenly vanished.

Will Bek feel the same way?

She had only lived in Claysville for a few years; she'd moved there with her mother at the start of high school, and they were gone before graduation. Somehow those three years were the ones that set the events for the last nine years of his life. Ella died, Rebekkah left, and Byron spent the next nine years missing them both.

Byron heard his father's voice in their office manager's office.

He listened to William ask about the preparations for the wake and burial. After William was sure all was in order, he would go down to the preparation room to visit Maylene. She had been bathed and dressed; her hair and makeup made her look more lifelike. However, as was traditional in Claysville, she had not been embalmed. Her body would be returned to the earth with no toxins other than the lingering traces of those she'd ingested over the years.

Tradition.

That was the only answer he'd ever been offered to this and myriad other questions. There were times he'd thought the very word was nothing more than a convenient excuse, a way to say "this is not a point we will discuss," but the truth was that, as far as Byron could tell, most of the town saw no need to alter tradition. It wasn't as simple as a generational dispute: everyone seemed confused when he questioned town traditions.

Byron pushed his chair back with a *thunk* and went after his father, catching the older man at the top of the staircase leading down to the prep and storage rooms. "Dad, I'm going to head out, go over to the Barrow house to look around. Unless you need me . . ."

"I always need you." The wrinkles in William's face were divided between laugh and worry lines, but call them what one would, they still reminded Byron that his father was growing old. He'd been almost fifty when Byron had been born, so while most of his friends were minding grandchildren, William had been a first-time father. More than a few of his friends—like Maylene—were now gone; although, unlike her, all of them had died of natural causes.

Byron softened his tone. "Here. Do you need anything from me *here*?"

"I'm sorry I can't tell you all the answers you want right now, but"—William's grip on the doorknob tightened slightly—"there are rules."

"I came home," Byron said. "I'm here for you."

William nodded. "I know."

"You knew I would."

It wasn't a question, not truly, but William answered it all the same. "I did. Claysville is where we belong, Byron. It's a good town. Safe. You can raise a family here, and you can know that you and yours will be protected from the world beyond."

"Protected?" Byron echoed. "Maylene was just murdered."

William's already age-worn features looked years older for a moment. "She shouldn't have been. If I'd known, if she'd known . . ." The elder Mr. Montgomery blinked away obvious tears. "Things like that don't happen here often, Byron. It's a safe place . . . unlike anywhere else out there. You've been out there. You know."

"You talk like it's another world outside Claysville."

William's sigh said what he didn't: he was as frustrated by their circular conversations as Byron was. "Give me a couple more days, and you'll have your answers. I wish . . . I wish you didn't ask so many questions, Byron."

"You know what would help with that? Answers." Byron closed his eyes for a moment before looking at his father and saying, "I need air."

William nodded and turned away—but not quickly enough for Byron to miss his look of regret. He opened the door and vanished inside, pulling it closed with a soft *snick*.

Byron turned and walked out the side door of the funeral home. His Triumph was parked behind the house just under a big willow. From the back, the funeral home looked like most of the other homes in the neighborhood. The yard was fenced in by faded wooden pickets, and a long covered porch had two rockers and a swing. Azaleas, an herb garden, and flower beds—carefully planned and replanned by his mother for years—still flourished now as they had when she was still alive. The oaks and willow looked just as they had in his childhood, shading the yard and part of the porch. The normalcy of it didn't hint that the dead were cared for inside the building.

Gravel crunched under his boots as he walked the bike forward a few yards. Old habits were hard to escape even now, and the roar of motorcycles outside the kitchen window had always bothered his mother. He shook his head. Sometimes he wished she would walk out the door to give him hell for tracking mud on the floor or spitting gravel when he left, pissed off at his father again, but the dead don't come back.

As a boy, he used to think they did. He'd sworn he'd seen Lily English sitting out on the porch one night, but his father had shushed him and sent him back to bed while his mother sat at the kitchen table and wept. Later that week, she'd torn out the entire flower bed and replanted it, and Byron suspected that his imagination and nightmares weren't the only upsets resulting from living too near the dead. His parents didn't argue often, but he'd have to have been clueless to miss the tension between them over the years. They'd loved each other, but being the undertaker's wife wore on his mother.

Byron eased out into the scant traffic and opened the throttle. The wind slammed into him like he was hitting a wall. The vibrations of the engine and twists of the road allowed him to slip into a Zen-like state of simply being. When he rode, there were no thoughts—not about Lily English, or his mother, or Rebekkah.

Well, maybe still Rebekkah.

But he could outrun that, too. He might not be able to run from Claysville, but he could run from memories for a little while. He sped up, topping out the speedometer and whipping around curves fast enough that he needed to tilt dangerously close to the pavement. It wasn't freedom, but it was the closest thing to it that he'd found.

4

WILLIAM STOOD IN THE QUIET OF THE PREPARATION ROOM. MAYLENE WAS silent on the table in front of him. She was gone. He knew that. The body wasn't her, wasn't the woman he'd loved for most of his life.

"Even now, I want to ask your opinion. I hate taking the next step without you." He stood beside the cold steel table where they'd stood together over the years more times than he could rightly count.

"Do you ever regret it?" She didn't look up as she asked the question. Her hand rested on her son's chest. Jimmy hadn't coped well with the loss of his family. Unlike his parents, he was made of softer stuff. Maylene and James were strong-willed. They had to be in order to raise a family and make a life.

"No, not what we do."

Maylene lifted her gaze from her son. "You regret what we didn't do?"

"Mae . . . you know that's not a conversation that's going to help either one of us." He put his arm around her shoulders. "We were who we were when we got called. You were already spoken for. I found Annie. I loved her. Still do."

"Sometimes I wonder . . . if I hadn't tried to build a life so different from what we could've had—"

"Don't. You and James had a good life; Annie and I did, too." He didn't pull Maylene closer. After several decades as her partner, he knew to wait until she was ready to be comforted.

"My husband's dead, my granddaughter's dead, now my son." The tears slipped over the lines in her face. "My Cissy and both my blood-granddaughters are angry at the world. Beks isn't Jimmy's daughter by blood, but she's family now. She's mine. She's all I've got left."

"And me. I'm with you till the end," he reminded her as he had so many times before.

Maylene turned away from her son's body and let William fold her into his embrace. "I can't have her hate me, Liam. I can't. She can't know yet. She wasn't even born here."

"Mae, we're getting too old to keep this up. The kids are more than old enough—"

"No." She pushed away. "I've got one daughter who hates me, two granddaughters who can't handle being this, and Beks. She's only lived in Claysville a few years. I'm going to let her go for now. Byron wants to stay away from here, live a little. You know he does. Let them both have some time away."

And William did what he'd always done when Maylene needed anything: he agreed. "A few more years."

Now he was standing in the same spot—only this time they had no more choices. Byron needed to know; Rebekkah needed to know. In the years since Jimmy's death, William had suggested it often enough, but Maylene had refused every time.

"No more choices, Mae." He looked down at her lifeless body. "I wish I could protect them longer. I wish I could've protected you."

That was the crux of it, though: he hadn't. After half a lifetime of being by her side, they'd both gotten complacent. She'd handled so much that he'd almost forgotten what could happen.

Almost.

Every month the chance was there, and until he introduced his son to Mr. D, the town was unprotected. He loathed what Byron and Rebekkah were being asked to handle, but it was past time.

"They're strong enough." William brushed his fingers over Maylene's cheek. "And she'll forgive you, Mae, just as we forgave those before us."

5

WHEN BYRON PULLED INTO MAYLENE'S DRIVE AND SHUT OFF THE ENGINE, he wasn't surprised to see Chris leaning against his patrol car. He'd seen the sheriff in traffic an hour earlier and wondered at the time if he was going to get a ticket or just a lecture.

"Your mama would have your ass the way you were driving." Chris had his arms folded over his chest. "You know that."

Byron pulled off his helmet. "She would at that."

"You trying to get arrested?" Chris scowled.

"No." Byron got off the bike.

"Killed?"

"No, not that either. Just needed to relax. *You* ought to understand that," Byron said lightly. "I watched you crash enough times in high school."

"Well, I got some sense . . . and kids to look after now. You got a pass on a ticket today, but don't think my looking the other way will be a regular thing." Chris shook his head and then pushed off his car. "Guess you want to go inside again?"

The simplicity of it made Byron pause. The law was relative in Claysville. Chris and the town council were the first and last step for all legal matters—and sometimes for social ones, too. If they had been anywhere else Byron had lived, he wouldn't have been able to just walk into a dead woman's house; if they had been in a proper city, he couldn't expect the police to open a door for his curiosity. Here, if Chris said he could go in, that was as good as having a warrant.

Byron shrugged off his jacket and laid it over the seat. "Tell me you collected evidence that makes *some* sort of sense of this."

Chris had gone up Maylene's walk, but he paused and looked back at Byron with challenge clear in his posture—shoulders back, chin up, and lips curved in a smile that was not genuinely friendly. "Why are you being difficult? There's nothing to this, Byron." Chris waited until Byron caught up with him and then he said, "Maylene's gone, and whatever happened, it's happened and done. She died, the door was open, and something bit on her."

"You can't think that. I *saw* her. We can look for fingerprints or . . . something." Byron wasn't a detective, didn't know what clues he'd even look for—or if he'd recognize them if he saw any. "Let me call up some people I met. One of the women I knew in Atlanta was just finishing up a program in forensics. Maybe she could come here and—"

"Why?"

"*Why?*" Byron stopped midstep. "To find out who killed Maylene."

Chris gave him the same sort of inscrutable look that William always did. It was galling to see it on the face of a man he'd once partied with. "They're probably long gone. No sense chasing up the road after some vagrant. Maylene's dead and gone. It won't help anything to go asking questions. Not you or Bek."

Byron paused. He hadn't said it, but that *was* part of it: he wanted to have something to say when he faced Rebekkah. At least he'd had that when his mother died, an explanation, an answer of some sort. It hadn't made the loss any less, but it helped.

I can't protect her from this. I can't fix it . . . I can't deal with her blaming me again either.

"Just open the door." Byron motioned at the key in Chris' hand.

Chris shoved the key in the lock and pushed the door open. "Go on, then."

For the second time in twenty-four hours, Byron crossed the threshold he hadn't crossed in almost a decade. One of the last times he'd been in there was when Ella and Rebekkah had tried to sneak him in the upstairs window. The girls had shushed him and giggled; they had all tumbled together into an untidy pile, too high to do much more than that.

"She's going to need a friend more than anything. I know you've had your . . . whatever it is, but you need to be there for her." Chris stood just inside the door. The kitchen was now immaculate. No dishes waited in the drying rack. No blood remained on the floor.

"They cleaned already." Byron wasn't sure what he'd expected, but the simple fact of the situation was that any clue he might possibly have found had been wiped away with the bleach he could still smell.

"'Course they did." Chris shook his head. "Can't have Rebekkah coming back to Maylene's blood on the wall. Would you want that?"

"No, but"—Byron swept his hand around—"how are we going to find who did this if everything's all bleached and vacuumed and whatever else they did? Maylene was *killed*."

"Maybe you ought to take your concerns to the council." Chris didn't follow him any farther into the house. "If it makes you feel better to look around, go ahead. Just pull the door behind you when you're done."

Byron took a calming breath, but didn't reply.

"I'll see you at the service tomorrow . . . with Rebekkah?" In that one short phrase, Chris asked all of the questions that he wasn't verbalizing: did you reach her and is she coming and will you help her?

"Yes," Byron confirmed.

"Good." The sheriff turned and left Byron alone.

Because there is no crime scene to preserve. No sense of law or privacy or any damn thing that makes sense.

Byron walked through the house. If he knew what was normal for Maylene's house these days, it would be easier to see what was amiss. *Or if they hadn't already cleaned.* The kitchen had always seemed uncommonly large, but in an old farmhouse, that wasn't too peculiar. The pantry, on the other hand, was enough to make him wonder if every single person in Claysville was hiding some sort of eccentricity. Years ago, the girls had been adamant that they weren't ever to open the door to it, and at the time, he hadn't cared. Now he stood speechless. The room itself was the size of some of the kitchens he'd had outside of Claysville. Shelves ran from floor to ceiling, and as he looked he realized that there were runners in the floor so as to slide any of the front shelves forward and to the side. Behind these were another set of equally stocked shelves. Maylene had enough food to cook for the whole town.

He slid a shelf forward and to the left.

"Damn," he whispered. Floor to ceiling was stocked with whiskey and Scotch. Bottle upon bottle lined the shelf, all label forward, sorted by brand, five deep.

Maylene had never seemed drunk, didn't smell like the bottle, but unless she was running some sort of speakeasy, there was no way any one person could need this much liquor. If she got drunk every night, it still would've taken years to drink this much. If it had always been so, it wasn't any wonder now where Ella and Rebekkah had found their never-ending supply of liquor all those years ago.

Byron slid the next shelf over and saw the same sort of overstocked shelf, this one full of unmarked bottles of clear liquid. He took down a bottle and twisted the cap. There was no seal to break.

Moonshine?

He sniffed. It didn't have any scent.

Not shine.

He dipped a finger in the neck of the bottle and touched his finger to his tongue.

"Water?"

The town's water was tested regularly. There wasn't a thing wrong with it. The grocers didn't carry much in the way of bottled water, finding the idea of buying water foolish, and *these* bottles were clearly not from any store.

"I don't get it." Byron examined the bottle in his hand, turning it around, looking on the bottom and under the lid. The only identifying mark was a date written in black indelible marker on the bottom. *Home-bottled water, a distillery worth of whiskeys, and enough food for years of living.* Short of preparing for End of Days–style catastrophes, this didn't make sense. Maylene wasn't any more religious than the rest of Claysville, and she certainly hadn't seemed like she was planning for any sort of Armageddon.

And stockpiling food and booze doesn't explain why anyone would kill her.

Byron closed the pantry door, set the bottle of water down on the countertop, and walked upstairs. He didn't know where to send a sample for testing, but it was something.

Except bad water doesn't result in torn-up bodies.

Upstairs, everything looked perfectly in order. Even the beds were made. In the bathroom that Ella and Rebekkah once shared, someone had set out a hand towel, bath towel, washcloth, and one of those little seashell-shaped soaps. It looked homey.

The guest bedroom that was once Rebekkah's room had a quilt folded at the foot of the bed, and Maylene's bed had fresh linens on the night table as if whoever tidied up wasn't sure if changing the linens was a good idea or not. Byron wasn't sure either. His father had kept his mother's things out for months, even going so far as to spray her perfume in the air every so often. The shadow of her presence had lingered long after she was gone.

For a moment he considered sitting down, but he couldn't bring himself to do so. It was one thing to come into Rebekkah's home to look for something, some clue, some *anything* to answer the questions he knew she'd have. It was another altogether to make himself at home.

He paused in the doorway, remembering the first time Rebekkah had dealt with the death of a loved one.

Rebekkah sat on the edge of her bed. Her face was wet with tears, and her sobs were the gulping-gasping kind. He'd seen grief before; sobbing people were normal in a funeral home. Those people weren't Rebekkah, though; seeing her in pain was different.

Byron went over and pulled her into his arms.

"She's gone," Rebekkah said against his chest. "Dead, B. She's dead."

"I know." He could see Maylene watching them from the hallway. She didn't come in; instead, she nodded at him approvingly.

Rebekkah clutched his shirt in her hands, holding him to her, so he kept his arms around her until her cries faded to sniffles.

"Why?" She lifted her face and looked up at him. "Why is she dead?"

But he didn't have any more answers than she did. Ella had been acting strange the past few days. Without warning, she'd broken up with him in the morning. They'd never fought, never argued, and until that week, he'd thought she was happy.

What happened?

He'd hardly thought about anything else since she'd told him she was done with him. She hadn't been angry, just sad. He didn't tell Rebekkah any of that, not yet. In the span of a few days, he'd gone from having a girlfriend and a good friend, to being afraid he'd lose both of them because he and Rebekkah had kissed, to holding Rebekkah as they both tried to make sense of Ella's death.

Was it our fault?

"Don't leave me. Promise." Rebekkah pushed away from him, but kept her hand fisted in his shirt as she stared at him. "She left us, and now . . . She could've told us what was wrong. She could've told me anything. Why didn't she tell me?"

"I don't know, Bek."

"Promise me, Byron." Rebekkah wiped her cheeks angrily. "Promise you won't keep secrets or leave or—"

"I promise." He felt a guilty twinge at how right it felt to make that promise to Rebekkah. Her sister, his girlfriend, was dead. Byron shouldn't think of Rebekkah as anything but a friend—except that he had been thinking of her like that long before Ella had died.

And Ella had known.

"I promise," he repeated. "No secrets, no leaving you. Ever."

It was Rebekkah who had left, not quite a year later. She'd left Claysville and left him.

"How do I tell her you were killed, Maylene?" he asked the empty room.

He opened the doors to the other rooms. The third bedroom, Ella's old room, wasn't made up. The bed sat in an anonymous room that was overfilled with clutter. Maylene hadn't built a shrine to her dead granddaughter—nor had she done so with her dead son. The room that had been Jimmy's was a storage room now. In it, there were more boxes and plenty of clutter, but no bed at all. Both Ella's room and Jimmy's room looked untouched by the murderer and by the townsfolk who'd cleaned the house.

Byron went downstairs and grabbed the bottle of water. He let himself out, checked that the door was locked behind him—and then stopped.

A teenage girl sat astride his bike, kicking her foot back and forth.

"Hey!"

She cocked her head. "Yeah?"

"Off my bike." He leaped off the porch and crossed the lawn, but when he reached her, he hesitated. Grabbing hold of a girl—regardless of the reason—wasn't something to do lightly.

She hopped up so her feet were tucked under her and then sprang backward, putting the bike between them. For a moment she stared at him. Her forehead furrowed in apparent confusion. "She's dead. The woman that lives here."

"Do you know her?" Byron tried to place the girl, but he'd been back in Claysville only a few months, and he didn't recall seeing her anywhere. She didn't look like anyone he knew either, so he couldn't peg her as someone's daughter or sister.

"They stopped bringing her milk." The girl's expression turned wistful as she stared past him to the porch. "Yesterday there was milk, and today there's not. I'm hungry."

"I see." Byron took in her frayed jeans and dirty face. There weren't any homeless shelters in Claysville. He wasn't sure if there was even a foster-care system. Relatives took in those that needed taking in, and neighbors handed over whatever extra they had to the folks who lacked.

He opened his jacket and pulled out his phone. "Do you have a home? Relatives here in town? I can call someone to come for you."

"No, I'm not going anywhere. Not now," she whispered.

The skin at the back of Byron's neck prickled, but when he lifted his gaze from his phone to look at her, she was already gone.

6

C HRISTOPHER HAD DRIVEN FROM MAYLENE'S HOUSE DIRECTLY TO RABBI Wolffe's. The young rabbi was on the duty roster this week.

From what Christopher had read in books and seen on the television, he knew that Claysville was peculiar in the way they ran things. Their mayor was joined in his governance by a joint secular and spiritual town council; any resigning council members picked their own replacements—as did the mayor. Between the town proper and the outskirts there were fewer than four thousand living citizens, but under the leadership of Mayor Whittaker and the council, Claysville had next to no serious crime. Hardly anyone moved away, and those few who did always came back. It was a safe, predictable town, and to assure that it stayed that way, the town leaders had policies in place for anomalies. The sheriff had only to follow protocol.

"I hate this part." Christopher cut off his engine, but he stayed in the car for an extra minute. The rabbi was relatively new to town, so he tended to forget that there were topics that most of the town couldn't discuss. He, and the rest of the council, never got the headaches that everyone *not* on the councils got when forbidden subjects were broached.

The door to the well-kept Craftsman house opened, and the

rabbi stepped out onto the wide front porch. He'd obviously been working: a pencil was tucked behind his ear, and his shirtsleeves were rolled back. For the rabbi, book work was as distracting as the carpentry projects he had started up in town: both sorts of activities required folding up his sleeves.

Christopher got out of the car and closed the door.

"Everything in order, Sheriff?" Rabbi Wolffe called. The question wasn't said in any alarming way, but they both knew Christopher wouldn't be stopping by if things were in order.

"I thought we might talk a minute, if you have the time." Christopher made his way up the flagstone walk.

"Always." The rabbi stepped aside and motioned Christopher into the house.

"I'd just as soon stay outside, Rabbi." Christopher smiled. He liked the young rabbi, and he was glad the man had chosen to come to Claysville, but longer talks with him always made the headaches come.

"What can I do for you?"

"There are a few odd details about Mrs. Barrow's passing." Christopher kept his voice bland. "Not that I think the whole town needs to know, but I thought you might mention it to the council. Maybe one of you all could pay a visit to William."

"Is there something in particular that we should tell him?"

Christopher lifted his shoulder in a small shrug. "Suspect he knows. He's seen her body."

Rabbi Wolffe nodded. "I'll call the council to a meeting tonight, then. Do you know—"

"No. I don't know a thing," Christopher interrupted. "I don't want to either."

"Right." The rabbi's features were unreadable. "Thank you, Sheriff."

Christopher shrugged again. "Just doing my job, Rabbi."

Then he turned and got back in his car as quickly as he could. He didn't run from fights or anything like that, but he didn't want to know what he didn't need to know. Anyone who paid attention understood that there were plenty of times that avoiding questions was the best way for things to work out.

7

AFTER TAKING CARE OF ERRANDS AND GOING FOR A LONG RIDE TO CLEAR his head, Byron settled in at Gallagher's, his regular evening hideaway. Gallagher's was the best sort of tavern: wooden floor and wooden bar, pool tables and dartboards, cold beer and good liquor. Here, he could believe he was in one of any number of neighborhood bars in any town or city, and usually he could relax—both during open hours and after the bar was closed.

Not tonight.

He did all right at first, but as the night stretched on, his nerves became increasingly jangled. He looked at the clock for the third time in as many minutes; he considered going to the airport. Hell, he'd started *driving* there earlier, only to pull over and turn around again. *Twice.* As much as he wanted to see Rebekkah, he wasn't sure that being there was going to help, so he sat at the bar and told himself that being met by an undertaker—*especially me*—wasn't liable to help her mood.

"Are you drinking or just taking up a stool, Byron?" Amity smiled to ease the bite in her words. She'd been a welcome diversion since he'd been home, never demanding, never asking for more than he could offer.

"Byron?" she prompted, her tone a little less sure this time.

"Drinking." He tapped his empty glass.

After an assessing look, Amity took his glass and scooped ice into it. She was pretty, with plenty of attitude. Skeleton-hand barrettes held back pale blond hair; thick-rimmed red glasses framed dark eyes heavily made up in purples and grays. Her curves were accented by a tight black shirt decorated with a picture of a cartoon monster and the words GOT STAKES? on the front and GOT SILVER? on the back. She was four years younger than he was, so she wasn't old enough to notice when he was in high school, but in the few months he'd been home, he'd definitely been noticing her. Amity was uncomplicated, and he was able to give her exactly what Rebekkah had asked for from him: no strings, no hang-ups, no future talk.

Maybe I've changed.

Amity darted a glance at him, but didn't speak as she tipped the bottle over the glass, pouring a triple shot of Scotch.

He held out a credit card.

She set the glass on a new coaster in front of him with one hand and took his card with the other. "It'll be okay."

"What?"

She shrugged and turned to the cash register. "Things."

"Things," he repeated slowly.

She nodded but didn't look up. "Yeah. Things will be okay. You have to believe that . . . it's what we're all doing since she died."

Byron froze. Amity's words emphasized how little they actually talked. He knew very little about her life, her interests, her. "Maylene?"

"Yeah." She swiped his card and while it was printing slid the Scotch into the empty space on the shelf. "Maylene was good people."

Byron paused, took a drink, and then asked, "Did she come in here? I didn't see her around."

"She came in, but not much." Amity leaned on the counter for a moment and leveled her gaze on him. "I mostly know her through my sister. Maylene went to council meetings, and Bonnie Jean took a seat on the council last year. So . . ."

Byron looked at the clock again. Rebekkah's flight should've landed.

"Hey." A soft touch drew his attention: Amity covered his hand with hers. He glanced at it, and then his gaze flickered between her hand and her eyes.

"Things will be okay. You *need* to believe that," Amity assured him.

"Why does it seem like you know something I don't?"

"Most folks don't get to leave like you did. Sometimes a person who stays around here knows things . . . different things than those who were able to go." She squeezed his hand. "But I'm guessing you know things *I* don't."

Byron didn't pull away, but he did pause. Amity usually kept the conversation light—if they even talked at all. He took a long drink to stall.

"Relax." She laughed. "No strings, right? You think I'm changing the rules on you or something?"

He felt his tension drain away as she laughed.

"No," he lied.

"So . . . after I close . . ." She let the offer hang in the air.

Most nights he stayed until closing only if he intended to accept that offer. Tonight he couldn't. It was foolish to feel guilty, but he did. He couldn't be with Amity when Rebekkah was in town. He also couldn't say that to Amity. Instead he smiled and said, "Rain check?"

"Maybe." Amity leaned over and kissed his cheek. "Go see her."

He gripped his glass tightly, but tried to keep his expression neutral. "Who?"

Amity shook her head. *"Rebekkah."*

"Rebek—"

"You'll feel better if you make sure she's home safe." Amity slid the credit-card slip and a pen over to him.

"How did you—"

"People talk, Byron, especially about you two." Amity's expression was unchanged. "Just so you know, though, *she* doesn't talk about you ever. When you were away and she visited, Maylene introduced us and we got to know each other, but she's never *once* mentioned you."

Byron stared at the credit-card slip for a moment. He wanted to ask if Amity still talked to Rebekkah, to ask if Rebekkah knew that he and Amity . . . *Not that it matters.* He shook his head. Rebekkah had made herself perfectly clear years ago, and they hadn't spoken since that night. Byron signed the slip and shoved his copy of the receipt into his pocket.

He looked at Amity. "I didn't know you knew each other."

"You and I don't exactly talk much, Byron." She grinned.

"I'm s—"

"No, you're *not*," she said firmly. "I don't want words, Byron, especially empty ones. I want the same things you usually offer. Don't stop coming to see me just 'cause Rebekkah's home."

"Rebekkah and I . . . We're not—"

"Come see me," Amity interrupted. "But not tonight. I already told Bonnie Jean I might need a ride. Go on."

Byron stepped up to the bar, reached out, and pulled her close. He dropped a quick kiss on her cheek.

"Your aim's off." Amity tapped her lips.

He leaned in and kissed her. "Better?"

She tilted her head and gave him a look that, most nights, would've meant that they didn't make it to her place after they locked the door. "Closer. Definitely closer to better."

"Next time, Ms. Blue." He picked up his helmet.

He was at the door when she answered, "I hope so, Byron."

8

REBEKKAH STOOD AT THE BAGGAGE CAROUSEL. THE AIRPORT WAS MOSTLY empty at this hour, shops closed and gates vacant. She wasn't quite alert, despite several cups of the nastiness the airline passed off as coffee, but she was upright, awake, and moving. At this point, that was about as much of a victory as could be hoped for.

Cherub, unhappy to be in her kitty carrier, mewed plaintively.

"Just a little longer, baby," Rebekkah promised. "I'll let you out when we get . . ." The words dried up as she imagined going home and finding it empty. Tonight there would be no rose-scented embrace to make everything less bleak: Maylene was gone. The tears that Rebekkah had kept in check the past few hours slipped down her cheeks as she watched the baggage carousel. *Maylene is gone. My home is gone.* The few short years Rebekkah had lived with Maylene, and the next nine years of visiting her, had made Claysville home, but without Maylene, there was no reason to come back here.

Rebekkah leaned against the faded green wall and stared blindly while the rest of the passengers got their bags and left. Eventually hers was the only bag circling. The carousel stopped.

"Do you need help?"

Rebekkah looked up at a man in an airport uniform. She blinked.

"Is that your bag?" He pointed.

"It is." She stood up. "Thank you. I'm fine."

He stared at her, and she realized that her face was wet with tears. Hastily she wiped them away.

"Why don't you let me—"

"Thank you, but I'm fine. Really." She smiled to take the sting out of the words and walked over to heft her bag off the carousel.

Looking unconvinced, he walked away.

Rebekkah extended the handle of her bag, picked up Cherub, and headed toward the rental-car desk. *One step at a time.* A few minutes later, keys in hand, she turned away from the counter and almost dropped Cherub.

A man in a pair of jeans, boots, and a well-worn leather jacket stood in front of her. His hair was a little longer than usual, brushing his collar, but the familiar green eyes watching her warily hadn't changed.

"Byron?"

The temptation to throw herself into his arms the way she once had was overwhelming, but he kept his distance.

"It's been a while," he started, and then paused. He raked his hand through his hair and gave her a tense smile before continuing, "I know we didn't part on the best terms, but I thought I'd make sure you were settled in."

She stared at him, her Byron, here. The past few years had given him more edges, shadows where his cheeks looked too sharp and his eyes too worried, but the gestures were unchanged—so was the wariness.

I earned that.

"I didn't know you were back," she said foolishly. Her hand tightened on Cherub's carrier as they stood there in the sort of awkward silence she'd dreaded when she thought about seeing him again.

After a few moments, he held out a hand for her bag. "Let me get that."

When he reached out, she jerked her hand away quickly so as to avoid touching him.

The tightening of his expression made clear that he noticed, but he took the bag and motioned for her to precede him.

They'd gone several silent steps when he said, "I've been here for a few months now."

"I didn't know. Maylene didn't tell me." She didn't tell him that she hadn't—*wouldn't have*—asked Maylene either. Rebekkah had figured out that dealing with Byron was best done by pretending he didn't exist, that he was as dead to her as Ella. Managing that feat was a lot harder with him walking beside her. Rather than look at him, she looked at the tag on the keys in her hand, staring at them even though she knew the make and model. "The last she'd mentioned you was . . . I don't know when. I thought you lived in Nashville or somewhere down that way—not that I was checking up on you."

"I know that." He gave her a wry smile, and then took a deep breath and changed the conversation back to safer territory. "I've only been back a few months. Since late December."

"Oh." Lack of sleep and grief were apparently making her foolish because she admitted, "I was here at Christmas."

"I thought you might be, so I didn't come back until after Christmas." He walked with her to the rental-car lot. "I didn't figure either of us needed to deal with . . . any of it then, so I waited till I thought you'd be gone back to wherever you were."

She wasn't sure what to say. *This is what I wanted, what I asked of him.* Unfortunately, standing in the deserted lot, jet-lagged, grief-stricken, and lost, made her want to forget all of that. *You're the one who told him to stay out of your life*, she lectured herself as if the words would keep her good sense intact.

But as they walked, his already whiskey-deep voice broke the silence: "I told myself I'd stay out of your way, and I will if you want, but I couldn't . . . I needed to make sure you got in safely. I said I'd give you your distance, and I *have*. I will. I just want you to know I'm here if you need a friend the next few days."

Rebekkah didn't know how to reply. They had said words much like those to each other for almost a decade. *Since when Ella was still alive.* Rebekkah knew it was safer not to look at him, wiser not to let herself go there. She glanced at him and then quickly looked at the car in front of them. "It's this one."

"Pop the trunk."

She did so, and he put the bag in while she put Cherub's carrier in the backseat. Then she stood unsurely at the door.

He held out a hand, which she looked at blankly. When she didn't move, he said, "You've been up all night. You're exhausted and upset." He uncurled her fingers and gently took the keys. "Let me drive you to the house. No strings, Bek."

"Your car—"

"Bike. It's a bike, not the same one I had before but . . . Anyhow, it'll be fine here." He walked around and opened the passenger door. "Let me do this. I can't fix much of anything, but . . . It's a good hour or more to town, and . . . well, I'm *here* already. Let me be a friend tonight. After that, if you want me gone, I'll do my best to stay out of your sight."

"Thanks for meeting me and for offering to—for *being* a friend," she said, and then she got into the passenger seat before she did throw herself into his arms. He was the one person who had stood by her side during the two worst things in her life—Ella's death and Jimmy's—and now he was here, ready to help her get through a third one. Despite the times she'd stolen away in the middle of the night, the words she'd hurled at him, the calls and visits she'd ignored, he was still willing to help her keep it together.

There were a lot of things she ought to say, apologies, explanations, maybe even excuses, but she was silent as he opened the driver's-side door and got into the car—and he didn't push her. He never had.

As they left the lot, Rebekkah relaxed for the first time since she'd received the call. He was the one person left in the world who truly knew her, flaws and all. It felt both comforting and unreal to sit next to Byron. When she'd moved to Claysville during high school, he'd been Ella's boyfriend, but instead of ignoring Rebekkah, he made sure to include her—enough that she'd thought about him being more than a friend, enough that once, just once, she'd crossed that line.

Then Ella had died.

Afterward, Rebekkah had had a difficult time staying on the right side of the line, and over the years, she'd been in and out of his bed, but it always ended the same way: Byron wanted more than she could give him.

She stole a fleeting look at his ring finger, and he pretended not to notice.

"Do you need to stop anywhere?" he asked.

"No. Maybe. I'm not really sure." She took a deep breath. "I expect that the cupboards . . . that food isn't an issue."

"No." Byron tore his gaze from the dark road only long enough to glance her way. A hesitant look flickered over his shadowed face. "They haven't started bringing too many covered dishes, but there's sure to be a few in the fridge."

"Nothing changes here, does it?" she murmured.

"Not really." He made a sound that might've been a laugh. "It's like the world outside stops at the town line."

"Is your dad okay?"

"He's pretending to be." Byron paused as if weighing his words and then settled on, "You know he loved her?"

"I do."

Rebekkah rested her head against the passenger-door window. "I feel like I've come untethered. She is—*was* . . ."

When her voice faltered, he reached over and laced his fingers with hers.

"She was my rock. No matter how often I moved, how many jobs I failed at, how much I fucked up *everything*. She was my home, my whole family—not that Mom's not great, she is, but she's . . . I don't know, after Ella, then Jimmy . . . Sometimes, I don't think Mom ever recovered from losing them. Maylene believed in me. She thought I was better than I am, better than I could ever be. Her love wasn't choking, but it wasn't something I had to feel guilty asking for either." Rebekkah felt the tears well up again and blinked against blurred vision. "I feel like everything's just *gone*. They're all gone. The whole Barrow family. All I have left is Mom."

Technically, Rebekkah wasn't a Barrow: she'd taken the name as her own when her mother had married Jimmy. She kept it because it was Maylene's name, Ella's name, Jimmy's name. They were her family, not by blood, but by choice. The only Barrows left—*other than me*—were the ones who hated her: Jimmy's sister, Cissy, and her daughters.

Briefly, Rebekkah wished her mother had come with her, but she wasn't even sure where Julia was right now. Like Rebekkah, her mother had serious wanderlust. Unlike Rebekkah, Julia didn't ever return to Claysville; she hadn't even come to Jimmy's funeral. Sometimes Julia talked about him, and it was clear that she still loved him, but whatever had happened between them was enough to keep her from ever setting foot in Claysville again.

Rebekkah pulled her hand away from Byron. "I'm sorry."

"For what?"

She shrugged. "You get enough people weeping on your shoulder at work."

"Don't. Please?" His voice was harsh, but he held his hand out, palm up. "Don't use my job as an excuse."

She wanted to be stronger, to not let him in again, to not open a door that she'd need to close again in a few days, but she couldn't.

At the best of times, it was a challenge to resist the pull she felt to him, and right now was far from the best of times. She slid her hand back into his.

For the next forty minutes, he drove silently while she stared out the window and watched for Claysville to come into view. The stretch of road between the airport and the town limits was desolate. For miles, there was nothing but shadowed trees and the occasional road that seemed to lead into deeper darkness. Then, she saw it ahead of them: the sign that said WELCOME TO CLAYSVILLE. She always felt a pressure that she hadn't even realized she was carrying ease when she passed that line. She'd used to think that it was because she was going to see Maylene, but tonight, with Byron beside her, the feeling of relief was stronger than it had ever been. Before she'd even realized she'd done it, her hand tightened on his—or maybe his grip tightened first.

She pulled her hand away from his as he turned into the drive in front of Maylene's house and cut off the engine.

Silently, he got out and carried her bag and Cherub's carrier to the porch. When he started to walk back over to the car, Rebekkah opened the side door and a sob escaped her. She refused to lean on him, but for a moment, the thought of going into the house was too much. She stopped at the door, unable to cross the threshold.

Maylene isn't here.

Byron didn't touch her, and she wasn't sure if she was grateful for that or not. If he did, she'd fall apart, and some part of her needed to stay in control. Another, less stable part wanted nothing more than to crumble.

Quietly he said, "If you need to stay somewhere else, I can take you over to the Baptistes' B and B, or you can stay at my apartment and I can stay somewhere else. It's okay if you need time to get your feet under you."

"No." She took a deep breath, unlocked the door, and walked inside. Byron followed her in. Once the door was closed, she set Cherub free.

And then she just stood there. Byron waited in the doorway between the kitchen and living room, and for a moment, it was as if
time had wound backward.

She looked helplessly at him. "I don't know what to do. It seems
like I should be doing something. She's dead, B, and I don't know
what I'm to do."

"Honestly? You should get some sleep." He took a step toward
her and then stopped. Time *hadn't* wound backward: they had years
of distance and words they couldn't undo. "You're jet-lagged and in
shock. Why don't we get you settled in, and—"

"No." She walked past him and snatched an afghan from the
rocker. "I will. Just . . . I can't. Not yet . . . I'm going out front to
watch the stars. You can join me, or you can go. I'll be on the swing."

The look of surprise on Byron's face vanished before it was even
fully there, and she didn't wait to see what he decided. It was selfish
of her to want him to stay, but she wasn't going to try to convince
him. *He came to pick me up. It's not like he hates me.* She slipped off
her shoes, opened the front door, and went out to the porch that
stretched the length of the house. The weathered wood was familiar
under her feet. As always, one of boards, not quite halfway between
the door and the swing, moaned as she stepped on it.

Maybe it was foolish, but she wanted to at least pretend something was normal. Going out to watch the stars was normal, even if
Maylene's absence wasn't. She wanted—*needed*—some part of coming home to be like it always was.

Rebekkah sat down on the porch swing. The chains creaked as
she set it to swaying, and she smiled a little. *This* was right. It was
home. She wrapped the afghan around her, looked up at the flickers
of light in the sky, and whispered, "What am I going to do without
you?"

"You all right?"

The voice in the darkness drew Rebekkah's attention. A girl
of no more than seventeen—*older than Ella ever was*—stood on the

front lawn. Her features were drawn tight with tension, and her posture was wary.

"No, not so much." Rebekkah looked past her, seeking the girl's friends, but she seemed to be alone.

"You're Maylene's kin, right? The one not from here?"

Rebekkah put her feet down, stopping the movement of the swing. "Do I know you?"

"Nope."

"So . . . you knew my grandmother, then? She's gone. Died."

"I know." The girl stepped forward. Her gait was awkward, like she was trying to force herself to move slower than was natural. "I wanted to come here."

"By yourself? At three-thirty in the morning? Things must have changed if your parents let you get away with that." Rebekkah felt a ghost of a smile on her lips. "I thought curfew was still at sunset unless you were with a group."

The screen door slapped shut with a sharp crack as Byron came outside. His expression was cast in shadows, but she didn't need to see his face to know he was tense. His tone told her everything as he said, "Do you need us to call someone for you?"

"No." The girl stepped backward, away from the porch and deeper into the darkness.

Byron stepped to the edge of the porch, positioning himself in front of Rebekkah. "I'm not sure what you're looking for here, but . . ."

The girl turned and vanished, disappearing so suddenly that if Rebekkah didn't know better she'd think the girl had been a hallucination.

"She's just *gone*." Rebekkah shivered. "Do you think she'll be all right?"

"Why wouldn't she?" Byron didn't turn to face her; instead, he stood staring out into the darkness where the girl had disappeared.

Rebekkah pulled her afghan tighter around her. "Byron? Should we go after her? Do you know her? I felt like . . . I don't know. Should we call Chris or her family or—"

"No." He looked over his shoulder at her. "We were out after hours half the time when we were her age."

"Not alone."

"Yes, we were." Byron laughed, but it sounded forced. "How many times did I walk you two home and then haul ass to get back before Dad caught me out alone after curfew?"

In a guilty flash, Rebekkah remembered running inside so she didn't have to see him kissing Ella good night. She forced herself to hold his gaze. "Maybe I was braver then." She paused, frowned, and stared past him into the darkness. "God, listen to me. I'm not even back a day, and I'm worrying about curfew. Most towns, most cities don't have sunset curfews."

"There's nowhere quite like Claysville, is there?" He came to sit on the far end of the swing.

"Between the two of us, I think we'd have found it if there was." With one foot, she pushed against the porch and set the swing to swaying again. "Do you feel the . . . I don't know . . . *click* when you come back here?"

Byron didn't pretend to misunderstand. "I do."

"I hate that feeling sometimes; it made me want to stay away *more*. But Maylene is—*was* everything. I'd see her and sometimes I could forget that Ella was . . ."

"Gone."

"Right. Gone," she whispered. "Now Maylene and Jimmy are both *gone*, too. My family is gone, so why does it still feel right coming home? It feels *right* the moment I cross that line. All those prickling feelings that I feel everywhere else I go vanish when I pass that stupid sign."

"I know." He pushed the swing again; the chains creaked from the force of it. "I don't have any answers . . . at least not the ones you want."

"Do you have other ones?"

For several moments, he was silent. Then he said, "At least one, but you never like that one when I bring it up."

9

Nicolas Whittaker wasn't the sort of man to patrol the streets; he had people who handled that, people who were out doing it while he waited in the comfort of the mayoral office. *It's the natural order of things.* He'd grown up secure in the fact that his hometown was a place where a person could grow up healthy and together. His children, when he was selected to have some, would be safe. They wouldn't move to some city and get mugged. They wouldn't have any of those childhood diseases that killed other people's children. They would be protected. The town founders had made sure of it. Only one real threat to the family he intended to have someday ever existed in Claysville— and only when the Graveminder failed to keep that threat in check.

Mayor Whittaker paced to the small mahogany bar that his father had added to the mayoral office during his tenure. The soft clink of ice in his glass seemed loud in the empty office. At this hour, his secretary was long gone. He poured himself another bourbon, absently thinking he was lucky that alcoholism didn't strike the townsfolk either.

A tap at the door was followed by the entrance of two of the councilors, Bonnie Jean and Daniel. At twenty-six, Bonnie Jean was the youngest of the council members. Her youth made her fearless in a way the other members weren't, but then again, she hadn't been on the council the last time they'd had a problem.

Now her cheeks were flushed, and her eyes were widened. "We didn't see anything, you know, *weird* while we were out."

Behind her, Daniel shook his head.

"We put out the mountain-lion flyers," Bonnie Jean added.

"Good." Nicolas smiled at her. He couldn't help himself—*or see any reason to*—she was a lovely girl, albeit not necessarily breeding material. He held up an empty glass. "Would you like a drink to warm up a bit?"

The young councilwoman flashed a smile at him, even as Daniel caught Nicolas' gaze and scowled. "It's getting late, *Mayor.*"

Nicolas arched a brow. "Well then, I'll see you later, Mr. Greeley."

"Bonnie Jean doesn't need to be walking alone with a murderer out there, sir." Daniel stepped forward so he was standing beside Bonnie Jean. "A young woman doesn't need—"

"Um, right *here,* guys." Bonnie Jean slipped her hand into her handbag and showed them a .38 gripped in her manicured hand.

"I see," Nicolas murmured. "Maybe we should be asking the lady to escort us, Daniel."

Bonnie Jean grinned. "Dan's driving, and he's more than able to handle himself. What about you, Mayor?"

With the same showmanship he relied on in meetings, Nicolas patted his trouser pockets and then opened his suit jacket. "Actually, I'm afraid I'm unarmed, my dear. Perhaps I do need an escort." He smiled at her. "Unfortunately, I'm not quite ready to leave the office. Could I impose upon you to wait?"

"You could." She turned to Daniel. "I'm perfectly able to handle whatever's out there"—she flashed Nicolas a smile—"or in here."

After a pointed look at Bonnie Jean, which she ignored, Daniel shook his head and left. She followed him to the door, kissed him on the cheek, and closed the door.

Nicolas poured Bonnie Jean a glass of Scotch and held it out to her.

10

Byron thought about the things he ought to tell Rebekkah, about the things he wanted to tell her, and the fact that none of what he had to say was what she needed to hear tonight. They sat in the dark, listening to the insects and frogs and being as careful as they always were when they were trying not to talk. Even sitting beside her made him realize that he'd lied to himself when he'd said he had changed.

Almost three years had passed since she asked him not to call her anymore. He'd tried several relationships, and then he'd told himself that he wasn't meant to fall in love. He'd pretended that—like his need to return to Claysville—his need to be with Rebekkah was something he could outrun. The difference, of course, was that when he gave in and went to Claysville, it hadn't run *from* him. Rebekkah would run by morning if she wasn't grieving. She still might.

Tonight she'd let down her defenses, though. She leaned her head on his shoulder. The adrenaline and grief that had held her upright seemed to fail her all at once. She slouched down—shoulders drooped, one hand falling limp into her lap—like a marionette with cut strings. The dim porch light hid the pallor of her skin, and the messy knot she'd twisted her hair into hid how long it was

these days. In all, though, she didn't look much different than she
had three years ago when she'd walked away from him: she was
fit enough that he figured she still ran or swam regularly. *Or both.*
Rebekkah had always buried stress with exercise and emotion with
flight. *Among other things.*

"Byron?" she said sleepily.

"I'm right here." He didn't add that he always *would* be if she
wasn't so damn difficult or that he hadn't ever pushed her away when
she wanted him there. That was Rebekkah's area of expertise, pulling him to her and then shoving him away when she realized that
she actually wanted him there. He sighed, feeling guilty contem-
plating those things when she was feeling vulnerable but knowing
full well that once she wasn't feeling lost, she'd be off and running.

"Bek?"

"I wish it was a bad dream, B," she whispered. "Why do they all
keep dying and leaving me?"

"I'm sorry," he said. Even with a lifetime of being surrounded by
the grieving he hadn't found any better answer. There wasn't one:
people died, and it hurt. No words could truly ease that ache. Byron
wrapped his arm around her shoulders and held her while tears slid
down her cheeks.

She didn't pull away, but she did turn her head to look at the
slowly lightening sky.

They sat there for several minutes watching the night end. She
had her feet curled up under her, and one hand clutched the chain
of the swing as if she were a small child afraid of falling. The afghan
was tucked around her, adding to her vulnerable appearance.

And he felt like a jackass for wanting to tell her the things that
she always tried to keep unspoken between them. The problem with
Rebekkah was that there wasn't ever a good time to talk. She only
let her walls down when she was hurt, and when she wasn't hurt she
ran—either literally or by chasing emotions away with sex. He used

to think that there would be a time when the sex wasn't an excuse to run from intimacy, but she'd disabused him of that notion the last time he'd seen her. Carefully keeping his own emotions in check, he said, "You'll sleep better in a bed than out here on the swing. Come on."

For a moment he thought she'd refuse, but instead she said, "I know."

As she stood, he wrapped the afghan around her shoulders, and she whispered, "Will you stay?"

When he frowned, she hastily added, "Not like . . . not *with* me, just in the house. It's almost dawn, and I don't want to be alone here. The guest beds are probably made up."

Instead of calling her out on the lie she was trying to sell, he opened the door. "Sure. It's probably easier. I had planned to pick you up for the service."

She stopped and kissed his cheek. "Thank you."

He nodded.

But she didn't move. One foot was on the step into the house; the other was still on the porch.

"Bek?"

Her lips parted, and she leaned toward him and said, "Tonight doesn't have to count. Right?"

He didn't pretend to misunderstand her question. "I don't know."

She pulled him to her almost desperately, and he wasn't sure whether it was a cry or an apology she whispered as she wrapped herself around him. The screen door hit him as he let go of it to hold her tighter to him. A part of him—a very insistent part—wanted to ignore her grief and the inevitable this-is-a-mistake that morning would bring. Another more responsible part knew she would be running by morning and he would be kicking himself for ending up back where they always were if he did that.

They stepped into the house, and the door snapped shut with a bang. Rebekkah pulled back. "I'm sorry; I shouldn't—" She stopped, shook her head, and all but ran up the stairs.

He followed. If he were a different sort of man, he wouldn't let things end there, or maybe if she were a different sort of person, but he knew them both well enough to know that what she was inviting him to do was take the responsibility for the choice out of her hands so later she could blame him.

Not this time.

It was difficult for either of them to have any sort of resolve where the other was concerned. They both claimed they did, but inevitably his decision not to repeat the same pattern and her insistence that they were just friends failed. Over the years, they'd avoided talking by ending up in bed, and they'd ended fights in bed, but they'd always circled back to Rebekkah's running and his deciding he was a fool for thinking this time was going to be different.

But here I am.

The difference was that this time he was standing outside her room, not in it.

At the top of the stairs, he asked, "Are you sleeping in your old room?"

She paused. "I can stay in Maylene's room, so you . . . that way you have a bed, too, or . . . I could sleep in Ella's—in the *other* room so . . . you—"

"No." He put a hand on her forearm. "You don't need to sleep in Maylene's room *or* in Ella's room. I'll sleep on the sofa."

She shook her head. "You don't need to . . . I'm okay. I mean . . . I'm *not*, but—"

"It's fine." Gently he put a hand on either side of her face and looked at her. "You need to get some sleep."

Indecision flickered in her expression, but after a moment, she nodded and went into her room. She pushed the door partway closed, but it was still open enough that he could follow. He consid-

ered it. In the past, he would've. She needed him, and he had repeatedly told himself that need was enough. With any other woman, it
was all *he* wanted.

With Amity, it is enough, but Bek is not Amity.

Resolutely Byron pulled her door shut and went back downstairs. He sat on the sofa for a minute, lowered his head to his hands,
and thought about everything that they needed to talk about, about
all the things that were a mess, about the reasons that he wasn't
going to go right back upstairs.

He couldn't sleep in Ella's old room. She had been gone a long
time, but sometimes he didn't think Rebekkah would ever truly her
let go. In death, Ella stood between them in a way she never would
have in life. That, like so many other topics, wasn't something Rebekkah was willing to discuss. Of course, there were also plenty of
topics *he* was grateful not to discuss tonight. He was dreading telling Rebekkah that Maylene was murdered—and that Chris seemed
unwilling to investigate it.

Byron thought about the homeless girl he'd seen lingering at
the house yesterday afternoon and again tonight. She was young,
a teenager, and too slight to have inflicted the injuries he'd seen on
Maylene. He wondered if she traveled with someone, maybe a man.
Byron checked the windows and doors again, but saw no sign of in-
trusion. *Probably just hungry,* he decided. She'd known that the house
was empty, and when a person has no home, finding an empty house
is surely tempting. He made a mental note to suggest that Chris talk
to the girl. Maybe she'd seen something. Even if she hadn't, letting
her wander around alone in town without resources was a sure way
to turn her into a criminal. Claysville took care of its own. Whether
she had been born here or not, she was here now, so she'd need looking after. *Which I should've thought of earlier.* Right now, he suspected
that the worst she was guilty of was theft of milk from Maylene's
porch. If she had nowhere to go, no food, and no family, there would
be more serious problems in time.

11

ONLY A FEW HOURS LATER, REBEKKAH woke after a fitful sleep in her old room. It was technically a guest room now, had been since she'd stopped spending summers there, but it was still hers. She showered, dressed, and went downstairs to find Byron rubbing his eyes.

He didn't say anything about the half-assed invitation he'd refused last night, and she didn't tell him it didn't freak her out to walk downstairs and find him waiting for her today. Instead, for a moment, neither spoke, and then he said, "I hate that you don't have time to get your feet under you, but the final viewing will have started, and if we want—"

"Let's go." She motioned to her black dress and shoes. "I'm as ready as I'll ever be. What do you need to do?"

He held up the key to her rental car. "Walk out the door."

Byron drove her to Montgomery and Sons. They pulled around back and went in the kitchen door. He must've phoned ahead because William was waiting. Over his somber suit, the older man wore a frilled apron covered in pictures of bright yellow ducks. He held a wooden spoon in one hand.

"Go on." With the spoon, he motioned at Byron and then at the stairs. "I'll look after her."

William turned to Rebekkah and gestured to the table.

She sat, and he poured her a cup of coffee. Momentarily she could hear the shower upstairs. It felt comforting to be there, like being in a real home—as long as she didn't think about the other part of the house where mourners were gathering around Maylene's body.

William set down a plate he'd just filled with scrambled eggs and bacon. "If you want to see her, you can. I know you and Maylene had your traditions, though, so we can wait till the rest of them are gone."

Rebekkah nodded. "Thank you. I'm not going to hide all day, but the . . ." She felt the tears build up again. "I'll be fine at the service. I'll handle the funeral breakfast. I can do this."

"I know you can," William said. "Can I tell the ladies that they can get the meal set up at your house?"

Rebekkah paused. *My house.* It was still Maylene's house. Calling it "hers" felt wrong, but arguing semantics wouldn't help.

William looked at her expectantly.

"Sure," she whispered. "That's the right place to have it. I just . . . They took care of everything already, didn't they?"

"Everything but bringing it into the house. They *are* efficient," William said. "They have to be with the short time between death and burial."

His words weren't cruel, nor was his tone, but it still made her chest tighten. "I just heard yesterday and then the flight and coming home and . . ."

She heard herself, listened to the excuses pouring from her lips. The truth was that she didn't want to see Maylene in her casket, still and lifeless, and she surely didn't want to do it around other people.

"And there's the jet lag," William added. "No one will fault you for not being out there. Not many folks even know you're home yet."

"Thank you. For everything. You and Byron are both being

so . . . I'd be even more lost without you." She offered him a smile, a watery one, but a smile nonetheless.

William smiled gently at her. "Montgomerys will always look after Barrows, Rebekkah. I would've done anything for Maylene, just as Byron would do anything for you."

Rebekkah didn't know what to say to that. She wondered if William thought she and Byron had stayed in touch. *Really not what I want to ponder.* She pushed that topic away and looked at the elder Mr. Montgomery's tired eyes. The dark circles under them could be normal, for all she knew, but his red-shot eyes revealed that he'd been crying. He and Maylene had been friends forever, and they'd been in love almost as long.

Rebekkah realized that she was staring at him. "Are you . . . doing okay?" she asked—and then immediately felt like an idiot. Of course he wasn't doing "okay." *If anything happened to Byr—* She shook her head as if it would erase that thought.

William patted Rebekkah's hand and turned away to refill her coffee cup. "As well as you are, I imagine. The world is lot less worth being in without her here. Maylene has meant the world to me for a long time." She heard the threat of tears in his voice as he said, "I need to go out front. You stay in here and eat. When they go, I'll come fetch you, so you have a few private moments with her."

At the thought of suddenly being alone, she blurted, "Do I need to do anything? I mean, are there papers or . . . something? Anything?"

He turned back to face her. "No, not now. Maylene's orders were very precise. She didn't want you to have to deal with those things, so we made sure everything was taken care of in advance." William brushed Rebekkah's hair back as if she were still a small child. "Byron will be down in a few moments, and if you need him you are welcome to go upstairs. The house hasn't changed. I'll be out there with Maylene."

"She's not here," Rebekkah whispered. "Just her empty shell."

"I know, but I still need to look after her. She's gone to a well-earned rest, Rebekkah. I promise." He had tears in his eyes. "She was more amazing than most anyone we'll ever meet. Strong. Good. Brave. And she saw all of those traits in you. You need to be brave now. Make her proud."

Rebekkah nodded. "I will."

Then William left her in his kitchen alone with her grief. Her first instinct was to find Byron.

Coward.

Being alone was wiser. She'd lived alone for years; she'd traveled alone. The problem was that it was easier to keep her grief at bay when she had witnesses. Maylene had taught her the importance of hiding the hard parts years ago: *Don't let the world see your soft underbelly, lovie,* she'd reminded when the barbs of strangers and classmates had hurt. *Part of being strong is knowing when to hide your weaknesses, and when to admit them. When it's just us, you can cry. In front of the world, you keep that chin up.*

"I'm strong. I remember," Rebekkah whispered.

Byron hadn't come down by the time she finished breakfast, so she walked through the door separating the private part of the house and the public space and joined the crowd of mourners, accepting their nods and hugs without a flinch as she approached Maylene's body.

I know you're gone. I know it's not really you.

But the body still looked like her grandmother. The familiar keen gaze was absent; the smile was absent; but the form was still Maylene.

Rebekkah knew what she needed to say. The flask was in her bag, but she couldn't. *Not yet. Not in front of everyone.* There were words, traditions that she'd observed with Maylene time and again. *Soon.*

Rebekkah leaned down to kiss Maylene's cheek. "Sleep now, Grandmama," she whispered. "Sleep well, and stay where I put you."

12

REBEKKAH WENT THROUGH THE MOTIONS, ACCEPTING CONDOLENCES AND listening to the reminiscences of strangers and of those vaguely familiar. She did so alone.

Byron had come down to the viewing area, now dressed in one of his dark suits. He and William both kept an eye on her, and she knew that at any time they would extricate her if she sent them a pleading glance. Instead, she gave Byron a small shake of her head when he started to approach her.

I am Maylene's granddaughter, and I will do as we have always done. Together with her grandmother, she'd gone to innumerable viewings and funerals. She politely nodded and calmly accepted hugs and arm pats. *I can do this.* She was only there for the last hour of the wake, but it felt longer than any she could recall. *Even Ella's.*

Thankfully, Cissy and her daughters had left just before Rebekkah had arrived. *Overcome by grief,* William had said with a stoic expression.

Then the viewing was over. William took charge of the mourners, and Byron came over to her side.

"Do you want a minute with her?" he asked.

"No. Not yet." Rebekkah glanced over at him. "Later. At the gravesite."

"Come on." Byron deftly avoided several people who wanted to speak with her and led her back into his home.

"I could've stayed," she murmured as he closed the door behind them.

"No one's doubting you," he assured her. "We have a few minutes before we go to the cemetery, and I thought you might want to catch a breath."

She followed him into the kitchen. Her dishes still sat on the table. "Thank you. I know I keep saying it, but you really have been better to me than I deserve."

To avoid looking at him, she busied herself rinsing her cup and plate.

"Our . . . friendship didn't die for me," he said, "even when you decided to stop returning my calls. It never will."

When she didn't reply, he came over and took the cup from her hand.

"Bek?"

She turned, and he folded her into his arms.

"You're *not* alone. Dad and I are both here," he said. "Not just last night. Not just today. But for as long as you need."

Rebekkah rested her cheek against his chest and closed her eyes for a minute. It would be so easy to let herself give in to the irrational urge to stay next to Byron. In all her life, no one else had ever made her want to stay in one place; no one she'd met since she left Claysville had made her want to think about commitments. *Only you*, she thought as she pulled away. She didn't admit that. *Not to him.* He wasn't hers. *Not really. Not ever.*

Rebekkah smiled and said, "I'm going to freshen up before we go."

She felt his gaze on her as she walked away, but he didn't say anything as she fled.

When she returned from the washroom, William and Byron stood waiting.

"She didn't want a procession. It's just us. Everyone else has gone ahead." William held out his hand. In it was the tarnished silver bell Maylene had carried with her to the graveside.

Rebekkah felt foolish for not wanting to take it. She'd stood here innumerable times when William wordlessly held that same bell out to Maylene. Slowly she wrapped her hand around it, tucking one finger inside to keep the clapper still. It was meant to be rung at the grave, not here.

She turned to Byron to escort her to the car for the graveside service, just as William had once escorted Maylene. Byron would take her where she needed to go. His presence at her side since she'd returned last night felt right, just as it had when she first moved to Claysville, just as it had when Ella died, just as it did every time she saw him.

I can't stay here. I can't stay with him. I won't.

As she clutched the bell in her hand, Rebekkah slid into the slick black interior. She put a hand out for the door, effectively blocking him from joining her. "Please, I would prefer being alone."

A flash of irritation flared in his eyes, but he said nothing about her rejection. Instead, his professional guise reappeared. "We'll meet you at the cemetery," he said.

Then he closed the door and went over to the waiting hearse.

I can get through this without him . . . and then leave.

Without Maylene, Claysville was just another town. It wasn't really home. She'd tricked herself into thinking there was something special about it, but she'd lived in enough places to know better: one town was no different from the next. Claysville had some odd rules, but none of that mattered anymore. Maylene was dead, and Rebekkah had no reason to keep returning here now.

Except for Byron.

Except that it's still home.

Rebekkah watched out the window as the hearse pulled into the street; her driver eased out behind it, following William as he drove Maylene to her final resting place.

When the driver came around and opened her door, Rebekkah could already hear the overdramatic wailing. *Cissy's here.* Ringing the bell as she walked, Rebekkah made her way across the grass to the chairs that were lined up under the awning. She reminded herself that Maylene would expect her to be on her best behavior. She'd arranged everything, no doubt hoping that easing the stress would make this moment more bearable, but even careful planning couldn't negate the headache that Cissy would inevitably cause. Maylene's daughter was contentious under the best of circumstances. Her venomous attitude toward Rebekkah had been a source of irritation to Maylene, but no one would explain to Rebekkah why the woman hated her so much. *She'll come around*, Maylene had assured her. To date, that hadn't happened; in fact, the animosity had grown to the point that Rebekkah hadn't exchanged words with Cissy in years. Her absence at the end of the viewing had been a wonderful respite, but it wasn't a kindness: it was merely a way for her to be first at the gravesite.

As Rebekkah approached the grave, she swung the bell more forcefully.

The volume of Cissy's caterwauling increased.

One hour. I can handle her for one hour. Rebekkah couldn't toss her out as she so dearly wanted to do, so she walked to the front and took her seat.

I can be polite.

That resolve lessened when Cissy approached the now-closed casket.

Lilies and roses swayed atop Maylene's casket as Cissy clutched it, her short fingernails skittering over the wood like insects running from light. "Mama, don't *go*." Cissy wrapped her fingers around a handle on the side of the casket, assuring that no one would be able to pull her away from it.

Rebekkah uncrossed her ankles.

Cissy let out another plaintive cry. The woman couldn't see a casket without wailing like a wet cat. Her daughters, Liz and Teresa, stood by uselessly. The twins, in their late twenties now, only just older than Rebekkah, had also gotten to the gravesite early, but they didn't try to calm their mother. They knew as well as Rebekkah did that Cissy was putting on a show.

Liz whispered to Teresa, who only shrugged. No one really expected them to try to convince Cissy to stop making a spectacle of herself. Some people couldn't be reasoned with, and Cecilia Barrow was very much one of those people.

Beside Maylene's casket, Father Ness put an arm around Cissy's shoulder. She shook him off. "You can't make me leave her."

Rebekkah closed her eyes. She had to stay, to say the words, to follow the traditions. The urge to do that pushed away most everything else. Even if Maylene hadn't made her swear on it enough times over the years, preparing her for this day, Rebekkah would feel it like a nagging ache drawing her attention. The tradition she'd learned at her grandmother's side was as much a part of funerals as the coffin itself. At each death they'd been together for, she and Maylene had each taken three sips—no more, no less—out of that rose flask. Each time Maylene had whispered words to the corpse. Each time she refused to answer any of the questions Rebekkah had asked.

Now it was too late.

Cissy's shrieks were overpowering the minister's attempt to speak. The Reverend McLendon was too soft-spoken for her voice to be heard. Beside the minister, the priest was trying again to console Cissy. Neither one was getting very far.

"Fuck this," Rebekkah muttered. She stood and walked toward Cissy. At the edge of the hole where they'd inter Maylene, Rebekkah stopped.

The priest looked almost as frustrated as she felt. He'd dealt with Cissy's performances often enough to know that until someone took her in hand, there wasn't a thing they could do. Maylene had handled that, too, but Maylene was gone.

Rebekkah wrapped her arms around Cissy in an embrace and—with her lips close to Cissy's ear—whispered, "Shut your mouth, and sit your ass down. *Now.*" Then she released Cissy, offered her an elbow, and added, at a normal volume this time, "Let me help you to your seat."

"No." Cissy glared at the proffered arm.

Rebekkah leaned in closer again. "Take my arm and let me help you to your seat in *silence,* or I'll tie up Maylene's estate until your daughters die bitter old bitches like you."

Cissy covered her mouth with a handkerchief. Her cheeks grew red as she looked around. To the rest of the mourners, it looked like she was embarrassed. Rebekkah knew better; she'd just poked a rattlesnake. *And I'll pay for it later.* Just then, however, Cissy let herself be escorted to her seat. The expression on Liz's face was one of relief, but neither twin looked directly at Rebekkah. Teresa took Cissy's hand, and Liz wrapped her arm around her mother. They knew their roles in their mother's melodramatic performances.

Rebekkah returned to her own seat and bowed her head. Across the aisle, Cissy kept her silence, so the only sounds beyond the prayers of the priest and the minister were the sobs of mourners and the cries of crows. Rebekkah didn't move, not when Father Ness stopped speaking, not when the casket was lowered into the earth, not until she felt a gentle touch at her wrist and heard, "Come on, Rebekkah."

Amity, one of the only people in Claysville Rebekkah kept in sort of contact with, gave her a sympathetic smile. People were standing and moving. Faces she knew and faces she had seen only in passing before turned toward her with expressions of support, of sympathy, and of some sort of hope that Rebekkah didn't understand. She stared at them all uncomprehendingly.

Amity repeated, "Let's get you out of here."

"I need to stay here." Rebekkah moistened suddenly dry lips. "I need to stay here alone."

Amity leaned closer and hugged her. "I'll see you back at your grandmother's house."

Rebekkah nodded, and Amity joined the crowd of people who were leaving. Semi-strangers and family, friends and others, they walked past the casket and dropped flowers and earth into the yawning hole. Lilies and roses rained down on Maylene's casket.

"Wasting all that beauty," Maylene whispered as they dropped flowers on another casket. "Like corpses have any need of flowers."

She turned to Rebekkah with her serious look. "What do the dead need?"

"Prayers, tea, and a little bit of whiskey," then-seventeen-year-old Rebekkah answered. "They need nourishment."

"Memories. Love. Letting go," Maylene added.

Rebekkah waved away Father Ness and Reverend McLendon as they tried to stop and comfort her. They were used to Maylene's eccentricities—and Rebekkah's staying with Maylene while she lingered with the dead. They'd leave Rebekkah alone, too.

Once everyone was gone, once the casket was covered, once it was just her and Maylene alone in the cemetery, Rebekkah opened her clutch and took out the rose-etched flask. She walked up to the grave and knelt down on the earth.

"I've been carrying it since it arrived in the mail," she told Maylene. "I did what the letter said."

It had seemed wrong to put Holy Water in with good whiskey, but Rebekkah did exactly as she'd been told. There were always plenty of bottles of Holy Water in Maylene's pantry. *Holy Water and heavenly whiskey.* She opened the flask, took a sip, and then tilted it over the grave once. Tears streamed over her cheeks as she said, "She's been well loved."

She took a second sip and then lifted the flask in a toast to the sky. "From my lips to your ears, you old bastard." Then she tilted it over the grave a second time.

"Sleep well, Maylene. Stay where I put you, you hear?" She took a third sip and then poured the flask's contents onto the earth a third time. "I'll miss you."

Then Rebekkah finally wept.

13

D AISHA STAYED OUT OF SIGHT DURING THE FUNERAL. SHE'D STOLEN A black hoodie and jeans—*and some food*—from a woman who'd been taking out her trash that morning. The woman didn't stand up after Daisha had finished eating, but her heart was still beating. *And most of her skin was still on her.* The thought of skin and blood shouldn't make Daisha's stomach growl, but it did. Afterward, the thought of it was gross, but in the moment, it was . . . exactly right.

It made her mind clearer, too. That part was important. The longer she went between meals, the less focus she had. *Less body, too.* She felt like she was being pulled and pushed in every direction all at once. Earlier she'd fallen apart, scattered like smoke in the breeze.

This morning she stood in a cemetery and watched them put Maylene in the ground. It seemed so permanent, being killed and being buried, but obviously it wasn't.

Daisha kept herself behind a tree as she watched. She'd had to come. When she'd heard the bell, her body was as pulled to this spot as it had been when she'd met Maylene there. The inability to refuse the strange compulsions, the impossibility of holding on to thoughts or memories, the hungers that filled her, everything had become wrong. Daisha wanted answers, wanted company, wanted to be *right*. Only Maylene had understood, but she was dead now.

Maybe Maylene will wake up, too.

Daisha stood waiting, but no one stepped up out of the earth. No one came to join her. She was as alone now as she'd been when she was alive for real. Daisha didn't remember crawling out of the ground. She didn't really know when she'd woken up, but she was awake. That part she knew.

She leaned her head against the tree.

The shrieking woman was carrying on something fierce, and the Undertaker was scowling at her. He had scanned the crowd and the cemetery. Every so often, his gaze had paused on the woman who had come to stay in Maylene's house.

Now *she* glowed like Maylene had. Maylene's skin seemed to be filled with moonlight, a beacon that drew Daisha even before she saw her. All Daisha had known was that there was a light, and she had to go toward it. As the new woman had poured her flask onto the soil, she had started glowing until her whole body was filled with brightness.

The rest of the mourners had left, but even if they weren't gone, Daisha couldn't walk up to them and ask. Only the Undertaker and the wailing woman waited.

Daisha started shaking, and the focus that she'd had started to fade. *She* started to fade, so she fled before her body could dissipate again.

14

A S THEY WALKED TOWARD THE CAR, LIZ HELD ON TO HER MOTHER, NOT in a protective way, but as a please-Mama-don't-make-another-scene measure. The supportive arm she offered was accepted only as long as there were people watching; once they reached the car, Cissy shook her off.

Liz pushed down her guilty relief. There was no good way to handle funerals: each and every one was a reminder of what Liz and her sister weren't.

Not good enough.

Not chosen.

Not the Graveminder.

Truth be told, Liz had no actual desire to be the Graveminder. She knew all about it, the contract, the duties, but knowing didn't make her eager to *be* a Graveminder. Her mother and sister seemed to feel that they'd been slighted, but spending life worrying about the dead didn't appeal to Liz. *At all.* She talked the talk well enough—because the alternative was feeling the back side of her mother's hand—but she wanted the same things that most women in Claysville wanted: a chance at a good man who would agree to enter the birthing queue for the right to be a parent sooner than later.

Not that Byron would be a bad man to bed.

She stole another glance at him. He was lovestruck with Rebekkah, but that was an inevitable result of the whole Graveminder-Undertaker gig. Her grandmother and Byron's father had made eyes at each other for as long as Liz could remember. *Like to like.* She shook her head. Despite everything, Maylene had been her grandmother, and she ought to be ashamed of thinking ill of her when she wasn't even cold in the ground. *And for thinking lustful thoughts at a funeral.* She shot a glance at Byron again.

"Look at him," Teresa muttered. "Can't take his attention off her. I don't think I'd have any struggle resisting him if I were . . . *you know.*"

Liz nodded, but she silently thought that she wouldn't *want* to resist Byron. "Not every Graveminder marries the Undertaker. Grandmama Maylene didn't. You wouldn't have to . . . be with him."

Teresa snorted. "It's a good thing, too. I don't know that I want a man who has fucked both our cousins."

"*She* is not your cousin." Cissy dabbed at her eyes. "Your uncle married that woman, but that doesn't make her brat your cousin. Rebekkah isn't family."

"Grandmama Maylene thought—"

"Your grandmother was wrong." Cissy held her lace-edged handkerchief so that it covered the ugly snarl that twisted her mouth.

Liz repressed a sigh. Their mother, for all of her strengths, had an old-fashioned notion of family. *Blood first.* Cissy hadn't approved of Jimmy taking a wife with a child, and she certainly hadn't approved of Rebekkah's continuing to visit a few years after that wife left him. Rebekkah had arrived during her freshman year of high school and left before graduation, yet she'd continued to visit Claysville after Jimmy and Julia divorced and then after Jimmy died. Whether or not anyone liked it, Rebekkah was as much Maylene's granddaughter as the twins were—which was the issue.

Blood-family matters, especially for a Barrow.

Unfortunately, Liz suspected that her own blood made her the next likely candidate for the very thing that both Teresa and their mother wanted, and she was torn between the desire to please her mother and the desire to have her freedom. Of course, she wasn't fool enough to admit that. *She* knew better than to call Rebekkah family; she knew better than to admit that she wouldn't mind getting to know Byron Montgomery.

With a determined look, Cissy started across the cemetery.

"She's in a mood," Teresa muttered.

"Our grandmother, her *mother*, just died." Liz wasn't sure whether following or staying out of it was wiser. Years of trying to play peacemaker in the house made her want to go after her mother, but just as many years of trying to dodge her mother's vitriol attested to the wisdom of letting someone else be the target.

"She's not crying, Liz; she's itching for a fight."

"Are we going after her?"

Teresa rolled her eyes. "Shit, I don't want to be the one she sets her sights on. You know she's going to be a bear once Rebekkah finds out that she's the Graveminder. Every council meeting will end with a tantrum then. You're welcome to go after her, but I'm staying right here." Teresa leaned on the car. "We'll get plenty of time listening to her rant after the funeral breakfast."

"Maybe—"

"Nope. If you want to go after her, you go ahead, but she's about to be face-to-face with the both of them. Grandmama Maylene isn't here to calm her down. You think you're able to?" Teresa shook her head. "I don't need to draw her temper. Neither do you. Let *them* handle her."

15

BYRON HAD BEEN SO FOCUSED ON WATCHING REBEKKAH THAT HE'D AS-sumed that all of the mourners had left. He bit back a decid-edly uncharitable remark as he saw that Cissy was marching back toward him. Behind her, the twins stood—and were apparently arguing, from the looks of it—beside the car. Liz threw her hands in the air and followed her mother. Teresa leaned on the car and watched.

Cissy had a determined look on her face, and he braced himself for her temper. However, she passed him without a glance, heading for Rebekkah.

"Cecilia!" Byron grabbed her arm. "She needs a moment."

Cissy's eyes widened; she moistened her lips. "But she needs to know. Someone ought to tell her about the . . . what happened, and I'm Maylene's family—"

"You needn't worry about it," he interrupted. He put an arm around her and steered her back toward the car. "You've had enough to deal with, Cissy. Let your girls take you on home. I'll bring Re-bekkah back to the house."

Byron looked back at Cissy's daughters. Teresa still watched from beside the car; Liz stood anxiously behind her mother. "Eliza-beth, please help your mother to the car."

Cissy glared at him. "I really should talk to Becky. She needs to know what happened, and I doubt that *you've* told her. Have you?"

"Told her . . ." Byron shook his head at the unpleasant realization that of all the people in Claysville, it seemed that Cissy was the only one other than him who thought the circumstances around Maylene's death warranted discussion. "This is *not* the time or place."

"Mama," Liz started.

Cissy stepped to the side to go around Byron. "I think Becky should hear what happened."

At that, Liz held her hands up in defeat. She was the more reasonable of Cissy's daughters, but she also had the sense to not want to be the object of her mother's temper.

"I said *no*. Not here, not now." Byron clamped his hand on Cissy's elbow and steered her toward the car.

Cissy glared at her daughters—who remained motionless, one at the car, one beside her—before giving in. "Fine. I'll see her at the house, then." She pulled her arm out of his grasp. "You can't keep me away from her, boy."

Byron knew well enough that responding wasn't going to get the result he wanted, so he forced a polite smile to his lips and stayed silent.

Liz shot a relieved look at Byron and mouthed, "Thank you."

Byron turned his back on them and returned to the gravestone where he had been waiting before Cissy had approached. He was trying not to watch Rebekkah, but he couldn't leave her here alone. He wished he didn't have to tell Rebekkah about Maylene's murder, but he wasn't willing to let her hear it casually—or cruelly—spoken.

A black blur to his left drew his attention, but when he turned, he didn't see anyone or anything. So he leaned on the tree beside the grave and waited.

He'd never realized that the ways of death in Claysville were peculiar. When he'd moved to Chicago, he was surprised that there was no designated final mourner. He'd decided then that it must've been a trait of small towns, but eighteen months later—after living in Brookside and Springfield—he'd realized that it wasn't the size of the town. Claysville was simply unique in the way it mourned the dead. He'd watched carefully as he traveled, becoming almost a funeral-tourist of sorts for a few months. Nowhere else was like Claysville. Here, graveside services regularly had several religious representatives in attendance. Here, the graves were meticulously kept in order: graveyards and cemeteries mowed, trimmed, and planted. Here, a woman walked in funeral processions ringing a bell.

Once, as a child, he'd thought Maylene worked for Montgomery and Sons. As a teen, he simply decided that his girlfriend's grand-mother was a little odd. She had her own way of saying good-bye, and folks in town just accepted that she would be the last mourner for each and every person who passed. Now he wasn't sure what to think, especially as Rebekkah seemed to be standing in for the last Barrow woman.

What am I missing here?

Once she stood, Rebekkah composed herself and turned to walk away. Only then did Byron step out from the shadow of the tree and move toward her.

"I didn't know anyone was still here until"—Rebekkah mo-tioned up the hill—"I heard the disturbance."

He rubbed his hand over his face. "Cissy and the twins were here and . . ."

"Thank you." Rebekkah blushed. "I doubt that any conversation between us could go *well* just now. I was a bit less than patient with her."

Byron hesitated. "She wanted to tell you . . . to be the one to . . ."

"To tell me whatever you've been avoiding." She lifted her chin and looked pointedly at him. "You haven't mentioned anything about Maylene's being sick . . . I know it was sudden. You didn't want to tell me last night, this morning. William didn't mention it. No one at the wake did. So, what are you not telling me?"

He'd been trying to come up with a way to tell her since it had happened. There was no nice way to say it. "She was murdered."

Rebekkah thought she was prepared for whatever Byron said, thought that things couldn't hurt any worse than they already did. She was wrong. Her knees gave way, and if not for Byron, she would've fallen to the ground.

He slid an arm around her waist and steadied her. "I'm sorry, Bek."

"Murdered?" she repeated.

He nodded. "I'm sorry."

"But . . . she was *buried already*!" Rebekkah stepped away from him and waved her hand behind her where her grandmother's body was now interred. "What about an autopsy? There's no way to do one with her . . . *there*. Tell me what—"

"I can't tell you anything." Byron raked his hair back in a familiar gesture of frustration. "I tried to get answers from Chris, but there's nothing."

"And you tell me this *after she's buried*?"

"It's been forty-eight hours, Bek. If we didn't inter her"—Byron looked past her to the freshly turned soil—"she would need to be embalmed. Do you think they'd agree to *that*? It's against the law here."

Rebekkah brushed the graveyard dirt from her hands off on her skirt. "You know that's fucked up, too. Nowhere else has such bizarre funeral laws. I'm not sure there *are* funeral laws elsewhere."

"Oh, there are, just not like here." He pressed his lips together in a way she remembered from the times she'd seen him force his temper away. "Here they clean up murder scenes with bleach and vinegar. Here they take the body away and work to make the house look untouched."

"House?" She felt herself sway. "She was killed at the *house*?"

He took her elbow again, steadying her. "That wasn't a very good attempt at 'breaking it to you gently,' was it?"

Rebekkah sat down in the grass. "How could they not tell me? How could *you* not tell me?"

Byron sat down with her. His tone wasn't cruel, but there was a bite to it as he asked, "And when should I have done that? When you were standing at the baggage carousel or when you were jet-lagged and needing to sleep or just now at the service?"

"No." Rebekkah plucked at the grass. "I just . . . why aren't they telling me? I get the trying to be gentle. I really do. I might even appreciate it, but when someone is *murdered*, shouldn't they tell me? Shouldn't someone have called, or I don't know, *something*?"

"I don't know." He took a deep breath, and then he told her that he'd come into her house and tried to find a clue, a hint, something—and had no luck. Then he added, "The laws on burial make everything happen so fast, and I'm an undertaker, not a detective."

"Right." She wiped her hands off on her dress. "Knowing isn't going to bring her back to me. Let me get through today first, or at least the funeral breakfast."

He stood and helped her to her feet. Still holding her hand in his, he looked directly at her and said, "Just say the word. I'm here . . . despite your insistence on trying to shove me so far away that we aren't even friends. I promised I'd always be here, and that hasn't changed."

Rebekkah stopped and looked at him. He had—when Ella died. He'd held her and promised exactly that. Those first few weeks after Ella died, he'd been her lifeline, and when her mother had decided they needed to move, Rebekkah had thought that losing Byron would tear her in two.

"That was a long time ago," she said somewhat uselessly.

He let go of her hand. "I don't remember it having a time limit, do you?"

Whatever I need.

"Ella would've appreciated it, too," she murmured. She resumed walking.

Beside her, Byron shook his head. "I'm not doing it for Ella. I'm here for *you*."

For a moment, Rebekkah felt the weight of losing his friendship. In that one day, she'd lost both of them. She hadn't known it at the time, but losing Ella had led to losing Byron. Not long after Ella died, her mom left Jimmy, and they'd moved away. Afterward, her mother had hated it when Rebekkah talked to Byron; she'd never tried to keep Rebekkah away from Maylene, but any mention of Claysville—or anyone there—was a source of conflict.

As if none of it had ever happened.

She glanced at Byron. "We *are* friends. I know that. Not like we were then, but . . . a lot has changed."

"It has," he agreed in that neutral tone he adopted when they both suspected she was about to say something that would lead to an argument.

Not this time.

Softly she admitted, "Sometimes I think about then . . . about all of us . . . I think Maylene knew exactly what we did every time we thought we were so smart. Your mom was just as bad."

"They were good people, Bek. That's how I remember Mam. If you'd have told me I'd miss the sharp side of her as much as the rest . . ." He shook his head, but he was smiling now. "That's how I cope. I don't stop missing her, but I remember her. The good and the bad—just like I remember Ella. She wasn't the angel you want to remember her as."

Rebekkah stopped. "I know that. I just thought you . . . I figured that's how you still thought of her. We're a pair, aren't we?"

"I remember the bickering between you, and that she stole my cigarettes—and my stash—every time I left her alone in my room.

That fight after school sophomore year? It was *not* her defending herself. I was there. She threw the first punch." Byron laughed. "No one had a shorter temper. No one was going to outdrink, outsmoke, outcuss Ella Mae Barrow. I loved her, but I saw who she was, too. She couldn't resist a dare, but she would refuse a party so she could plant flowers with my mother. She cussed enough that I probably blushed then, and she sang to herself, but mouthed the words in church because she wasn't sure of her voice. There's no sense in building a shrine, especially to an illusion."

"She was so alive." Rebekkah looked away, her gaze lingering on the stones that marked Ella and Jimmy's graves. "I don't understand how someone that alive could choose to die."

"I don't know either, but I do know that she—and Maylene and your dad—wouldn't want you remembering them as anything other than who they really were." Byron gestured for her to precede him toward the one remaining black car. "Loving someone means admitting the good and the bad."

He opened the back door, and she slid into the car before he could see the panic in her eyes when he mentioned *that* topic.

16

D AISHA STEPPED INTO THE BUILDING, CROSSING THE THRESHOLD WITH the assurance of one who knows she is safe. It was an unfamiliar feeling. After years of flinching at every sound, the security of her new *life* was heady.

She was in a cloakroom, an antechamber for the mourners who hadn't yet readied themselves for the viewing. Even out here, beige carpet and leafy green plants were positioned for a calculatingly soothing atmosphere.

Beyond the doorway stood the man she needed to find. Mr. Montgomery knew she was different; she could tell by the cautious way he watched her. No one else in town—*except Maylene*—had looked at her that way.

"You shouldn't be here," he said.

Her body had known she needed to come here, just as it had known she needed to find Maylene. She'd walked for days, not knowing where she was going or why, just that she was going to the place where things could be made better. Her body belonged here in Claysville.

"But I *am* here," Daisha told Mr. Montgomery. She stepped into the viewing room, where he waited. Once she'd sat in this same room mourning an uncle who'd been in a wreck after too many drinks and who knows what else. The smell of it was the same as it had been then, a lingering perfume of flowers and something sweeter. Once she'd thought that this was the scent of death, an almost sickly sweet odor. Then she had died. Now she knew that sometimes death smells like copper and leaves.

"I can help you." His voice was comforting, confident.

"How?"

"Help you get where you need to be," William said. If not for the fine trembling in his hands, Daisha would think he was unaffected by her.

Daisha shook her head. "The other one that tried that . . ."

"You killed Maylene."

"She offered to feed me," Daisha whispered.

William raised his voice then: "So you *murdered* her."

She frowned. It wasn't supposed to go like this. He wasn't supposed to be so mean. *Maylene* hadn't been.

"What else could I have done?" She wasn't objecting; she was asking. William didn't see that, though. Maylene would've. She *did* before she died.

Maylene offered Daisha a glass of whiskey and water.

"I'm not old enough to drink that."

Maylene smiled. "You're a bit beyond their rules now."

Daisha paused. "Why?"

"You know why." Maylene was gentle but firm. "Take it. It'll help."

Daisha took the glass and tossed it back. It didn't burn like whiskey usually did; instead, it felt heavy, like some sort of syrup coating her throat all the way down to her stomach. "Nasty." She tossed the glass at the wall.

Maylene poured another. This one she lifted in a toast. "You might finally have me, you old bastard." She emptied the glass and then looked at Daisha. "Let me help you."

"You are."

"I need you to trust me. If I'd known you were . . . gone, I would've minded your grave. We still can do that. Tell me where—"

"My grave." Daisha stepped backward. The truth that hadn't taken shape yet hit her. My grave. She looked down at her hands. Her fingernails were dirty. She hadn't crawled out of anything, though. She mightn't remember everything, but she knew that. "I wasn't in a grave."

"I know." Maylene poured another glass, tilting both the whiskey and the water bottles over the cup. "That's why you're so thirsty. The dead always are if they haven't been minded properly."

"I'm not . . ." Daisha stared at her. "I'm not."

Maylene cut a thick slice of bread, laid it on a plate, and poured honey over it. She slid the plate forward. Her fingertips were right next to the handle of the bread knife. "Eat."

"I don't . . . how can I be dead if I'm hungry?" Daisha felt the truth in Maylene's words, though. She knew.

Maylene nodded toward the glass and the plate. "Eat, child."

"I don't want to be dead."

"I know."

"I don't want to be in a grave either." Daisha pushed away from the table. The chair fell backward to the floor.

Maylene didn't react.

"That's what you want, though, isn't it?" Daisha understood. She knew why she'd come here, knew why the old woman was giving her the whiskey and the bread.

"It's what I do." Maylene stood. "I keep the dead in their place and I send them back when they wake. You shouldn't have been left outside Claysville. You shouldn't have been . . ."

"Killed. I shouldn't've been killed." Daisha was shaking. Her head felt like it was full of bees buzzing so loud her thoughts weren't staying clear. "That's what you want. You want to kill me."

"You're already dead."

The next thing Daisha knew she was kneeling over Maylene, the floor hard under her knees. "I don't want to be dead."

"*Me either.*" Maylene smiled. Blood ran down a cut by her eye. "*But you already are, child.*"

"*Why you? Why did I come to you? I couldn't stop myself from coming,*" Daisha whispered.

"*I'm the Graveminder. It's what I do. The dead come knocking, and I set things right.*"

"*Put us back.*"

"*Word, drink, and food,*" Maylene murmured. "*I gave you all three. If you'd been buried here . . .*"

Slowly Daisha walked farther into the room. All the while, she watched William. He didn't seem like a threat, but she wasn't sure.

"He doesn't know what I am . . . the other Undertaker. He doesn't know any of this," Daisha guessed. She took a step forward.

William didn't back up, but the tension in his body said he wanted to. His gaze narrowed. "Leave them out of it."

Daisha ran a hand over the back of a chair beside her. "I can't. You know that, don't you? Some things aren't choices."

"We can end this before anyone else gets hurt." William held his hands out to the sides as if to show her he was unarmed. "You don't want to hurt people, do you? You will if you don't come away with me. You know that."

"I'm not bad," Daisha whispered.

"I believe you." He held out a hand to her. He curled his fingers toward him in a beckoning gesture. "You can do the right thing here. Just come with me. We'll go meet some people who can help us."

"*Her. The new Graveminder.*"

"No, not her. You and I can fix this all on our own." He took another step forward, hand outstretched. "Maylene gave you food and drink, didn't she?"

Suspiciously Daisha said, "Yeah, but not enough. I'm so hungry."

"Do you need me fix you something?" William's breathing was ragged. "Would that help?"

Without meaning to, Daisha took his hand and pulled him to her. He was so close; it wasn't as if she'd even meant to move, but she had. She was shaking her head. He trembled. *Like Maylene did.* Daisha sank her teeth into his wrist, and he made a sound, a hurt animal noise.

He pulled something out of his pocket and tried to stick it in her arm. *A needle.* He'd offered her hope, but he was trying to hurt her. *Poison.* She pushed him away. "That wasn't nice."

He clutched his bleeding arm to his chest. Little red drops fell to the floor; more sank into his shirt.

"Let me help," he said. He reached for the needle, which had fallen from his hand. "Please, child. Let me help."

Daisha couldn't stop looking at his wrist. The skin was torn. "I did that," she whispered.

"We can make it okay." He picked up the needle. His face was pale, and he dropped to the floor so that he was half kneeling, half sitting in front of her. Despite his obvious pain, he reached out to grab her wrist. "Please. I can . . . help you."

"No." She wiped her mouth with the back of her hand. Her mind felt clearer now. Everything made more sense when she wasn't so hungry. "I don't think I want the help you have."

He cradled his bloody arm and tried to stand. "This isn't right. *You* aren't right. You aren't supposed to be here."

"But I *am*." Daisha shoved him down. She was still hungry, but she was more afraid of him than she was hungry. *He doesn't understand.* Afraid meant falling apart. She didn't like that. She wasn't going to let that happen. Daisha might not have chosen to be dead— or to be awake after dying—but she could make a few choices now.

Quietly Daisha left the room and closed the door behind her.

William didn't follow.

She thought about visiting the woman who was humming in her office, but staying here seemed unwise. William might not be strong enough to stop her, but he knew things and people who might be able to hurt her.

Daisha slipped out the door.

Someone else would feed her, someone who didn't make her afraid. She'd find them, and then she'd decide what to do next.

17

Rebekkah was grateful for Byron's silence as they rode the short distance to Maylene's house. Some part of her rebelled at how easy it always was to pick up where they'd left off. At the beginning, Byron had been her guilty secret. *And Ella knew.* Rebekkah didn't mean for anything to happen; she'd loved her stepsister. *One night. One kiss. That was it.* She shouldn't have, and she knew it then, but it was only once. *It wouldn't have happened again. We wouldn't have . . .* It took years before she could even talk to Byron without feeling guilty. Then one night, too many drinks and years of wanting edged her across the line she swore she wouldn't cross. Afterward, he'd become the one addiction she couldn't shake, but every time she let him in she thought about her sister. *Ella knew how I felt, how he felt, and she died knowing it.*

The car stopped. Byron opened the door and got out.

"You ready for this?" he asked.

"No, not really." Rebekkah took a deep breath and followed him to the front porch and into her grandmother's home. *My home.* She didn't want to know where in the house Maylene had died, but knowing that she had died there made it hard not to wonder. *Later.* She would ask questions later—of Byron, of Sheriff McInney, of William.

Cissy sat in Maylene's chair, and by the look on her face, she wasn't feeling the least bit friendly. She glared fixedly at Rebekkah and Byron as they entered the room.

"Aunt Cissy," Rebekkah murmured.

"Becky." Cisssy held a cup of tea in one hand and a saucer in the other. Her tone was scathing as she said, "I assume *he* told you."

Rebekkah paused. This wasn't the time or place. "Please don't."

"My mother was killed here in her home. *My* home . . . Right there." Cissy closed her eyes for a moment and then opened them to glare at Rebekkah. "They found her out there in the kitchen. Did he tell you that part?"

"Cecilia! Please, not now." Daniel Greeley, one of the councilmen, had walked into the room. Rebekkah had met him a few times during her visits to Maylene, and she was grateful to see him today. He stood like a sentinel in front of Cissy.

"Oh, it's fine for me to know? It's okay for my daughters to know? But we have to protect *her*?" Cissy stood up so abruptly that the rocker clattered into the wall. She glared at Rebekkah. "You aren't even *family*. You don't need to be here. Just say you don't want it, Rebekkah. That's all you have to do."

Everyone stopped talking. People were politely leaving the room or turning their backs as if they couldn't hear the conversation. However, Cissy was loud enough that there was no way not to hear her.

"Mother." Liz stepped up beside Cissy. "You're upset, and—"

"If she had any morals, she'd leave." Cissy glared at Rebekkah. "She'd let Maylene's real family have what's rightly theirs."

For a moment, Rebekkah was too stunned to react. She was sickened by the idea that Cissy's hostility was over something as petty as money and things. Had the years of anger toward Rebekkah and her mother been because of Cissy's greed?

"Get out," Rebekkah said softly. "Now."

"Excuse me?"

"Get out." Rebekkah stepped away from Byron, putting herself closer to Cissy, but not too close; she kept her arms at her sides to stop herself from grabbing hold of the woman and tossing her out. "I am not going to stand in Maylene's home and have you do this. I get that you're angry about the funeral, but you know what? I've watched Maylene do the *exact same thing* when you started caterwauling, but she's not here now to tell you to stop making a spectacle of yourself."

Both twins were now standing beside their mother. Teresa had taken Cissy's arm in her hand in a gesture that could be either supportive or restrictive. Liz stood with her arms folded over her chest. The twins, like everyone else in the room, were silent.

Rebekkah didn't move. "I never wanted you to hate me, and God knows I've tried to make nice with you, but right now, I don't care. What I care about is that you are disrespecting Maylene in her own home. You have two choices: you can act civil, or you can get out."

Cissy shook off Liz's hold and stepped forward. Her voice was lower now as she said, "I'll never bother you again if you release your claim on my mother's bequests. Just walk away from here, Rebekkah."

Rebekkah frowned. *Release the claim on her bequests?*

"Cissy?" The sheriff walked up beside them. "How about we get a little air?"

Rebekkah didn't stay to find out if Cissy went with him. She turned and walked into her grandmother's kitchen. It was full of people, some familiar and some not. Her visits home weren't that frequent, and it had been years since she lived there, but every time she came home, Maylene seemed to want her to accompany her everywhere. The result was that she knew a fair number of the Claysville residents even though she had only truly lived there a few years.

"Ladies." Byron had followed her into the kitchen. "Would you give us a minute?"

"So, I thought that went fairly well." Rebekkah forced an I'm-not-falling-apart expression to her face before she turned to look at him. She knew he'd see through it, but she wanted the illusion that she hadn't already slipped into the habit of letting down her guard around him.

He snorted. "She was waiting for that."

"I'd ask why, but I don't think you know any better than I do." Rebekkah looked at the kitchen floor. "The rug's gone. My grandmother died right here, and they had to get rid of the rug because of it, didn't they?"

"Don't do this to yourself, not right now. " Byron wrapped his arms around her.

"That was a yes." Rebekkah leaned into his embrace. "I don't understand why Cissy wants to hurt me. I don't want to know that Maylene . . ." She closed her eyes for a moment. "I don't want her to be dead."

"I can't change that." He held her for a few moments, and when she relaxed a little, he asked, "Want me to kick Cissy's ass?"

Rebekkah laughed a little, but the laugh didn't completely hide the sob.

They were still standing like that when Evelyn came in a few minutes later. She was only a few years older than they were, but she'd always had a maternal streak to her. When Byron had spilled his first bike during a race out at the reservoir, it was Evelyn who hovered over him until Chris got him to promise he'd go to the doctor *and* got Ella and Rebekkah to promise to call him to wake him every forty-five minutes to make sure he wasn't concussed. Being the sheriff's wife and mother of four kids had made her even more of a nurturer.

"Cissy and her daughters agreed that it was probably for the best if she went home to rest a bit," Evelyn said.

With a watery smile, Rebekkah turned to face her. "Thank you."

Evelyn waved it off. "It wasn't me, shug. Christopher does a good job of handling difficult women." She lowered her voice. "He had to learn that skill with his sisters. He comes from high-strung women."

"Well, please thank him, too." Rebekkah gave a small laugh. When she'd lived here, the McInney family had been responsible for more than its fair share of disturbing the peace, and to hear Maylene talk, one of the reasons the town council made Chris sheriff was that he knew all the troublemakers—or was related to them.

"Everything will be okay, Rebekkah." Evelyn pulled out a chair. "And it will be easier once you get a little food in you. Grief is exhausting, and you can't keep up your strength on an empty stomach. Come on." She patted the chair. "Sit."

Obediently, Rebekkah did so.

Evelyn looked at Byron. "You go on and see if your father's here yet. He's hiding it well enough, but he's having a rough time of it, too. Those two were always thick as thieves." She made a shooing motion at Byron. "Go on. I'll stay with her for a bit."

Byron glanced at Rebekkah, who nodded. Leaning on Evelyn didn't feel as dangerous as leaning on Byron. With Evelyn, there was no confusion, no conflict. She was simply being kind. Most likely, she'd do the same for every person currently in the house if they were grieving.

"I'll be right out there," he said.

Evelyn started fixing a plate for Rebekkah, filling the kitchen with the same sort of easy chatter that Maylene always used to when Rebekkah was upset. *Which is why she's doing it*, Rebekkah realized. She smiled gratefully at Evelyn. "Thank you."

"Shush." Evelyn patted her hand.

Over the next hour, a number of people flowed in and out of the kitchen, telling little tidbits of stories about Maylene—a fair number

of them about conversations in that very room—and generally helping Rebekkah erase the thought of her grandmother dying there.

Then Rebekkah felt a tug, as if she were being drawn along a
cord she couldn't see. She walked back into the living room, trying
to make sense of the utterly unfamiliar feeling inside of her. She'd
grieved before, but grief didn't compel you to follow unseen paths.

"Bek?" Amity stepped toward her. "Rebekkah? What are you
doing?"

Rebekkah ignored her and kept walking. She opened the door
and stepped onto the porch. Vaguely, she realized that she should
say *something*, explain herself in some way, but a pressure inside insisted that she keep moving.

Amity followed. "What are you . . . Oh my gods." She turned
and ran back inside yelling, "Sheriff? Daniel? Somebody?"

A child Rebekkah didn't know was lying on the ground. She had
several long gashes in her arm, at least one tear in her shoulder, and
scrapes on her legs as if she'd been dragged over the ground. The
child's eyes were closed, and her face was turned away.

In a haze, Rebekkah knelt down beside the girl and felt for a
pulse. It was thready, but there. It took all of her efforts to force herself to focus on the child.

This isn't what I am looking for.

"Oh my God." A woman, presumably the child's mother, sobbed
the words as she shoved in front of Rebekkah and scooped the little
girl into her arms. "Call an ambulance. Oh my God, Hope . . ."

Sheriff McInney helped the woman over to the porch. "Let me
see her."

Then Father Ness and Lady Penelope, the local spiritualist, were
both there. Evelyn was steering the crowd. Someone had come outside with a kitchen towel and was using it as a makeshift bandage on
the little girl's arm. Everything was as under control as possible, but
the compulsion Rebekkah was feeling hadn't abated.

It's farther away now.

Rebekkah walked past the child and the people clustered in the yard. Beyond her was a small patch of woods. At the front of the woods were trees and bare ground; Maylene had always kept the front-most bit clear of underbrush. Beyond that, it grew wild. *That's where it went.* Rebekkah searched the trees and underbrush for movement, eyes, something to help her locate the animal that did this.

Why would I feel an animal outside?

Byron came up beside her. "The EMTs are on the way. Evelyn called them the minute she heard Amity. The station is close enough that they should be here in a couple minutes." He paused. "Bek? Are you okay?"

She kept watching the shadows in front of her.

"Do you see something?"

"No," she said.

"*Did* you see anything?" Byron looked out into the small wooded area. "Cougar? Dog of some sort?"

"No, I didn't see anything." She felt like her voice wasn't entirely her own, as if the sound of the words echoed around her.

For several moments, they both stood silently. Then the tug that had pulled Rebekkah outside released all at once. She rubbed her hands up her arms, trying to chase away the prickled feeling on her skin.

"There were a couple other children out here. Are they all here? I don't know a lot of these people. I'd think their parents would check, but . . . I don't know." She kept her voice low, as much in hopes of not spooking anything that waited in the trees as not to alarm anyone who overheard her. "Can you check?"

"Sure. Let me go ask Chris. Are you—"

"I need a minute," she told him.

Obviously, the shock of the past two days had hit her. *I was in California yesterday.* Today she was at her grandmother's funeral breakfast staring into the woods in some strange attempt to find an animal that had attacked a child. Grief wasn't always the same, and if she was acting irrationally, it was to be expected. *That didn't feel like grief.* She wasn't sure what else it could be, though—or if she wanted to know. What she wanted was to kick everyone out, go upstairs, grab a shotgun, and sit on the porch watching for whatever big cat or feral dog had bitten the child.

The EMTs pulled up. Right behind them were William Montgomery and the young rabbi who'd moved to town a few years ago. William's gaze immediately sought first Byron and then Rebekkah.

The rabbi went over to the child's mother, but William walked past the small crowd until he was beside Rebekkah. "Are you okay?"

"I am." Rebekkah gestured to the crowd. "A little girl got bit by some sort of animal."

Daniel came over and took charge of keeping the bystanders out of the way. He paused and gave Rebekkah and William an almost accusatory look.

Rebekkah flinched. She hadn't been gawking, but she hadn't been much use either—but neither had anyone else. They'd wrapped the wound and called for help; there wasn't much else anyone could do. *What did he expect?*

"Why don't you go on over to the house, Bek," William said.

There was no graceful way to refuse William's suggestion, and she didn't want to argue with him—he was the only other person who'd lost as much as she had when Maylene died—so Rebekkah did as William suggested.

She walked toward Byron, and as she approached she caught the tail end of his comment. " . . . just like Maylene," he said in a low voice to Christopher. "So don't tell me to calm down, Chris."

Rebekkah blanched. *Like Maylene?* That didn't make sense. Byron had said Maylene was murdered; animals didn't *murder* people. "Byron?"

Byron looked over his shoulder. "Bek . . ." He rubbed his hand over his face. "I didn't realize you were behind me."

She looked from him to the sheriff, who shook his head and remained silent, and then back at Byron.

Lady Penelope came up beside Rebekkah and put an arm around her. The spiritualist was gentle but insistent. "Come inside. It's been a stressful morning. Evelyn already put on the kettle. Why don't we get a nice cup of herbal tea? I brought several blends that should soothe your nerves."

Rebekkah gently extricated herself. "You go ahead. I need a minute."

The reverend came up and gave Penelope a questioning look that Rebekkah pretended not to notice. Penelope shook her head once.

Sheriff McInney said, "There's nothing we can do here, and Evelyn could probably use our help. Come on, Reverend." He glanced at Penelope. "Lady P."

Penelope embraced Rebekkah quickly and whispered, "Byron is a good man, Rebekkah. You can trust him . . . and yourself." Then she stepped away. With an implacable smile, she turned to the reverend. "Did Cecilia get escorted out peacefully? That detail was unclear."

"Of course. Thank you for the warning," Reverend McLendon murmured.

Then the three of them went inside. The porch door closed with a small snap, and Byron and Rebekkah were left alone on the porch.

Byron started, "About what I said to Chris—"

"No. I can't. Not right now. I can't hear anything else today." She shook her head. "Please?"

Byron put his arm around her shoulder as they watched the EMTs load the stretcher into the ambulance. The child's mother and the rabbi climbed in after them.

Rebekkah leaned against Byron.

The rabbi leaned out and said something to Father Ness and William; then the doors closed on them. Father Ness kept his back to the house as the ambulance left the drive, and William walked over to where they stood on the porch. He cradled his arm awkwardly, but said nothing for a moment. He looked weary and suddenly far older than he had that morning, but he gave her a warm smile. "Maylene would've been proud at the way you're handling yourself, Rebekkah. You're stronger than you realize."

"I don't feel very strong, but I'm glad it looks like that at least."

"Mae knew strong, and I've never had reason to doubt her where you were concerned . . . either of you." William glanced at Byron for a moment, and then pulled a thick envelope out of his jacket pocket and held it out to Rebekkah. "She wanted me to give you this."

She accepted the envelope. "Thank you."

He nodded, and then looked to the side as Father Ness came over to the porch. The priest stopped on the bottom step. "There are limits to what we can forestall, William. The council will step in soon."

"I know." William's face was drawn and pained; his posture was tense. "I'm handling it."

Rebekkah and Byron exchanged a confused look, but before they could ask any questions, William told Byron, "We need to talk about some things. I need you to come with me now."

"*Now?* But Rebekkah—"

"I'm okay," she assured them both. She stepped forward, leaned up, and kissed William on the cheek. "Thank you for everything."

"Maylene was right about you, Rebekkah: you've grown into a fine woman. Byron is lucky to have you." William pulled her into a firm embrace. "It'll get easier. I promise."

He pulled back and stared at her silently, and she didn't have the heart to tell him that she and Byron weren't . . . whatever he thought they were. All she said was, "Thank you."

She turned to Byron. "I'll see you tomorrow."

Then she fled into her house before she had to think about William's words or the look of hope that came over Byron's face when she said she'd see him tomorrow.

18

S ILENTLY, BYRON FOLLOWED HIS FATHER. WILLIAM HADN'T BEEN WILL-
ing to talk at Rebekkah's house, and Byron hadn't felt much like
arguing, so he accompanied his father to the funeral home in silence. They didn't stop in the part of the house that was their home;
instead, William proceeded to the door that separated the living
quarters from the funeral home. He winced as he opened the door.

"Are you okay?" Byron reached out, but his father dodged him.

William called out, "Elaine, we'll be in the basement. There are
memos on your desk."

Elaine poked her head out of her office. "Most of them are already done."

"Of course they are." William paused for a moment and gave his
office manager a smile. "Thank you . . . for everything."

"The package you ordered came in earlier. I'll take care of it."

"Good." William nodded once before resuming his steps. He
paused at the door of his office, pulled out a key, and locked the door.
Instead of pocketing his keys, he held them out to Byron. "Put these
in your pocket for me."

"Why?" Byron took the keys and held them in his hand.

His father ignored his question. "Come on."

Byron stood in the hallway. The list of things that didn't make sense grew longer every day, but all of those were unimportant as he noticed the increasing caution with which William held his arm against his chest. "What happened to your arm?"

"It'll be fine. That's not what we need to talk about right now." William opened the door to the basement and started down the steps.

Byron shoved the keys in his pocket and followed his father downstairs. "What's going on?"

William opened the door to the storage room and flicked on the lights. "Close the door."

Byron pulled the door shut.

"Lock it."

"You're worrying me, Dad." Byron locked the door. "Do you want to tell me what's going on?"

William laughed humorlessly. "No, not really, but we're past the point where I can keep it from you."

"Dad? What's wrong?" Byron went to stand beside his father. He reached out again toward the arm his father was holding against his body.

"Stop that."

"Sure, if you tell me what's wrong with your arm." Byron glanced at his father's ashen face. "Is it a heart attack or—"

"No, it's not. Let me start at the beginning." William paused, and when Byron nodded reluctantly, he continued, "A long time ago, the town founders made an agreement, and it's been honored ever since. There are terms, responsibilities that some of us must bear. A select few of us can ask questions that not everyone can"—he stared pointedly at Byron—"but it also means that we are held accountable for keeping the town safe when there is trouble. We are what stands between the living and the dead. Being an Undertaker is an honor, son."

"I know." Byron grew increasingly alarmed. His father was making less sense by the minute. *Wasn't it a stroke that made patients have illogical thoughts?* Byron wasn't used to diagnosing anything; his "patients" were already dead when he met them. *Arm pain can be a sign of a stroke, too.* He stepped toward his father. "Dad, let's go upstairs. Let me call Dr. Pefferman."

William ignored him. "I'm telling you what you need to know. I wish this wasn't such a shock, son. I'm truly sorry about that."

"What are you talking about?" Byron debated running upstairs to call for the ambulance. Nothing about his father's behavior made sense. *Is he grieving? In denial? Having a heart attack? A stroke?* Byron tried to remember symptoms beyond arm pain, but he couldn't.

"Listen. Stay focused." William slid his hand down the outside of a pale blue metal cabinet that sat against the back wall.

"On what?"

The cabinet made a clicking noise, and as it slid to the side, a tunnel became visible. William added, "And trust your instincts."

"Holy f—"

"No." William's gaze snapped to Byron's face. "Reverence here."

"Here?" Byron stepped up to stand shoulder to shoulder with his father. Of all the answers he had imagined for the myriad unanswered questions, a tunnel behind a cabinet in a storage room wasn't anywhere on the list. "Where *is* here? Where does this go?"

William stepped into the tunnel and took a torch that looked like it belonged in a medieval dungeon—gray rags wrapped around a weathered bit of wood—from the wall. The torch flamed to life as if a switch had been thrown. *Torches don't do that.* The touch of his father's hand had caused flame to appear and cast some scant light into the tunnel. On the ground was what looked to be an abandoned stretch of railroad track, overgrown with mosses and covered in dirt. The walls of the tunnel looked like nothing so much as a rough-hewn access shaft into a cave. The abandoned coal mine tunnels Byron had once gone exploring with spelunker friends might've looked less safe, but not by much.

Byron stared at the tunnel and then at his father. "Is it a Prohibition tunnel? From a war? From . . . I don't know. What is this? What does it have do with your arm? Were you down here explor—"

"No. It's the entrance to the land of the dead," William told him.

"*What* did you say?" Byron stared at his father. He must have slipped into some sort of grief-induced dementia or shock or something. "Let's go upstairs. Maybe we can go for a drive and—"

"Come on." William beckoned. "I'm not crazy. I know it seems . . . I know exactly how odd it seems, but you need to come with me now. The dead don't get any more patient for having forever at their disposal. Step into the tunnel."

Byron hesitated. It was probably just an old, unused tunnel, an escape route or something. Tunnels to the dead didn't exist.

It's not real. It's . . . Faces appeared in the frosty air; hands stretched out toward his father; and Byron wasn't sure if they were welcoming or threatening. Terror rose up in him as the ghostly figures hurtled toward his father. Byron stepped into the tunnel and in front of his father. "Dad?"

William leaned close to him and yelled in his ear, "Just stay with me. They aren't always like this."

They?

William strode off into the swirling darkness in front of them. Any words he might have said were lost in a gust of wind that came tearing at them. The sheer force of the wind was like teeth sinking into skin, like cold breath on Byron's neck, like viscous wet things pressed on his lips.

The flickering light didn't seem touched by the screaming wind, but the air was cold with it. Frost had started to creep over the walls, covering them with a growing white rime.

And then the shrieking wind died as suddenly as it had begun. The hands and voices dissipated, and Byron wondered if he'd imagined them.

Am I hallucinating?

"You wanted answers," William said in a breath of white air. "You're about to get a few of them."

Byron jumped as he heard the slam of a door closing behind him. As it did so, the landscape around them seemed to shift. The already hazy tunnel grew dimmer and then flared with light. An opening, an end to the previously dark tunnel, appeared.

Beside him, his father said only, "Some days the way is long, and some days the way is brief. When it's quick as today, it means they want to talk *now*."

Byron turned quickly as something ran past him and into the shadows along the tunnel walls. "They?"

"The dead, son." William started walking toward the vague shape of buildings that had become apparent at the end of the tunnel. As they walked, or maybe as time passed, the wooden storefronts became clearer. "This is their world. They've been waiting to meet you."

"The dead?" Byron peered into the darkness of the tunnel to try to see whatever had hidden itself there, but the torch in his father's hand only illuminated a small space around them. Even if the torch did cast light farther into the tunnel, Byron wasn't sure that the light would help. Warily, he said, "We're here to see the *dead* who want to *meet me*."

"Not all of them," William murmured. "There are those we can't meet here. You won't see your mother. If you have children who die . . . or close friends . . . or other Undertakers."

"You are saying that we're in the land of the dead . . . That hell is under our house." Byron kept his voice low, but the absolute silence in the tunnel made it echo nonetheless.

"Not hell. Not heaven." William mostly watched the ground in front of them, but he swept his gaze along the walls a few times as if he saw things at the edge of the light, too. "Those are other places maybe, but this is the place we can reach."

"We?"

"You are the next Undertaker, Byron." William paused for a moment. His hand tightened on the torch he clutched. Light flickered over his face. "I'd thought of revealing it some other way, but seeing is believing. You need to see, and after . . . then we can talk."

Then William increased his pace, and Byron was left with the choice to follow or to be left alone in the dark.

The dead.

Byron bit back a few words that he was pretty sure weren't anywhere near the reverence his father had demanded while here. He wasn't sure what was stranger—that his father was leading him to meet the dead or that he felt betrayed that this had been in his home all of these years. It was one thing to keep a bottle of booze tucked in a hidden nook or to hide a flirtation or a hobby. This was an entire world.

At the end of the tunnel, William stopped. He held his hand behind him, fingers outstretched and flat, in a stilling gesture, and said, "I want you to meet someone."

He sounded nervous for the first time. A tremor threaded through his voice, and those outstretched fingers seemed poised to tremble. They didn't, but Byron knew his father well enough to read the signs of worry.

William put the torch into a hole in the wall; it extinguished as soon as he released it. He stepped out of the tunnel and said, "Charlie."

Standing in front of what looked to be a fully functioning mining town was a man who didn't blend with the crude buildings around him. The man, Charlie presumably, wore a 1930s-style suit complete with silk pocket square, wide-brimmed fedora, and silk tie. Byron suspected that the tie and pocket square matched, but the world had taken on shades of gray: all color had vanished.

"It took you long enough. Shake a leg, son," Charlie said. "We have places to go and people to see."

William opened his mouth to reply, but Byron spoke first. "What? Why?"

Charlie stopped and grinned. "Because the alternative isn't one you'll like much. You might be set to be the new Undertaker, but he"—the man gestured at William with an unlit cigar—"hasn't finished his living just yet, so there's still time to fetch a new one if you are found lacking."

William put a hand on Byron's shoulder.

Byron glanced back and could see blood seeping through the sleeve of his father's suit. The sight of that blood scared Byron more than anything else. "What happened?"

William ignored him. He looked past Byron and said, "I'm not long for the other side, Charlie. You and I both know that the time has come for change."

Charlie nodded once. A flicker of regret seemed to cross his features, but before it was clearly there, it was gone. The dead man gestured widely with the hand still holding the unlit cigar. "I reserved a table."

"Dad?" Byron pulled up his father's sleeve. A blood-soaked bandage covered his wrist. "Shit. We need to get you to the hospital."

Charlie looked at William's arm, and then caught William's gaze. "Do you need a medic?"

"No." William gently loosened Byron's grip. "This can wait."

An inexplicable look passed between William and Charlie; then Charlie nodded. "As you will."

He turned and walked away into the gray landscape. William motioned for Byron to follow. Byron wanted to take his father and leave this place, but he trusted William, so, reluctantly, he walked after Charlie.

Soot looked different when there were only shades of gray: that was the first realization Byron had as he walked through a city that had neither modernity nor antiquity to distinguish it. As they went farther into its precincts, wooden structures gave way to brick buildings and steel-and-glass structures. Horse-drawn curricles and barouches shared space with bicycles and Model Ts and 1950s Thunderbirds. The costumes varied as much as the conveyances: women in flapper dresses strolled past others who sported punk and belle époque attire. There was something unsettling about the unnatural beauty of these coexisting eras.

The streets, storefronts, and windows were all crowded with people—many of whom were watching them with open curiosity. Byron noticed more than a few guns carried openly, not always in holsters, but he also saw women with children in baby carriages or clutching their skirts. Couples, the men not always in the garb that matched the era of their partners', talked or in several cases pushed the boundaries of public displays of affection, regardless of the mores of the era their clothes belonged to.

"Been a while since we had a tourist." Charlie's voice was laced with obvious amusement.

"He's not a tourist," William said. "He belongs here as much as any of us ever do."

"That remains to be seen, doesn't it?" Charlie stopped at an intersection and tilted his head, the cigar clamped between his teeth. The street was completely clear. He held up his hand and motioned for them to wait. "Just a moment."

No more than six heartbeats later, a train tore through the intersection in front of them. It was absolutely soundless; no tracks or rail lined the street; and in moments, it was just a speck in the distance.

Charlie pulled a pocket watch out of his waistcoat, glanced at it, tucked it back into his pocket, and then stepped into the now crowded street. "The way will be clear now."

"Because a train passed?"

Charlie fixed him with a stare, and then looked at William. "Boy's not too sharp, is he?"

William smiled, but not in any way that could be mistaken for friendliness. "I suspect he's more than sharp enough to do the job better than I have. If you're after picking a fight, Charles, we can do that after we talk."

After a tense moment, Charlie laughed. "I'll welcome you any day, old man. Maybe you'll feel like lingering with us awhile."

William shook his head. "I go to where Ann is, and I doubt that my wife is *here*."

Charlie stopped at a glass door with the words MR. D'S TIP-TOP TAVERN painted on it. He reached out and grabbed the brass bar that served as a door handle, tugged it open, and gestured them inside. As William passed, Byron heard Charlie ask in a low voice, "What about your Graveminder?"

"Don't." William lifted a fist as if to strike Charlie.

"Relax, boy." The menace in Charlie's voice grew gravel thick. He didn't flinch, but he grinned around his cigar. "Your Graveminder's safe enough, but she can't go on till *you* get here. Rules are rules."

Byron stepped in front of his father, hoping to defuse the tension between them. "What's a Graveminder?"

Between one step and the next, a blur of expressions crossed Charlie's face—surprise, doubt, and then amusement. "You didn't tell the boy *anything*, old man?" He paused and looked straight at William. "And the other one?"

At his side, William's hand unclenched. "Maylene and I decided to let them have their peace while they could."

"And now Maylene's dead." Charlie whistled.

Byron had just about reached the end of his patience. "Someone want to fill me in?"

"Boy, I wouldn't want to be in your"—Charlie looked down—"ugly boots for love or money. I would, however, pay dearly to have a good seat for the show. It's a real shame I'm stuck over here."

Then he walked past Byron into the shadowed interior of the tavern. It looked well past its prime: faded wallpaper, tattered in places, lined the walls; exposed pipes ran the length of the ceiling; and more than a few of the velvet-covered sofas sagged. The front of the room was taken up by a low stage; on it sat a drum kit and a baby grand piano, the only things in the room that didn't show signs of wear, age, or neglect. Throughout the room, linen-draped tables were surrounded by high-backed chairs. On each table, a small candle flickered. At the far side of the room were a long wooden bar and a curtained doorway. The curtain, like the tablecloths, was threadbare in places. The place had a sort of tired elegance that spoke of better days. What it didn't have was a crowd: the entire room was empty save for one waitress and one bartender.

"Ahhh, there's our table." Charlie swept his arm forward, gesturing them to the front of the room.

When they reached the table, Byron noticed a placard in the center of the table. It read, in precise calligraphic letters: RESERVED FOR MR. D AND GUESTS.

William glanced at the waitress, who had followed them to the table. "Scotch. Three of them."

She looked at Charlie. "Mr. D?"

Mr. D? Byron looked at the man who'd escorted them to the club, at the placard in front of them, and at his father.

Charlie—*Mr. D*—nodded. "From my reserve."

The waitress glided away.

"And keep them coming," Charlie called after her. Then he clapped Byron on the shoulder. "You're going to need them."

19

D AISHA WAS STANDING OUTSIDE THE FUNERAL HOME WHEN SHE FELT AN insistent pull. Inside that building was a yawning mouth stretching open; she hadn't known it existed until that moment, but she felt it now. It wanted to swallow her whole, take her to wherever that place was that the not-walking dead went, and keep her there forever.

Make me truly dead.

Something like loneliness crept up on her as she stood there trying not to clutch the tree beside her. Once, she'd seen *him*, the Undertaker, scurry up the tree and shimmy onto one of the branches to get a kite that was all tangled up. He had been a teenager then, and he had dropped to the ground to give the kite back to the kids she was with, not looking at them like they were less because they didn't have money like his family did, not looking at her like she was something disgusting. He had been a hero that day.

Not yet a monster.

Now he'd kill her if he knew what she was. Now he'd end everything.

Hours passed as she stood trying to ignore the temptation to go into the building, to find the mouth of the hungry abyss inside of it.

She needed something to keep from falling apart. *Food. Words.*

Drink. The things she wanted since she woke up dead were weird, but weird or not, she needed them like she'd once needed air. The blood and flesh weren't so hard to find, but stories were a little different. She'd never done too well talking to people before she'd died; doing it *now* was even harder.

There was a woman, though, a stranger. She walked purposefully, as if she knew exactly where to go, as if she knew things. She was only a few years older than Daisha, not even as old as the new Graveminder.

Daisha followed her for a few moments, watched her walk and pause. She stapled papers to poles, and as she went she listened to whatever music pulsed in her earbuds. Daisha could hear the bass, but nothing more.

She approached the woman, stepped in front of her, and said, "I think I'm lost."

The woman let out a small squeak and yanked out one of her earbuds.

Startled, Daisha stepped away quickly.

"Sorry. I didn't hear you come up." The woman blushed. "I probably shouldn't play the music so loud."

"Why?"

The woman held up the stack of papers she clutched in one hand. "There's a, um, wild animal roaming around."

"Oh." Daisha looked behind her. "I had no idea."

"I'm on the town council. We're trying to alert everyone, but it takes a while." She smiled self-consciously. "I was going to wait, but I have plans later and . . . Sorry. You probably don't want to hear." She broke off with a laugh. "I'm pitiful, aren't I? Nerves."

"I can help." Daisha extended a hand. "If there's an animal out here, I don't want to be alone either."

"Thank you." The woman handed her a few flyers. "I'm Bonnie Jean."

"I'll put one on that pole." Daisha started to walk toward a light pole.

"Hold up." The woman followed. "You forgot the stapler."

"Sorry." Daisha kept walking until they were in the shadows, until they were farther away from the already empty street.

"It's okay," Bonnie Jean said. "If we hurry . . . I have a date."

It's okay. Daisha heard the words, the permission. *It's okay. Like Maylene. She wants to help.*

"Thank you," Daisha whispered before she accepted Bonnie Jean's help.

Afterward, Daisha walked through the peaceful streets, wishing that Maylene were still alive. She'd *tell me stories. Bonnie Jean didn't tell me anything before she was empty.* After a few moments, she'd become motionless while Daisha ate. She didn't share any words. She wasted her breath on whimpering noises, and then she stopping making any sounds.

20

REBEKKAH SAT AT MAYLENE'S WRITING DESK. SEVERAL PAPERS WERE stacked to the side of the blotter, and a note to "pick up oranges" was scrawled across the topmost paper. Absently, Rebekkah ran her fingertips over the wood of the desk. Maylene had refused to let anyone refinish it, arguing that the pattern of the scratches and wear marks earned from years of use made it uniquely hers. *Years leave stories written on every surface*, she'd said. The room, Maylene's bedroom, was filled with stories. The tatting on the pillow shams and on the delicate doilies atop the chest of drawers had been done by Maylene's great-grandmother. The noticeable chip at the foot of the Tudor four-poster bed was from when Jimmy threw a toy car at it when he was a toddler.

Family.

Sometimes it felt odd to know so much about her stepfather's family tree and nothing about her biological father's, but Jimmy had been a part of her life, and her bio-father was just a name on her birth certificate. Jimmy had been the only real father she'd had—even though he hadn't been in her life more than a few years—and after he died, Maylene had been her closest family. Rebekkah and her mother were close: they talked and visited and got along well enough, but they'd never had the kind of bond Rebekkah and Maylene shared.

And now it's gone. Maylene is gone.

Rebekkah ran her hand over the desktop. Stories hovered like ghosts in Maylene's room, and Rebekkah wished she could hear them all one more time, that she could hear the ones Maylene hadn't spoken yet, that she could hear Maylene's voice.

Instead, she'd spent hours listening to people tell her that Maylene would be missed. *No shit.* She'd smiled while they told her how wonderful Maylene was. *As if I didn't know that.* She'd tried not to scream while they assured her that they knew how hard it must be for her. *How could they?*

After much badgering, Rebekkah had resorted to flat-out rudeness to get the last of the mourners out of the house. It wasn't that she didn't appreciate the solicitousness of some of Maylene's friends and neighbors—okay, maybe she *did* resent it a bit. Maylene had never been altogether accepted by the community. They'd all been kind enough, but they'd never simply stopped by for a cup of tea or piece of pie. For reasons Rebekkah never understood, the community was always slightly reserved where Maylene and her family were concerned.

Not that Maylene ever complained. If anything, Maylene defended the peculiar distance the town kept from the Barrow family. "They have their reasons, lovie," she'd murmured every time Rebekkah mentioned it. Rebekkah, however, wasn't quite so willing to accept that there was any reason *not* to want to have Maylene at their tables.

The stillness of the house felt calming, despite everything. There was something right about Maylene's home—*my home*—that had always soothed whatever upset Rebekkah felt. Even now, being in the old farmhouse eased the weight of Maylene's loss more than Rebekkah could've anticipated. She stroked a hand over Maylene's writing desk and opened the envelope Mr. Montgomery had handed her earlier.

> *April 1993*
>   *I can't say that I'm liking writing this letter, Beks, any more than you're liking reading it. I'm not sure I'll be ready to*

*talk about any of this stuff anytime soon. If that changes . . .
perhaps I'll become a braver soul. If not, try to look kindly on
me when I'm gone.*

*You're the child of my heart as much as Ella Mae ~~is~~ was.
You're stronger, though. Never doubt that strength. There's no
shame in admitting it, no disrespect to Ella Mae. I love her,
but I don't pretend she was something she wasn't. You can't
either. A day will come when you might hate her for the choice
she made. A day might come when you'll hate me. I hope you'll
forgive us all.*

*Everything I have, everything I am, and everything the
women before me had—it's all yours. The paperwork is all in
order. Cissy and the girls have known for years. Your mother
has, too. When Ella Mae died, you became my sole heir. The
house, the contents, everything: it's yours and yours alone
now. The good and the bad, unfortunately, are both part and
parcel of the deal. I'd ask your permission if I thought there
were other options, but you're my only choice now. Once I'd
thought it would be Ella Mae and you both who could've made
the decision for yourselves.*

*Someday you'll read this, and God willing, you'll be ready
for it. I hope my dying wasn't a surprise. If it was, the answers
you'll need are in the house. Trust the Montgomerys. Trust
Father Ness. Look to the past. All those before you kept records.
The journals are here in the house. Every question you're
having—I hope—will be answered between these . . . except
of course, why I'm too much a coward to tell you all of this in
person. That one I'll answer now: I am afraid, my dear. I am
afraid that you will look at me the way Ella Mae did. I am
afraid you will look at me the way I looked at my grandmother.
I am afraid that you will abandon me, and I'm too selfish to lose
you. I'd rather we go on as we are right now, with you loving me.*

*Forgive me, lovie, for all my mistakes, and think of me
after I'm gone. The alternative is too horrible to bear.
All my love and hopes are with you.
Grandmama Maylene*

The tight script of Maylene's handwriting was as familiar as her own. The words, however, made little sense. Rebekkah could think of nothing that would change her love for Maylene, nothing that would turn her affection to hate.

The second item in the envelope was a copy of Maylene's will, which Rebekkah gave a perfunctory read to verify what Maylene had said in her letter. Maylene had, indeed, left every item, every cent, and the house solely to Rebekkah. *Everything?* Rebekkah wondered how long Cissy had known. *Is this why she's always hated me?* Rebekkah stopped herself from dwelling too long on that train of thought: Cecilia Barrow had taken up more than enough of her energy today.

Instead, she turned her thoughts toward the journals that were somewhere in the house; she also couldn't figure how the answers to her grandmother's murder would be found in journals—or where in the rambling farmhouse they would be. A cursory glance around the room revealed nothing so much as the fact that Maylene had lived a long time in one spot. Shelves were built close to the ceiling and above the door frames, and lined the perimeter of the room. They were packed full of books, some well worn from repeated readings or advanced age, none looking like journals. A wardrobe sat on either side of Maylene's bed. At the foot of the bed sat a wooden chest. They were obvious storage spots, but neither the wardrobe nor the chest held any journals.

Rebekkah began looking through the three other bedrooms on the second floor—her own, Ella's room, and the one Jimmy and her mother had shared. Although her own room wasn't cluttered, the other two were packed. The third-floor attic was worse. It over-flowed with Maylene's accumulated possessions from decades of living—and decades of living by those who'd been here before May-lene. The downstairs was equally stuffed. The secret "cubbyhole" in one wall of the living room was crammed to the point that Rebek-kah had closed it with a grimace almost instantly upon opening it, and the pantry had always been near overflowing—a topic Maylene had dismissed with vague words of "never knowing what a body might crave." Nowhere in the morass of belongings in the house did Rebekkah see anything resembling journals. What she did see were reminders of the amazing woman whose life had been ended before Rebekkah had a chance to say good-bye. Death of a loved one hurt, that was a constant, but the suddenness and the violence made this death seem worse.

Jimmy's was sudden. So was Ella's. Rebekkah could picture them all here in the house. *Never again.* She looked around her, and sud-denly the memories were too much—and the memory that wasn't hers, Maylene's last memory, felt like it tainted everything.

Maylene was killed here.

The walls felt too close, and every sound made her skittish. The place she'd felt safe, the place she ran to when the world was too much, suddenly had shadows in it that stretched like threats loom-ing around her. The fear wasn't logical, but she couldn't say it was foolishness either. Someone had murdered Maylene in their home.

Is it someone I know?

Is it someone who stood there at the grave?

Did he—or she—offer me words of comfort?

The wind set the swing to creaking on the porch. When she was a girl, that sound used to comfort her. As a grown woman alone in the house where her grandmother had been murdered, she found it a lot less comforting.

Rebekkah picked up Cherub, who was winding around her ankles, and went to the window. She pulled the sheer curtains aside and looked out. It was getting toward late afternoon, but the sun hadn't set yet. The porch was empty.

Nothing but shadows and air.

"I'm going walking," Rebekkah announced.

Cherub meowed.

"Shush, you. I'll be back soon." She kissed his head and lowered him to the floor.

She changed into something slightly less funereal—jeans, a dark gray pullover, boots, and a black jacket. Then she gathered up her wallet, keys, and a canister of pepper spray. Pepper spray wouldn't be ideal against an animal, but it would buy her a moment if the person who'd hurt—*killed*—Maylene tried to hurt her. *A gun would be a lot better.* She'd grown up around guns, but the only one she knew of in the house was a shotgun, and even in Claysville, someone walking around town with a shotgun in hand would seem downright odd. *Pepper spray it is.* She shoved everything into her jacket pockets and slammed the door.

She had no destination in mind, other than being out of the house. Too much was changing too fast. She'd thought Cissy would inherit something. *Like she needed* another *reason to hate me.* Despite feeling slightly guilty that Cissy and the twins hadn't been left anything, Rebekkah felt a relief that the house she'd come to think of as home was still hers.

Several times, Rebekkah thought she'd heard someone behind her, but when she turned, no one was there. She walked faster, staying along the well-lit sidewalks. Thoughts of the little girl's injured arm made her pause: well-lit paths might be a deterrent to human "animals," but she wasn't sure that they'd be a concern to a wild animal. If there was someone or something following her, turning back seemed unwise.

Now what?

She started running; the thud of pavement under her boots had the illusion of echoing louder with each step. By the time she'd reached the familiar neon lights of Gallagher's, her legs ached and sweat trickled down her spine. No one and nothing had grabbed her, and the run had made her feel better than she'd felt since she'd gotten the call yesterday.

That was only yesterday. Rebekkah shook her head. *Too much change too soon.* She pulled open the door and stepped into the dim bar.

Faces, familiar and not, turned toward her. No one looked hostile, but their scrutiny wasn't comfortable. People there knew her, knew more than she wanted them to know. She'd remembered that objectively, but the reality of being watched, being studied, was more unnerving than the memory had allowed her to expect—or maybe the pity rankled more than the studious stares.

"Beks?" Amity called. "Come sit up here."

Rebekkah could've hugged Amity for the invitation. It was the bartender's job to be friendly, but Rebekkah didn't care. She smiled and went toward the bar.

Amity stood with her hands on her hips; a bar rag dangled from one hand. The look on her face wasn't one of pity. "You looking for someone?"

Rebekkah shook her head. "Air and a drink. I . . . I needed to be out."

Amity gestured at a stool. "You want to talk?"

"No." Rebekkah pulled the stool out and sat. "I've had more than enough talk."

"Got it. No talking." Amity slid a bowl of bar mix to her. "So . . . beer, wine, or liquor?"

"Just wine. House white. Whatever."

"We have—"

"I don't care," Rebekkah interrupted. "I just need to hold a glass of something so I can sit here not looking *quite* as pitiful."

Amity stared at her for a moment, turned, and pulled a partially empty bottle of white wine out of a cooler. She twisted the cork out of the bottle. "You don't want to drink or talk."

"Nope."

Amity poured the pale liquid into a glass, shoved the cork back into the mouth of the bottle, and brought the wine to the bar. "What are you looking for?"

"I don't know." Rebekkah wrapped her fingers around the glass. It felt fragile in her hands, enough so that for a moment she considered squeezing hard, driving shards of glass into her skin. She lifted the glass and drank half of it.

"A little space, boys?" Amity uncorked the bottle and refilled the glass. "Should I have asked, 'Who are you looking for?'"

"No." Behind her, Rebekkah could hear the door opening and closing. Footsteps clomped across the room. The door opened and closed. More footsteps sounded. The door opened again. It clicked.

"Bek?" Amity's hand came down on Rebekkah's. "You can handle this."

Rebekkah nodded.

After a couple of silent minutes had passed, Rebekkah looked around. The room was empty. Bar rag in hand, Amity came out from behind the bar. From the way she was dressed, the bartender looked like she had been expecting a half-decent crowd: her short skirt and tall boots were look-at-me fare. On slow nights, Amity wore jeans—not that she looked slouchy even then—but a generous glimpse of skin helped part patrons from more of their money, so busy nights meant skirts.

"You kicked them out," Rebekkah said.

"They didn't have to obey me." Amity tossed a bottle toward the trash bin as if it were a ball through a hoop.

Rebekkah left her drink behind and walked over to stand beside Amity, who was now singing softly to herself while she tossed bottles, emptied ashtrays, and swished crumbs onto the floor. Rebekkah gathered up several half-full glasses that patrons had left behind and carried them over to the bar. "Nothing shakes you, does it?"

For a moment, Amity stilled. A flicker of fear crossed her face. Then she lobbed another bottle. "Oh, you'd be surprised."

Rebekkah wasn't sure if she wanted to ask or let it go. She paused, and the moment stretched. "Maybe some night you can tell me what frightens the invincible Amity Blue."

"Maybe," Amity murmured. "Not tonight."

"No, not tonight." Rebekkah walked over to the bar. She put her hand on the pass-through. "May I?"

"Sure. Hell, if you want, you can have a few shifts for as long as you're here . . . It might help keep your mind off the claustrophobia of being in Claysville," Amity said.

"I don't know about all of that." Rebekkah lifted the bar flap and went behind the counter. Then she flipped it back, once more making the bartender's domain separate from the rest of the main room. She and Amity were now on opposite sides of where they'd started the evening.

A job? In one place? Rebekkah couldn't remember the last time she'd had a regular job. Portions of the alimony checks her mother received from her various ex-husbands and Jimmy's very generous insurance had left her with a bank balance that never seemed to decrease much. She'd added to it with the proceeds from a few commissioned art contracts, but that was about her own self-esteem, not about need. *Jobs mean staying.* The thought of staying in one place never made sense. *Except when I'm here.*

"I have questions about Maylene's death, but that doesn't mean . . ." Rebekkah shook her head: she knew she wasn't leaving right away. She needed answers. Weakly, she finished, "I don't know how long I'll be around."

Amity's dry tone filled the suddenly awkward pause: "Temporary is not shocking in this business, Bek. If nothing else, I'll give you a few Bar Wench 101 classes to distract you . . . unless you have another distraction lined up?"

The thought of Byron came unbidden to her mind, but using him as a distraction was wrong. *Is it?* She shoved that thought away and looked at Amity. "No. I have nothing else in mind to distract me."

"I thought maybe you and By—"

"We're old friends, but he's a relationship guy and . . ." Rebekkah paused at the tight smile Amity offered her. "Am I missing something?"

Amity shook her head. "I think you know a different Byron than I do."

Rebekkah felt an awkward burst of jealousy. She didn't look at Amity while she opened the cooler, uncorked the wine, and poured two glasses. Once she was sure the undeserved jealousy wasn't visible in her expression, she looked at Amity. "So you know Byron?"

"There are only a few thousand people in Claysville, Bek. Most of them aren't anywhere near as interesting as Byron." Amity opened her arms wide. "Plus, Gallagher's is the hottest bar in town—and I *am* the hottest barmaid in town—which means I know everyone old enough to drink."

Rebekkah laughed. "Maybe you ought to visit me when I go . . . wherever I go next."

"I don't think I'm the sort to go anywhere, but thanks."

Glass in hand, Rebekkah half sat, half leaned on one of the hip-tall beer coolers and braced her feet against the stool Amity had placed behind the bar for that very purpose. "You running the place now? Last time you wrote, you said Troy was the manager. Are you two . . ."

"No. Troy's not really the commitment sort, or maybe I'm not the sort of girl guys want to commit to." Amity shrugged. "We split up a few months ago. We're cool, though . . . or we *were*. He needed a week for personal stuff, but he was supposed to be back to work almost a month ago. No show, no call. And Daniel . . . well, he might *own* the place, but he's not saying much other than 'Amity, you handle things.' So I'm handling them."

"Troy just vanished? Did he leave town?" Rebekkah's heart felt constricted. He'd never been the responsible type, but he loved the bar. Gallagher's and Amity were the only two reasons she'd ever seen him get excited—or possessive. In high school, they'd been in art class together, but after Ella's death, they hadn't really talked until she'd come back for a visit and found him slinging drinks at Gallagher's. He'd introduced her to Amity, his younger coworker and his very obvious infatuation.

"I don't know." Amity wiped down the last of the tables that had been occupied earlier. "He's just gone. Considering how rarely anyone leaves, *I* think it's something to worry about, but what do I know, right? Daniel acts like it's a 'lovers' quarrel' thing, but Troy and me . . . we weren't like that. He wouldn't take off because I started seeing someone new."

"Do you think the new guy said something to Troy? Did you ask him? Troy's a sweetie, but that might be an issue. Do they know each other? Or—"

"He . . . the *new guy* is just filling time with me, Bek. Trust me on this."

Rebekkah couldn't make herself ask, but she wanted to know. She wanted to not care if it was Byron, but she did care. "Maybe I ought to give him a talking-to. Have I met him?"

Amity came over to the bar, put both hands on it, and pushed up so her feet were off the floor. She leaned forward, reached under the bar, and pulled out the jukebox remote. She hopped back down and aimed the remote. "Credits. Go pick us some songs. If you're here, might as well dance or shoot."

"My pool skills still suck." Rebekkah came back through the bar door. She paused beside Amity. "Did you tell Sheriff McInney?"

Amity's smile was strained. "About Troy? Yeah, he knows."

"And?"

"And Troy's a bit . . . unreliable, so the sheriff's not thinking any-thing of it. I asked Bonnie Jean to mention it at the next town coun-cil meeting, but"—Amity shrugged—"my sister's so worried about impressing the mayor that I'm not really counting on her."

The door opened. A half-dozen men stood there. The one in the front of the group looked at the two of them; he took off his hat and held it in his hands. "Ma'am?"

Amity's barmaid smile returned instantly; she motioned them forward. Then she murmured, "Break's over, Bek. Set us up with something loud. Nothing country or blues tonight."

Rebekkah nodded and went over to the old jukebox. She glanced over her shoulder to look at Amity, but the bartender was beckoning to the men tromping into the bar, acting as if the two of them hadn't had any sort of personal conversation.

"Belly up, boys. Those tip jars don't fill themselves, and we've got a new barmaid to train. Can't train her if you don't order up a bunch of drinks." Amity hopped up onto the bar, swung her legs over, and jumped down. "What'll it be?"

21

Byron sat at the table with Charlie and his father. A woman in a floor-length dress with charcoal-dark hair and smoldering appeal reminiscent of Bettie Page sashayed across the room. She paused at their table.

"You wanted me, Charlie?" Her voice was breathy, but that could've been a result of the corset and bustier that cinched and lifted her breasts so they were a gasp away from spilling out of the deep-V cut of her dress.

"Be a good girl, and go sing for us." Charlie patted her ass absently. "I can't stand the quiet."

A single spotlight came on with a sharp click. The curtain over the doorway opened, and three dead musicians came through it to join the singer onstage. One carried a cello, and the other two took their places on the stools in front of the piano and drums.

"Graveminder?" Byron prompted.

Charlie lifted his glass in a toast as the breathy girl started singing. "Ahhh, that's what we needed. Now, back to business . . . Graveminder: the woman who keeps the dead from going out on rampages; the partner of the Undertaker. Maylene's replacement is"—he tilted his head as if thinking—"Rebekkah."

Byron looked from Charlie to his father. *"Rebekkah?"*

"Yes." Charlie snapped his fingers.

The waitress came over carrying a dark wood box. She placed it in front of Charlie, glanced at him, and then turned away when he neither spoke nor acknowledged her presence. As she walked away, the singer sang-whispered something almost too soft to hear into the mic.

Charlie reached in his pocket and drew out a key. He slid the key into the box's lock. "The Graveminder keeps the dead in the earth or brings them to me if they go out walking. You need a new one to replace Maylene." He unfastened the latches on either side of the box. "The Graveminder is the only living person—other than you now—who can come here."

"Why would she do that?" Byron stood. "Why would *I*, for that matter?"

The spotlight seemed to brighten as the pianist's fingers danced over the keys. The rhythm from the drums added a sense of urgency to the music as Charlie opened the lid of the box.

"Because the alternative is violating the contract." Charlie reached into the box and grabbed a scroll. "Because the alternative is that the dead will kill the lot of you." He unrolled the scroll, pulled a pen out of the box, and tapped the pen on the scroll. "You sign here."

Charlie held out the pen, and the musicians stopped all at once as if they'd been cut off. They, much like everything else since Byron had arrived in the land of the dead, seemed to be under the control of the man currently watching him expectantly. Byron wasn't eager to be under anyone's control. "What's my part? You talked about the Graveminder, but what is it that I'm supposed to be promising to do?"

Charlie smiled magnanimously. "The very thing you want, Byron, the thing you've wanted since Ella died: you protect our Rebekkah. You love her. You keep her from wanting death."

Byron fixed his gaze on Charlie. "Can you come to our side?"

"If the Undertaker and the Graveminder do their job, *none* of the dead will come to your town. Your children will stay in the town, be safe from . . . well, quite a few things. Your town will stay strong, safe, flourish, all that rot." Charlie tapped the scroll. "It's all there in the fine print, spelled out in black and white."

"It's simply the order of things, Byron." William's voice was weary. "Go ahead."

"Why? You expect me just to . . ." Byron backed from the table. "No. You're not thinking clearly, but I am. Let's go."

He turned and made it as far as the door before he heard his father's voice: "You drank with the dead, son. You sign, or you stay."

Byron put his hand on the door, but he didn't open it. His father had *knowingly* brought him here and put him in this predicament.

"I'm sorry," William added softly. "There are traditions. This is one of them."

"Your old man is right." Charlie's voice echoed in the quiet room. "Make your choice."

Slowly, Byron turned around to face them. "And if I don't sign?"

"You die. It won't hurt: you simply stay here. He finds a new Undertaker over in the land of the living. His Graveminder died; he's done with his duty now." Charlie didn't rise from his seat. Nothing in his expression offered any clue to what the dead man thought. "I can't force your hand. If you stay, you won't lack for entertainment, and if you sign, you'll go back and forth between worlds. It's no matter to me in the end."

While Charlie spoke, the cellist and pianist had begun to play, and the girl started singing again softly. She stared only at Byron.

He took a step back toward the table. He looked at his father. "How could you—" He stopped, not even certain what he wanted to ask. "Help me understand, Dad. Tell me . . . *something*."

"After Ella Mae died, Maylene and I agreed that it was for the best to delay telling you until you were ready . . . or it was necessary." William looked as implacable as he had looked during all the years Byron asked questions without answers. "She was a child. We couldn't risk losing you or Rebekkah, too. Now here we are."

"Ella died because of *this*?" Byron's mouth went dry. His heart-beat pounded too loud under his skin. "She knew. That's what she wouldn't tell us. I thought . . . I thought all sorts of things. That someone hurt her or that she saw something or . . . but it was this."

"It was," William admitted.

Gracelessly, Byron walked over to the table and dropped into the chair he'd vacated.

William tossed back the rest of his whisky. "Being the Grave-minder is a family burden."

"Bek's not Maylene's blood-family." Byron felt stupid saying it, but it was true. If blood-family was the criterion, that would leave the role to Cissy or one of her twins. He grimaced at the thought.

"Ahhh, yes, Cissy," Charlie said. "She'd make of mess of it, but it would be entertaining nonetheless. Her Elizabeth's not a bad sort, though. Do you fancy her?"

"Why?" Byron tasted his Scotch; it had the delicate aroma and slight saltiness that bespoke a Northern Highlands origin, one of his favorites. *That's probably not accidental either. Is anything coincidence?*

"If your Bek dies, it'll be one of the others. That's how it works. Chain of command and all. Maylene was a clever old bird. She desig-nated Rebekkah, but if she'd let things fall as they might . . . things aren't always predictable with so many women in the family. One of the girls would be your partner then . . . you *are* signing, aren't you, Byron? Going back, keeping the girl safe and all that? Doing your part?"

"You're a bastard." Byron reached out his hand, though.

"Atta boy." Charlie extended a pen and then smoothed out the scroll. "Right here on the line, son."

For a moment, Byron paused. His fingers played at the edge of the scroll.

"Sign it," William instructed. "The terms don't change the truth: you sign or you stay. You can read it later in search of the loophole. We all do. None of it changes what you need to do right now."

Byron ran his finger over the column of names.

> 1953–2011 William B.
>
> 1908–1953 Joseph
>
> 1880–1908 Alexander
>
> 1872–1880 Conner
>
> 1859–1872 Hugh
>
> 1826–1859 Timothy
>
> 1803–1826 Mason
>
> 1779–1803 Jakob
>
> 1750–1779 Nathaniel
>
> 1712–1750 William

Some of the signatures were in tight script; others were jagged. He wondered how many of the men on the list had been as clueless as he felt, how many wondered at their sanity. *How could they bear to sentence their own sons to this? How had his father?* Byron let his gaze lift to William for a moment. William didn't flinch or look away.

"I don't have all day," Charlie nudged. "Actually I *do*, but I'm getting bored. Sign, or send your father back to find a new Undertaker. Rebekkah needs a partner, and until she's brought here to my domain, she is only a shadow of what she needs to be. They will see her, but she won't know what they are or what she is. She's vulnerable to them. Either be her partner or move out of the way."

Byron wasn't going to abandon her, or his father, or accept dying. He scrawled his name beneath his father's.

Charlie flipped the page over, and on it, Byron read THE BARROW WOMAN followed by another list. This time, the names were all written in the same hand. These weren't signatures, but a list of women who were selected to fill a role. For them, there was no real choice.

> 2011 Rebekkah
> 1999 ~~Ella~~
> 1953–2011 Maylene
> 1908–1953 Elizabeth Anne (called "Bitty")
> 1880–1908 Ruth
> 1872–1880 Alicia
> 1859–1872 Maria
> 1826–1859 Clara
> 1803–1826 Grace
> 1779–1803 Eleanor
> 1750–1779 Drusilla
> 1712–1750 Abigail

Byron's gaze lingered on Ella's scratched-out name. *She was to be the one.* He clutched the edge of the paper. "Why? Why don't they get a choice?"

"I wasn't going to make *everything* easy." Charlie rolled up the scroll, returned it to the box, and locked it.

The waitress came over and took the box away.

Abruptly, Charlie stood. "Feel free to stay and enjoy the show." He nodded at them both and put his hat on his head. "Be seeing you soon, William."

As soon as Charlie left, the bar started filling up. Whatever privacy they'd had before vanished as dead men and women sat down at the tables. Many of them nodded to William.

Byron turned to his father. "I have questions."

"I don't know that I have answers you'll like." William motioned to the waitress. "The bottle."

After she was gone, Byron stared at his father. "Did Mom know?"

"She did."

"But what about Maylene? If Graveminders and Undertakers are *together*, and each job's passed on in families . . ." He paused, thinking. "It doesn't work after one generation."

"Love doesn't mean marriage, son. If they choose to be together, one of them has to pick a new family to pass his or her duty on to. The son or the daughter is spared. That's the benefit of the contract. You pick one of the children to let free of it." William laughed, but there was only bitterness in the sound. "If I'd married Maylene, one of our children would have been chosen, and the other role would've moved to another family in town—someone we chose. If we had no children, or if we had no blood-heirs we deemed worthy and capable, we could *pick* a successor. That's the loophole that Maylene was clever enough to use to choose Rebekkah: she decided that *the choice to be Graveminder* was part of being worthy, so she decided to give Ella and Rebekkah both the choice, but Ella made a different choice before Maylene even told Rebekkah."

"So you could've . . ."

"Only if you were a wastrel. Only if you couldn't handle it. Only if it was—*in my heart's truth*—better for the town. There's no one I'd trust more with the duty; you've always been meant to be the new Undertaker." William accepted the bottle from the waitress before she had a chance to set it on the table. Silently, he poured Scotch into their glasses.

When Byron realized that the waitress was still beside the table, he looked up at her.

She bent down and whispered, "If you want"—she flicked her tongue along the curve of his ear—"Mr. D says you can have a full night on the house." She straightened up and gestured around the room. *"Anyone. Anything.* No kink too bizarre."

Most of the club's occupants were staring at him. Amused smiles, parted lips, heavy-lidded eyes, disdainful glares, and raw hunger—

there was no continuity in expression. Byron felt curiously exposed and uncertain of how to react.

The waitress pressed an envelope into his hand. "Here's a chit. It's got no expiration date . . . unless you die, of course. As long as you're alive, though, we're available."

"Thank you," he said, not because he was truly grateful, but because she looked at him expectantly. "I'm just not . . . I don't know what to say."

She bent closer and brushed her lips over his cheek, quickly tucking a book of matches into his hand as she did so. "Welcome to our world, Undertaker."

22

DAISHA LIFTED HER HAND TO KNOCK ON THE TRAILER DOOR. SHE FELT odd knocking, but the alternative was walking in unannounced and that didn't feel comfortable either. Nothing felt quite right: being here wasn't right, but not-being-here was wrong. So she knocked.

The door opened, and her mother stood in front of her. She wore a clingy T-shirt and too-tight jeans. Makeup hid some of the splotchiness of her skin, but it couldn't do anything for her bloodshot eyes. She had both a cigarette and a beer bottle in her hand. For a moment, she simply stared at her daughter.

"You're gone. You left." Behind her, the light from the television flickered and cast blue-tinged shadows on the wall.

"Well, I'm back." Daisha thought about shoving her mother aside and going into the trailer, but the idea of touching Gail made her hesitate.

"How come?" Gail leaned again the doorjamb and studied Daisha. "I don't have the time to be bailing you out if you're in some sort of trouble, you hear?"

"Where's Paul?"

Gail narrowed her gaze. "He's at work."

"Good." Daisha stepped past her mother.

"I didn't say you could come in." Gail let the door slam closed even as she said the words. Absently she flicked the ash from her barely smoked cigarette in the general direction of one of the over-full ashtrays on the scarred coffee table.

"Why?"

"I'm not running a motel. You left and—"

"No. I didn't *leave*. You sent me away." Daisha didn't feel the confusion she'd been feeling since she'd woken up. The walls had the dirty tinge of too much smoke trapped in a small space; the carpet had the burn marks and stains of too many drunken nights; and the furniture had the cracks and tears that told of fights and poverty. As she stood in the tiny structure that had once been her home, she understood more than she had so far: this was where she belonged. It was hers, her home, her space.

"He said he'd be good to you, and it's not like I was sending you off to some stranger." Gail lit another cigarette and then flopped back onto the sagging sofa with the same bottle of beer and the cigarette in hand. "Paul said he was good people."

Daisha stayed standing. "You knew better, though, didn't you, *Mom?*"

Gail lifted the beer bottle to her lips and drank. Then, with a vague up-and-down gesture, she motioned at Daisha. "You look fine, so what are you bitching about?"

"For starters? I'm dead."

"You're what?"

Daisha stepped across the small room to stand at the edge of the sofa. She looked down at her mother and hoped to see some sort of emotion, some hint that Gail was relieved to see her. There was nothing. Daisha repeated, "I'm dead."

"Right." Gail snorted. "And I'm the fucking queen of Rome."

"Rome doesn't have a queen. It's a city, but"—Daisha sat down beside her mother—"I *am* dead."

The words felt unnatural, admitting them felt impossible, but they were right. Her body didn't live. Her heart didn't beat in her chest; her breath didn't fill her lungs. The things that made a person alive had stopped—because her mother had let someone make her dead.

"Dead," Daisha whispered. "I am dead, not alive, not right, and you're the reason why."

"You think that's funny?" Gail started to stand, but Daisha shoved her back before she was all the way upright.

"No," Daisha said. "It's not funny at all."

Gail raised a hand, the one holding the cigarette, as if to slap her daughter. The cherry of the cigarette was almost pretty.

For a tense moment, Gail's hand stayed upraised and open, but she didn't touch Daisha. Instead, she took a drag off the cigarette and exhaled noisily. "I'm not laughing."

"Good. It's not funny." Daisha took her mother's wrist and forced her arm back down. The bones under her mother's skin felt like brittle twigs wrapped in sweet flesh and warm blood. It was hard to believe she'd ever thought her mother was strong.

Daisha kept hold of Gail's stick-thin wrist and scooted closer. She pressed her knee hard into Gail's leg, pinning her. "Tell me. Did you honestly think—even for a moment—that I would be safe?"

Gail's eyes widened, but she didn't say any of the words that would help. Instead, she shoved ineffectually at Daisha with the hand that held the bottle and muttered, "You look fine to me." She shoved again, harder this time. "Let me up."

"No." Daisha took the beer bottle and tossed it at the opposite wall, hard enough that it shattered. The glass shards fell to the carpet like glitter. "Did you know what he was going to do?"

"Paul said—"

"No," Daisha repeated. She pinched the cherry off the tip of the cigarette and dropped it on her mother's lap.

Gail shrieked and tried to swat it out. "You little bitch. How dare you?"

"You sent me away with someone you didn't know, and you didn't expect me to come back." Daisha squashed the smoldering ember before it did any real damage. "You knew."

"Paul said that a lot of countries still do arranged marriages and bride prices, and it's not like you were making a contribution. Food and electricity and . . . kids are expensive. We can't afford another baby if you're here." Gail's chin jutted out. "If you were gone, we'd jump to the front of the wait to have a baby. Paul wants a baby, and I'm getting old."

"So you were just recouping your losses, right?" Daisha stared into her mother's eyes. This woman had given her life. All she saw was irritation. "He *hurt* me, and then he left me in the woods like trash . . . He left me there bleeding, and when I thought I'd found help, when I thought the people from *here* who found me were going to help, they *killed me*. All because you wanted rid of me. All because *Paul* wants a baby."

"You don't understand."

"You're right," Daisha whispered, "but the longer I'm awake, the more I *do* understand. Seeing you here, it helps. Being here helps. You're helping me now, Gail, but you know how you can help me more?"

"I can't let you stay here, but I can . . . I can not tell Paul you were here. Maybe I could get you some money or something."

"No." Daisha leaned her forehead against Gail's and whispered, "I need more than that from you."

"I don't have anything else to give you." Gail squirmed and batted at Daisha. "I can't let Paul know you're back."

When her mother's hand made contact with her cheek, Daisha caught both wrists and held them with one hand; she pressed harder on her mother's leg. "Paul will figure it out when he gets here."

Daisha covered her mother's mouth with her hand, squeezing to make sure that the sound was muffled. She leaned forward and bit a hole in the side of her mother's throat. It was messy, the way the blood came pouring out too fast. By the time Daisha had swallowed the first bite, Gail's shirt was soaked.

But Daisha's mind felt increasingly clear, and her mood was improved now that her hunger was silenced. The more she ate and drank, the clearer her mind became. Hunger made her get confused, just like fear made her drift away.

I am safe here. Now.

Eating helped; drinking helped; words helped. Gail had given her all three.

23

A S THEY WALKED BACK TOWARD THE TUNNEL, BYRON TRIED TO TAKE IN as many details as he could. He wondered if the city itself shifted, because the streets they traversed didn't look at all like the ones he thought they'd come in on. The area around him was definitely not modern, but he could see what looked to be a 1950s suburb at one intersection. Some blocks belonged to eras he couldn't identify, but the residents didn't always fit the landscape: flappers and apron-clad women were accompanied by miners from another century and modern businessmen.

"I'm going to need a map or a guide or something," he muttered. "Otherwise, how will I ever find my way around here?"

"It gets easier," William assured him.

"After how long? How long have you been coming here? How *often?*" Byron stopped at an intersection. Two women riding late-nineteenth-century high-wheeled bicycles passed. The first woman smiled at them, but the second seemed not to see them at all.

"I've been coming for most of my life." William rubbed a hand over his face. "I was eighteen. My grandfather was the last Under-taker."

"Not your father?"

"No," William said. "He was too old, or maybe it was that I was old enough. It's hard to say."

Byron saw the mouth of the tunnel ahead of them. Within it, flickers of red and blue blinked at him like the eyes of some great beast. In a world of gray, the brightness of the tunnel was a beacon.

"Your mother and I thought about not marrying, not having children, not passing this to our own child. If I'd married young, I might've been old enough that you would be spared, but then my grandson would need to be next in line, and I couldn't stand the thought of my grandson dealing with this so young . . . and your mother and I wanted a child, wanted *you*." William shook his head, looking more than a bit sorrowful.

Not sure what to say, Byron stepped into the tunnel. William followed. Unlike when they had entered the land of the dead, the tunnel now stretched quite a ways in front of them.

"Take the light," William instructed. "You lead."

Byron lifted the torch from the wall. It flared to life in his hand.

"Your touch will light the way. Her touch will not. You light the way; you open the gate. Without you, she cannot enter their world."

"Why?"

"To keep her safe. She's drawn to the dead." William gave him a rueful smile. "And you are drawn to her. You'd give your life for your Graveminder, to keep her apart from death, yet some part of her wants desperately to hurtle toward it. She can choose not to be with you, but you and you alone will be able to tempt her as the dead can." He shook his head. "Ella felt the call of the dead far sooner than anyone expected. Maylene brought her over. Charlie agreed to it; the old bastard never liked saying no to Mae. She was going to bring both of the girls, and let them make the choice over the next few years, but after Ella came over . . . We didn't expect her to do that, but when she did, we decided not to tell you and Rebekkah. I don't know if it was the right choice, but that world is a temptation I don't understand for Graveminders . . . and I never did much better at telling Mae no than the old bastard did."

William looked at Byron, waiting for something—forgiveness or questions or Byron wasn't sure what. He couldn't say that he was all right with everything or that he even understood everything. He didn't even know if he was angry. Later he might be all of those things; later they'd have to talk; but just then Byron was still to trying to make sense of the enormity of the secrets that his father—and mother *and* Maylene *and* Ella—had kept from him.

And from Bek.

For another ten minutes, Byron and his father walked in silence, but the entrance appeared no closer. Byron looked over at his father and noticed that he was no longer cradling his arm. "Is it feeling better? Your arm, I mean."

"It doesn't hurt at all," William assured him.

"It looked like it was bleeding pretty badly." Byron frowned. "Whether it hurts or not, you're getting stitches. Can you still feel it? I mean—"

"I don't need stitches."

"Shots, too," Byron continued. "Did you clean it? Was there rust on whatever you cut it on? What *did* you cut it on? Was it sterile? What—"

"Byron, stop." William unwound the bandage and dropped it to the floor on the tunnel.

As Byron watched, the bandage disintegrated and drifted away like smoke.

"The dead did this." William held out his arm. A piece of skin was missing like it had been peeled back. Muscles were exposed and ravaged. "Shots don't help. Bites from the dead *can* heal. The child will be fine, but like any other open wound, bites are vulnerable to regular infection."

"The child . . ." Byron stared at his father. "You and that child were bitten by a *dead* person."

"As was Maylene."

"A dead person is loose in our world . . . *biting* people. The ones we saw seemed normal enough." Byron paused as he realized the peculiarity of what he'd just said. "Aside from the *dead* part."

"They're different if they wake here." William lowered his arm, so it hung loosely by his side. "She's only newly awake. They come to the Graveminder as soon as they can—if they wake, and they usually don't. Maylene's not had one wake in years. This one wasn't minded. They *need* minding, so they don't wake. This girl . . . she had to have died out there alone somewhere. She's young, not much older than seventeen, I'd guess. Skittish."

Byron thought about the girl he'd seen. *Twice.* He opened and closed his mouth.

Around them, the tunnel suddenly compressed, and then they were standing just outside the storage room again. Byron put the torch back into a space in the wall. "I think I met her. The dead girl."

"Good. You and Rebekkah have to work together to bring her through the tunnel. I'm not sure what Rebekkah needs to do once she reaches the girl, but Maylene will have taught her or left instructions." William suddenly clasped Byron, pulling him into a tight hug, and asked, "Forgive me my faults, son."

Byron held on to his father for a long silent moment. "Yeah. Of course I do. We just need to figure out how to tell Bek all of—"

"No." William released him and stepped back deeper into the tunnel. "*You* need to tell her. You are her Undertaker."

"But . . ." Byron's words faded as he saw the sorrow in his father's eyes.

"I can't come with you." William took another step back into the shadows. "You'll do fine."

The emotional overload he'd thought he felt mere moments ago was nothing compared to the rush of conflicted emotions that consumed him now. Charlie had told him that he could die, "simply stay here"; Byron had seen his father's name on the list *with an end date.* William had never intended to come back to the world. Byron looked at his father, the last living member of his family, and said, "You knew when we went there . . . that going meant dying."

"I did. Only one Undertaker. Only one Graveminder. You're able to go back and forth without a problem, up until you bring your replacement to see Charlie. Once the next Undertaker signs . . ." William smiled reassuringly. "It's a painless way to die."

"I don't want you to be dead . . . what if I pull you through the gate?" Byron felt desperate. Too much was happening too fast. "Maybe—"

"No. I'd still be dead, but it would hurt. Heart attack, probably. Stroke maybe." William shrugged. "For all intents and purposes, I died over there. My pain left when you signed the contract. If you force me back, the pain will return, and I'll still die. Only one Undertaker at a time can sit at Mr. D's table. You signed, and I died."

Byron felt the weight of William's admission settle on him. He'd killed his father.

"You didn't know," William said, drawing Byron's gaze to his father's face. "It was *my* choice. I took you to see Mr. D. We drank with the dead. You're safe to do so now, up until the day you bring the next Undertaker to his table. That's the way it's always been . . . If you're lucky, it's what you'll do one day. Your son—or your heir, if your successor isn't by blood—will walk through this door alone, and you'll stay behind."

"My successor?"

"If you and Rebekkah—the Graveminder and the Undertaker are drawn together—if you need to pick a successor because you marry her or have children with her"—William paused as if he was weighing his words—"it's like arranged marriage. Watch their interests. Be wise."

"You and Mom and Maylene . . ." Byron couldn't finish the words.

"We wanted you all to have some choice. It could've been either of the girls. That's why you were drawn to them both, but Ella's death changed things." William's expression grew stern. His brow furrowed, and his chin lifted. "You and Rebekkah will be good together."

And at that, every thread of interest Byron had for Rebekkah became tainted. What he wanted, what he felt, the protectiveness and the longing—it had all been programmed in him. *How could they?* Byron couldn't think about it then. *Practicality first.* If he thought about it, he'd be furious, and he couldn't walk away from his father with anger between them. *Later when . . . my dad is dead.* Then he could let himself feel the anger that threatened.

"How do I . . . what about your service?" Byron felt foolish asking his father about his own burial, but it mattered more now than it ever had. The dead walked. That much he understood. He couldn't have his dead father walking the earth biting people.

"We Undertakers don't often die in the same way as most folk. Graveminders don't either unless"—William blanched—"they don't make it . . . Sometimes they walk into the land of the dead, but it's unpredictable."

"You're dying because Maylene died."

"She's not replaced your mother *ever*, but she is my partner. I made two vows, one to Ann and one to be the Undertaker. I made the same vow you just made." William kept his voice gentle, but there was no mistaking the firmness in it as he said, "I don't have any business being Undertaker now. There's a new Graveminder. She needs *her* Undertaker, not some old man."

"But—"

"And Maylene needs her rest," William interrupted. "She's earned it. I go easy to my death. She went in pain, consumed by the dead who shouldn't have walked. It needs fixing. That's your job. Yours and Rebekkah's."

"Dad—"

"Go to Rebekkah. Open the gate for her. She needs to meet

Charlie before anything else can be done." William clasped Byron's forearm. "Then bring her home and put the dead to rest where they belong."

"I need you." Byron pulled his father closer. "You're the only one I have. The only family. Maybe—"

"You know better than that. There are no maybes. I need to go." William embraced him again. "There's papers and things for you in the trunk in my room. The rest . . . you'll figure it out. Trust your instincts. Think about the lessons you've had. I've done what I could to prepare you. Don't ever forget what the dead are capable of. You saw Maylene's body. The one that did this to my arm, to Maylene, she looks harmless, but she's not." He caught Byron's gaze. "Don't let them wake, but if they do . . . show no mercy. Protect each other and the town. You hear me?"

"I do."

"Make me proud." William turned his back and started walking back into the shadows. His voice came clearly through the emptiness even as he walked away: "You've *always* made me proud, Byron."

And then he was gone.

Dead.

Byron stepped into his funeral home, his home again, and stumbled a few steps. He crashed to knees as the weight of what just happened settled on him.

My father.

He understood grief. He'd felt it when his mother died, when Ella died; he'd seen it in other people his whole life, but this was different. His father was the last tie to the world he'd known, his childhood, his memories. Everything Byron had been—the "and Son" part of the family business and of his life—was now changed.

Gone.

There was no son. With William's death, he was Mr. Montgomery.

The Undertaker.

He'd known that he'd follow his father's path since he was a child. At mortuary school, he'd met those who rebelled against it, who followed because it was expected, but for him, it was something else. It was a calling.

Byron stared at the still-open cabinet. The plastic bottles and their multitoned liquids were as familiar as the sterility and scents of the basement rooms of his childhood home. Even though embalming was atypical, they still had supplies on hand for those not born in Claysville. Only the town-born residents had to be buried unembalmed. The door was hidden behind the things they rarely used. It seemed an obvious clue now, but before that day, Byron couldn't have guessed at the secrets hidden behind those chunky bottles.

So now what? That was the real question. He needed to move forward, explain his father's absence, talk to Rebekkah. *Who else knows?*

The enormity of the day, of the future, of the things left undone, hit him.

Sitting around won't get anything done.

He stood and brushed himself off, although there was no dirt to remove. Carefully, he closed the cabinet. He sealed the tunnel to the land of the dead, where his father had gone.

My father is dead.

24

IN A FEW HOURS, AMITY HAD TAUGHT REBEKKAH ABOUT MIXING THE BA-
sics or at least following the instructions in the dusty recipe box
behind the bar. Now Amity stretched up to pull down a couple more
bottles for her next demonstration. She'd explained enough about
the flavors of liquors and liqueurs that Rebekkah had a new appre-
ciation for the difficulty of creating new drinks.

"What's the house special?" Amity prompted.

"The alternate version of any drink I can't remember," Rebekkah repeated. "If I add too much triple sec instead of upping the
tequila, I call it as a 'special 'rita' and add it to the recipe box if I have
time. Unless they don't even notice, which they usually don't."

"And if you pour the altogether wrong thing?"

"Unless it goes together, toss it and log it." Rebekkah grinned
and repeated one of the odder bits of advice. "And if *they* ask for
things that don't go together, don't refuse. 'It takes all kinds, even
those who have sick tastes.'"

"Good girl." Amity grabbed a bottle from the well and poured a
double shot of gin in a glass. She topped it off with a splash of tonic
and set it on the bar just as one of the men approached.

"Thanks, hon." He dropped money on the bar and took his
drink.

Rebekkah waited until the man walked away and then said, "You make it look easy."

Amity rung up the drink, pocketed the change, and shrugged. "I've been doing this since before I was legal. There aren't a lot of things I can do without leaving Claysville, and there are fewer that I would enjoy. This job is my life . . . There are other things I want in life, but not many of them."

The tone in her voice made Rebekkah pause; Amity wasn't as blasé as she was pretending to be. "Should I ask what those are?"

Amity hugged her. "Family, friends, you know, just the normal stuff."

Only half jokingly, Rebekkah shuddered. "No thanks. Cages don't appeal to me. Never have, never will."

"People change, Bek," Amity murmured as she turned away and busied herself at straightening the top-shelf liquor.

"Not if I can help it." Rebekkah tossed the ice out of several glasses that had been brought back up to the bar. "If it works for you, though, good luck with whoever he is. There is a specific *he*, right?"

Amity glanced over her shoulder at Rebekkah. "Tonight was to be about me cheering *you* up. So let's drop that subject, okay?"

"Sure." Rebekkah felt increasingly uncomfortable, suspecting that the "he" in question was Byron. She tucked her hands into her pockets. "I think I need to crash. I'm going to head out."

"I'm sorry."

"For what? It's just been a long day and—"

"And my mood-swinging on you didn't help, did it?" Amity glanced at the tables again, presumably to make sure they weren't in need of attention. "I was serious, you know: I really could use the extra hands here if you decide to stick around for a while. I have a few temp people, and I'm happy to step up as a manager till Troy turns up again . . . if he does . . . but another bartender on call would be great."

"Sure." Rebekkah forced a smile to her lips. "Add me to the list. I'm guessing I'll be around for a few days while I figure out what I'm doing about . . . everything."

Maylene's house. Maylene's things. How do I box it all up? Rebekkah felt the returned weight of decisions she didn't want to make—or know how to make. *How do I not box it up?* Cissy's claims that Rebekkah wasn't real family came back with an almost physical slap. *I am Maylene's family. Family isn't only blood.* Maylene had told her that over and over, and just then, Rebekkah was even more grateful than usual for that particular sentiment.

"Bek?"

Rebekkah pulled her thoughts back to the here and now. "Sorry. I'm tired . . . and overwhelmed."

"I know." Amity glanced toward the door. "Hey, do you want to call someone to walk with you? Or maybe one of the guys—"

"I'm good. I got here on my own, right?"

"You know Maylene didn't die of natural causes, don't you?" Amity lowered her voice and added, "Somebody killed her, Bek. That means that you need to be careful. *Everyone* does."

Rebekkah pushed the queasiness down. "Drop it."

"Ignoring it doesn't change it. You aren't safe," Amity insisted.

"Me specifically?"

Amity hesitated. It was only a fraction of a moment, but it was there. "Everyone, but everyone's not grieving and walking home alone."

"Right." Rebekkah didn't believe her. She felt cold chills run down her spine. Without another word, she grabbed her jacket and ducked out from behind the bar. She caught Amity's gaze. "I want to ask you questions. I want to know that you're . . . I don't know . . . the person I thought I knew, but right now I'm burned out. It's been a long day, and I'm going to hope that whatever you're hiding right now is because you're trying to look out for me—or that I'm just being paranoid. I'm not even sure right now."

"Just be careful. That's all I'm saying." Amity spoke the words softly.

"I am." Rebekkah shrugged on her jacket and walked out without another word.

The walk between Gallagher's and home wasn't that far, but it was still a little stupid to think about walking alone when both an animal and a murderer were loose in town. Rebekkah reminded herself that she had done far stupider things in the past and suspected she would do so again. Most of her bad decisions after being in a bar were a lot worse than walking home in the dark in the small town where she'd come for respite over the years.

Of course, her grandmother had just been murdered in this small town, so she couldn't shake her discomfort as easily as she would have been able to do on prior visits. Streetlights were spaced so far apart that the darker shadows seemed omnipresent. Passing cars made her tense. Far-off unidentified noises as well as the sound of dogs barking raised chills on her skin, so when she saw Troy sitting on the stoop of Once in a Blue Moon Antiques, the sense of relief she felt was palpable.

The shop was across the street and partway up the tiny block, but she recognized him easily enough. Few men in Claysville had the combination of bulky muscles and pretty-boy hair that Troy had. His long curls were tied back with a red bandanna, and he had on his usual bartender garb: black jeans and a button-up shirt worn like a jacket over a formfitting T-shirt. That particular look made Amity call him "cougar bait" when they'd gone out dancing, and a group of much older women spent the night eyeing him like he was a particularly decadent treat. Troy was too good-natured to mind, especially as Amity was several years younger than him. "Barely old enough to *be* in a bar, much less working in one," Troy had pointed out.

"Hey," Rebekkah called.

He looked up, but not at her. Rebekkah couldn't read his expression under the dim light that reached into the shadowy stoop. He didn't move.

"Troy!" She was still across the street, but not so far away that he shouldn't be able to recognize her. "It's me. Rebekkah."

Still, Troy didn't move or reply.

The nerves that had been eased by seeing him became unsettled again. "Troy?"

He stood then. His movements were awkward, so much so that he seemed to stumble as he took a step forward. He lifted his head and stared straight at her.

"Are you okay?" She stopped with more than an arm's length between them. "Amity was worried about you."

Troy lifted a hand like he was going to reach out to her, but he simply stood there with his hand upraised. He looked at his hand and then at her. His brow wrinkled, and he scowled.

"You're freaking me out a little," Rebekkah told him.

She reached out to touch his wrist, and he knocked her arm aside with his already upraised hand. Before Rebekkah could react, he pivoted and lunged forward. With his other hand, he grabbed her shoulder.

"What the fuck, Troy?" Rebekkah put the flat of her hand against his chest and shoved.

Troy's fingers clutched at her as she shoved him backward into the brick front of the store, but he still didn't speak. His lips parted in a soundless snarl.

"Don't try me." Rebekkah backed up, though: she wasn't a fighter. She'd taken some basic self-defense courses, but she also knew that he outweighed her by half again her body weight—and he seemed strung out on something.

She reached in her pocket for her pepper spray. If not for whatever adrenaline burst she'd just had, she wasn't sure she could have pushed him away, and adrenaline wasn't a reliable fight tool. She stepped back again. "Whatever you're on, it's not doing you any good."

He stared at her silently.

"Get some help." She kept hold of the pepper spray, but didn't raise it.

"Rebekkah." He said her name as if the act of speech was a challenge; the word came out in broken syllables.

She swallowed nervously. "Yeah . . ."

"Fix it." He lunged at her a second time; this time, his mouth came down on her shoulder.

The weight of his body against hers made her knees bend, and she started to fall backward. Instinctively, she pressed her other hand against his throat and pushed. She felt something under her hand give, and then before she could do anything else, Troy was gone.

She stood, cautiously, and looked around. In a fraction of a second, Troy had vanished. For someone so obviously unsteady on his feet, that kind of quick exit made little sense.

Rebekkah looked up and down the street. There was no sign of him or anyone else. He could've ducked into any one of a number of shadowed doorways or down an alley, but it had felt like he'd evaporated when she'd pushed against his throat.

Which is impossible.

She shivered, as much from the cold as from fear, and then she continued walking home. It felt like every hour since Maylene died brought new questions. The only answer she had just then was that standing alone in the street wasn't going to help matters, especially if Troy came back.

With a small sigh of relief, she let herself back into the house. The temptation to call Amity—and Byron—was outweighed by the fact that she simply didn't want to stay awake for either conversation. The adrenaline rush was gone, and the combination of the crash and her already pressing exhaustion meant that she wanted nothing more than to topple over onto whatever flat surface she could find. Tomorrow she could make those calls. Morning would come soon enough.

25

F LIP THE SIGN, WOULD YOU?" PENELOPE CALLED OUT FROM THE BACK
hall when Xavier entered.

"I could've been anyone. You shouldn't leave the door unlocked,
especially right now. There are monsters out there and—"

"I left it unlocked because I knew you were coming," she interrupted.

One of these days, she suspected she'd tire of provoking Xavier,
but until such time, she'd enjoy herself. Father Xavier Ness could
accept that the dead walked, that Death himself had made a bargain
with Claysville, that the townsfolk knowingly accepted such a bargain in exchange for health and semisealed borders, but the idea that
she could foretell the future caused him to furrow his brow. As far
as she was concerned, that degree of mulishness simply begged for
provocation, and she was happy to provide it.

"Penelope?"

"Still changing. You can wait or watch." She dropped her skirt
and slipped on her jeans. She wasn't about to go walking around
this town in a voluminous skirt that would hamper any running she
might need to do.

The sound of the priest's pacing made her pause. She brushed
the beaded curtain aside and said, "There's chamomile or that mild

mint you liked already out on the counter. I couldn't tell which you'd want."

He kept his back to her, but she knew he lifted the mint. The chamomile was for her, but it was more fun if she let him think she had wavered. Once she was sure he'd put the tea ball in his cup, she grabbed her boots and said, "I thought you might surprise me, for a minute. Put the chamomile in my cup, would you?"

"Surprise . . ." He glanced at the tea balls. "You dislike the mint."

"I do, but it's always nice to test myself." She twisted her hair into a knot on top of her head. "Don't worry about the mess." She grabbed the broom just before he accidentally knocked the jar to the floor.

"I find that infuriating." He snatched the broom from her hand. "You set up these ridiculous scenarios simply to . . . provoke me."

"And to prove that I'm not a charlatan, Xavier." She squatted down with the dustpan and held it in front of the pile of tea. "You doubt me every time we go too long without these 'ridiculous scenarios,' and we both know it."

He swept the spilled tea onto the dustpan and said quietly, "I don't mean to doubt you."

"But you do." She stood and dumped the tea into the waste bin. "You won't eventually, but until then"—she took the broom and put it and the dustpan aside—"we will do this. It causes you far more consternation than it does me."

He took a deep breath and looked directly at her. "Tell me why I came, then."

Side by side, they washed their hands. She filled both of their cups with boiling water, took hers, and walked to the front of the shop. Standing in front of the window looking out at the darkened streets, she whispered, "To tell me that William has died."

Behind her, she heard Xavier's footsteps, the slide of the chair, and the soft clack of his cup against the mosaic-covered table he preferred. She waited for him to ask the question he needed answered.

Moments passed. She sipped her tea and waited. Xavier hated that he wanted to ask her these things, struggled with it, so she gave him the space to do so on his own terms. Like everyone else in Claysville, he had to come to his decisions in his own time and way.

Finally, he said, "Tell me that everything will be resolved soon."

"I can't." She turned and walked to the table. "I can only see so far out most of the time, especially on matters of the dead. I can't see when the end is, only that we aren't near it yet."

"And Byron?"

"He needs to talk tonight." Penelope stood beside the table. "Not to a council member, but to someone who knew his father. You should go."

"I wish you could tell me where the monster is," he admitted. "It seems wrong that you can tell that I'll knock over the tea, but can't tell me . . . You make me question things, Pen. I don't like that."

"I know." Penelope took her seat. "I don't always like it either, but I am only what the Goddess allows me to be. If I knew everything"—she smiled at him—"I wouldn't be human . . . or here."

"Be safe."

She nodded, and the priest stood and left.

26

Late that night, he sat at his parents' kitchen table trying to make sense of what had just happened. Byron heard a soft knock on the kitchen door. He stood and opened it.

"Father Ness." He stepped aside to let the priest in.

"How are you?"

"Fine." Byron pulled out a chair and gestured to it.

The priest sat. "And William?"

The question was spoken softly, but the answer wasn't one Byron knew. *Do I say he's stayed in the land of the dead? That I killed him?* Byron took his seat.

"I'll be staying here for a while. Dad had to go . . . he . . ." Byron faltered.

"Died." Father Ness patted his hand.

Byron stared at the priest. "You know."

"Some of us are tasked with knowing. I can't tell you this will get easier, but if it helps, we—myself and the other clergy—can do a memorial. William was a good man." Father Ness had the look in his eyes that Byron had seen at innumerable funerals. It was only the second time it had been directed at him. The first time, when his mother died, it had been for both Byron and William. Grief shared was easier than grieving alone.

"He was a good man." Byron walked away and pulled open the fridge. A six-pack sat inside. He grabbed two bottles, popped the tops off on the edge of the counter, and set one in front of Father Ness.

The priest lifted his bottle. "To William, may God protect and keep him."

"To Dad." Byron clinked his bottle against Father Ness'.

They drank in silence. The priest let him have his quiet and his memories for the space of one slowly swallowed beer. When Byron slid his empty bottle away, Father Ness pushed his mostly full beer aside, too.

"A service would be great. Not right now, though." Byron had thought about the things he knew so far, and as much as he wanted to grieve, to hide and nurse the sense of loss, he couldn't.

Neither can Bek.

"No one will ask after William," Father Ness mentioned. "The inability to question things tied to the town contract is a typical consequence of being born here. People accept any anomalies that spring from the contract. Once you're settled, the town council will help you better understand the minutiae."

"Town contract?"

Father Ness gave him a wry smile. "When the town founders settled here in Claysville, they made an agreement with an entity whom they—mistakenly—thought was a devil. When I moved here, fresh out of seminary and ready to tackle the evils of the world, the previous Mayor Whittaker explained everything to me in rather tedious detail. I have no doubt that Nicolas will follow in his father's footsteps and tell you. The gist of it is that we're safe from a lot of things, and children born here won't be able to leave, but sometimes the dead refuse to stay dead."

"'They' made a pact and 'sometimes' the dead don't 'stay dead'? You say it like it's no big deal. You just *accept* all of this?" Byron wrapped his hand around the empty bottle, holding it as if to reassure himself of *something*'s solidarity. "How do I know I'm even *sane*? I walked through a gate in—"

"Don't tell me," Father Ness interrupted. "The diocese sent me here because of my openness to the less *modern* parts of the Catholic faith. However, unless there is due cause, only two people are meant to know where the gateway is. I am not one of them. There are things the members of the council know and things we should *never* be told."

Byron tossed the bottle into the sink. It broke in the stainless-steel basin. Brown glass shards bounced up and across the counter. "I hate this."

"I know, but what you do keeps us safe. Your father did God's work."

"Really? Because what I saw over there sure didn't look like heaven."

"Please, Byron, what's over there isn't something I should know. I wish I could ease your burden on this, but it's not my place. I *can* be here to help you through your grief . . . or your anger." Father Ness didn't look any less sympathetic and understanding than he had before. If anything, he looked more sympathetic. "Either way, you can call me or any of the spiritual leaders at any hour."

"For?"

"Talking. Whatever you need. *You* do God's work now." Father Ness stood. He laid his hand on Byron's shoulder and squeezed. "We can't carry the burden, but you are not alone."

Byron felt his anger flee at the kindness the priest offered. It wasn't Father Ness' fault that Byron was in this situation. The priest didn't deserve anger or disdain. "Thank you."

Father Ness nodded.

"They know, too? Lady Penelope, Reverend McLendon, and Rabbi Wolffe?" Byron asked.

"They do." Father Ness nodded. "We've known that you and Rebekkah would replace the previous generation one day. It's unfortunate that it should happen under such circumstances, but we have faith that you will handle this challenge—as did Maylene and William."

Byron stared at him blankly. *This challenge?* He was being asked to stop a murderous dead girl, tell the woman he'd loved for years that she was going to spend her life "minding" the dead with him as her companion, and figure out how to cope with his father's death. He wasn't quite sure which of those *challenges* was the most daunting.

"I'm not even sure how to get started," Byron said weakly.

"Start with some sleep. In the morning, go see Rebekkah. The details of the living will work out as they do, but the dead are walking. We all need the Graveminder to set things right, and she needs an Undertaker to open the gate."

Byron caught Father Ness' arm before the priest could step away. "I didn't learn as much as I want to know, and I need answers now. Tell me what you know."

Father Ness paused, but he nodded after a moment. "The terms of the contract aren't as clear as we'd like, but over the years we've gleaned some things. Those born here can't *stay* gone; many can't leave at all. They are stricken with illness if they try." The priest gave Byron a sad smile. "Rebekkah can't leave Claysville now. Neither can you—unless you must pursue the dead *or* retrieve the body of a town member."

"Rebekkah can't leave," Byron repeated. "She has no idea. Maylene's dead, and she's got to deal with all this, and she's trapped, and . . . I have to tell her."

"Go to her," Father Ness urged. "Tell her what she needs to know, so you can put the dead to rest. We count on you to keep each other—and us—safe."

Then the priest let himself out, and Byron was left trying to make sense of more things than he could process. If his father was right, a teenage girl was killing people in his town. If his own sanity was intact—a thing he wasn't entirely sure of—he'd stepped into a land where the dead walked, and he'd signed a contract he hadn't read. If his father, the priest, and a dead man could be believed, Rebekkah was caught up in the same contract, and his job was to not only break this news to her but also keep her safe—and take her to meet the dead.

No problem.

He sat in the same kitchen where his mother had once offered him after-school cookies and advice. *How had they kept it a secret?* He thought back to the years before his mother had died, to the years after Ella had died, to the past months when he felt compelled to return home. In pieces, it all fit. There had been whispered conversations and late-night visitors for as long as he could remember, and after Ella's death, Maylene had been at the house more and more often. Understanding the lies and secrets didn't alleviate the anger that threatened to spill out.

"Mam? What were you and Dad talking about with Ella's grandmother?"

"Nothing that you need to hear right now," she assured him. She'd paused then. "You know that Rebekkah's going to need you even more, don't you?"

"I'll always be there for Bek. She knows that." Byron felt tears on his cheeks. It was okay to cry for Ella, for Rebekkah, for all of them, here with his mother. Ann Montgomery wouldn't ever think him weak for grieving.

"She's lost more than anyone knows." Ann pulled him into her arms. The scent of vanilla and something else that he didn't know other than the fact that it was home filled the air. "She'll need you."

"I was friends with Bek before—not just because she is . . . was Ella's sister. That won't change." Byron pulled away from his mother's embrace. "I'm not a jerk."

"Oh, I know, baby." She'd cupped his face in her hands. *"I know who you are. I couldn't be prouder of you. I just . . . it's confusing sometimes being . . ."* She'd stopped herself then and hugged him.

At the time Byron thought she'd meant "being a teenager" or "being a guy" or even "being a girl's friend." He hadn't known that she meant being the Undertaker to a Graveminder. He hadn't thought she meant having your future mapped out for you without your consent. She'd known, then, known since he was born.

Once, he'd thought he and Ella had ended up dating because his parents had been close with her grandmother. They'd been thrown together so often that he wasn't even sure when they'd *started* dating. They'd slipped from being best friends to being girlfriend and boyfriend without any real discussion. They were meant for each other, a perfect fit. *How had she felt when she learned the truth?* He wished, not for the first or even the fiftieth time, that Ella had talked to him then.

The second line rang.

"Byron?" his mother called.

"Got it." He'd grabbed the phone.

Because the family telephone was used primarily for business purposes, his parents had gotten a second line for his birthday a couple of years ago. At the time, he didn't see the big deal, but over the past year, it had become increasingly important. When he wasn't with Ella, he was on the phone with her.

"Hi."

"Hey, I was just getting ready to leave to meet y—"

"No," she interrupted. "I can't see you anymore."

"What?" He sat down. "Ella . . ." The sentences were twisting in his head too fast to speak. "I don't . . . why? If it's what I said about Bek, what happened, it was just a kiss, we didn't mean to. I love you, and—"

"I know." She made a sound that was half a laugh. "Actually, that's one of the few things that made me think about not *breaking up with you. It's*

good that you had those thoughts about my sister. It means you're human, normal, not just programmed, right?"

"Programmed?"

"We can think for ourselves. You aren't just doing things you were forced to do. Neither am I." She was sniffling now. "That's good. Having a choice about what you do, who you are, what you love, who you . . ." Her words drifted off, and Byron felt suddenly sick.

"Did someone hurt you?" He hated speaking the words, but he kept going. "Were you forced to do something? Talk to me, Ells."

"I think I loved you before I even understood what love meant," she whispered. "I really do, Byron. I love you with my whole heart, with my body, with everything."

Byron leaned his head back against the wall. Ella had said those words to him more times than he could remember. She'd whispered them over and over their first time. She'd laughed and said them the other night. She said them so often, in so many places, that he hadn't felt lame when she'd said them in front of his friends.

"It's not enough. I wish it was, but it's not. I'm sorry. I'm sorry for what . . . I'm sorry for how it'll change things for you and for Bek." Ella's voice was steadier now. "I'm making my choice, though. Now."

"You're scaring me," he admitted. "I'm going to come over, and we'll talk and—"

"I won't be here." She took a gulping breath. "I need to go . . . somewhere. Oh, I wish you could come, that you could see it. You can someday. Just not now . . . and I can't wait. It's not fair to see it and be told I can't have it for years . . . or maybe at all. I need to go."

"Wait!" He shoved his feet in his shoes and cursed his inability to keep her on the phone while he ran to her house. "I'll go wherever you want me to, Ells."

"I love you. Promise you'll take care of Rebekkah for me." She paused and sniffled again. "Promise it. She needs love."

"Ells, she's your sister. I'm not—"

"Promise it," Ella insisted. "That's my last request. Take care of her. Say you will."

"No, not if . . . your last request? What are you talking about?" Byron clutched the phone.

"Do you love me?"

"You know I do."

"Then promise me that you'll always take care of Bek," Ella demanded.

"I will, but—"

She hung up.

Byron had dropped the phone and taken off running to her house, but by the time he got there, she was gone, and no one knew where she went. They didn't know until the next day when her body was found.

Now Byron understood: Ella hadn't been running away from something; she was running to something. Whatever she had seen in the land of the dead was more alluring than her life in the land of the living.

And now I need to take Bek to that world.

27

REBEKKAH HAD TRIED TO SLEEP BUT COULDN'T. AFTER A FEW FITFUL hours, she was outside walking again. This time, however, she watched the sun rise as she walked toward the cemetery. *Day two without Maylene.* Over the years, she'd lived a lot of places and spent many days—*weeks*—without speaking to her grandmother, but now that she was home, each day stretched out in front of her forebodingly.

When she'd visited Maylene, they'd gone from cemetery to cemetery plucking weeds and planting flowers. They'd buried food just under the soil and poured whiskey or gin or bourbon or any number of other drinks onto the ground. It hadn't felt *normal* exactly, but it hadn't felt peculiar either.

Rebekkah couldn't fill the gap in her life that existed now that Maylene was gone, but following the routine she'd shared over the years with her grandmother helped. *Like a handful of dirt to fill in a chasm.* She shifted the weight of her messenger bag on her shoulder again. The clink of tiny glass bottles was almost too soft to hear over the sounds of cars and birds, but she listened to them. The whole of it—the birds singing, car engines humming to life, and liquid sloshing in the bottles—felt right. The familiarity was comforting.

At the gate of Sweet Rest, she jiggled the heavy lock until it clunked open. She lifted a hand to the tall iron gate and pushed. It swung inward with a mild creak, and she drew a deep breath. The peace she needed was here. She knew this with a surety that made little sense. Her feet moved over the soil as if a cord had pulled her forward, not to Maylene's grave, which was in the nearby Oak Hill Cemetery, but toward a grass-covered plot in Sweet Rest. Once she reached it, reached Pete Williams, she stopped. The string that had pulled her there had vanished.

"Pete," she started. "I have some bad news."

She knelt and flipped open her bag.

"Maylene couldn't come see you," she told the month-dead man. "I came in her stead."

Rebekkah pulled out a bottle and twisted off the cap. Silently, she upended it over a tiny ivy plant that had started to creep up the side of Pete Williams' memorial stone.

"My grandmother died, Pete," she whispered. "Would you miss her?"

She paused and leaned her forehead against the gray stone. Tears fell on the soil, not many, but enough that she had to blink them away.

"I'm not crying for you, but with you," she said with a sniff. "You'd cry with me, wouldn't you, Pete?"

Her tears fell to the soil, where the whiskey had already vanished, and then she took several steadying breaths and wiped her cheeks with the back of her hand. "Places to go, people to meet," she told the absent man. "Hope your drink was good."

Then she patted the top of the stone. "See you around, Mr. Williams."

Nine graves, nine bottles, and quite a few more tears later, Rebekkah realized she wasn't alone: Byron Montgomery was walking up the hill toward her. A five o'clock shadow made obvious that he'd not stopped to shave since yesterday morning. He looked exhausted: clothes wrinkled, steps heavy, and eyes red-rimmed.

"Did you sleep? I mean . . . you look about as tired as I feel."

He fell into step beside her. "Some things came up, and . . . I slept, just not enough. You?"

"The same," she admitted.

He reached out as if to touch her arm, but didn't complete the gesture. "The grief will get easier. It *has* to, right?"

"I hope so. I miss her," Rebekkah murmured. That was the truth, the whole of it: Maylene's being gone hurt.

He nodded. "When Mam passed . . . it felt wrong to be happy, to move on. I felt like a jackass for even trying to let go. In my line of work, you'd think—" He stopped himself. "It's not the same when it's family. Some deaths are harder than others."

Rebekkah's gaze drifted over the cemetery as she and Byron wound their way down toward the old mausoleums. Irises spotted the overgrown grass in bursts of purple and blue. Morning glories and ivy crept up trees and over the stone sides of the mausoleums. A few of the squat buildings had weathered benches, stone steps, and columns. Doors of ornate iron and bronze sealed some; others had lost their doors and had only wire mesh affixed to the entryways to keep out would-be visitors.

At the bottom of the hill, Rebekkah sat down on the grassy earth. She wondered briefly if Byron had become one of those people who thought resting too close a grave was bad manners. "Will you sit with me?"

He lowered himself to the ground and sat with his legs stretched in front of him.

She pulled at the long grass beside her. It needed trimming. No one was minding this grave. She glanced at Byron. "How did you know where I was?"

Byron gave her an inscrutable look. "Maybe we're both meant to be here."

"I came here because . . ." She shook her head as she realized that the words she was about to say would sound freakish.

"You came here"—he reached out and laid a hand on the side of her satchel—"to visit the dead."

The bottles clinked as he slid his hand over the bag.

Rebekkah swatted his hand away. "Maylene used to bring me. I thought it would . . . it's silly, but I thought she'd like it if I came here."

"It's not silly." Byron caught her gaze. "I knew you'd be here."

"Because of Maylene," she said.

"And because of who *you* are." Byron caught her hand in his. He laced his fingers with hers and held on. "We need to talk, Rebekkah. I know the timing sucks, but— "

"Stop right there. You said you'd give me my space, that you were my friend, and I know I . . . that I'm the one who kissed you, but"—she tugged her hand free—"I'm not staying here. I'm not staying anywhere or with anyone, and you're the relationship type."

"That wasn't what I wanted to talk about, but for the record, no. I never was the relationship type, not with any woman I've met outside of Claysville. Just you." He stood up. "But I understand now."

"Understand what?"

"I was waiting on *you*, Rebekkah." He shook his head and laughed humorlessly. "I'll *always* be waiting on you, and I guess I need to either accept the crumbs you're willing to give me or pretend I'm over you. Maybe that's been the choice for years, and I was too damn stupid to realize it. What I have with you I'm not going to experience with anyone else alive."

"Byron, I'm sorry, but—"

"No." He cut her off. "Don't lie to me right now."

She stayed on the ground, staring up at him. With the sun rising behind him, he looked like a graveyard angel, carved and dark, silhouetted against the morning sky. He belonged here, in the quiet of the cemetery.

With me.

She shoved that thought away as quickly as it formed and, speaking as much to herself as to him, said, "I don't plan on staying here forever. I'm already going to be here a lot longer than I thought I'd be."

He raked his hand through his hair. "I don't know that you *can* leave. That's what we need to talk about, Bek."

She couldn't see the expression on his face for the sunlight behind him, but he sounded serious. It made her nervous. *"What?"*

He looked past her. "Did you ever think that the obstacles to what you want multiply the closer you come to getting it? If you say the wrong thing . . . if you had done the smallest thing differently . . . if you were *better* . . . if you were *enough* . . ."

"Byron?" She said his name softly.

He looked back at her. "My father died last night, and before he did, he showed me some things I need to tell you . . . and show you."

"Oh my God . . . Why didn't you say something when you got here? Why didn't you call me last night?" She scrambled to her feet and wrapped her arms around him. "I'm so sorry. What happened? He seemed fine when you guys left."

"He . . . It sounds crazy, Bek. Dad's gone, and . . . I need you." He cupped the back of her head in his hand and with his other arm held her close. "I need you, Rebekkah. I've always needed you—as much as you need me."

She laid her cheek against his shoulder. Despite the tangled mess between them, he was still her friend, had always been her friend, and he was clearly in some sort of shock. She pulled back and looked up at him. "Do you want to talk? I'm not much for sharing my feelings, but Mom certainly is, so if you need to . . . I've had *lots* of practice listening. I'll listen if you want to talk."

"I do," he admitted, "but not about Dad. There's a man you're going to meet. His name is Mr. D or Charlie. He lives over there."

"Over where?"

"In the land of the dead," Byron said.

"The . . . *what?*"

"Please? Just listen." He paused, and when she nodded, he told her: about Charlie, about the Graveminder, about his being the Undertaker, and about the contract between Claysville and the dead. He told her about the strange multi-era world, the club where he'd shared drinks with the dead, and his father staying behind. Then he added, "And the only two people who can go there are the Graveminder and the Undertaker. They're partners. The Undertaker opens the gate, and the Graveminder escorts the Hungry Dead to their rightful place."

"Uh-huh."

Byron ignored her tone. "The goal is that the dead don't get out of their graves, but—"

"Out of their graves?" she repeated. "Byron, sweetie, I think you're in shock. Don't you think we'd notice zombies?"

"They're not zombies, Bek." He understood why his father hadn't told him, but as he tried to explain to Rebekkah, he also understood why the new Graveminder and Undertaker should've been told years ago.

"Okay . . . Not zombies. Dead folk crawl out of the graves. Graveminder puts them back, by taking them through the gate that the Undertaker opens. William stayed behind; you're the new Undertaker."

"Right, and then she, *you*, take them to the land of the dead," he added.

"Me?"

"Yes. The Graveminder is supposed to keep them in their graves by way of . . . I'm not sure how. There are things you do when people die, ways to pin them or something. I'm hoping Maylene left you instructions on that part or Charlie tells you or—"

"Whiskey," she whispered. "Prayers, tea, and whiskey. Memories, love, and letting go . . . oh, fuck."

28

Rebekkah stopped. Her knees felt weak. "You're not crazy, are you? Or if you are, Maylene was crazy, too, and . . . *fuck*."

"I wish I *was* crazy," he said. His arm helped hold her upright, even as his words caused her to falter.

She shook her head. "Show me."

Silently then, he led her to Montgomery and Son's Funeral Home. Elaine—the receptionist, manager, and general assistant—marched toward them as they came in. Her silver-shot hair was swept up in its usual chignon. Her steel-gray skirt, pale rose-colored blouse, and low heels were her standard office wear. When Rebekkah was younger, Elaine had frightened her. The office manager was unlike anyone she had known: forceful, efficient, and stern. Time hadn't changed that.

"Your father's absence means it's just the two of us full-time now," Elaine began.

"I can't deal with this today," Byron muttered. "Is there a body?"

Elaine frowned. "No, but—"

"Then it'll wait." He rubbed his face.

"We need—"

"Fine. Call Amity," he said.

At the sound of Amity's name, a stab of jealousy went through

Rebekkah. *Amity has every right to . . . whatever.* She knew that Byron was the man Amity hadn't wanted to discuss. In their admittedly sporadic e-mail conversations, Amity had never once mentioned him or the funeral home. She hadn't even mentioned splitting up with Troy.

The silence stretched out a moment too long, and then Elaine said, "I will call Miss Blue, and you, Byron Montgomery, better get some sleep. I tolerate a lot, but whether you are my boss now or not, I will not be snarled at, young man."

Elaine turned and disappeared into her office.

"She's as frightening as I remembered," Rebekkah whispered.

"She is." Byron nodded. "And we couldn't function here without her. I think it would take three people to accomplish what she does in an average day. I will apologize later. First . . ." He took a deep breath and gestured for her to follow him.

He led her to the basement and into a storage room. Just inside the door, he turned on the overhead light and locked the door behind them. "I'm not crazy. I wish I was. I really, really wish this was all a delusion or a bad dream, Bek."

Then he walked over to a pale blue metal cabinet, reached behind it, and pulled it toward him. As he did so, Rebekkah felt her heart race. Her skin tingled all over as if tiny electrical pulses were being forced into her body. *This is real.* Her lips parted on a sigh as he slid the cabinet to the side.

"Oh . . . my . . . God." She breathed the words. "It's . . ."

The tunnel stretched in front of her, beckoning her, and only willpower kept her from racing to it. She stepped toward it as slowly as she could. Something in it hummed, a song sung by a thousand soft voices, and in that song, she heard her name.

She reached forward—and hit a wall.

Byron touched her face. "You're frightening me right now, Bek."

Rebekkah forced her gaze away from the tunnel. "Why?"

"I don't want you to look this happy about going toward death. There are reasons here in this world, *good reasons*, to feel happy. You need to let yourself free to feel that here." Byron leaned closer and covered her lips with his.

Rebekkah put both hands on his chest, neither pushing him away nor holding him closer. He put one hand lightly on her hip, and she leaned into his embrace.

The tension in his body relaxed, and he pulled her against him. He kissed her throat. "I wanted you before now, before this week, before this moment. I loved you before this—whether or not you liked hearing it."

Before she could object, he kissed her again. When he pulled back, he added, "Remember. Please remember what we've both known for years, Bek. Even if you weren't that and I wasn't this, I would love you. I thought I was awful for it, but I thought of you *then* . . . years ago. You were Ella's sister, and I thought it was wrong of me, but I couldn't *not* want to be nearer to you. The night you kissed me . . . If I'd been with anyone else, I wouldn't have tried to talk to her before I told you what I felt about you. But it was Ella. I needed to tell her first, and then . . . then she was gone, and you didn't want to hear it. You stop me every time I try to talk about it, but I can't *not* tell you now. I want to be with you forever. I love you. And you l—"

"No! Stop." Rebekkah grabbed his arm.

He cupped her cheek and continued as if she hadn't objected. "I love you, and *you* love me. We both know it. The problem is that you're determined not to."

She stared at him. *Not love.* She felt a lot of things for him. They were friends; they'd been lovers. That wasn't love. He'd said it once, but after that first time, he'd avoided the word. *It's not love.* She shook her head. "Byron, don't. You're upset."

"I am, but that doesn't change the facts." He caressed her cheek with thumb. "Lie to me later if you need to, but right now, before we go over there, you need to listen to me. I *know*. I've known for years, Bek. You love me just as much as I love you. You need to stop lying to both of us about it."

She stared at him, trying to find words to prove him wrong. There weren't any. She settled on: "You're confused. I don't want to hurt you. Ella died. We . . . and then she . . . *you're hers*. I don't deserve . . ."

He sighed. "She didn't die because of us, and even if she had, do you think she'd really want us to stay apart? She wasn't like that. You know that."

Tears were streaking down Rebekkah's face. In nine years, they'd never talked about it; she wouldn't, couldn't, bear the thought of that conversation. "You were not mine, and she was my *sister*. What I feel isn't love. It can't be. Ever. I don't have any right to . . ."

"Love me?" Byron took both of her hands. "But you do, and it's well past time for you to accept it. What we have is not about her . . . or anything else. It's about *us*. Remember that."

They stood there, at the entrance to the land of the dead, and she tried to think about the things he was saying. *I care about him. That doesn't make it love.* She shook her head and looked past him. Her gaze fell on the tunnel; instinctively, she took a step toward it.

His grip on her hands tightened. "Bek?"

The pulsing energy of the tunnel tugged at her; the song just on the other side of the barrier grew louder.

"Rebekkah!"

She pulled her attention from the tunnel and stared directly at him.

"Tell me you won't stay there," he demanded. "Promise me that when I walk out of there, you will come with me."

"I promise."

"I love you, Rebekkah Barrow." He released her hands and stepped into the tunnel. "I will take you there, but I *will* bring you home."

29

Byron?" Rebekkah tried to follow him, but was stopped by an invisible barrier in front of the tunnel. She put both hands on the air and leaned into it. She watched Byron take a torch from the wall. It flared to life as his hand wrapped around it. "Byron!"

He reached back through the barrier and held out his hand. "You gave me your word, Bek."

She slid her hand into his and tried to ignore how right it felt.

For a moment he stared at her, his features unreadable, and then he pulled her into the tunnel. "When we get to the other side, we need to find Mr. D. Later, at home, we will talk . . . about us. No matter what, though, you need to trust me."

"I *do* trust you. I always have." She wasn't sure of much, but she knew that. In the moment she'd stepped into the tunnel, she also knew that Byron was meant to be beside her. He would lead her home. She knew with a certainty that she had never felt before that he was meant to be at her side—he was *hers*.

The voices in the tunnel lifted and fell in waves; they spoke words she couldn't quite understand. *They are trapped.* The air around her was filled with invisible hands petting her cheeks and hair. *They are the dead who were abandoned.*

Byron's hand held fast to hers; their fingers were intertwined.

She squeezed. A chill wind pressed against her, bringing tears to her eyes, stinging her face. The wind swept the tears from her cheeks and the breath from her lips.

"Byron?" she called.

"I'm with you," he assured her.

At the end of the tunnel, she gasped. The colors she could see were so vibrant that it almost hurt to look around her. The sky was streaked in violet and gold. The buildings around her were breathtaking. Even the drabbest of them was cloaked in shades of colors that surely couldn't exist. She let go of his hand and stepped forward. Slowly, she turned around in a circle, taking in the sights of impossible glass buildings gleaming like jewels in the distance and nearer wooden buildings and brownstones. Everything was richer in hue than her mind could process.

Rebekkah looked around. "Byron?"

"Can't join us just now," a man said. He shook his head. "It's a real shame. He's entertaining."

"Where is Byron?" She looked around her, but she couldn't see the tunnel either. It had vanished when she'd stepped out of it. "What just happened?"

"Your Undertaker seems to have been detained. He will meet us at the house, my dear. I will escort you there."

"You . . . No, I need to find Byron," she insisted.

"My dear, he was escorting you here to meet *me.*" The man took off his hat, holding it by the brim, swept his arm gallantly, and simultaneously bowed from the waist. A lock of dark hair fell forward as he did so. Still in his bow, he lifted his earth-dark gaze to stare at her. "Charles."

He straightened, still holding her gaze, and added, "And you, my lovely one, are my *Rebekkah.*"

She shivered. Her name sounded different on his lips, like a prayer, an incantation, a holy plea.

"Mr. D," she murmured. "Byron told me—"

"Half-truths, my dear." Mr. D extended an elbow to her. "Let me escort you to the house while we await your Byron."

She paused, looking from his crooked arm to his face.

He smiled. "I'd rather not leave you here alone, Rebekkah. The streets can be treacherous."

"And you?"

Mr. D laughed. "Well, yes. I can, too, but you *are* here to see me, aren't you?"

The things Byron had told her didn't inspire a lot of faith in the charming man beside her, but her instincts warred with Byron's words. She *wanted* to trust Mr. D, even though she had no reason to do so. Cautiously, she laid her hand on his forearm. "I'm not sure why, but . . ."

"Ahhh, the devil you know," he stage-whispered. "You know me. Whether we've met or not, my Graveminders always know me."

"And do they like what they know?"

Charles laughed. "That, my dear girl, remains to be seen. Come now. Let me show you our world."

Rebekkah looked around one more time. There was nothing even remotely like a tunnel anywhere as far as she could see. A wooden walkway twisted off to one side; a cobblestone walk intersected it a short distance away. To her left, a dirt path and a paved city street extended into what looked like different neighborhoods. As she turned to look behind her, a river appeared. There were more paths than she'd first noticed, and none of them stood out. She turned her attention back to the man beside her. "You're certain that Byron will come to your house? Today? Soon?"

"Most definitely."

Unsure of what else to do—and guiltily curious about the world that spiraled out all around her—Rebekkah nodded and started walking with him, hoping that she wasn't making a mistake and trying diligently to focus on the warnings Byron had shared with her. This was the man who had manipulated Byron, who knew the answers to the questions she hadn't even known they should be asking until earlier today—and at that moment he was carefully guiding her through a city the likes of which she couldn't have conceived.

She alternated between gawking at the sights and feeling oddly self-conscious of her jeans and T-shirt. *Or perhaps longing for something else.* Mr D wore a well-tailored suit, and the women around her were dressed in a variety of eighteenth- and nineteenth-century gowns. She could hear the swish of fabrics, see the jewel tones and muted shades. She wanted to reach out and touch them. With more effort than she could've imagined, she resisted.

"It's normal."

She darted a glance at him. "What?"

"Our world is different to you." He gestured with a sweep of his hand. "Your senses are alive here. No other mortal experiences this world as you do. You are the Graveminder. *My* Graveminder. This is your world more than that other one ever will be. Shades and ashes, that's all you can find over *there*. But this"—he took a scarlet poppy from a street peddler and held it to her face—"is your domain."

The touch of the poppy was dizzying. The petals against her cheek felt like raw silk, and the vibrant color seemed too extreme to be real. She closed her eyes against the intensity.

"Over there you are a mere shade of what you are in our world." Mr. D stroked her cheek with the flower. "Death is a part of you. It's the future you've been headed toward all these years. It's the path our dear Maylene chose for you."

At her grandmother's name, Rebekkah opened her eyes. "Is she here?"

"She was waiting until William came to meet her." Mr. D dropped the poppy to the ground. "He joined her yesterday."

"And now?" Rebekkah felt like her eyes were burning from the tears she didn't want to let fall. "Can I see her?"

"Even if she *was* here, Graveminders may not see their own dead, girl." Mr. D patted her hand, which was still clutching his crooked elbow. "You are such predictable creatures."

She pulled her hand away. "Humans?"

"Graveminders," he corrected. "Although humans are often predictable as well. Shall we perambulate awhile? Take in a show?" He tipped his hat to a woman who wore nothing more than a pale gray chemise and cascading necklaces and bracelets of diamonds.

Rebekkah watched her walk away. The people on the streets paid her no more attention than anyone else. "I'm not here to . . . is she dead?"

"Everyone here is." Mr. D stopped in front of an immense set of marble steps that swept down from a high arched doorway. "Well, all save you, and your Undertaker, when he finally arrives."

"Do you know where he is?"

With Rebekkah beside him, Mr. D started up the steps. At the top, two men in uniforms stood, one on either side of a medieval-looking door. The men watched Rebekkah and Mr. D ascend with implacable expressions.

They were only a few steps up when an old-fashioned black roadster with whitewalled tires came careening around the corner. Four men in dark suits stood on the running boards; two others clung half in, half out of the passenger-side windows. In their hands, they had long-barreled guns—aimed at her.

"Guns?" She breathed the word. "They have—"

"Hold very still now, my dear," he interrupted as he swept her up into his arms and turned his back to the street.

She felt the bullets strike him as he held her aloft, and she screamed. The impact of the bullets as they penetrated his body made her flinch, but he shifted slightly from side to side. In doing so, he seemed to be keeping the bullets from hitting her, and all the while, he held her aloft and continued to ascend the stairs.

Killed in the land of the dead. She felt hysterical laughter threaten. *I'm going to die here.*

Then, as quickly as it started, it ended. She heard the car as it sped off, but she couldn't see anything. Charles had cradled her against him, and she'd closed her eyes in panic. She opened her eyes and looked up at him now, her eyes wet with sudden tears.

"I don't understand," she whispered as Charles lowered her so her feet touched the stairs.

One of the men who had stood at the door was gone. As Rebekkah looked toward the street, she saw him jump into another black roadster, which tore out, presumably following the men who had shot at Charles.

"Mind your step," Charles instructed as he swept his foot to the side, brushing several bullets away. They tinkled like chimes as they rolled down the stairs.

She stared at him. There was no blood on him, but his suit was in tatters. "Charles?"

A crowd of people paused at the foot of the steps, watching them with varied expressions. The other man at the door hadn't moved toward them. No one in the crowd seemed alarmed. *Is this normal?* Rebekkah forced herself to treat it as if it were—perhaps doing so would quell the panic still fluttering under her skin. She brushed back her hair and looked directly at the face of the man who had been shot shielding her body from bullets.

"I don't understand what just happened." She heard the tremor in her voice, but she tried to ignore it—and the shock that was making her shiver—as she straightened her clothes.

"They shot at us. Why . . ." Her shirt was ripped on the side, and when she reached a hand over, she felt that the skin was torn as well. She looked at her hand and saw blood. "Charles?"

Charles looked at her bloodied hand, and then at her side. He wrapped an arm around her waist carefully. "Ward," he called. "Retrieve a physician."

The remaining man at the door was beside them in an instant. "She appears likely to faint, sir," he said. "Shall I carry her?"

"I have her, Ward."

"I don't faint," Rebekkah protested.

"Sleep, Rebekkah," Charles said. "Let go, and sleep now."

"It's just a scratch," someone said.

A voice—*Charles' voice*—said, "First the physician, and then find them. This sort of carelessness is unacceptable."

Then Rebekkah gave in to the darkness. *It's a dream*, she rationalized, *a very, very bad dream*.

WITHIN THE TUNNEL, BYRON HAD ALTERNATED BETWEEN CURSING AND pleading. He'd thrown himself at the transparent barricade that had sprung up between the tunnel's opening and the gray world of the dead.

"Charlie!" he yelled.

No one came, of course. Byron was pretty certain that the barrier was Charlie's doing. Whatever he was, he'd seemed to be the only one running the show.

Futilely, Byron punched the wall, and then turned back to explore the tunnel with the scant hope that he might find a clue. The tunnel appeared to be a damp cave now; slick-wet walls with phosphorescent mold of some sort stretched into the gloom behind him. The ground under his feet was a slab of stone, smooth as if formed by a glacier.

When he heard Rebekkah scream from the other side of the barrier, he spun around, clawing at the invisible barrier, scraping his fingertips over it to find an opening of some sort. Nothing helped:

he was trapped outside the land of the dead. His choices were to wait or to go back, and going back seemed exceptionally unwise.

WHEN SHE WOKE, REBEKKAH WAS LYING ON A MASSIVE FOUR-POSTER BED. She looked around, but saw nothing beyond the perimeter of the bed, which was hung with thick brocade drapes. Reaching out, she slid the material between two fingers, enjoying the feel of each thread and the weight of the fabric. *It's just a drape.* She stroked her fingertips over the material, though—until a laugh made her recoil.

"The fabrics were selected for the pleasure of one of your long-gone predecessors. I'm glad they please you. Although"—Charles pulled back a drape and looked down at her—"I do apologize for the reason you are in my bed. It's not the reason I would've preferred."

She didn't look away, nor did she acknowledge the underlying meaning. She wasn't going to deny that Charles was handsome, or that he'd just saved her from far more injuries than she could fathom. He was tempting in the way that she imagined the devil himself—if there was such a man—would be: polished charm, wicked smiles, and easy arrogance. However, she wasn't sure what game he was playing, and the idea of looking at a dead man with any sort of lustful thoughts seemed inherently twisted.

Rebekkah smiled at him briefly before saying only, "I am *alive* and unharmed . . . thanks to you." She winced as she moved. "Mostly unharmed," she amended.

"I assure you that they will be dealt with, Rebekkah." Charles' earlier flirtatious look was replaced with an expression of tenderness. "I do apologize for the scratch. I had the physician clean and bind it."

Rebekkah reached under the sheet that covered her to feel the bandage that was wrapped around her ribs, covering the tender spot. In doing so, she realized that she was not wearing a shirt over the bandage. "Oh."

"My physician is not recently deceased." Charles' grin was wry. "He refuses to apply newer-style bandages . . . The dead are often intractable when it comes to adapting to modernity."

"So does that mean you were alive in . . ." She peered at him, studying his silk tie and matching handkerchief, assessing his well-cut suit, and admitted, "I have no idea when."

"The Great Depression, 1930s and '40s . . . but no. I have been around *far* longer than that. I am merely fond of that era."

Clutching the sheet to her chest, she sat up and realized that her legs were bare, too. "Where are my jeans?"

"Being laundered. There are other clothes here for you." He looked behind him and made a come-here gesture. A young woman stepped up beside him. "Marie will help you dress."

Then, before she could ask any questions of him, he bowed and left.

"Would you like to select your dress, miss?" The girl held up a robe.

For a moment, Rebekkah stared at Marie. She looked to be about twenty. Her hair was drawn back severely, and her face was without makeup. A sober-looking black high-waisted skirt fell to the floor; a pale gray blouse topped it; and at the collar, a black tie of sorts was fitted around her neck. The tips of plain black shoes showed under the edge of her skirt, and a gray bonnet covered the crown of her head.

"Miss?" The girl hadn't moved.

Rebekkah swung her feet to the floor, slipped her arms into the robe, and went over to the wardrobe. "I can dress myself."

Maria followed and opened the massive wardrobe. "Begging your pardon, miss, but I don't think you understand."

Rebekkah stared at the clothes. "It's like a costume shop."

"Graveminders like texture, miss. The master likes to assure your pleasure if he can . . . which he definitely *can*." Marie said the last words hurriedly—and with a blush.

As the girl started pulling out the edges of dresses, Rebekkah fought the urge to reach out and stroke them.

Maria continued. "I know they're not ones you've picked, but the seamstresses are on standby. We have your measurements sent to all of them, but there are some lovely gowns here already." She pulled out the edge of a dark purple skirt. A second sheer layer in pale lavender shifted over the underskirt. "This one would flatter you."

Rebekkah gave in and took the material in her hand. Tiny jewels were scattered over the underskirt. It took effort not to sigh, but she dropped the material. "I'd like a pair of jeans. I don't have time for this."

"I'm sorry, miss," Marie said. "What about this one?"

With a grimace, Rebekkah shoved her hands into the wardrobe and flicked through the amazing textures of fabrics she'd never be able to afford and some she couldn't even identify. She settled on a two-layer green dress with sheer sleeves. It covered everything—from shoulder to wrist, from chest to ankle; it had neither a plummeting neckline nor back; and it was loose enough to allow free movement. All told, it seemed to be the plainest, most utilitarian option.

Hurriedly, Rebekkah dropped the robe and stepped into the dress. Marie fastened it, and Rebekkah turned to see herself in the large cheval glass. The dress had looked innocuous in the wardrobe, but when Marie held out the second layer, its innocence vanished. The outer layer of diaphanous material with sheer sleeves tightened just under her breasts. Like the skirt under it, the outer layer fell straight to the floor, where the extra length of material would puddle or trail behind her. As Rebekkah moved, the sheer layer flared to the sides and revealed more of the dark green silk of the dress.

While Rebekkah debated the possibility of finding a more sedate dress, Maria retrieved a pair of comfortable green low-heeled slingbacks that matched the gown—and were Rebekkah's size.

Like the dresses . . . and who knows what else.

She folded the robe and laid it on the foot of the bed. "Can you take me to see Charles?"

"There are ear bobs and—"

"Please?" Rebekkah interrupted.

After a small nod that might've been more bow than sign of accord, Marie opened the door and gestured for her to follow. Silently, the girl led her to an immense ballroom. At the far side of it, double doors opened onto a balcony. And standing with his back to her was Charles.

He stepped aside and gestured to a table on the balcony beyond him. "Come. I thought we could dine out here tonight."

Rebekkah could see two place settings on a linen-draped table. A bottle of wine chilled in a silver bucket, and crystal glasses sat waiting. Arrangements of orchids and verdant plants covered every conceivable space on the balcony; the effect was of a small hothouse gone slightly wild.

"Marie, tell Ward that Ms. Barrow and I are on the east balcony." Charles pulled out a chair. "Rebekkah?"

Rebekkah crossed the room and stepped onto the balcony. "It's not that I don't appreciate what you did, but I'm not here to be your friend." She took her seat. "I'm here because I *had* to come."

"True, but why should that have anything to do with our being friends?" He poured them each a drink.

She accepted her glass. "I was just shot at. My grandmother died. I'm sitting with a dead man. Byron is somewhere out there"—she motioned to the seemingly endless city that sprawled as far as she could see and then looked back at Charles—"and I'm almost certain you know a whole hell of a lot more than you're saying about *all* of it. Byron's father brought him here, and then *died*. People . . . *dead people* shot at us. Something is attacking people at home and . . . I'm here to make sense of what's going on, not have dinner."

"Perhaps I can clarify parts of your confusion. The Undertaker will be here shortly; you have my word on that. Until he arrives, you shall stay here, where I can be certain of your safety. Some of my unrulier citizens shot at you, and they will be dealt with for causing you harm. A dead child is killing people in Claysville—and you, my dear girl, are exhausted and in need of a meal." He motioned to the man who stood waiting with a tray full of salads and bread, and then he looked back at her. "So we shall eat, and then we shall discuss work."

Rebekkah waited while the dead man stepped onto the balcony and served their food. Charles stayed silent the entire time, and she felt his gaze on her all the while. His attention felt like an almost physical assessment—and a challenge.

Once the server had returned inside the opulent house, she slid her plate aside. "I was taught to give food and drink to the already dead. I never knew that Maylene did that to keep them from waking, but I do now. So what happens to me if I eat with you?"

"You enjoy yourself, I hope," Charles replied. "The food here is delicious in a way that you'll never find over there."

She folded her hands in her lap to keep them from shaking. "Why did those people shoot at us?"

Charles lifted his napkin and dabbed his lips. "They aren't always obedient. Do know that I'll be addressing this matter with them."

"Who were they? Why were they shooting? Why did you keep them from hitting me?"

Charles caught her gaze. "Because you are *mine*, Rebekkah."

When she didn't reply, he broke a piece of bread from the loaf and held it out to her. "Please do eat. The food here is safe for you. My vow on it. Afterward, we shall deal with a few of those questions you're trying to make sense of. But you must keep your strength up if you're to go off to battle, right?"

Ignoring his offered food, she lifted her own fork. "Your vow that this is safe and that it has no consequences in any way?"

"My vow. It is only food. Delicious food, of course, fit to serve my lovely new Graveminder, but food nonetheless." Charles took a bite of the bread he'd offered her. "Not everyone here is civilized, but their sovereign is."

"Their sovereign?"

"Did I not mention that?" Charles' eyes widened in feigned shock. "They call me Mr. D, and this, my dear, is my demesne. All that you see is under my control. Only one person"—he smiled at her—"has the ability to truly stand against me . . . or beside me."

Rebekkah wasn't quite ready to ask what it meant to stand against him. "Who are you? *What* are you?"

Charles looked at the city behind her, but she was pretty sure that he was looking far beyond the landscape she could see. "I've been called many things, in many cultures. The name doesn't matter—not really. It all means the same thing: they believe in me, and I exist. Death happens. Everywhere, to everyone."

"*Death?*" Rebekkah stared at him. "You're saying that you are *Death* and that you exist because people believe that Death . . . that it . . . *you* exist?"

"No, my dear. Death simply *exists.*" He swept his hand out in a wide arc. "This exists." He laid his hand over his chest, where his heart would be if he were truly a man. "*I* simply exist . . . and you, Graveminder, exist because of me."

30

BYRON FELT THE WALL VANISH AS HE FELL FORWARD ONTO HIS HANDS and knees. He hadn't done anything differently in the past moment than he had been doing the past couple of hours. There was no sense in questioning it, though: he was free now, and he needed to get to Rebekkah.

He stepped into the gray world of the dead and wished he had a map. Unlike his first trip to the land of the dead, Charlie wasn't waiting; nor did Byron have his father to lead the way. What he did have was a fearlessness that he hadn't felt the first time. All that mattered was assuring that his Graveminder—*that Rebekkah*—was safe.

Byron grabbed hold of the arm of the first person he saw. "Where is Charlie? Mr D? Do you know where he is?"

The man grinned, shook loose of Byron's hold, and walked away.

"Thanks," Byron muttered.

He looked around, but the area outside the tunnel seemed deserted. *Now what?* He'd had a vague sense that the streets weren't laid out as they had been the first time, which, considering the haphazardness of the rest of what he'd seen, wasn't entirely unexpected.

Byron followed the man, figuring that any direction was better than none at all.

This part of the dead's city was desolate. Store windows had "Closed" signs in them; drapes were drawn. No one lingered in the alleys.

"Where is everyone?" Byron asked.

The dead man he followed glanced back, but did not answer. They went around another corner, and then the man held up a hand in a halting gesture. "Stay."

One shop appeared to be open. Three men sat on chairs outside, as if it were a sidewalk café or pub. It wasn't. It also wasn't a nineteenth-century mining town, but two of the three were dressed in cowboy boots, battered hats, and worn jackets.

The third man, in ripped jeans and a faded black concert tee, stood out from his companions. He muttered something to the other men. All three stood.

"Alicia?" one called.

A rough-looking woman in snug jeans and a half-buttoned man's shirt came to the doorway. A gun holster hung around her lean hips, and a knife long enough to be a sword was strapped to her thigh. She cocked one hip and said, "Come on in, Undertaker."

"I need to find Charlie," Byron started.

"And you will, but it's better for everyone if you stop in here first." Alicia glanced at the men. "Boys? Go on."

One man nodded and went to stand at the corner. Another walked off in the opposite direction. The third sat down, propped his boots on the table, and angled his hat so it was tilted over his face.

Byron didn't know if he was walking into a trap or not. He was more than able to fight, but he wasn't a fool. He was outnumbered—as well as unsure of the wisdom of fighting several armed men.

He walked over to the doorway and stopped in front of Alicia. "You have me at a disadvantage."

"In more ways than you can guess, Undertaker, but you're welcome among us." Alicia motioned for him to enter the store. She didn't move out of the doorway, so he had to brush uncomfortably close to her.

Just inside the doorway of the shadowy shop, Byron had to remind himself that he hadn't stepped into the past. He'd entered a general goods shop. Tins of various foods and supplies sat in rows from floor to ceiling behind the counter. An oversize cash register sat on a wooden ledge that abutted a glass-and-wood cabinet. Inside it, pistols and knives sat alongside pocket watches and lockets.

Alicia leaned against his back. Her chin rested on his shoulder and the butt of one of her pistols dug into his lower back. She whispered in his ear, "You need a few supplies, Undertaker?"

"I don't know. *Do* I?"

"Unless you're smarter than most of your sort are when they start, you do." She stepped around in front of him as she spoke. Her hand came down flat on the glass cabinet. "Most of the arms we carry here aren't much compared to what's over in your world. New arrivals bitch about it."

"But over here?"

"Over here, sugar, you need to have a few choices." She squeezed his biceps. "You're not frail. Always a plus."

"I boxed for a while," he admitted.

Alicia nodded. "Nice, but this isn't always a gentleman's game. How are you in an alley or a bar?"

Byron shrugged. "I've never had reason to know."

"You will." Alicia went around the counter and reached down by her feet. "Don't let misplaced ethics get in the way, Undertaker." She plunked a worn duffel on the glass cabinet in between them. "The dead don't have as much to lose as you do—on either side of the gate."

"Why are you helping me?"

Alicia flashed him a smile that was half challenging, half amused. "You sure I am?"

And as she asked, Byron *was* sure. He didn't know who she was, why she was, or much of anything, but he'd grown up hearing his father repeat "trust your instincts" enough times that he was confident in his own gut feelings.

"I am," he said.

"Good boy." She unzipped the bag. "Some of this won't be very useful anymore, but you can replace it with its like over there."

She pulled out a mason jar filled with a white crystalline substance, a few vials with faded handwritten labels, a Smith & Wesson revolver with a mother-of-pearl grip, a box of bullets, a sheathed six-inch knife.

"What is all of this?"

Alicia stopped mid-movement; her hand still held a tin canister with a stylized cross on it. "What does it look like? *Weapons.*"

"Weapons."

"Some of what you do is as much instinct as knowledge. You know that, right?" Alicia paused and looked expectantly at him. He nodded once, and she continued. "But sometimes there's a bit of science to it."

"Science?"

"There are many purposes for a good blade." She unsheathed the knife. "Hack a man's feet off, and he won't run." She held it out so the tip was dangerously close to his throat. "You can silence a dead woman for a while with a good cut."

When Byron didn't respond, Alicia lifted the gun and aimed into the street. "If you're a good shot, take the eyes. Can't see, can't follow." She flicked the swing-out cylinder open and then closed. "This is a turn-of-the-century piece, Undertaker." She laid it on the counter and slid a finger down the pearl grip. "Well cared for. Straight shooter." Then she looked him in the eye. "I *only* deal in quality merchandise."

"Good to know," Byron said.

She held up the white crystals. "Sea salt. Anchor the dead in solid shape. It makes them easier to drag through the gate."

Byron held up the vials. "And this?"

"Temporary death. Dosed with top-shelf Haitian zombie powder—the real stuff—and ground corpses, actually. Works great on stopping the hearts of the living. One drop for every fifteen minutes of death." She held up the bullets. "Now, *these* are for—"

"Why would I kill the living?"

"Not *kill*, Undertaker. It's for pausing. In case you need to get into a morgue to get a Claysville citizen who dies away from home. It shuts your body down. Don't do it for more than a few hours."

"Right." Byron stared at her. "Tell me again why you're helping me?"

"Don't think I told you the first time, did I?" She tilted her head and flashed him a grin. "Pay attention. You need to go on over to Charlie's soon. We can sort out the other things another time."

"Right." Byron stared at her. "Another time?"

"Sure. Bring me a few of the guns that we don't have here yet, and you can buy whatever you want of my time. We'll do a little business, and then"—she gave him a slow, thorough once-over—"talk."

He opened his mouth, thought better of the question he was going to ask, and closed it. She was being helpful, and he didn't want to risk offending her to satisfy his curiosity. On the other hand, that was the second time so far that he'd been blatantly and lasciviously assessed by a stranger, first at the Tip-Top Tavern and now by Alicia.

Alicia laughed. "Go ahead. Ask."

"Ask what?"

"Yes, that will happen a lot here. There's only one live man who comes here. You're easy on the eyes, but even if you weren't, you're *alive*. It makes you tempting." Alicia licked her lips. "Young. Living. New."

"I'm not looking for—"

"Oh, I know, shug: your Graveminder's all you can see, think of, dream of. It's always like that, but sometimes that don't work out, so"—she shrugged—"never hurts to throw the invite out there, does it?"

Byron wasn't sure how to respond, so he did as Alicia had done earlier: he ignored the question. "The bullets?"

She laughed. "Work on the dead. Not permanent-like, but they can knock a body out for a good forty-eight hours. That's more than enough time for you to get out of here. Aim for the head or heart for the longest incapacitation."

"Where do I get more of those or the powder if I run out?" He was pretty sure he knew the answer even as he asked.

Alicia spread her hands wide. "Right here."

"Seller's market, I'm guessing?"

"You do catch on quick." Alicia opened the duffel wide and started to settle the jars and vials back inside. "I'm here to help, Undertaker, but even a dead girl's got to make a living."

Byron slid the revolver to the side. "And where does Charlie fit into this?"

"The old bastard runs this world, but he isn't big on global laws. I'm within rights to help you as much as I see fit . . . or not. We all are." Alicia opened the box and handed him a few bullets. "Extras."

He put the bullets in his pocket. "And you're not going to tell me *why* you're helping unless I buy that answer."

Alicia put her elbows on the counter behind her and leaned back. The gesture had the—not accidental, Byron was sure—effect of emphasizing her physical assets as well as her apparent flexibility. "Only one thing I'd give you for free, and I'm pretty sure you wouldn't take it. Least not right now."

"No," he admitted. "You're a beautiful woman, but . . . no."

At a sound in the street, Alicia looked toward the door. One of the cowboy-hat-wearing men ducked inside. "Time for him to move out, boss."

Alicia straightened up. "Five minutes."

"Two. Three tops." The man stepped back outside.

Alicia shoved the knife and the box of bullets into the bag. "Everything else has a fee. Barter." She held up a hand before he spoke. "Not sex. I'm not asking you to whore yourself. Bring me guns. Boots. Be creative. We'll sort it out in the ledger."

"And this?" He put his hand on the duffel.

"Credit." Alicia zipped it up. "You good for it?"

"I am." He slung it over his shoulder. "Now I need to know where Charlie is."

"Boyd will take you most of the way to Charlie's." As she spoke, the man, presumably Boyd, came back to the doorway. Alicia looked at him. "See you next trip, Undertaker."

31

DAISHA SAW THE MAN COMING TOWARD HER. HE STUMBLED AS HE walked, not steady on his feet or maybe not sure of where to step. She felt bad for him. Since she'd come home to Claysville, sometimes the ground didn't feel right under her feet either. She'd felt better since she'd gone to her home, but she still felt a disconnect with the world around her.

The man stopped just in front of her and sniffed.

"Hey." She jumped backward, out of his reach.

With a sound that might've been a word, he reached out and grabbed the back of her neck. His other hand clutched her shoulder at the same time, and he pulled her against him. The hand holding her neck caught in her hair, and he forced her head to the side.

Daisha shoved against him, but he didn't seem to notice. It was the first time since she woke up that anyone had been unmoved by her touch.

Then he buried his face against her throat and inhaled.

"What are you—" Her words ended in a yelp as he shifted his hold. He shoved his face up against her lips and sniffed again.

"Stop this," she hissed.

The hand he'd had on the back of her head moved to her jaw, cupping her chin. His other hand shifted from her shoulder to her lower back, holding her securely against him. She could feel his arm like a vise around her side.

Then he squeezed and forced her mouth to stay open. He peered into her mouth and then sniffed.

Daisha couldn't move away.

For the first time since she woke up dead, she wished she could control that dissipating thing that happened sometimes. *Fear.* Fear was what she thought caused it, and she was very afraid. *Why am I not fading?*

She needed to swallow, but couldn't with her mouth held open like this.

He inhaled, drawing as much breath as he could from between her lips. He didn't touch her mouth. He just breathed in.

And it hurt like he was pulling things out of her.

She remembered *hurt,* and in remembering hurt, she remembered what could stop it. She pulled her knee up as fast and as hard as she could.

He gargled and dropped her.

And as soon as he let go of her, she faded into nothingness and was gone.

32

Partway into the multicourse meal, Rebekkah's frustration had reached uncontainable levels. Charles had steadfastly refused to talk about anything of consequence; Byron had not yet arrived; and she herself sat at an elegant table, eating some of the most mouth-wateringly good dishes she'd ever tasted.

Wasting time.

"I'm not trying to be difficult, but I don't know who you are, what this place is. Byron could be in trouble for all I know, and we're just *sitting* here." She gestured around them, and then took a moment to try to quell her emotions. She folded her napkin, concentrating on the square of linen rather than the anger and fear roiling inside her. "You're asking a lot of me . . . and I'm not sure why I should trust you."

Charles frowned. "My being shot multiple times ought to give you *some* reason to trust me. That's not something I would do for just anyone, Rebekkah."

Ward removed their dishes.

Charles reached out as if to touch her arm. "You are special to me. This world can be yours to rule alongside me if you so desire."

"No." Rebekkah pulled away. She shoved back her chair and stepped back from the table. "I'm not going to *stay* here."

"Of course, but you are going to come here repeatedly." Charles came to stand beside her. "I am not asking for your hand, Rebekkah, and I'm most assuredly not asking for your death. I would prefer you alive."

She stepped away and turned to face the city that sprawled out around them. She could see the tops of buildings stretching as far as her vision allowed. *And beyond.* Architecture from various cultures and eras clashed and blended. A medieval castle stood not far from a massive glass building. Squat wooden cabins abutted stern brownstones. The only continuity was that the whole of the city was bustling. Throngs of people and various conveyances filled the streets as far as she could see.

Quietly, Charles said, "You are of the dead, Rebekkah Barrow, and thus you are *mine.*"

Pulling her gaze from the city, she looked over her shoulder as he walked back to the table. She watched him pour the wine.

"When you are here, you will sup at my table, and you will attend the theater at my side. As Graveminder, you can spend as much time as you want here. You simply need to convince your Undertaker to bring you through the tunnel."

Rebekkah laughed. "Convince Byron to bring me here to see *you?*"

Charles held out her glass.

She accepted the drink, but she didn't lift it to her lips. "I feel the pull . . . to it, to you. You know it, so there's no point in lying. You've met how many Graveminders now?"

"Eleven or twelve, depending on if one counts your sister." Charles sipped his drink. "Ella wanted to be here the moment she crossed through the tunnel. You . . . Maylene kept you out of my reach all these years. Typically, I meet the intended Graveminder when she is much younger. You, however, have been a mystery to me."

The implications in those words—that Maylene had hidden her and that Ella had been here—made Rebekkah shiver. "So Ella . . . you're why she—"

"No, not me," Charles corrected. "This." He swept his arm in front of him. "The land of the dead calls to Graveminders. Maylene felt it, Ella felt it, and you, Rebekkah, are trying very hard *not* to feel it."

She wanted to run through the city streets, to get lost in the landscape that beckoned from every direction, but she'd traveled enough to know that doing so would be supremely stupid. A person didn't arrive in a new country—which for all intents and purposes this was—and go haring about without any information, at least not if she wanted to avoid trouble.

And bullets.

"I do, but"—she turned her back on the beguiling city—"I'm not going to be hanging on your arm."

"Why?"

"*Why?*" she repeated.

"Yes." He didn't look away from her while he took a drink from his glass. "Why refuse the protection, the escort, the *guide* to a world you don't know? Am I offensive in some way? Was I too rough when I protected you from the bullets—"

"No." She sat back down. Rebekkah felt her thread of mistrust twine with guilt. Charles *had* saved her. He hadn't picked her, or shot at her, or forced her to come here. In truth, he'd done nothing but protect her and offer her a safe space to rest. *And clothes and food and answers.* She couldn't ignore the nagging worries, but she couldn't ignore facts either. "You saved me. I am indebted to you for that. I don't mean to insult you . . ."

"All is forgiven." He smiled magnanimously. "I need you to know that while the Undertaker looks after you over there, here you can find respite from the trials of that world."

"The trials?"

"If you are not good enough, they will eat you alive. Literally, I'm afraid. You're what stands between the dead and the living. My champion. Theirs, too." Charles reached out and took her hand. "It's a trying job, and you are ever welcome to come among your people and rest."

Silently, Ward stepped out and delivered another dish. A dozen different desserts sat on a circular tray that he placed in the center of the table. Silver knives, spoons, and forks lay beside the luscious-looking treats.

"The boys from earlier will be dealt with, and you will have guards, of course." Charles released her hand, took one of the knives, and cut into one of the pies. "He always offers far too many desserts; it's his way of trying to figure out your tastes."

"Ward?"

"No, dear. Ward is hopeless in the kitchen. He's my personal guard." Charles gestured at a cream pie with his fork. "That one is usually quite good."

"Everyone here seems to know who I am, what I am, and I had no idea. Maylene didn't . . ." Her words dried up. She didn't know much, if anything, about Charles, yet she was speaking freely as if she trusted him. She pushed away from the table and went to the edge of the balcony again.

This time he came to stand beside her, so they were standing shoulder to shoulder. "Maylene is an amazing woman. She fulfilled her role with the dead with aplomb." He frowned at a car with a blaring siren that rushed by in the street below. "She had good reasons for not telling you the things you want to know."

"I'm not seeing how keeping this all a secret was a *good* idea." Rebekkah felt disloyal for saying it, but it was true.

"She had her reasons." Charles put a hand on her forearm. "Did you know your mother had an abortion?"

Rebekkah looked at him. "No . . . a lot of women—"

"She did so because Jimmy didn't want another daughter born to be *this*." He squeezed her wrist. "Ella, his daughter, died because of Maylene. That meant the next Graveminder was destined to be one of his nieces or you . . . unless your mother had the baby she carried when Ella died. He asked her to not have the child."

"You're saying he knew about all of this." She thought about Julia's attitude toward Claysville, her refusal to return to it, her refusal to come to Jimmy's funeral. "Jimmy knew about the land of the dead?"

"Not many over there can think on what you are, but exceptions are made for the Graveminder's family. Maylene's mother was a Graveminder, so she always knew what was coming. Bitty died easy, by the way, came walking through my door when Maylene was ready." Charles sighed. "Now, *there* was a woman. Feisty thing. Had no objection to what she was. Didn't flinch. She stuck a hat pin in a man's eye once, poor bastard." Charles paused and then continued, "Your mother lost Ella and her baby that same year. Jimmy lost her as result. He lost everything because of what Maylene was, what you are. He was afraid, and he destroyed himself because of it."

Tears burned in Rebekkah's eyes, but she didn't let them fall. Her whole family had been destroyed because of this, because of being Graveminders: her parents' marriage, her mother's sorrow, Jimmy's death, Ella's death . . . and now Maylene. That knowledge made it difficult to blame Maylene for her secrecy.

"I want you to understand why Maylene didn't tell you," Charles said gently. "It was her choice, and I allowed it. However, that means you don't have time to make sense of this. Afterward, if you survive, this home, *my* home, is open to you." He took Rebekkah's hands in his and forced her to face him. "This *world* is yours. Over there, your needs will be provided for as well. The town will see to it. It's part of the agreement we made a couple centuries ago. First, though, you must attend to the unpleasant matters: Daisha needs to be brought here. She was left to walk, and with every passing day, with every swallow of food and drink and every breath she takes from them, she's growing stronger."

Rebekkah pulled her hands free of his and wrapped her arms around herself, but she still started shivering. "Daisha? You know the murderer's *name*?"

"Of course I do: I'm Mr D. I know those who are of the dead . . . including you. I know you as no one else in either world can." He reached out to cup her chin.

She stepped back again, putting herself out of reach. "Don't touch me."

He paused, hand still outstretched. "You're being foolish, Rebekkah."

For a moment they stood motionless, and then he shrugged. "Your other escort is due to be here any moment. I'll see you next time."

He walked away and left her standing shivering on his balcony.

BYRON FELT THE WEIGHT OF STRANGERS' GAZES ON HIM AS HE WALKED through the streets with Boyd. The man hadn't spoken at all, and truth be told, Byron wasn't feeling much like talking anyhow. He'd taken the gun Alicia had given him out of the duffel, checked that it was loaded, and carried it openly in his hand.

He was a bit out of practice, but years of target practice with his father left him confident that he'd be able to hit most targets he aimed at. The purpose of strange hobbies he'd shared with his father for years suddenly became obvious: preparation for a career that hadn't been named until now. Byron was grateful, but the knowledge cast an unpleasant pall over his memories.

Still, the weight of the revolver was comforting. He'd prefer to have it holstered, but he didn't have a holster and he wasn't about to shove the revolver in his waistband. That was a pretty gesture in fiction, but in reality, it wasn't the wisest place to carry a loaded weapon.

"Am I likely to need to be armed every time I come here?" he asked Boyd in a low voice.

"Nah. Transition period's always a little tense. Folks'll get used to you," Boyd said. "You're new. Some will want to test your mettle."

"Any punishment if I shoot them?"

"Not unless they take it personal." Boyd's tone was dry enough that Byron couldn't tell if he was joking until he added, "Shoot them right. No pansy-ass wounds. Give them a good scar. Makes for story credit at the bars, you know?"

"*Story* credit?" Byron darted a glance at Boyd. "Seriously?"

"Hell, yeah. A man can drink for free if he has a good enough story, and you're the news, Undertaker. You and the woman. Not a lot new happens here. Same shit, *every* day." Boyd ducked into an alcove and pointed across the street. "That's it. I stop here. I'm not welcome inside his house."

Despite the beauty of some of the other buildings, Mr. D's house still stood out like a mansion among rubble. Marble steps, columns, and an enormous door all assured that the house wouldn't be missed. Above the third floor a rooftop garden held towering trees and plants that draped over the sides. And on the second floor, a long balcony stretched half the length of the building. Standing at the edge of the balcony looking out over the city was Rebekkah.

She's alive. She's safe. She's . . . wearing a gown like the dead women in the streets.

Byron frowned. It was one thing to see the residents of the city dressed in the fashions of earlier eras, but seeing Rebekkah looking out of time was unsettling. He'd seen her in dresses, but in the silk-and-gauze dress she was wearing now, she looked as if she belonged in Charlie's mansion. Her lips were parted as she stared out at the city as if she were a member of a royal family surveying her kingdom.

I'm panicking over her safety, and she's standing on a balcony looking at the city. Byron wasn't sure whether this realization made him more or less worried. He did know he didn't like seeing her looking like she belonged here. *She's not staying. She promised to come back home.* He didn't look away from her as he asked Boyd, "What happens if I'm shot?"

"Here? It'll hurt. Same as with us. Over there? Normal rules."

"And Rebekkah?" Byron forced himself to look away from her.

"She can be killed here." Boyd shrugged. "She's different."

"*Why?*"

Boyd shrugged again. "I don't make rules. Wasn't even here when the rules were made. Some things just are."

Then he turned and ambled off down the street. People moved out of his way as he walked, and Byron had a moment of wondering whether they were afraid of Boyd or simply realized that he wouldn't veer, so they had to move.

Byron looked back at the house, not entirely sure of the protocol. *Is she a prisoner?* A guard of stood on either side of the massive doors to Mr. D's house. *Do I knock?* There was only one way to find out.

With the revolver still in hand, he crossed the street and ascended the stairs. He didn't raise the gun, but just as he did when he'd walked through the city, he didn't make any effort to hide it. The street at the foot of the steps was littered with bullet casings, and a wet gray stain on one step made Byron pause. *Blood?* The inability to distinguish color in this world was something he'd adjusted to relatively easily, but as he saw the fluid on the step, he realized that it could be any number of things. Without color, the possibilities were harder to narrow in on. *Rebekkah is on the balcony. She's alive.* He paused as the absurdity of his thought hit him: he couldn't be sure she was alive. *She can die here.*

He ran the rest of the way up the stairs.

The guards both stepped in front of the door in perfect sync. "No."

"Yes." Byron lifted the gun and aimed it at one of the guards. "Rebekkah . . . the Graveminder is in there, and I'm going in to get her. *Now.*"

The guards exchanged a look, but they didn't move or reply.

"I *will* shoot," he assured them. "Open the doors."

"We have orders," the guard he'd aimed at said.

The other added, "No one simply walks into his house. You are no exception."

Byron cocked the hammer. "Are you going to let me in?"

"Mr. D directed that we don't. *That*"—the first guard pointed at the gun—"doesn't change his orders."

"I don't want to shoot." Byron lowered his gun marginally and reached for the door handle. The guard grabbed his arm.

"But I *will*," he added.

The first bullet entered between the guard's eyes, and in another instant, another bullet pierced the second guard's throat. Both men slumped, and Byron hoped that Alicia had been honest when she told him that he wasn't truly killing the dead men.

Can you kill the already dead?

It didn't matter. He wasn't going to be turned away at Mr. D's door. His job was to keep Rebekkah safe, keep her by his side, take her home to the world of the living.

Byron pushed open the door. Mr. D was sitting in a velvet-covered wing-back chair in the middle of a vast foyer. An enormous chandelier dangled high over his head, and for a moment, Byron considered seeing how good his aim still was. *Could I break the chain?* The idea of sending the crystal monstrosity down atop Mr. D was exceptionally tempting.

Mr. D followed his gaze. "Difficult shot, that one. You want to try it?"

"Where is Rebekkah?"

Mr. D motioned upward. "Top of the stairs. Straight back, big doors, balcony. Can't miss it."

"If you hurt her—"

"You'll do what, boy?" Mr. D flashed his teeth in a smile of sorts. "Go fetch her. I've work to tend to. Unless you want to take the shot?"

For a moment, Byron hesitated. He looked back up at the chain holding the chandelier up over Mr. D's head. *Could I? Should I?* He looked back at Mr. D and said, "Maybe next time."

Mr. D's laughter followed him up the stairs.

33

REBEKKAH?"

She turned from the street and saw Byron striding down the short hallway toward her. She was confused, tired, and scared. Her side stung from the bullet that had grazed her, and her head was so full of worries that she couldn't even name them all. Yet, in that instant, everything else went on hold.

He stopped at the threshold between the room and the balcony. "Are you okay?"

He studied her as he spoke. There was no tenderness in his expression, and seeing that coldness in his eyes made her shiver.

"I am." She stepped toward him, suddenly self-conscious in the dress, unsure of him as she hadn't been when they entered the tunnel, guilty even though she hadn't done anything more than dine with Charles. "Take me home. Please?"

"That's the plan." Byron's tone wasn't any warmer than his gaze.

"Are *you* okay?" she asked.

"I will be once we get out of here." He stood at an angle and watched the hallway he'd just come through and the balcony. He held a white-handled revolver in his right hand and an unfamiliar dingy duffel bag slung over his shoulder. Flecks of blood were spattered on his shirt.

"I have no idea how to find the exit . . . to the house or to the world," she admitted.

"Just stay beside me." He reached into his pocket and pulled out two bullets. Then he opened the cylinder of the old-fashioned revolver in his hand.

She stared as he removed two empty casings and then slid bullets into the two chambers.

He repositioned the strap of the duffel bag on his shoulder. "Stay beside me, okay? If anyone . . . if anyone fires at us, you step behind me."

"But—"

"Over here, bullets are only a threat to you. I'm safe." He caught her gaze and demanded, "Promise me."

She nodded. *How had Maylene done this?* It wasn't anywhere near the sort of life that she could've imagined her grandmother living.

Byron walked down the hallway of Charles' house. The plush carpet under their feet, the elaborate stamped tin ceiling, the murals on the wall, none of it drew Byron's attention. He paused at the top of a curving staircase Rebekkah didn't remember.

I was unconscious when I came in.

"Stay with me," Byron reminded her.

At the foot of the stairs, Charles stood waiting. As she and Byron approached, he stepped forward.

"My lovely Rebekkah, it was a pleasure." Charles took her hand and lifted it to his lips. "I trust that you'll let me know if anything was unsatisfactory. Our meal? My bed?"

She pulled her hand free of his. "Only you."

Charles nodded. "Then I shall work harder. The first time together isn't always one's *best* performance." Then he turned his gaze to Byron, who was standing stiffly beside her. "Undertaker."

Rebekkah had thought Byron's tone couldn't have been colder, but it chilled even more as he said, "Charlie. Should I expect an attack on the way to the gate? Or are we safe?"

"I expect that they'll behave for now, but do try to keep our girl safe. My domain is dangerous." Charles walked over to the door and opened it. "And don't leave too many bodies for me to clean up."

Two men lay sprawled outside on either side of the doorway. Rebekkah gasped and covered her mouth. She looked from the men to Byron and then to Charles.

Expression unreadable, Charles leaned against the doorway. All he said was, "Mind your hem, dear. Blood does stain."

Byron put a hand on her lower back. "Come on, Bek."

The Byron she'd known wasn't someone who walked around shooting people, but as she looked at him now, she thought about the two bullets he'd loaded into the cylinder of the gun. *What happens when the already dead are shot?* Had Byron taken away their afterlives? Were there layers of realities for the dead?

After another glance back at Charles, Rebekkah walked down the marble steps that led to the street. She didn't want to stay with him, didn't want to hear the things he told her, didn't want to be caught in a world where people shot at her. Spent rounds and discharged casings were scattered on the steps and in the street. There were bright drops of red on the stairs as well, and she wondered if it was her blood or Charles'. *Did he bleed?* She tried to remember. *Why didn't the bullets go* through *him into me?* She stopped midstep and looked back again.

Charles leaned casually against the doorjamb watching them.

"I have more questions," she said.

The smile that came over his face was beatific. "Of course you do."

"So—"

"So you'll come back." Charles descended the stairs with poise. He didn't hurry, but each step conveyed an eagerness that made her want to flee.

"You'll come to my door with your questions and your theories, and I"—he paused and glanced at Byron—"will tell you what you need to know."

"When they shot at us, why didn't you get hurt?" Rebekkah pointed at the slumped bodies outside his door. *"They* are hurt."

"Ahhh, that question you may need to ask your Undertaker." Charles' tone held suspicion. "Your partner has secrets of his own. Don't you, Byron?"

Byron nodded curtly. He visibly scanned the street even as he listened to their conversation. All he said was, "We all do."

Charles kept a slight distance from them. "True."

"If Byron shot you, would it hurt?" Rebekkah pressed.

"*All* bullets hurt, Rebekkah." Charles held her gaze. "They didn't kill me, but that doesn't mean it didn't hurt when they were tearing through my skin."

She stilled. The memory of the gunfire and the number of casings on the ground made her wince. She gestured toward the blood on the steps. "You mean . . ."

Charles gave her a terse nod.

"And why were they shooting in the first place?" Byron's words drew Rebekkah's attention.

"It's a deadly world, Undertaker, as I'm sure you're learning." Then Charles turned back to Rebekkah. "For now, you'd best be going, unless"—he gave her a wistful smile—"you'd like to linger?"

Byron's gaze snapped to Charles. "No."

"Maybe next time," Charles murmured.

"No," Byron repeated. "Not now. Not then."

The look that came into Charles' eyes wasn't friendly. "That isn't your choice, Undertaker. You open the gate. You bring her back and forth. That doesn't mean you make her decisions . . . any more than I do."

"Stop." A wave of exhaustion washed over Rebekkah. "Can you not do this right now? I'm tired, cold, and sore. We can all argue later, but right now, I need to find Daisha and bring her here before she hurts anyone else."

"And that, Byron, is why she is the Graveminder. Now that she has come here and become what she is meant to be, her focus is on the mission. They're all like this eventually. Some"—Charles paused and his voice softened—"are more so from the first. Go to the land of the living, Rebekkah, and find Daisha. The Hungry Dead shouldn't be this strong this fast. Bring her home."

34

CHARLES WORRIED ABOUT ALL OF THEM, HIS NOT-ENTIRELY-DEAD-OR-alive Graveminders. Such was the nature of their arrangement. They were his responsibility, his warriors, and he could do little to protect them. His interference several centuries ago had given them a touch of death, but he couldn't shelter them from everything.

"You said if I needed help . . ."

"I did. I would do anything in my power for you." Charles pulled his newest Graveminder into an embrace. "This, however, I cannot fix."

"My son is dead, and you—"

"I cannot let the dead return as if they were still alive. That is forbidden." He brushed his hand over her damp cheek. His Graveminders were among the strongest and most courageous of women, yet like all mortals, they were still so fragile.

She stepped back and looked into Charles' eyes. "If you don't help me so he can come back right, I'll let him come back as Hungry Dead."

"Alicia . . ."

"No. I do everything asked of me. I am . . . this, here"—she made a sweeping gesture at the storefronts along the streets in the land of the dead—"as your Graveminder, without choice. I accepted it. I did as you asked, as my aunt asked when she designated me as her heir. All I ever wanted was a family and . . ." Tears started to slide down her cheeks again. "He's my son."

"I'm sorry," Charles said.

"No. The rules are that we are safe until eighty years. Brendan was just a child. He was to be safe."

"Accidents are not within my control. Poverty, accidents, murders, fire, these I cannot stop." Charles knew that the particulars weren't all remembered. The contract he had with Claysville wasn't a written document. They'd been too afraid of outsiders learning of it, of bringing witchcraft persecutions to Claysville.

"I am sorry for your loss." Charles reached out, but she moved away. He watched her, knew her with the same certainty that he'd known every Graveminder since the first, Abigail. They were strong, not afraid to test the rules that didn't make sense to them. Life and Death, all in the hands of these women. He was only Death. He'd tried to give life back once.

For Abigail.

And the results had been disastrous.

"There has to be something . . . Please?"

"I cannot return his life," Charles told her. "And if you do this thing, you'll be dead by the next day. I can promise you that. You keep the dead from walking, Alicia. You do not ever invite them to return."

"I hate you."

"I understand." He nodded. "If you wish, you can spend eternity taking it out on me, but if you do this, you will be sentencing yourself and your Undertaker to die."

Despite every bit of common sense, Charles still regretted his choice. Hurting Alicia—hurting any of his Graveminders—wasn't something he did lightly. If he could've given Alicia her child with impunity, he would've, but he was bound by rules. He'd broken those rules for Abigail, a mortal who had opened a gate to the land of the dead.

And look where that's landed us.

35

BYRON WAS GRATEFUL THAT REBEKKAH HAD BEEN SILENT AS THEY'D LEFT the land of the dead. His relief at seeing her unharmed vied with a fury that she'd been in the land of the dead alone. *Charlie arranged that,* Byron reminded himself. Unfortunately, he was also aware that Charlie couldn't have arranged it if Rebekkah hadn't let go of his hand: she was so entranced by what she'd seen there that she'd stepped away from him.

The world she seemed to see was unlike the one he'd experienced, and now, even as she stayed at his side, she was lost in thoughts he wasn't privy to. He'd known that her experience there would differ from his, but he hadn't thought about what that meant. He had absolutely no desire to step foot there again.

Except for the need to keep Rebekkah safe.

He considered the possibility of opening the gate and simply shoving the dead into the tunnel, but the image of tossing the dead girl—Daisha—into a tunnel without walking her into the land of the dead made him feel like a criminal. Good men didn't abduct people. Good men didn't truss them up and throw them into hidden chambers.

Daisha is dead. The girl is dead already.

The warnings his father had shared had sounded far less challenging at the time. *The monsters need to be stopped.* The dead girl had bitten a child, had injured William, had killed Maylene.

This time, Rebekkah kept her fingers laced with his as they stepped back into the storage room, so he used only one hand as he closed the cabinet and hid the tunnel. The room felt different the moment the tunnel was out of sight, as if removing the visual temptation of it changed the threat.

It doesn't.

He'd seen Rebekkah's face when she stood on the balcony looking out over the city of the dead. She was afraid, but underneath the fear, she was enamored. Her cheeks had been flushed, and her eyes had glimmered like she had a fever. For a chest-tightening moment, he'd wondered if that's what Ella had looked like when she'd gazed out at the land of the dead. He might not understand it, but *something* they'd seen there had been alluring enough to cause Ella to rush to the end of her life.

Will Rebekkah do the same thing?

With carefully controlled movements, he lowered the duffel bag of supplies from Alicia to the floor and kept his voice even as he asked, "What happened to your clothes?"

Still holding his hand, she turned away from the cabinet and blinked at him. The gown that was gray in the land of the dead was suddenly vibrant in the world of the living. The rich green fabric stood out in the sterile steel and muted tones of the storage room.

"Bullets. Blood." She put her free hand against her side. "Just a graze. Charles kept me safe. It doesn't even hurt now."

Byron paused at the familiarity in her tone. His opinion of Charlie was far from a positive one, but Rebekkah seemed to think differently. Their entire experiences of the land of the dead were dissimilar. It added to Byron's dislike of the place. All he said, however, was, "I don't trust him, but I'm glad he protected you."

"Me, too." She took her hand away from her side. "I feel fine, but if he hadn't . . ."

"He kept the bullets from you. That's what matters. If he hadn't trapped me in the tunnel—" He stopped himself. "I can look at the injury if you want."

"Really, I'm okay." Her eyes widened briefly. "It should still hurt. It did when I was over there, but now"—she put a hand on her side—"it's . . . fine." She looked into his eyes. "It's gone."

He wasn't sure whether he was alarmed that the injury seemed to be tied to her time in the land of the dead or grateful that her pain was gone. *Would it return when she went back there? Or had it truly healed by passing through the tunnel?* As with so much else, there were more questions than answers. Obviously, things could cross between the two worlds. If not, Alicia wouldn't be making requests of him.

Byron tried to keep the worry from his voice as he said, "It's probably a good idea to look at the wound."

"Right . . . but I'm not wearing underwear under this, so that means it'll wait till elsewhere or I'm going to need to get naked." Rebekkah plucked at the skirt. "*All* of my clothes were ruined."

"Oh." The thought of Rebekkah injured was briefly replaced by the idea of Rebekkah vulnerable in Charlie's bed.

He was just trying to provoke me when he said that. She wouldn't. *Would she?*

Byron wasn't sure what had actually happened, and he wasn't sure that he wanted to ask just then, wasn't sure he could handle knowing. Instead, he said, "You're not in danger from me, Bek. I can be professional. If you'd prefer, I can ask Elaine to look—"

"No." Rebekkah shuddered. "She'd probably make me lie on the prep table."

Byron smiled a little at Rebekkah's attempt to lighten the mood. "Be nice."

"Anyone that efficient isn't going to be gentle."

Byron pulled open the utility closet where he'd stored extra clothes since he'd moved back. He reached inside and grabbed a few things, shoving most of them into the bag Alicia had given him. "I can be efficient and gentle."

"And professional?" Rebekkah prompted.

"Do you want me to be professional?" He pulled his shirt off. There wasn't a lot of blood on it, but there was enough that he wanted a clean one. "Is that the lie you still want to hear?"

"You're heading into dangerous territory, B," Rebekkah cautioned, but she'd made no pretense of looking away as he stripped off his shirt and put it into the biohazard bin.

He grabbed a clean shirt from the closet, but didn't put it on. "And?"

She pulled her gaze away from his chest and studiously looked at the floor in front of her. "I don't need you to look at my side. It's fine."

He walked across the room and stopped in front of her. "That's not what I asked."

She lifted her gaze. "You do know that I wasn't . . . when Charles said those things . . . I mean, I *slept* there, and—"

"It's fine," he interrupted. The last thing he wanted to hear just then was Rebekkah talking about Charlie. "You don't owe me an explanation; you've made that abundantly clear."

"Sure." She put her hands on his bare chest. "And I've known you too long to believe for a minute that you'd be fine with me being with Charles . . . or anyone else."

"Maybe I've changed." Byron ran his hand over her hip. "Maybe—"

She stretched up and kissed him, carefully and slowly, and all of her repeated protestations that she didn't do relationships felt empty. She didn't touch him as if this was casual. He'd had friends with benefits; this felt like more. It always had.

For both of us.

She pulled away. "No."

"No what?" he prompted.

"No, I don't want you to be professional, and no, you haven't changed, but right now I'd probably ignore that . . . again. Then tomorrow we'd regret it." She stepped back.

The temper he'd been trying to keep in check slipped a little then. "Bullshit. *I* never regret it the next morning. You're the only one with that issue."

And as she had done for the past nine years when he tried to talk about things she didn't want to discuss, Rebekkah changed the subject. "I need to find Maylene's journal. She left me a letter that said there were answers in it. I started to look for it, but I didn't realize how important it was. Now I need . . . I'm not even sure what I need, but there's a dead girl out there and I have no idea how to stop her."

"Right," he bit off.

He pulled on his shirt, lifted the bag, and walked toward the doorway that led into the hall. He felt like he was walking a thin line between pushing her to face facts and going along with her habitual avoidance. The problem was that *he* knew they were past the point where ignoring their relationship was an option.

She can accept murderers and hidden worlds, but us . . . that she can't accept.

Frustration barely in check, Byron stepped aside for her to pass him.

She caught up the hem of her skirt and stepped into the hall. Once he pulled the door shut, she asked, "Will you come with me? To look through the house, I mean."

"I was planning on it. First, though, I need to grab something." He locked the storage room behind them. "Last night, before Dad . . . before I came back from there without him, Dad said he left some things up in his room."

"And you didn't get them yet?" She gave him an incredulous look. *"Why?"*

He stared back at her for a moment. "Because I thought finding you was a bit more important, all things considered. Dad said that nothing else could be done until you met Charlie, and the whole thing was a bit surreal. I just wanted . . . I needed to find you before anything else." Byron took her hand in his. "Whatever else happens, however infuriating I find your refusal to admit what's between us, you are my first priority for the rest of my life. That's what it means to be the Undertaker. You, my Graveminder, are my first, last, and most important priority. Before my life, before anyone else's life, *you.*"

Rebekkah stared at him silently. "What?"

"My *job*, Rebekkah, is to put your life before mine."

"I don't want . . ." She shook her head.

"Don't let go of my hand in the tunnel again. You can *die* there." He gave her a tight smile and then added, "I, however, can get shot repeatedly and live, apparently."

She opened and closed her mouth, and tears filled her eyes.

And, as had happened so many times when she wept, his temper vanished. He sighed. "I love you, and I would rather be the one trying to keep you safe than let anyone else in this world . . . or *that* one . . . do it, but I need you to work with me. I don't trust Charlie, and I don't know what game he's playing, but I do know that it didn't even occur to me to hesitate when I had to shoot two men to reach you."

"B, I didn't—"

"No. I don't want to hear all the reasons you can't this or that. Just tell me that whether or not you can give *us* a chance, you will work with me on this Graveminder thing." Byron stared at her. "I'm the only one that can open the gate, Bek, and I'll let the whole town die before I let you go over there and get killed because you're being stubborn."

"I promise," she whispered.

He hated the way she was staring at him, as if he was somehow a stranger to her, but he hated the thought of failing her even more. Rebekkah's safety was the most important thing in both worlds. *I won't fail you.* Byron thought about the bullets that had been fired toward Rebekkah, about the certainty he'd had earlier that she was in danger. *I can't be sure she is safe ever again.* The dead walked, and her job was to find them. The man who controlled the land of the dead was not to be trusted. The only thing Byron knew for sure was that he would die rather than fail Rebekkah—and that if he *did* die, he was failing her.

36

REBEKKAH WAS SPEECHLESS AS THEY WALKED UPSTAIRS AND INTO THE private part of the house. She followed Byron and tried not to notice the tense way he held himself. It wasn't like they hadn't had their share of arguments, but there were topics he'd always allowed her to avoid. After the immediate shock of Ella's death had passed, Byron would look at Rebekkah sometimes with an expectant expression—and she would pretend that she didn't know the conversation they should have. Years later, when they ended up in bed the first time, she ignored the "what-does-this-mean" conversation. He'd pushed a few times, but every time, she'd walked out or silenced the conversation with sex. *I don't deserve him.* That was the truth of it, and she knew it.

"I'm sorry," she said quietly as they went up the second set of stairs.

At the top of the steps, Byron glanced at her and sighed. "I know."

"Truce?" She held out a hand.

"We're still going to talk," he warned her.

She kept her hand extended. "And I'm going to hold your hand when we cross the tunnel to the land of the dead, and"—her voice cracked—"do my best not to get either of us shot."

Byron took her hand, but instead of shaking it, he pulled her to him in a quick hug. "That wasn't your fault. Not you getting shot or my killing those men." His voice was rough as he added, "It would destroy me if I lost you, Bek."

The truth was that she would feel the same way if she lost him, but before she could admit that, he pulled away. Brusquely he walked down the hall and opened a door. "Come on. Dad said we'd find some answers here."

Byron tossed his jacket on the bed and looked around the room briefly. At the foot of the bed was a dark wooden chest. It looked like something that had been passed down from generation to generation. The brass latch was dented and scratched, and several spots looked like they'd seen water damage over the years. He knelt in front of the chest, lifted the latch, and opened the lid.

Inside was an old black leather physician's satchel. Alongside it was a small wooden box that, when opened, revealed two old derringers. Several wicked-looking knives rested in sheaths.

"Well . . ." Byron opened a strongbox filled with ID tags from various hospitals. As he sifted through them, there was a note that read: "Ask Chris when you need new ones."

Tentatively, Rebekkah sat next to him on the floor. "I don't understand."

"In case I need to retrieve a body that has to be brought home and don't have time for paperwork," Byron told her. "There are other ways, too."

Then he told her about the woman he'd met in the land of the dead, Alicia, and the vials she had given him that caused temporary death. As he spoke, Rebekkah started shivering.

If they failed to find Daisha, people would die; if residents of Claysville died elsewhere and were left unminded, they would wake—and more people would die. The staggering list of things that could go wrong made her shoulders feel heavy. She had to keep the dead in their graves, and she had to stop them if they awoke. People who had no idea of the contract, people who had no idea

Claysville existed, people who had no idea that the dead *could* wake: all of them were depending on her not to fail them.

And I am depending on Byron.

Byron was the one person in all the world whom she could trust; he was the only man she'd ever loved. That was the truth she shouldn't say: she did love him. In a few short—albeit intense— days, years of running from him had been negated. She wasn't sure if laughing or crying would be more fitting at this moment: she'd finally faced the fact that she'd been in love with Byron Montgomery her whole life.

Because of what we are.

She realized then that Byron was staring at her, waiting for something, waiting for her. He'd been waiting for her for nearly a decade. "I'm sorry," she whispered.

He shook his head. "How did they do it?"

"The same way we will." Rebekkah squeezed his hand.

They both looked at the physician's bag and then at each other again. With obvious trepidation, Byron opened it and looked inside. An old box of syringes, bandages, various antibiotics, sterile gauze, a small scalpel, antibiotic ointment, peroxide, and myriad other emergency aid equipment filled the bag. It wasn't all modern, but most of it was.

Also inside the satchel was an envelope. She held it out.

"Open it," Byron said.

She did so, pulled out a small sheet of paper, unfolded it, and read the words aloud: "'You can also pay Alicia with medicinal supplies.' Does that make sense?"

"It does," he said.

Rebekkah flipped the paper over. "On the back it says, 'The syringes will stop *them*. Save for emergencies.'"

He snorted. "Which means what? When *aren't* dead people who are trying to kill us an emergency?"

She shrugged. "I have absolutely no idea."

Byron took the paper and stared at it. He lifted it up to the light and peered at it closely. As he did so, Rebekkah could make out a faint watermark.

"That's not Dad's handwriting," Byron said. "Which one was it? His grandfather? Someone else?"

He held out the paper, and Rebekkah took it. She refolded it and tucked it back in the envelope.

Byron reached in the trunk for one last item: an accordion file labeled MISTER D. He opened it. Inside were two plain brown journals, letters, news clippings, and some papers.

"We may have just found some answers." He held up a carefully clipped article with the headline MOUNTAIN LION ATTACK CLAIMS THREE. Setting it aside, he opened an envelope. He looked at each item it contained and then handed them one by one to Rebekkah. There were receipts for handguns, ammunition, and one pair of women's size-seven boots.

Byron continued passing items to her, and Rebekkah read the mishmash of notes. One slip of paper read: "for Alicia." Another piece of paper listed questions and answers: "Human? No. Age? Not what is visible *or* what era his clothes are from." After it was a scrawled note that read "Alicia has ulterior motives." Some would take longer to read. Letters and news clippings mixed with nearly illegible notes; going through all of it would take time.

Time we don't have.

When she yawned, Byron stopped passing her the papers. Silently, he collected those he had given her, slipped them all back into the file, and placed it and various other items from the trunk into the duffel he'd brought from the land of the dead.

"I'm good," she protested.

"You're exhausted," he corrected gently. He stared at her for a moment until she nodded.

Rebekkah stood and stretched. "Let's go home."

His look of surprise was masked almost immediately, and she was grateful that he didn't comment. Even when they'd been lovers over the years, she didn't use "we-speak," and she certainly didn't refer to the space where she was residing as "home."

She drifted off during the short drive from the funeral home to her house and woke as Byron turned off the engine. Instead of getting out of the hearse, she stayed with her head resting against the passenger-side window for a moment.

"You all right?" he asked.

She looked at him. "I am. Overwhelmed. Confused. Exhausted . . . but I'm not going to run screaming into the night. You?"

He opened his door. "I've never been much for screaming."

"I don't know. I remember a few movie nights—"

"I never screamed." Byron went around back and grabbed the duffel bag.

"Yelled, screamed, whatever." She got out, gathered her skirt in her hand, and climbed the steps to her front porch. She unlocked the front door and went inside. "I'm glad you're here with me. Maybe it's fear or partnership or grief or—"

"Or friendship. Let's not skip that one, Bek." He closed the door behind him. "This other stuff is going on, but we were friends before all of it. If you won't admit that you love me, at least admit that we're friends."

"We are, but we're friends who hadn't spoken in several years," she corrected.

His jaw clenched, but he didn't say whatever he'd thought. Instead, he carefully lowered the duffel bag to the coffee table. "Did you ask me to stay the night before last because of any of this?"

"Maybe," she admitted. That was the thing she hadn't spoken, the *other* fear that had lingered at the edges of her mind. "What makes you think that our . . . friendship is real?"

"A couple years of putting up with you, listening to you and

Ella talk boys and hair and music and books, watching movies you two outvoted me on." Looking more frustrated by the moment, he ticked each item off on his fingers. "A lot more years of hoping you'd come home, watching in every crowd for you, years of hoping every brunette that could possibly bear even the slightest resemblance to you would turn and say my name."

"But how much of that was out of your control?" She flopped on the sofa. "Was any of it real or was it just instinct? You are meant to protect the Graveminder—*me*—so maybe you were responding to that."

He stood in the middle of the room and stared at her. "Does it matter?"

She paused. *Does it matter?* The question wasn't one she was considering. The hows, the whens, the whys, the what-nexts, those she had been trying to ignore, but unfortunately those were things she couldn't overlook. *Does it matter?* If all of the things they'd shared were merely happenstance, if the fact that he was in the room right now trying to help her—if everything was a result of Maylene choosing her to be Ella's replacement, then yes, it mattered.

None of that was what she wanted to discuss, though, so she ignored it in favor of more pressing matters. "Do you want to help me tear the house apart? Or start looking at your dad's file?"

"You're dodging the question," Byron pointed out. "We need to talk about this, about us, Rebekkah. You've been ignoring it for more than eight years, but now . . . it's the two of us dealing with this. Do you honestly think ignoring what's between us is still an option?"

Rebekkah closed her eyes and leaned her head back. She knew that ignoring her feelings for Byron wasn't an option anymore; it probably never had been, but she wasn't sure what else to do. She loved him, but that didn't mean everything else was going to fall in place.

After several moments passed during which she didn't reply, he sighed. "I love you, but you're a pain in the ass sometimes, Bek."

She opened one eye and looked at him. "You, too. So . . . journals?"

He paused, and she waited for him to push. She wanted to say the words, but she wasn't sure how to. Years of trying to put him away on a shelf with the rest of Ella's things weren't going to fade in one day.

Instead of pushing her, he said, "I think we need to talk to the town council, read the contract, *and* ask Charlie some questions."

"I asked some questions, but being forthcoming isn't his first impulse," Rebekkah said, and then she filled Byron in on the little that she'd learned from Charles.

Byron, in turn, told her about his conversations with Charles, with William, and with Father Ness.

"So whatever this contract is with the town . . . it's over there in his world? You saw it?" she asked when he finished.

The expression on Byron's face grew oddly closed off. "I saw *a* contract, but I'm not sure if it was the one with the *town*. It had past Graveminders' and Undertakers' names, and . . . I don't know what else. Dad was there, and it was our last chance to talk . . . I didn't know it then, but they obviously did. Charlie boxed the contract up and left, but I guess every Undertaker reads it sooner or later."

"So we go back and tell him we want to see it."

"Pretty much," Byron agreed. "We need to talk to the council, too."

"Is it awful to be furious with all of them?" Rebekkah fisted her hands together. "I mean, I get it, but *damn*, it's not like we have much time to figure *anything* out and . . . I'm exhausted."

"We will," he said. "We'll find Daisha, and then figure out the rest."

Rebekkah nodded, but she wasn't entirely sure they *could* do everything they needed to do. *How do we find Daisha? How do we stop her? Why is there a contract in the first place? Is it breakable?* She closed her eyes and leaned her head on the back of the sofa.

She felt the cushion dip as Byron came to sit beside her. "How about we get a little sleep?"

"We can't. There are—"

"Just a couple hours. We aren't going to get anywhere if we're so exhausted we collapse. We're both running on next to no sleep."

She opened her eyes. "I know you're right, but . . . people are *dying*."

"I know, and if you can't focus, what good are you going to do them? The members of the council are asleep at this hour. Charlie refused to answer our questions. Between jet lag, Maylene's funeral, Dad's death, trips to Charlie's world, shootings . . . Catching a couple hours' sleep is going to do more good than anything else we can do right now."

For a moment, they stayed like that; then she stood. "You're right. I'm going to grab a quick shower."

Feeling foolish, she turned her back to him. "Can you unfasten this?"

She unhooked the clasp between her breasts, and then shrugged the outer layer of the dress off. She pulled her hair over one shoulder and stared steadfastly in front of her.

The first touch of his hands on her back made her draw in a sudden breath. They both froze for several heartbeats—each of which she was convinced he should be able to hear. Then, carefully, he began to unfasten the row of eyelets that ran along her spine. Her grip tightened on the sheer outer layer she held in her hand.

When the dress gaped open in the back, he pressed one kiss to her the back of her neck. She shivered and looked over her shoulder at him.

Say it. Tell him.

She took a steadying breath, stepped away from him—and fled.

37

BYRON LISTENED TO THE WATER TURN ON UPSTAIRS AND DEBATED THE foolishness of following Rebekkah. Unlike her, he couldn't care less *why* they were together, only that they were. He'd spent his life waiting on her, but had he known about Graveminders and Undertakers he'd have given her up rather than have her in danger. *She has no choice.* Because of the contract, they were tied together until death. *Which isn't going to make her any more likely to admit her feelings.* She was the Graveminder—but she was still the same woman who hated being trapped, the same woman who had let her dead sister stand between her and Byron for years, the same woman who was so afraid of losing the people she loved that she denied loving them. She was the same woman he'd loved for years. *And now she's going to be in danger for the rest of her life.* He wasn't sure if her vulnerability in the land of the dead was more or less frightening than the fact that a dead girl was in Claysville killing people. In both worlds, Rebekkah was a target.

How did you do this, Dad?

Everything had shifted in mere days—giving Byron what he wanted most, a future with Rebekkah, and putting that very same thing in a state of danger he couldn't have anticipated. He checked the doors, and then stood at the bay window in the living room looking at the dark. Daisha could be right outside, and he wouldn't know it. She could be killing someone. She *would* kill people.

He picked up the journal and flicked through the pages.

> *If Mae knew Lily had died, none of this would've happened. What kind of man hides his wife's death? Lily was kept there, and because of it, she came back. Mae was heartbroken.*

Byron turned to another section and read:

> *Charlie refused to tell me anything about Alicia's anger. She isn't much better. She's steered me wrong a few times, but most of her information is good . . .*

The number of secrets in the thin book was staggering. Byron skimmed, looking for Charlie's name.

> *Nick is a jackass. If he could, he'd let the ministers move here without any knowledge of the contract. He says, "The townsfolk don't know about it when they have children, so why should the ministers?" The difference is that the townsfolk are trapped here. New people aren't. They can come and go if they aren't born here.*
>
> *Ann brought up parenthood when I mentioned the fracas at the meeting. We're allowed to have a child whenever we choose. Undertakers don't have to wait for consent. How do I pass this on to my own son? How do I tell Ann no?*

Rebekkah came partway down the stairs. She was wearing a long nightshirt; the top of it was damp from her dripping-wet hair. "The shower's free."

If it wouldn't make her run, he'd be upstairs with her already. Instead, he nodded. "I'll be up in a minute."

He resumed reading:

Mae understood why Ella did it, but she didn't want to tell me. I saw her look at Ella. She knows the lure of Charlie's world. I don't understand it, but she tells me that the world she knows there is not what I see.

Sometimes I dream of killing Charlie.

Byron flipped forward again and read:

Mae was bitten. I wanted to kill the dead, but she's unable to remember that they are monsters. She lets them in her home, brings them to her table . . . I don't know how to reason with her sometimes. Sometimes I think she forgets that she is human. If they come here, they can kill her. They would kill all of us. She tells me I worry too much, but I exist to protect her. It's my job.

Carefully, Byron closed the book and went upstairs.

This wasn't a fantasy: there were no rules in place to protect the townsfolk while they rested. The monster could—and had—entered homes. Daisha had entered *this* house and killed Maylene. She'd entered Byron's home and bitten his father.

And we have no idea where she is.

He thought about Daisha coming into the house while Rebekkah was alone. His shower was brief. He'd barely dried before he yanked on a pair of jeans; he dried his hair with one hand as he opened the door of the bathroom.

Rebekkah stood in the doorway to her room watching him. She'd obviously made a decision of some sort because she'd brought his bag to her room. It sat on the floor at her feet.

"Will you stay with me?" she asked.

Without breaking their gaze, he came to stand in front of her. They'd been here, in this standoff, so many times over the years. She'd only ever had to look at him, and he was hers to have. She never admitted that what they shared was special. He couldn't count the number of rooms they'd shared and the number of nights they'd spent in various cities and towns, yet never once had she allowed herself to admit that *he* mattered, that *they* mattered.

"Is it that you don't want to sleep alone or that you want *me* here?"

"You," she whispered.

She backed away from him, and he stepped into her room. He unzipped his bag and pulled out the gun that Alicia had given him. He put it on the nightstand, and then put the bag against the wall where he wouldn't trip on it if he had to get up suddenly.

Rebekkah pushed the still-tangled bedcovers back and sat on the edge of the mattress.

He turned off the lights and went to her. With a small sigh, she curled into his arms. He lay back and held her.

"This doesn't mean anything," she murmured as her eyes drifted closed.

"Liar." He held her with one arm cradling her to him and the other free to smooth her hair back.

Or reach for the gun.

Rebekkah's eyes opened again. "Byron . . ."

He wrapped a damp strand of her hair around his finger, then let it fall onto her shoulder. Some part of him, the same part that had accepted the terms she'd set every time he'd held her, told him to keep quiet. The rest of him was tired of playing by her rules. "No changing. No commitments. This is meaningless. It's always meaningless."

She sighed. "That's not . . . never mind."

"I'm bound to you for the rest of our lives. I've loved you for years. You've loved me just as long." He didn't look away as he said it, and she didn't deny it this time. "You can protest all you want, but my *job* is to keep you safe, take a bullet over there if I have to. I signed a contract. I shot two men today."

She sat up and pulled away from him. "I didn't ask for this. I didn't ask you to do anything."

Byron watched her. "And you can't change who you are or what you feel. I get that, but I can't change who I am either. This is who we are. Regardless of what we do now, I'm in your life. Regardless of how you feel, I'm yours until our death. "

"If Ella hadn't died—"

"But she *did*."

Rebekkah scooted to the foot of the bed, putting herself out of reach. "She died knowing that I . . . that we . . ."

"*Kissed*. It was kissing, and we've done a hell of a lot more since then. It's not *Ella* standing between us. You feel guilty, and you're afraid. I understand, but you need to let it go. I won't ever leave you, Bek, no matter how often or how hard you push me. I've been waiting for you for most of my life, and I'll be here. That won't change whether you and I see where we can go or not. Tell me we're just friends, or friends with benefits, and"—he shrugged—"I'll try to accept that."

"You'll *try*?"

"Yeah, I'll *try*." He rolled onto his hip and slid to the far side of the bed. "I'm going to spend however long we have anchored to your side. I'm not going to pretend that I don't want you in my life *and* in my bed. I've lov—"

"Maybe you don't want *me*, Byron. Did you even consider that? You want the *Graveminder*." She glared at him. "If Ella hadn't killed herself, you'd—"

"She did, though, didn't she? And, in case you forgot, I felt like this *before she died*." He sat up and tugged her onto his lap. "I used to look for you every time I came home. I scanned Dad's letters looking for mentions of you. Not Ella, not the Graveminder. *You*, Rebekkah."

"Would you do it if I weren't the Graveminder? If you weren't the Undertaker?"

"I wish I could answer that, but there isn't an answer. We *are* those things. I can't undo any of it. Unless you die, you're the Graveminder, and"—he took her hand in his—"I don't think tossing yourself, your life, and the town to the side to figure out you and me is a very good idea. If you want to ignore this, ignore me for everything but the . . . job, I'll try to do that, but I think it's a mistake."

She didn't answer, and after a minute, he released her hand.

"We don't need to figure it out tonight. It's been a long"—he glanced at the red digits of the clock—"day, night . . . several days. Let's try to sleep."

"You're a good man." She crawled off his lap. "You deserve better."

At that, he paused. His resolve not to continue to push her tonight evaporated. "So now you're protecting me? Staying out of my bed and my life to keep me safe?"

"Yeah. I guess that's one way to put it." She slid to the opposite side of the bed, but she didn't lie down.

He stretched out and propped himself up on one arm. "You might be the woman I love, but it's not like I've exactly been celibate."

"So tell me it wouldn't mean anything to you. Tell me it wouldn't complicate everything; tell me it wouldn't be the start of a relationship." She slid off the bed and stood staring at him for a moment. When he didn't answer her, she put a hand to the hem of her nightshirt and lifted it slowly. "Or tell me no."

Byron watched her lift the shirt, enjoyed the sight of her bare hips and her flat stomach.

When he didn't speak, she continued to lift the nightshirt higher. All the while she held his gaze. "You don't want the same things I do."

"I'm not so sure about that." Without breaking their gaze, he moved toward her. He knelt on the mattress so he could reach out. Slowly, he trailed his fingertips over her stomach.

She paused.

"I didn't say stop," he whispered.

She pulled the shirt over her head and dropped it to the floor.

He cupped her breasts, and then kissed first one and then the other. "Beautiful."

She caught her breath and slid her hand around the back of his neck.

He slid his thumbs over her already hard nipples, and then he trailed his hands over the curve of her breasts and around her back. He didn't hold her fast, but he kept his hands on her bare back. His fingers splayed across her skin, and for a moment he couldn't think beyond the knowledge that he was finally touching Rebekkah again.

She didn't speak—or pull away. Her breathing was as uneven as his. Her lips parted, and she stared at him.

He moved upward, nipped her throat, and kissed his way to her ear. She sighed and tilted her head to give him better access.

"We both know"—he kissed the curve of her shoulder—"that if we made love"—he leaned back and watched her face as he slowly traced the contours of her right side—"it would mean something"— he kissed her gently—"to *both* of us."

Then he pulled away. "I'll agree to one thing, though: it wouldn't be the start of a relationship. We started a relationship years ago."

She stared at him, but still didn't say a word. The expression of shock on her face was almost enough to make him waver; he forced himself to hold her gaze—in part because the sight of her nearly naked body wasn't doing much for his resolve either.

Before he could give in, Byron stood, reached down, and pulled the bedcovers farther back. "I'm a grown man, Bek. Don't throw challenges at me unless you're sure you're ready for the results."

"You're telling me no?"

"I am," he said.

Wearing nothing but her panties now, she slipped into the bed. He pulled the covers up over her and walked away.

When he reached the door, she spoke. "Byron?"

He paused with his hand on the doorknob. "Yeah?"

"I'm not ready for any of this. For us or for being the Grave-minder."

"Being ready doesn't matter sometimes. There *is* an 'us,' and you *are* the Graveminder."

"I know," she whispered.

He opened the door.

"Byron?"

"Yeah?"

"I still want you to sleep in here."

He looked back at her. "Just sleep?"

Rebekkah didn't answer. He could see her chest rising and falling, and he counted each breath. Several moments passed, and then she said, "No, that's not what I want, but anything else would matter to both of us."

"I know." Byron smiled and closed the door. It wasn't exactly a full admission, but it was progress.

He climbed into bed and pulled Rebekkah close to him.

38

REBEKKAH SLIPPED OUT OF THE BED WHEN SHE AWOKE. IT WASN'T MUCH past sunrise. The light of the new morning poured through the curtains she'd forgotten to draw last night. She stepped past the worn board that had creaked for as long as she'd had a room at Maylene's. Sleep was out of reach, and if she was going to be awake with too many thoughts on her mind, she was going to do it with a cup of coffee in her hand.

She'd slipped on her discarded nightshirt and made it as far as the door when Byron spoke.

"Running or just can't sleep?"

"It's morning," she said in lieu of answering the question.

Byron squinted at the light outside. "Not by much, Bek."

"You don't have to get up." She curled her hand around the glass doorknob and opened the door. Somewhere downstairs Cherub had begun proclaiming his need for kitty food. The familiarity of the sound made Rebekkah smile. Some things were constant, and in light of the myriad oddities of the past two days, that constancy was very welcome.

Byron sat up and rubbed his eyes. "I'll make breakfast if you start coffee. We need to see the town council or the mayor. Might as well get started."

Rebekkah thought of the platters of food that Maylene's neighbors had left for her. Most of them weren't breakfast foods, but she'd seen at least two cold-cut trays in the fridge. Between the ham and cheese and various fruit baskets, she and Byron would find plenty to graze on. She told him as much.

"You can have cold food if you want. I'm making eggs and ham." He rubbed his face and blinked a few more times.

"Not everything changes, hmm? You're not any more alert when you first wake up than you used to be. "

Byron lunged out of the bed, covered the few feet to the doorway, and pulled her into his arms. "I can be when I need to."

Rebekkah put her hands flat against his chest and looked up at him. "Hmm. Byron or coffee? Sex or food?"

"If you have to think about it, there's no contest." He brushed his lips over hers in a brief, chaste kiss.

"I've been thinking about you for years, B." She ducked out of his arms and out the door.

In the kitchen, she fed Cherub, started the coffee brewing, and pulled out a tray of cold cuts and bread. While she waited for the coffee to percolate, she sat down and nibbled on the food she'd set out on the table. The sounds of the shower upstairs made her smile. Having another person there made it easier to avoid the thought of living alone in the big old house.

Living here alone.

With a start, she realized that she couldn't ever leave Claysville now. As the Graveminder, she was trapped. It wasn't that she wanted to go somewhere specific or do something specific; it was simply knowing she could go anywhere, do anything. She'd avoided entanglements for most of her life. *Run from them.* Now her future, her address, her connection to Byron, her commitment to Charles: so many things had suddenly been decided for her. *They had been decided already; I just didn't know it.* Rebekkah thought back to the letter Maylene had left for her. *These are the things she didn't want to tell me.*

Rebekkah rinsed two mugs, set one by the coffeepot, and then poured coffee in the other for herself.

Byron came down the stairs. His hair was damp and stuck out in tiny tufts revealing that he'd just finished towel-drying it. He didn't pause on his way to the coffee.

"I can't leave," she said aloud, testing the words, gauging the panic they'd bring.

"I know. That's what I was trying to tell you yesterday at Sweet Rest." His face was carefully expressionless as he poured his coffee. "I don't know how strict that is or . . . well, much of anything. I signed a contract, but that's binding me, not you."

She gaped at him. "You *signed* a *contract*? Promising what?"

"I don't know." He didn't make eye contact with her, but he came to sit across from her. He rolled a slice of ham and a slice of cheese together and ate the breadless sandwich.

"You don't know what you signed? How could you sign something you didn't read?"

He shrugged. "Situational factors."

"*Situa*— Are you serious?"

Still not looking at her, he rolled up several more pieces of cheese and ham. "Yep."

Rebekkah pushed away from the table and walked over to the window. He had no idea of what he'd agreed to, but he'd signed. She hadn't even been given that option. She folded her left arm over her stomach as she stood and sipped the coffee she held in the opposite hand. Behind her, she heard Byron push out his chair and pour himself more coffee.

"Do you want eggs?"

"No." She didn't look at him.

He opened cupboards; the clatter of bowls and pans were the

only sounds for a few moments. Then he said, "We were with Charlie. Dad told me that I either signed or I stayed behind. I drank with the dead. They set me up to do so, but I did it all the same. I didn't know that by signing, I was killing my father. All I really knew was that if I didn't sign, I was leaving you."

While he was talking, she turned away from the window to face him, but his back was to her as he shifted things around inside the oversize refrigerator. He turned around with a carton of eggs in his hand and said, "I couldn't do that. I *won't*."

She crossed the room, took the eggs out of his hand, and sat them on the counter beside him. "William died so you could be—"

"He died because Maylene died," Byron interrupted, "and because the new Graveminder needed *her* Undertaker."

Rebekkah took his hands. "I'm scared, and I'm sorry about your dad, and I'm angry about all of us being trapped, but I'm glad you're the one who's at my side."

"Me, too. I—" His cell phone rang, and he frowned. "Hold that thought. That's the ring tone for work." He grabbed the phone. "Montgomery . . . Yeah. Where? . . . No, I'll be there. Hold on." He looked at Rebekkah and made a writing gesture in the air.

She mouthed, "Coffee table."

"Sorry," Byron mouthed back. Then he walked into the living room.

Rebekkah fixed two ham-and-cheese sandwiches. Then she started putting the food away. Snatches of Byron's conversation stood out like beacons.

" . . . animal . . ."

" . . . missing family . . ."

She'd already caught enough details to know that she wanted to go with him to the scene of the death, so she turned off the coffeepot, pulled two travel mugs from the cupboard, and filled them both.

When he returned to the room with a scribbled note and a frown, she held out a mug and sandwich. "I need five minutes to throw on clothes and grab a ponytail holder."

"Bek—"

"Is it Daisha?"

"We can't know yet, but . . . yeah, it sounds like it." He blew his breath out in a heavy sigh. "You can see her at the funeral home. The scene of a murder is . . . Chris says this one is messy."

"I can do this," she assured him. "Five minutes?"

He nodded, and she hurried upstairs to change out of her night-shirt.

39

BYRON AND REBEKKAH DROVE TOWARD THE SUNNY GLADES TRAILER Park. The mobile-home community wasn't quite at the edge of the town limits, but it was a long enough drive that the silence started to feel awkward. Byron plugged his iPod into the hearse's stereo system.

"Your upgrade?" She nodded toward the stereo.

"Yeah. I added it a few months ago." He glanced sideways at her. "It was a bit of an admission that I moved back to stay. I knew that when I crossed the town limits in December, but it took a little longer to really admit it."

"Well, you're a few months ahead of me, then: I figured out that I'm staying less than an hour ago." Rebekkah stared out the window. "Tell me what you know."

"I know it'll be okay," he said.

"About the murder," she clarified, "not about living here."

He cut off the engine. "Chris got a call, an anonymous tip, that there were two bodies that needed removal."

"Two?"

"A couple. Man and a woman . . . Chris says that it was another animal attack or maybe a murder suicide." He opened the car door, but didn't get out.

"This is ridiculous." Rebekkah's tone was angry. "What if we told them?"

"Told them?" he repeated.

"That a monster was killing people, not an animal." She got out of the car and closed the door a little too forcefully, not quite slamming it.

Byron closed his door gently, walked around to stand beside her, and said softly, "You want to tell Chris that a dead girl killed these people and attacked the others?"

"Yes. That's exactly what I want to do. Either they believe it and can try to protect themselves or . . ."

"Or they just forget, or they think we're crazy," he finished.

When Rebekkah didn't reply, he went toward the door of the trailer. She followed silently.

The door was propped open, and he was grateful for the cool day. The smell of recent death filled the small structure, but if not for the open windows and breeze, it would've been worse. He handed her a pair of protective booties.

Once he'd put on his own, he looked over his shoulder. "Can you do this? Or do you want to wait outside?"

She frowned and stepped past him into the living room. Her eyes widened. "There are three death scents."

She drew in a deep breath, and then, seemingly unfazed by the blood that was on the walls and soaking into the sofa, she walked farther into the trailer. "Two bodies. Another death."

"A third murder? Chris said that—"

"No." She looked around the room as if she saw things he didn't. Her gaze was unfocused, even as she assessed the room. "Hungry Dead, not still dead."

A sound from the hallway drew Byron's attention. Chris had come out of one of the rooms and now stood in the doorway. He nodded. "Byron. Rebekkah."

Rebekkah wasn't looking at him; she walked in the opposite direction and stood in the kitchen area. Her hand was outstretched like she was feeling for something in the air.

After a moment, she turned around. Her eyes were shimmering silver. "Over here," she said calmly.

"Bek!" Byron all but leaped over the dead woman to reach Rebekkah.

"She's fine, Byron," Chris said. "Barrow women get like that. Maylene looked peculiar-like when your dad brought her around dead folk."

As Chris spoke, Rebekkah had become so vibrant that Byron's eyes hurt to look at her. The shades of brown that he saw in her hair were highlighted as individual tones: dark coppers and soft golds twined with strands of amber and honey.

The urge to go to her vied with the need to run from her. Like stepping into the tunnel to reach the dead, this moment felt both frightening and alluring. Byron swallowed against a suddenly dry mouth. She was still Rebekkah, still the woman he'd loved for years, still his partner in the strange task that lay before them. *And not entirely of this world.*

Byron forced himself to look away from her and asked Chris, "What?"

"I don't understand the particulars, but she'll be fine. Just like her grandmama. Their eyes get different, but it's not anything to worry over." The sheriff shook his head, and then he headed to the door, trying to step around the worst of the bloodied carpet. "Come on. I'll help you bag these two."

"Sheriff?" Rebekkah called. "This wasn't an animal." Her voice was different, too, thready in a way that reminded Byron of the wind in the tunnel to the land of the dead. "There's a—"

"Stop." Chris spun around and held up a hand. "Before you go saying anything more, here's the facts: I don't know as much as you, but the terms of my job let me accept things that most folks won't hold in their mind. Reverend McLendon and Father Ness and the rest of the council members are able to remember some stuff, but if you go talking about things we shouldn't know, it causes a hell of a migraine."

"A migraine?" Rebekkah repeated.

"Stripes and lost vision, vomiting sick. Nasty." Chris grimaced. "Don't go saying anything that isn't mine to know. What matters is this: something that shouldn't be here killed them. When someone dies, I call the Undertaker. You"—he nodded at Byron—"bring the Barrow woman when you need to. Any . . . *weird* stuff Maylene told me always made my head hurt, and I didn't remember it the next day anyhow."

"And you're okay with that?" Rebekkah's voice became softer still.

"No. That's why I don't want you telling me things that aren't any of my business."

"That's not what I meant," she whispered.

"I know that." Chris took off his hat and rubbed a hand over his hair. "Some things are out of our control, though. Trying to change them"—he put his hat back on—"it just doesn't make sense. I know my place. Asking questions isn't part of it."

Rebekkah frowned like she wanted to press the matter, but after a moment she sighed. "We'll need to talk about the other *animal attacks*, too."

The sheriff nodded. Then he stared first at Byron and then at Rebekkah. "I know you're not the ones who used to deal with this," he said to Byron, "but her eyes are strange like her grandmama's and you're the Undertaker. I called you. Sooner or later that means the animal attacks will stop, right?"

Byron did not flinch as he and Rebekkah exchanged a grim look. Then they both said, "Right."

Chris nodded. "Good. I'm going out to your car to get the body bags. You two do whatever you need to do here. Holler when you want my help with bagging the bodies."

Then he walked out.

40

REBEKKAH WATCHED THE SHERIFF LEAVE WITH A MIXTURE OF SYMPATHY and astonishment. Her skin felt almost uncomfortably prickled by the things she could feel in the tiny trailer. She made sure that the sheriff was well outside the trailer, out of earshot, before she turned to face Byron.

"It's cold where she walked. Over there"—she pointed at a spot near the refrigerator—"she stood still longer. It's like ice against my skin the closer I walk to it. I don't know for sure that it's Daisha, but"—Rebekkah walked toward Byron, following the trail that wanted to tug her right out of her skin—"I know that a dead person walked here."

Byron kept his distance, giving her space to maneuver in the tiny room. "Can you find her out in town?"

Rebekkah shook her head. "Maybe. I don't know. I just know that she killed people here. I feel her here." She pointed toward the sofa. "One of them died right there."

"It's bloody, so that makes—"

"No." Rebekkah walked to the edge of the sofa. She bent down to touch the air just over the tattered cushions. "She was here. Sat here. The blood might be from the attack that killed the . . . which-ever of them it was . . . but there's plenty of blood other places that

there's not death. Here." She ran her hand through the air in a diagonal, as if she were tracing down the back of someone who was bent
forward. "Right here."

"You can feel her death?" Byron stepped closer.

"Or his. I don't know which." Rebekkah looked away from the
almost black stain on the cushions. "It doesn't matter. They don't
matter. *She* matters." Rebekkah folded her arms over her chest as if
holding on to her own body would keep her from floating away. She
wasn't sure, though, if it would. Part of her felt like she could close
her eyes and drift into the air. "Daisha is strong from killing people.
Not just dead. Not vacant. She's stronger than a newborn dead girl
should be. I feel it. I feel her, and she's strong." Rebekkah put a hand
over her chest as she stepped past Byron into the hallway. She drew
in several breaths, wanting to fill herself up with air, weigh herself
down with this world.

There were only a few drops of blood on the carpet in this part
of the trailer, like dark tears had stained the dingy pile. The trail
of cold was far more obvious than the blood. *That* she could see: it
stretched out toward her like wisps of smoke from a barely smoldering fire. She pointed into the bathroom. "The other one died in
there."

"If we step outside, can you follow the same trail?" Byron was
still behind her. His voice was low, but it felt strange to her.

Not dead.

She looked over her shoulder. The smoky trails of death weren't
touching him; they wound into the air around him, but he didn't see
them. They were for her to follow.

"The bodies need to be taken from here," she whispered.

He nodded. "I know, but you . . . Bek? Your eyes aren't . . . they're
different."

She looked at the cracked mirror that hung on the bathroom
wall, but it wasn't herself that she saw reflected in it. Instead of the

features she knew as her own, a silvered shape looked back at her with blacked-out eyes. It was okay. She *got* it. To find them, to lead them home, to keep them in their graves, she needed to be kin to them. She wasn't part of the living world anymore, not truly, but she was tied to it. *Through Byron.* He was her tether.

"I'm not here," she whispered to herself.

"Bek?" Byron touched her shoulder, and in doing so, he became visible in the mirror. Unlike her, he was vibrant. His eyes were fiercely green, and she had the sudden sense that right then she could've seen him in the dark.

Like a light to lead me home.

"You're here, Rebekkah," he assured her. He didn't come any closer, however; he stood apart from her with his hand on her shoulder.

She couldn't speak, didn't know the words to make the whispery thoughts in her mind come clear to him. She nodded. It was the best she could do for a moment. His hand on her shoulder seemed to reduce her feeling of detachment. He was the rope that bound her to the world of the living.

And I need to keep him safe.

That meant finding Daisha.

Rebekkah closed her eyes for a moment. Her tongue felt too thick for her mouth, and the voice that she heard as her own somehow wasn't right, but she needed to explain things to Byron.

"Daisha was here . . . or someone like her." She opened her eyes and met his gaze in the mirror that reflected her still-hollow eyes. "Daisha needs me to help her find her way home."

Byron took his hand away. "I need to take care of the ones she killed. That's my job too."

Mutely, Rebekkah nodded.

"Chris!" Byron yelled. "We're ready."

Then Rebekkah went outside while Byron and Christopher

sealed the two dead people into the body bags. These wouldn't walk. At their wake, she would say the words, and then she would visit their graves over the next few months. Byron would handle the details of the living world, the wake and the burial, and when the bodies were in the earth, she would make sure that they stayed there.

Like Maylene should've done for Daisha.

If Daisha had been buried and tended to, she wouldn't have woken up. *Which means she wasn't minded. Was there an accident? Why hadn't someone reported it? Was she killed?* There was a reason the dead girl awoke, a reason she wasn't still resting where she should've been, and Rebekkah needed to figure that out.

After I take care of Daisha. Or maybe as part of taking care of her.

Rebekkah's first duty was to the dead, and as she stood in the brown grass outside the trailer, she understood that the dead girl who'd killed and partially eaten the couple inside needed something she hadn't been given: Rebekkah's job was to give her the peace she'd been denied.

41

ALICIA DIDN'T TAKE ANY OF THE BOYS WITH HER. BOYD BITCHED, BUT most days he acted like the older brother she'd never had, so his objections had stopped bothering her a few decades ago.

The guards the Undertaker had shot were still lying on either side of the door, but a new pair stood on the next step down. She leveled a sawed-off shotgun at the first one. "Do we need to discuss my invitation?"

Charlie's personal guard, Ward, opened the door. "Don't you get tired of shooting people, Alicia?"

She tilted her head. "Not really. You?"

"Depends on the day, I suppose." Ward motioned her inside. "He's expecting you."

"Figured he would be. Though I'd rather shoot my way in than pretend civility toward him."

Ward, wisely, said nothing.

Alicia slung her shotgun over her shoulder and into the holster she'd rigged for it. After a wicked grin at Ward, she yelled, "I'm looking for the miserable bastard who thinks he runs this place."

"Must you do that?"

"I could just start shooting things," she suggested. "That always seems to get his attention. Actually . . ." She reached back for the shotgun, but Charlie came to the top of the stairs and looked down at her.

"My dear, what a lovely surprise."

She snorted and aimed her gun at him. "Why did you let the girl get shot?"

"I did not 'let' her get shot, Alicia." He sighed. "Why would I allow her to be injured?"

"Why did you allow them to shoot at her in the first damn place?" She shifted the barrel a touch and fired.

Charlie didn't flinch as splinters from the carved wooden handrail flew through the air beside him. "It was meant to be a deterrent; she was not to get injured, just encouraged to stay in protective care. I don't need her running all over the place asking questions, having her head filled with the wrong things."

"The truth, you mean?"

"Not all truths are equal, Alicia." Charlie's gaze didn't waver. "Shall I tell her *your* secrets?"

Alicia lowered her gun. "No, but don't think I'm waiting around."

"I saw." He scowled. "You couldn't let them get oriented before you tried to get him under your thumb?"

"Why should I? You weren't wasting any time, were you? The poor girl is barely here a minute, and you have yourself set up like some knight. Wine her and dine her—after a conveniently planned rescue scenario that chases her into your arms. You're predictable." Alicia shook her head.

"If I were predictable, my dear, you would've outmaneuvered me decades ago . . . unless"—Charlie started down the stairs toward her—"perhaps you *like* trying to outwit me. Is that it, Alicia? Do you—"

The rest of his words were lost in the blast of her next shot. She didn't hit him, of course, but she aimed close enough that splinters from the banister cut him.

Bloodless bastard. Not human. Not right.

He continued down the stairs as if the splinters didn't hurt. He might not bleed, but he felt pain. They both knew that. They both also knew that he'd allow her to hurt him repeatedly if it would ease the anger that festered inside her.

She couldn't look at the placid expression on his face any more than she could forgive him. Although they both knew she could reload with her eyes closed, she looked steadfastly at her shotgun as she broke open the barrel, removed the cases, and slid in two new shells. When she closed the breech and lifted her gaze, he was standing in front of her, waiting.

"Whatever's happening over there isn't business as normal," she said. "You and I both know it. Dead walking is one thing, but killing the dead so as to make them walk is altogether different. You ought to step in this time."

For a moment, Charlie stared at her, and Alicia saw the person she'd thought he was when she was still alive. Back then, he'd seemed almost human. Back then, he'd seemed like a powerful man who ruled an unruly empire.

A man I could trust.

He shook his head. "I won't break the rules. I wouldn't do it for you, and I won't do it for them either."

"You're a fool." She swung her shotgun up and shot the god-awful chandelier. Crystal shards rained down on him as she turned to leave.

42

A SHORT WHILE LATER, AS BYRON DROVE TO MONTGOMERY AND SONS, Rebekkah felt the weight of the living world begin to settle back into her body. She could still feel a lingering connection to the dead, and it somehow made the air feel different; everything smelled richer.

When Byron stopped the hearse, Rebekkah went into the funeral parlor. Somewhere in her town, Daisha was waiting. She was starving. The whole time she'd been dead, no one had seen to her needs. She'd been alone. She'd been hidden from Maylene somehow.

"Your weekly update." Elaine held out a thick manila envelope.

"My . . . right. My update. I need the records of the deaths for the last six months." Rebekkah forced her tongue and lips to make words.

Byron stepped in behind her, and Elaine called, "Mr. Montgomery? The mayor's office called. There was another animal attack, a fatal one this time. He'd like to schedule an appointment with you."

Byron stopped, and he and Rebekkah exchanged a look.

"Did you get ahold of Allan?" he asked.

"He's on his way to the pickup now." Elaine softened for a moment. "After I get Rebekkah updated, I thought I might run over to Cherry's Pies and grab a few sandwiches."

"And coffee?"

"Of course."

"Thank you. I'll be in the prep room." Byron nodded and walked away. A moment later, the door to the basement opened and closed.

Elaine took up her key ring, motioned at Rebekkah, and led her to another office. She opened the door and pointed at a tall gray cabinet. "Every week the backup copy is filed. There is a cross-reference that lists the family name of the deceased."

As Rebekkah looked on silently, Elaine pulled out a file and opened it.

"Each decedent has a separate entry within their family. In it, you will find the date, cause, and any peculiar details." As she spoke, she stabbed a finger at examples of the various details she recited. "Of course, the decedent's surname is the primary file category, but subreferences are listed in the appropriate box on the fact sheet." She snapped the file shut.

Rebekkah stared at her. "You are amazing."

"The electronic version is easier," Elaine added, "but the late Mrs. Barrow preferred her hard copies."

"She liked things the way they were," Rebekkah murmured.

Elaine's stern expression softened. "She was a good woman. I hoped—no disrespect to Ann—that she and William would wed after Ann passed, but they scoffed at the suggestion. She loved him, though, and he loved her."

"I know," Rebekkah murmured.

"But they were stubborn." Elaine shook her head, but her smile was a yearning one. "Love like that is a rarity, and to think they both found it twice."

Rebekkah clutched the file in her hand. "I'm not sure that love means having to marry. She loved him, but that didn't mean—"

"It's not my place. If it were, I'd nag the younger Mr. Montgomery to marry you already. The two of you have been pretending not to be in love for years. Sheer foolishness, if you ask me, but"—Elaine gave Rebekkah a look that would make most people flinch—"no one's asking me, are they?"

"No," Rebekkah said. "I don't think anyone's asking."

Elaine sighed. "Well, sooner or later, one of you will be bright enough to ask my opinion."

For a moment, Rebekkah wasn't sure whether to laugh or tell Elaine to back off. Laughter won. "I'm sure if we ever reach that point, we'll be able to find you."

"Good." Elaine smiled as she pointed at the barren desk. "This is your workspace. I don't suppose you'd like it outfitted for this decade?"

Rebekkah bit her cheek to keep herself from laughing again. "Electronic files would probably be easier to search."

"They're all backed up on the server. I took a course last summer, you know." Elaine's excitement became obvious. Her eyes glimmered, and her smile widened. "I'll get you set up this week. In the meantime, if you need help with the filing system, I'll be in my office."

"I'm sure I'll have no trouble. Something tells me your system is foolproof." Rebekkah opened the envelope in her hands and sat down at her new desk.

BYRON STOOD SILENTLY IN THE PREPARATION ROOM. HE HATED TO ADMIT that he was disconcerted by Rebekkah's reaction to the murder scene. She was still his Rebekkah, but seeing her become something *other* had left him unnerved.

He went about his job, grateful for the habitual steps. The body of the man on the table was relatively fit. His appearance spoke of years of physical labor and of hard living: he was thin with well-defined musculature and had a knife scar on his left biceps and a puckered scar where a bullet had entered his right thigh. Daisha's attack on the man had obviously been more brutal than her attack on Maylene. One forearm was bitten to the bone, and the throat and neck were bared to the collarbone on both sides. The right biceps was also ravaged.

She looked so harmless.

The murderer, the *dead* murderer, was too small to seem capable of such savagery. This body would not be made available for an open-casket viewing.

She's a monster, not a girl. His father had reminded him of that, reminded him that the dead weren't to be treated mercifully, and as Byron looked at the proof of her strength and violence, he understood why.

Are they this much stronger in the land of the dead, too? He felt a wave of exhaustion at the thought. He wasn't ready for this. *Will I ever be?* Resentment that he didn't want to feel for his father welled up in him. William had been a good man and a good father, but his choosing to keep such life-altering secrets threatened to negate everything else.

Byron looked up as Elaine walked into the room.

"Allan is here," she said. "He'll be down in a moment. You go on upstairs. The body . . . It's Bonnie Jean."

"Amity's sister?"

Elaine nodded. "Allan will handle things here."

Byron turned his back and stripped off his disposable coveralls. "I ought to—"

"No. You ought to go to Maylene's old office and see Rebekkah," Elaine said firmly. "Amity will be with family. I'll take care of the funeral arrangements."

Byron glanced at Elaine as he walked over to the biohazard bin and shoved the barely used protective garment into it. "Right, and I ought to do this because . . . ?"

"Because . . . because the Barrow woman's office is where the decedent files are kept. It'll makes things easier if . . ." Elaine's words trailed off.

"What things?" he asked.

Elaine frowned. Her usual peremptory and bossy manner was absent. Instead, she rubbed her temples before saying, "Work things. The Barrows . . . do things. Help."

"Right. Those things." Byron felt guilty as he saw Elaine rub her head. "I'm sorry."

She waved him off. "I don't expect you to be at her side as she gets settled in the office, but I think she needs assistance. William assisted Maylene, and"—Elaine winced—"Rebekkah requires you. Upstairs. Allan can do this, and you can't help Amity, but Rebekkah needs . . . I'm sorry. I think the light down here is aggravating my eyes again."

She turned away, and Byron swallowed back the guilt he was starting to feel. He hadn't *known* that he'd said anything that would hurt her. "Elaine?" he called after her. "My father thought a good day-spa visit helped with your headaches, didn't he?"

She paused. "A simple headache doesn't need pamper—"

"I'd be lost here without you. I know that, and *you* know that." He came to stand beside her. "You're right. Allan will handle the preparation down here, and I'll see what Rebekkah needs. *You* will go relax so you don't get ill and leave me floundering here."

Allan stepped into the preparation room as Byron took Elaine upstairs. As they walked past a spare office, Byron heard Rebekkah call for Elaine. At the doorway, he and Elaine both paused.

Rebekkah looked up from a stack of files on the desk. "Do you know of anyone born in town with the first name Daisha?"

Elaine motioned toward the bottom of the file cabinet. "Birth records are listed in there, but William had left a note on that same name. I'd only begun searching when you arrived today. Things were backed up, but . . . hold on."

She walked away, returning a minute later with a stack of papers. "I don't have all of the files sorted, but I do have two Daishas so far. One is five years old—mother, Chelsea; father, Robert."

"And the other?" Byron prompted.

"Seventeen—mother, Gail; father wasn't a Claysville native. She's been gone for a while. According to the note in her school file, her mother reported that she went to live with her father. I tried to call the mother yesterday several times, but there's been no answer." Elaine shook her head. "The address . . . it's . . ." She flipped the page.

"Sunny Glades Trailer Park," Rebekkah filled in. "That's her."

43

DAISHA RETURNED TO HER FORMER HOME. THE BODIES WERE GONE. She'd considered keeping them there, but the more she'd eaten, the more she'd remembered—and she wasn't entirely sure she *wanted* to remember much more. The people she'd met in town had helped her remember, so by the time she'd come to the trailer, she'd remembered so much more than she wished she had.

Leaves in her mouth.

Hands on her throat.

She knew that she had been killed.

She knew that when she woke up, she was stopped from coming home.

To find the shining woman. The Graveminder.

To hear the words, to find nourishment.

Someone had made it impossible for her to come back even though she'd felt the thread that grew from the center of her being, pulling her back to here, to home, to *her*. When she'd awakened, she had known where she was supposed to go.

Breath, drink, and food.

If she'd kept Gail and Paul here, they would've woken up in time: that's why she'd called the tip line to have their bodies removed. *I don't want them to wake up.* The Graveminder would stop that from

happening. Daisha understood that now. She understood most everything: the longer she'd been re-alive, the more she re-knew. The
better she was fed, the more she remembered.

She remembered the Cold Man. He was there, too.

And Daisha remembered *her*, the woman.

"Then let them go," the woman had said. "They'll fix everything, and when they're done, we'll kill them again."

Daisha remembered the voice, the woman. *She* was why Daisha
killed the last Graveminder: she had been sent to do just that.

It was why the woman made me dead.

44

NICOLAS HAD BECOME MAYOR AFTER THE LAST GRAVEMINDER AND UN-
dertaker were already in place, so the protocol for dealing with
the new ones was somewhat unclear to him. He'd never had to answer questions, fill in blanks, or explain anything.

"Sir?"

"Show them in," he said.

The words were barely out of his mouth when they came into
his office. Menace all but radiated from the new Undertaker, but the
Graveminder—like her predecessor—was far more sedate. Rebekkah Barrow hadn't been born in Claysville, nor had she spent her
life here. Some unexamined part of him wondered about the life
she could have known, about the possibilities among which anyone
born outside of town could choose, but he pushed those thoughts
away. He was Claysville born and bred, like the generations of men
before him. Whittaker men left town only for the acquisition of an
education or a spouse.

Nicolas came around the desk and gestured to the sofa and
chairs. "Please."

"We have questions," the Undertaker said.

His partner put a hand on his wrist. "You know who we are?"

"I do." Nicolas walked over to the bar in his office. "Drink?"

The Undertaker frowned. "It's a bit early in the day for that."

"Alcoholism is a disease; ergo, as with every other disease, Claysville natives are safe from it until we are eighty years old. After that, all protection expires. So . . ." Nicolas poured a generous measure in a glass. "Miss Barrow?"

"No, thank you." She sat on the sofa, and her Undertaker followed her lead.

Nicolas carried his drink over and sat in one of the chairs. "You know about the contract?" he asked. "The . . . situation here?"

"Some," the Graveminder said. "We know there *is* one."

"And we know that the thing killing people isn't an animal," the Undertaker added.

The mayor shook his head. "*That* remains to be seen. It might not be an animal the way that most of us would use that word, but any creature that savages humans . . . I'd say 'animal' is a fine term. One of my council members was killed. Your grandmother"—he nodded at the Graveminder—"was murdered. I've seen enough to say that it was more animal than person."

The Undertaker didn't say it, but the slight curve of his lips revealed his accord. The new Graveminder, however, frowned and said, "It's not their fault. If the dead are minded—"

"The animal doing this obviously was *not* minded, so you find it and you fix it." Nicolas didn't raise his voice, but the thought of Bonnie Jean dying made his stomach clench.

"That's all you've got to say? Find the dead and fix it?" The Undertaker scowled. "Do you know what we've been through this week? Who we've lost? And we're just to step in and *fix* everything? How about a little help? Information? Sympathy?"

"Byron," the Graveminder murmured. She took his hand in hers and squeezed it, and then she looked at Nicolas. "What can you tell us?"

Nicolas looked directly at them. "The first death was Mrs. Bar-

row; the most recent death was Bonnie Jean Blue. Why? I don't
know. Bad luck on Bonnie Jean's part, I suspect. There have been a
lot more attacks, but they've been . . . smoothed over. Not deaths,
of course. Those are harder to keep contained. More than a dozen
bites, though." The mayor paused, took a gulp of his whiskey, and
then continued. "Folks don't tie it all together. *Won't* because of the
contract. Unless they're on the council, they just can't put it all together. From what I know, it's always been that way."

"And there's no contract here that we can read?" the Graveminder asked.

"No. It's all passed down verbally. Outsiders might not understand if they were to read it, and . . . it's just not how we do things."
He felt oddly guilty as he spoke, as if he was being disloyal to his
position. Claysville was a good town. "We go years without issues.
If anyone wakes, Mrs. Barrow always handled it. No one was the
wiser."

"Why?" the Graveminder asked. "*Why* agree to this? Why do
people accept living like this?"

And, for a moment, Nicolas let the truths he didn't usually admit
come to the surface. "It's not like we can leave. The deal the founders made, the people that made it, they're all long gone. We are here.
We are born and die here, and in between those two moments, we
try to make the best of the lot we drew." He walked away and refilled his glass. "It's not all bad either."

They didn't answer, so he continued. "Think about your lives
here. No one gets sick. We die, but only from accidents or when
we reach an age for it . . . or choose to die so as to make room for
someone else."

At that, the Graveminder and Undertaker exchanged looks.

"For most folks, having a baby means waiting until there's a
death. Some families get exemptions." He looked at them pointedly. "Others earn them by community service, or they can get an-

other person's allotted birth if the one giving it up has sterilization surgery. We can only support so many bodies. The founders made some rules so we didn't exhaust our space. They wanted to be sure there was enough space for food and for the resources for those who live here."

"But that was a long time ago. We can get food and other things from outside town now," the Graveminder objected.

"Maybe, but there are still only so many jobs. We have some poverty now because we have more people than jobs." Nicolas gave them a strained smile. "There's a lot of good, but keeping it good takes managing. Part of that is relying on the resources we have—including you two."

The Undertaker spoke up then. "I'm not sure I agree with all of that."

"Why don't you do your job, and I'll do mine." Nicolas looked at each of them. "Unlike the rest of us, *you* are the only ones qualified for your . . . unique positions. The rest of us will handle the town. You need to resolve the animal problem."

The Graveminder stood; she was still holding the Undertaker's hand in hers, so he stood when she did. For a moment, Nicolas felt a surge of envy. They weren't ever alone.

Of course, they also had a higher likelihood of violent deaths than anyone else born in Claysville.

It's not worth the trade-off.

Nicolas stood. "You should also know that you will have no bills. Ever. I doubt that anyone's thought to tell you, but you don't pay for anything. Once you become *this*, your needs are"—he waved his hand—"handled, for all intents and purposes. It doesn't make up for what you are asked to do, but you will have your needs met. And when you're ready, you don't need to enter the parenting queue. You are allowed to have as many children as you want, whenever—"

"That's not going to be an issue," Rebekkah said firmly.

"Right." Nicolas gestured toward the door. "I'll see you at the meeting, but I would appreciate it if you let me know when the animal is contained."

The Graveminder tensed, but the Undertaker nodded.

And then they were gone.

45

AFTER THEY LEFT THE MAYOR'S OFFICE, THEY DROVE IN SILENCE FOR SEVeral minutes before Rebekkah smacked her hand on the dash. "Pull over."

"Here?"

"Now. Please." She glanced his way. Her eyes weren't quite silvered, but a ring of unearthly color surrounded her irises.

Byron parked the car, grabbed a gun and other supplies from the glove box, and then got out to join Rebekkah. He shoved the derringer in one pocket and a syringe in the other.

She walked with a purposeful stride; her gaze darted around. They walked for several blocks—toward her house—when Rebekkah stopped and drew a deep breath.

"She's come to me," she whispered in that hollowed-out voice.

Byron wanted to look at her, to see her as she became something not of this world, but keeping her safe was his first priority. Keeping alert for any signs of Daisha's presence, he slipped his hand inside his open jacket and unfastened the catch on his holster. His other hand was in his pocket holding a derringer.

They stopped at the edge of Rebekkah's yard. Daisha stood on the porch.

Byron didn't draw the gun in his shoulder holster, but his hand tensed on the derringer in his jacket pocket.

Could I kill her? What are the rules here?

"You're dead." Rebekkah extended her hand as if she'd call Daisha to her. "You came back . . . and . . ."

Daisha tensed, but she didn't flee. "I know I'm dead, but I'm not the only one."

"Daisha? That's your name, right?"

The dead girl nodded warily.

"I need you to listen to me." Rebekkah eased closer, not yet at the steps to the porch, but no longer at the edge of the yard. "You need to let me—"

"No, I don't. Whatever it is, I don't." Daisha held out her hand as if to ward off Rebekkah.

Byron couldn't decide whether it was better to pull out his weapons or wait. If he drew the gun, it would probably spook Daisha, but he wasn't sure how fast the dead girl was—or if he was quick enough to get to the gun before she was able to attack.

"I wanted to warn you," the girl murmured.

"Warn me?" Rebekkah asked in gentle voice. "About you?"

"No. Not me."

"You killed my grandmother." Rebekkah's voice didn't waver. "Here. You killed her here in my home."

"It wasn't on purpose. When we wake, we come to the Graveminder. I don't know why. Maybe you do . . . but you *shine*." Daisha walked to the edge of the porch. "You're filled with brightness, glowing inside, and I . . ." Daisha shook her head. "I *had* to go to her."

"And now?" Rebekkah stepped onto the first step.

Daisha smiled. "Now I don't have to see you. I don't need to come to your door, not ever again. I can leave."

Byron was near enough to help, but every instinct he wanted to ignore told him that Rebekkah had to touch the dead girl. "Then why are you here?" he asked, drawing Daisha's attention to him. "If you don't need to come, why did you?"

It took visible effort for Daisha to look away from Rebekkah and focus on him. She did, though, and then she said, "I'm not sure who he is, but someone else . . . like me. He's going to find you."

Rebekkah didn't back away. "You can't stay in this world. It's not where you belong."

"I didn't ask to be dead." Daisha frowned like she was trying to remember something. She bit down on her lip. Her hand tightened atop the porch railing.

"Daisha?" Rebekkah drew the girl's attention back to her. "Can I offer you a meal? Drink? That's what you need, isn't it?"

At that, Daisha laughed. "No, not from you. I won't drink or eat of you . . . no."

Rebekkah put a hand on Daisha's hand. "I meant regular food, not—"

"Only one chance for that," Daisha whispered. "I came. I ate. I drank. I listened. She wanted me to . . . but I couldn't get here. *Before.* Before here I couldn't get here. I felt it, though. I felt *her* calling me home."

"Maylene?"

Daisha nodded. "Like needing air, but I couldn't . . . Someone stopped me."

Byron felt cold chills come over him. "When you . . . woke up, someone stopped you from coming here?"

"I wanted to. I wanted to find her." Daisha sounded like a lost child. "I couldn't come."

"But you did," Byron reminded. "Who stopped you?"

"I did come," Daisha agreed. "But I was too hungry then. It was too late."

"Who stopped you?" Byron repeated.

A woman screamed somewhere nearby, and at the sound, Daisha jerked her hand away from Rebekkah.

"He's here." Daisha's eyes grew wide. She took several steps backward.

"Who?" Hand outstretched, Rebekkah stepped toward the dead girl. "Daisha, please!"

But Daisha's form wavered, and then she was gone as if she'd never been there.

As soon as Daisha had vanished, Byron and Rebekkah started toward the area from where the scream had seemed to come. They were already on their way when they heard a second scream, shriller than the first, and Byron grabbed Rebekkah's hand, and they began to run faster.

Whatever Rebekkah had expected to see, this wasn't it. In a narrow alley behind the local thrift shop, there was a clear presence of the Hungry Dead in the street—hanging in the air around a bleeding Amity Blue.

"Amity?" Byron pulled her into his arms. "What happened?"

She held her right arm crossways against her chest so that her hand was against her collarbone. Her black T-shirt was wet and clinging to her. *Blood.*

Amity shook almost violently. "In my bag."

"Got it." Rebekkah tore open Amity's bag and upended it. Tiny bottles of alcohol, a water gun, several small plastic bottles of water, a stun gun, and a notebook went clattering onto the sidewalk.

"Holy Water," Amity gasped. "I don't want to become like that."

"You won't. It's not conta—"

"Please?" Amity interrupted.

Byron was already twisting a cap off one of the plastic bottles. "Got it."

He poured the water over the wound. It ran off onto the sidewalk, pinkish tinged, catching a cigarette butt and a leaf.

"Hurry." Rebekkah glanced at Byron, and then at the crowd of people coming out to watch them. She couldn't focus on them. Her body felt like it was being pulled to move.

A woman whose name Rebekkah couldn't remember pushed

past the five or six people who were trying to see what had happened. "We called for help. I heard a scream, but Roger thought it was the TV. What do you need me to do?"

"Can you keep everyone back?" When the woman nodded, Byron turned his attention back to Amity. "Did you see . . . anything?"

"Troy." Amity gave them a wry smile. "He wasn't right. I know that. I saw him before . . . and I wrote notes to myself. Sometimes notes help me remember things. Usually."

With a frown, Amity reached into her jacket pocket. In her hand she clutched a small black notebook. "Here. This is what I know."

Byron flipped it open. The pages were filled with a scrawl that looked alternately frantic and calm. Words arched across pages as if they'd been slashed onto the paper, and around them tight script was woven into the empty spaces. Some of the writing appeared to be in some sort of code.

"The end. I saw him earlier, and I wrote it down." Amity stared at Byron as he turned the pages. When he reached the very last page, he turned the notebook toward Amity and Rebekkah.

Silently Rebekkah read the words Amity had written in heavy block print: "TROY. IS. DEAD. TELL BEK." The words were underlined several times.

The night I saw him. Rebekkah felt chilled. *He was trying to bite me.*

"Amity?" Byron said. "Talk to me."

Amity still had her head tucked between her upraised knees. Her voice was muffled. "He bit me. Earlier I saw him, and I ran. Maylene said to tell you if anything weird ever happened and she's gone." Amity turned her head to the side and looked directly at Rebekkah. "What does it mean? Is he a vampire?"

"No. It just means I need to stop him from hurting anyone," Rebekkah said. "I will, Amity. I promise."

"And me? Will I get . . . sick?" Amity didn't look away. "I feel queasy just trying to force myself to keep it in my head . . . or maybe because I'm missing a chunk of skin."

"Or both." Rebekkah put her hand on the side of Amity's head and smoothed back the bartender's hair. "Some things are easier to let yourself forget."

"I don't like forgetting. It's why I keep the journal." Amity laughed, but it sounded more like a sob.

Byron tucked Amity's journal in his pocket. "Here comes Chris."

The sheriff pulled up, a team of EMTs right behind him. Christopher got out of his car and stepped onto the sidewalk.

"What happened?"

Byron didn't hesitate. "A dog or something got her. We heard her scream, and we found her like this."

"Joe?" the sheriff yelled. "Another damn dog bite."

A young EMT took over, and Christopher leveled a glare at Rebekkah and Byron. "I'm hoping this will end soon."

"Me, too," Rebekkah told him.

Byron slipped his arm around her. "It will. I'm sure of it."

The comfort of his assurance was undercut by the way Amity watched them. She didn't call out, didn't ask Byron to go with her, but Rebekkah could see that she wanted to do just that.

"Why don't you go with Amity," Rebekkah suggested.

Byron gave her a look that conveyed exactly how foolish he thought *that* idea was. "Chris has it under control."

The sheriff nodded, and Byron went over to Amity and murmured something Rebekkah couldn't hear—and wasn't sure if she wanted to hear.

She rubbed her eyes and looked into the street. She could see a smoky trail winding out in front of her. She took a step toward it.

Byron came up behind her.

"I need to follow," she whispered.

46

BYRON FOLLOWED REBEKKAH OUT OF THE ALLEY AND AROUND THE COR-
ner. She was practically running. Whatever trail she was following was either fading fast enough that they needed to hurry or clear
enough that they had no need to pause. Byron wasn't sure which: he
saw nothing.

They entered a small intersection, and Rebekkah stepped into
the street without turning her attention in either direction. Byron
grabbed her arm.

She muttered, "We need to—"

"Not get run over," he interrupted. A car passed, and he let go of her.

This time, when she started following the trail, she did run.

"Damn it, Bek." He grabbed hold of her hand to keep her from
stepping in front of something or escaping him.

She said nothing, but she didn't shake off his hand either.

For the next twenty minutes, they ran in silence; the only sound
was the soft huff of Rebekkah's breathing. At the loading area of a
small grocery, she stopped.

"He's here."

She looked around the back lot, but didn't speak further.

Byron withdrew the gun and let his gaze wander around the
lot. Several cars made perfect spots to hide; so too did the two large
Dumpsters that had been placed in the lot for trash and recycling. A

small strip of grass filled the space between the lot and the river. A
picnic table and rusty grill stood in the sorry-looking grass. Farther
down the lot there was a netless basketball hoop.

"Troy?" Rebekkah called softly. She walked toward the Dumpsters. The gleam of her silver eyes made her seem inhuman, but
Byron was no longer unnerved by it. "I'm here," she called.

Gun in hand, Byron stayed beside her. He'd trusted his instincts
earlier when he'd gotten between her and Daisha, but this felt different. Troy *felt* dangerous in a way that Daisha didn't.

Rebekkah paused beside the Dumpsters. "I know you were looking for me the other night."

Byron shot a look at her. *"What?"*

She ignored him. "I'm here now. That's what you need, isn't it?
You need me. You came to find me."

Troy stepped out from behind the Dumpster. He looked no different than he had the last time Byron had seen him at Gallagher's:
he was wearing one of his bandannas, black jeans, and a too-tight
black T-shirt. What was missing was any sort of awareness in his
expression. He and Rebekkah were once close enough friends that
Byron had been jealous, but now, neither Troy's eyes nor his body
language indicated any sort of recognition. He didn't smile or speak.

"I can fix this, Troy." Rebekkah's voice was filled with the sort of
soft crooning tones people reserved for speaking to frightened animals.
"Just trust me. I wouldn't have let this happen to you if I'd known."

Troy stared at her. His lip curled in a soundless snarl.

"I understand that you're angry, Troy, but I didn't know. I wasn't
even here yet." She shook her head. "Let me give you food and drink,
Troy. You remember all the times you gave people food and drink?
You remember looking after me when I visited the bar?"

The dead man blinked at her.

"You do remember," she murmured. "I don't know how long
you've been hungry, but I can still help you . . . Let me help you."

He stepped forward.

"That's right," she encouraged him. "Come to me."

He frowned.

"Come on." She extended her hand. "Do you remember last year when I visited and we danced on the bar after hours? I thought Amity was going to hurt herself the way she twisted around. I stayed in touch with her. Did she tell you that?"

The look on Troy's face didn't express the recognition that Rebekkah was clearly seeking. He stepped forward, though, and he took her hand in his. For a moment, Byron thought she'd succeeded in luring him to her, that things were going well, that everything was going to be okay.

Then Troy yanked her to him and pulled her arm to his mouth.

"No!" Byron lunged forward.

"Byron, stop," Rebekkah said. She sounded calm. Byron looked at her closely. She'd shoved her arm so far back into Troy's mouth that his jaw was forced wide open. He had wrapped his other arm around her waist. He hefted her off the ground.

"Syringe? Now, please." Her voice cracked a bit.

Byron shoved the gun in the holster with one hand and grabbed a syringe with the other. "Where?"

The strain was clear in her voice now. "Anywhere."

Hoping she was right, Byron shoved the needle into Troy's neck just under his ear. Troy didn't react at all. He stared at Rebekkah, who still had her arm in his mouth, and blinked a few times.

Then his grip on her waist loosened, and her feet touched back down onto the ground. Troy's hand slid down her hip as his hold released; his arms dropped to his sides. All the while Rebekkah still had her arm in his mouth as if it were a bone in the jaws of a dog.

"Bek?" Byron wasn't sure what to do, but Troy didn't seem to be injuring her now. In fact, he seemed almost comatose.

Rebekkah lifted one foot and caught Troy behind the knee, then she pushed the whole of her weight forward and he fell. She fell with him, landing on top of him with her arm still in his mouth.

She turned her head and gazed up at Byron with her strange silver gaze. "Hold his jaw open."

Byron squatted down, put a hand on either side of Troy's face, and pressed his thumbs into the hinge of the dead man's jaw. This didn't force it to open any wider, but it would keep the jaw from snapping closed.

As Rebekkah pulled her arm out, Byron saw the teeth marks filled with blood imprinted on her skin.

Seemingly oblivious to her own bleeding arm, she stood up and looked at Troy. "He's been dead too long."

"You're bleeding." Byron didn't have any bandages, anything to help stanch the blood or ease the pain.

She ignored him. "I need to take him to Charles."

The dead man's gaze tracked Rebekkah, but he stared at her with absolutely no recognition. He seemed to be alert—at least as alert as he'd been when they'd found him—but motionless. *We'll have to carry him to the tunnel.*

Rebekkah took Troy's hands, and he came to his feet in a single fluid movement. He floated several inches above the ground as she laced her fingers with his.

Or not.

Byron repressed a shiver at the sight of the dead man gliding over the ground as Rebekkah walked forward. He'd thought that the things he'd seen in the land of the dead were disconcerting, but the clash of period clothing styles and the suspension of natural law were no longer the most abnormal sight of the week.

A few steps away, Rebekkah paused.

When he realized that she was waiting for him, he did a quick scan of the ground in case they'd left any mementos of their visit. Assured that there were no traces of their presence, he joined Rebekkah and said, "To Charlie's, then."

47

T HE WALK TO THE FUNERAL HOME WAS AT A SLOWER PACE THAN THEIR race to find Troy, but not by much. The pressure to get Troy to the land of the dead drove Rebekkah. She wasn't sure what it was that was holding Troy to her, how it was that he moved so carefully a few inches above the ground, but she was certain that it wouldn't last forever.

Rebekkah sped up. "We need to hurry, Byron."

Byron muttered something she couldn't hear. They walked through the town, people ignoring them on their return much as they had ignored them during their search. At the door of the funeral home, Byron went in first, making sure that no one was waiting to obstruct their progress.

Troy glided into the building and down the stairs with Rebekkah. "Almost," she whispered. "Close."

The words were spoken as much for herself as for Byron; she felt a trickle of fear that they wouldn't reach their destination, that Troy's cooperation would end, that the gate would be too far. Byron was there, though; he opened the door to the storage room and then he slid open the cabinet that hid the tunnel.

The expression on his face was strained as he took Rebekkah's other hand. "Don't let go. No matter what."

"I know." She felt the breath of the dead against her face, heard their whispering voices welcoming her home, and wished that it didn't feel so true.

"Bek?" Byron stepped in front of her. "Do *not* let go of my hand this time."

She nodded and whispered, "Or his."

"Honestly? I'd rather you let go of his than mine. He's here now, but you . . ." Byron's words were swept away in a scream of wind.

"He won't be trapped in the tunnel," Rebekkah told the whispering dead. "I won't let go of him." She looked at Byron. "If I let go of Troy, he'll be trapped like the others in the tunnel."

Byron winced. "Don't let go of either of us then."

Rebecca nodded. She held tightly to both Troy and Byron as she walked through the tunnel. The dead man didn't speak, didn't seem to react to anything around them. Byron led them forward, and the tunnel breathed around them.

"Are you okay?" Byron asked.

She wasn't sure if he was talking to her or to Troy. It didn't matter: in that tunnel, in that moment, she was the only one who could answer. "We are."

The sense of rightness filled her to bursting as they walked. This was what she was meant to do; it was what she needed to do in order to fill her place in the order of things. After years of feeling like every city, every man, every job was wrong, she knew that *this* was absolutely right. It wasn't that San Diego or the ad agency or Lexington or the tech writing job had been wrong. They just weren't the fit she was looking for. Here, with Byron, in Claysville, escorting the dead to Charles: that was right. Absently, she wondered if finding one's place in the world always felt like this, as if an audible *click* could be heard.

As they approached the tunnel's end, she stopped and took a deep breath. So far she'd been trusting instinct, but instinct began to war with desire as they neared the land of the dead. It felt like she was answering a siren's song, trying to still her feet as she was urged forward.

Would it still be so tempting if I were dead?

Rebekkah pushed those thoughts away and looked at Troy. "Come on."

For the first time since she'd seen Troy in the street, the person she remembered was looking back at her. He didn't speak, but he wasn't trying to attack her either. Instead, he looked hopeful.

"It'll be okay now," she assured him.

She felt Byron's hand squeeze hers tighter as they stepped into the land of the dead, together this time, and bringing the Hungry Dead with them.

"We're here," Byron said. "Now—"

Troy wrapped his arms around Rebekkah in a sudden hug. He seemed to be shaking as he held on to her. Byron reached out, but Rebekkah shook her head. It wasn't frightening.

"Thank you." Troy's voice was rough, but she wasn't sure if it was from disuse or tears.

"It's what I do: I bring the dead home."

"I wasn't sure where I was. I *died*, Bek." His eyes were wide as he realized what he'd said. He looked from her to Byron and back at her. "I'm dead."

"You are," she said gently. "I'm sorry."

"I don't know why." His brow furrowed. "I wasn't, and then I was, and then I wasn't *either*. I needed to find"—he sank to his knees—"you, but I couldn't."

"You did, though," Rebekkah told him. "You found me, and I brought you here. It's okay."

"But before . . ." Troy's eyes widened. "There was a girl. She's small. I tried to hurt her. After. Not before. She's not alive either. The girl I tried to hurt . . . I think I hurt her. Am I dreaming? Tell me I'm asleep. Is Amity okay?"

"She'll be fine." Rebekkah brushed his curls back. "You're not asleep."

"I'm dead." Troy backed away from Rebekkah, but she still held tight to his hand.

"I killed her," he said. "I think I killed a girl. I didn't want to, but I was so hungry. They wouldn't let me leave. They had me trapped . . . Poison all around the ground. It burned to touch. I wanted to disappear. Like smoke . . . drift away. I could do that, but they wouldn't let me."

"*Who* wouldn't let you?" Rebekkah squeezed his hand.

Troy furrowed his brow. "She hates you . . . the *you* that you were . . . or are. Are you two people? She wanted what you had, and wanted you not-alive so she could take it, but you aren't dead."

He reached out to cover Rebekkah's mouth, so her breath was against his palm. "You aren't dead, but she killed you." Troy looked increasingly horrified as he spoke, as if speaking brought him clarity, and clarity brought him horror. "Ms. Barrow wanted me to kill the grave woman. *You.* That's why she let me out. Not first . . . she let the girl out first to kill . . . the first grave woman. Her mother."

Beside her, Byron put a hand on Rebekkah's lower back, steadying her. She shook her head. The thoughts, the words Troy spoke, made an ugly sort of sense, but they couldn't be true. *Cissy?* Cissy *did this?* The thought made Rebekkah feel sick in a way that she couldn't quite verbalize. *Cissy killed him. Made him kill Daisha . . . who killed. . .*

Rebekkah grabbed Troy's other hand, so she was now holding both of his hands. "Are you sure? My aunt? Cecilia Barrow did this? Are you positive?"

Sadly, Troy nodded. "She kept me there. I couldn't leave. I couldn't think, but I knew where I needed to go. I needed to go home . . . find *you* . . . but not-you. The woman who could make it better. There was a different you. You aren't two yous, though, are you? You're real?" He pulled one hand from her grasp and stroked her face. "You are, and you saved me, but you aren't the one I was to find—except you are. I don't understand."

"I do." Rebekkah released his other hand. "You were looking for my grandmother, but she's gone and I'm . . . just like her."

He looked stricken. "Did I—"

"No." Rebekkah grabbed his arm as he started to step away from her. "Not you."

"I killed a girl, Bek." He looked heartsick. "I . . . I didn't think I could ever . . . what kind of man am I?"

"One who was used." Byron's expression held the anger that Rebekkah couldn't let herself feel yet.

Cissy caused Maylene's death.

"Troy." Rebekkah pulled his attention to her and then asked, "Can you tell me anything else about Cissy?"

"She . . . they . . . Twins . . ." Troy's eyes widened. He shook his head and pulled away. "I need to go."

"Wait." Rebekkah grabbed for his wrist, but he dodged away.

The moment she wasn't touching him, he vanished. She was left standing outside the tunnel with Byron.

"What happened?" she asked.

"We cannot see our own dead." Byron looked at her. "I'm guessing that means more than just those we call family."

"So everyone I bring here will vanish?" Rebekkah frowned. The city loomed just steps away, but she wasn't sure whether to walk toward it or go back home. Staying here meant that she could lose herself in the sensory excess that the land of the dead offered. *Hiding.* Going back meant she needed to find Daisha—and Cissy.

Cissy killed him.

Rebekkah opened her mouth to ask Byron what he thought, but as she did so, he said, "Alicia."

"Where?" Rebekkah looked around. Two men approached, but neither looked like an Alicia. One was in ripped jeans and a faded black concert tee. Rebekkah looked behind her. There was no one there either.

"That would be good," Byron said. "He needs a hand . . . He's a bartender by trade, though, not a . . ."

"Byron?" Rebekkah whispered. "Who are you talking to?"

"Sorry, this is—what do you mean? Of course she can . . ." Byron's expression was suddenly stricken. "Bek? Who do you see near me?"

"Two men I don't know. They aren't speaking, though. You're talking, and . . ."

"You don't see a woman?" Byron pointed to an empty spot and asked, "You can't see her?"

Rebekkah shook her head slowly. "No."

BYRON LOOKED AT ALICIA.

"No," Alicia echoed. She stood, hip cocked and chin tilted.

"Neither of you can see each other." He looked at each of the two women again and then he gestured at the men who'd come with Alicia. "Can you see them?"

Both Rebekkah and Alicia said, "Yes."

"And they see you?" he clarified.

"Boys?" Alicia asked.

"She's over there, Lish. Pretty thing," one of them said.

The other man nodded. "No weapons on her, though. Foolish."

Byron paused. "So . . . neither of you sees the other. They"—he pointed at Alicia's companions—"see both of you. You're not known to her, so you're . . ." He looked from one woman to the other. He thought about the list of names. *Was there an Alicia?*

"You were a Graveminder," Byron said.

Alicia's shoulders arched back. "I *am* a Graveminder. I'm dead, but I still am what I am."

"She's . . . why is she still here, Byron?" Rebekkah grabbed his arm. "Ask her. Does that mean that Maylene—"

"Why are you here?" he asked.

A flicker of pain crossed Alicia's face. "No reason to move on, and plenty to stay. It's a choice, Undertaker. I made this one. Tell her Maylene's moved on. Your dad has, too." She stepped up until she was uncomfortably close, but she didn't touch him. "If you want to spend a quiet evening sometime, I'll tell you all about it."

"I'll keep that in mind."

"What?" Rebekkah prompted. "Keep what in mind?"

"Alicia was explaining that she's here by choice. Maylene and Dad have moved on, but Alicia chose to stay," Byron said.

"Not telling her about my offer?" Alicia's smile was wicked. "Tsk. Tsk."

"I'm not in the mood for games," Byron cautioned her. "Is Troy, the one who came here with us, safe?"

"Safe as any are here." The man in ripped jeans looked behind him. "The man you brought says to tell you he's sorry he killed that girl, and that you need to go do something about Cissy." He paused. "Who's Cissy?"

Rebekkah let out a shaky breath. "Please tell him we'll fix it."

The second of Alicia's companions looked over his shoulder. "She says to tell you they'll fix it."

Alicia laid her hand against Byron's chest. "I'll look after the bartender."

"I don't have anything for you," Byron said. "The whole Hungry Dead business—"

"Next time. Your credit's good for a little while. Get your friend here set up with a few weapons, too, okay?" Alicia curled her hand so that her fingernails pressed into his shirt. "Don't linger here today."

"Why?"

Alicia ignored his question and said, "Boys?"

The men both turned to follow her. Byron suspected that Troy did, too, but he couldn't see the dead bartender. They walked away, and Byron was left deciding how much he trusted Alicia after all. She had taken Troy away, but he couldn't think of any good reason for a Graveminder to be lingering in this place if she *could* move on. Alicia had an agenda, and she seemed to be the source for weapons in the land of the dead.

Was she behind Bek's getting shot?

He stared after Alicia as she walked down the gray street. She might be a member of Rebekkah's family, but being family didn't mean that she was trustworthy. Alicia Barrow had secrets.

"B?" Rebekkah prompted.

"She said we need to go back now."

Rebekkah laced her fingers with his. "Do you trust her?"

"For now." He nodded, and together he and Rebekkah stepped back into the tunnel.

The walk back through the tunnel was a blink this time. They'd no more than stepped inside when they were back at Montgomery and Sons. Byron replaced the torch on the wall, and together they stepped back into the land of the living.

"Are you okay?" Byron asked.

"I think I'd really like for us to be able to stop asking that of each other." Rebekkah watched him close the cabinet.

"After we get things set back to normal, I promise to stop asking." He glanced at her before he walked to the door.

"Deal." She followed him out into the hall and pulled the door closed behind her. Being the Graveminder would become less exhausting—and bizarre. *It had to.* Maylene had lived a fairly calm life; at least it had seemed that way. When Rebekkah had lived in her house, her grandmother's restrictions were unusually stringent, but most of the time life was pretty calm. Maylene usually didn't fuss too much about curfew, but when she did, she was inflexible.

"Once they are put to rest, the Graveminder keeps the dead from waking, but with Daisha and Troy, Maylene couldn't because . . ."

"Because Cissy hid their bodies," Byron finished.

It all made a horrible sort of sense now: if they'd been buried, Maylene would've tended their graves, and they'd have rested. If they'd been able to come to the Graveminder when they awakened, they wouldn't have become feral. *Someone stopped me*: that's what Daisha had said. *She stopped me*, Troy had echoed. Cissy had stopped them. She'd intended for them to become *more* dangerous before they came to seek out the Graveminder.

She used the dead to murder Maylene.

They were partway up the stairs when Rebekkah announced, "I want to see if we can talk to Daisha. Troy couldn't tell us much, and I need to know how many people Cissy's killed, and where they are, and who all knows, and I want to know *why*."

Byron was silent as they went upstairs and exited the building. As they stood at the side of the Triumph, he said, "*Daisha* murdered Maylene."

"No," she corrected. "Cissy used the dead as weapons. They were no more than tools to her. *My* dead, mine to protect, and *my* grandmother . . . Cissy killed them."

His expression revealed nothing. "So you're *excusing* Daisha?"

Rebekkah paused. *Am I?* Daisha and Troy had both killed people; they'd injured people; they'd done so in ways that were both painful and grotesque. *Do I forgive that?* She wanted to. In some ways, she had: she'd hugged Troy and consoled him. Her reaction wasn't what she would've expected a week ago. *My dead.* The words she'd said were the truth of it, though; these were her dead. They were her responsibility. Being the Graveminder had tempered her—normal—responses; it hadn't negated them, merely blunted them.

"No." She reached out for Byron's hand. "I took Troy where he needed to go. I stopped him. I'll stop Daisha and as many of them as Cissy has made. I'm going to stop her, too. No matter what it takes. If that's too cruel or—"

"It's not," he interrupted with more than a little edge to his voice. "Let's be clear, though: are you telling me you're willing to *kill* Cissy?"

"Just hand me a gun." She picked up her helmet, put it on, and waited for him to climb onto the bike.

"Shooting someone over here isn't like it is in Charlie's world, Bek. They don't get back up." Byron slung his leg over the bike and put his helmet on. "If you do this—"

"If I don't, Cissy is going to keep hurting people. She murdered Maylene." Rebekkah felt a rage like she'd never known before. "She used the dead—my dead, *Maylene's* dead—to kill. If we need to, we'll take Cissy to Charles' world. If there's another answer, we try that, but we stop this."

Silently, she straddled the bike and wrapped her arms around him.

The bike roared to life, and Byron said nothing more. It wasn't like the last ride where he started out slow; this time he went through the gears, accelerating from stop to blur in what felt like a couple of heartbeats.

48

"B UT SHE HASN'T CALLED ME AT ALL THIS WEEK," LIZ STRESSED. "TERESA *never* goes this long without calling or visiting."

"Your sister doesn't consider how her actions affect others, Elizabeth." Cissy Barrow snipped a dead rose from the bush she stood beside and tossed it into a nearby bucket. "She thinks *her* interests are more important than duty."

"Do you know where she is?"

"We had a disagreement," Cissy admitted.

"About?"

Cissy waved dismissively, garden shears in her hand. "The usual. She thinks only of herself. You're not like that, are you, Elizabeth?"

The inflexible self-righteousness of her mother's voice made Liz tense. It wasn't that her mother was heartless, but she didn't believe in coddling anyone. *Children are to be obedient and devoted. Young women should respect their mother. Purposelessness leads to complacency.* Liz had heard her mother's reminders often enough that she knew the deceptively mild questions for what they were: tests.

Liz squared her shoulders and kept her voice even as she said, "No, Mama. I think of the family first."

Her mother nodded. "Good girl."

"Do you need me to do anything?" Liz offered tentatively. "I could talk to Teresa if you know where she is."

"Eventually, child. Right now, she's not quite ready to talk. She will be in a few more weeks, but she's *confused* right now." Cissy's gaze wandered over the garden that she had planned and cultivated in Liz's yard. It wasn't what Liz herself would've picked, but there were things worth defying her mother over and things easier to let slide. Floral placement fell in the latter category.

"Soon I'll have everything in place. Both of you will fulfill your roles." Cissy clipped another dead rose.

"Our roles?" Liz felt the fear inside of her growing by the moment. "What roles?"

"One of you will be the Graveminder, Liz. I realized that it would need to be you. Teresa understands that now. First, though, we need to remove Becky from the equation." Cissy stepped back to admire the rosebush. "Byron will do just fine if we can convince him. Better to work with known tools than start from scratch, right? He switched his loyalty from your cousin to that girl when Ella died. He'll switch to you just as easily." She tossed the shears into the bucket with the rose heads. "I'm going to wash up."

Liz stood in her tiny yard and watched her mother walk away. *She's talking about Rebekkah being dead. If I'm the next Graveminder, that would mean Rebekkah would be dead.* Trickles of fear grew into full-fledged terror. *What has she done? Teresa, where are you?*

Liz said that she didn't believe in "twin-sense" anymore, but in a town where dead people could—and did—come back, believing in a connection with a womb-mate wasn't that peculiar. *I don't want to believe it right now.* If she did believe it, if she thought about the real reason for her fear, she'd have to ask herself just *how* capable of murder her mother really was.

"Please be okay, Terry," Liz whispered.

49

BYRON KILLED THE ENGINE OUTSIDE THE TRAILER, WALKED OVER, AND jimmied the lock on the front door.

Rebekkah gave him a bemused look. "Do I want to ask why you know how to do that?"

"My father taught me." Years ago, Byron had thought that the peculiar lessons were signs of his father's laid-back nature, proof that having an older father was a better deal than the other kids had. In fanciful moments, he thought his father might even have some kind of secret life: lock picking, hot-wiring cars, and handgun proficiency were great preparation for a criminal. Byron smiled as he remembered how he used to imagine William as a comic-book villain training his son in his nefarious trade. *I never would've guessed the truth.* Now Byron saw these "hobbies" for what they were: preparation for the life he was now leading. *It is a family trade.*

The lock gave, and he turned the doorknob. He and Rebekkah stepped into the bloodstained trailer.

The dead girl sat on the end of the sofa where her mother's corpse had been found. The bloodstained seat cushions had been flipped over, and a blanket was folded over the side where Daisha sat with her feet propped on the coffee table.

She lowered the water-damaged paperback novel she was reading and looked at them. "You could've knocked."

"You knew we were here," Byron said.

"Stealthy you're not, Undertaker." Daisha dog-eared the page she'd been reading, closed the book, and set it to the side.

Rebekkah stepped farther into the room. She didn't sit, but she was close enough to Daisha that the dead girl could grab her without much effort.

"Troy is gone. He's been taken to where he needed to go," Rebekkah said.

"Thanks." Daisha picked her book back up.

The combination of stress and exhaustion pushed Byron to his limit. "Daisha!"

The book fell, and Daisha lowered her feet to the floor with a thump. She leaned forward. The illusion of a normal, albeit peculiar, teen girl vanished. Her voice dropped to an inhuman gravel-laden tone. "You do *not* want to yell at me." She stared directly at Byron. "Troy wasn't alert yet. He hadn't eaten enough *or* the right people. I did."

Rebekkah started, "The right—"

"Gail. Paul. They made all the difference." Daisha swept her arms out. "They talked to me. They gave me the food and drink I needed. I am myself, just . . . *different* now."

Silently, Rebekkah stepped closer to Daisha. She sat on the edge of the chair that was angled to the side of the sofa. "We didn't come to argue . . . or hunt you."

The tension in the room decreased. Daisha pulled her gaze away from Byron and looked at Rebekkah. "So what do you want?"

Rebekkah smiled at her. "I need to find Cissy . . . the woman who killed you."

"*Troy* killed me."

"Because she made him," Rebekkah said gently. "I need to find Cissy. I was hoping that you could take us to her, to where you were held." She spoke to Daisha calmly, just as she had spoken with Troy, as if their acts weren't deplorable. "I can find *you* and other dead. I can try that. Feeling for them, if there are others—"

"There are," Daisha interrupted. Abruptly she stood and walked into the kitchen. She yanked open a drawer, upended it on the counter, and sifted through the tangle of items that fell out. Keys and pencils and papers were knocked to the floor and stuck in the congealed blood as she searched. She kept knocking things to the floor until she found what she apparently sought: a map.

Byron watched with macabre fascination as the dead girl stepped into the blood and tracked it across the floor as she returned to the sofa.

"Here." Daisha spread out the map and stabbed a finger in an area against the farthest boundary of Claysville. "It was out here."

"Cissy doesn't live there," Byron pointed out.

"I know what I know." Daisha walked to the door and grabbed the doorknob. "Have a nice night, now."

"Daisha?" Rebekkah's voice drew both of their gazes. "My aunt is killing people."

"So am I."

"Yes, but you're doing it because of what she did to you." Rebekkah walked over and took Daisha's hand. "I'm not going to lie and say I'm okay with what you did. You killed my *grandmother* . . ."

No one spoke for a moment as Rebekkah's voice faded; then Daisha whispered, "I didn't want to. I couldn't think. I just—" She stopped herself. "I did, though."

"You did," Rebekkah agreed. "And now I need you to help me."

Daisha tilted her head. "Why?"

"Because I don't know where Cissy is, because she's already killed two people who then went out doing . . . this." Rebekkah pointed at the sofa where Gail had died. "She did this to you, and now I need your help. You warned me about Troy. I thought you might help me now. Help me find her?"

"And stop her?"

"Yes." Rebekkah's lips were pressed in a tight line, but she held the girl's gaze.

For several moments they simply looked at each other; then Byron pointed at the primer-gray truck parked outside the trailer. "Whose is that?"

Daisha flashed her teeth at him in a feral smile. "Some guy I killed. I think you took him out of here, didn't you?"

"I can start the truck, so she can ride with us."

Both Rebekkah and Daisha turned to look at him.

"I can start it, too . . . *without* hot-wiring it." Daisha scooped up a set of keys from the floor and tossed them at Byron.

As they walked out to the truck and climbed in, Byron hoped they weren't making a colossal mistake.

50

THE RIDE TO THE EDGE OF CLAYSVILLE WAS MOSTLY SILENT. THE TRUCK'S radio was stuck on a radio station that seemed to mostly involve angry preaching, and the only CDs in the vehicle were twangy country albums that Daisha tossed out the window with gleeful yells of "Screw you, Paul."

Rebekkah vacillated between the desire to protect Daisha and feeling anger toward her. Daisha was a victim, and Rebekkah's job was to protect the dead. It didn't matter whether they were in-the-grave dead, Hungry Dead, or those already in the land of the dead: they were hers to mind, to care for, and when necessary to take to the land of the dead.

"That way." The dead girl's voice was barely a whisper. "To the right there."

Rebekkah wasn't sure if it was fear or anger riding in the girl's voice, but she reached out and squeezed Daisha's hand. "What she did was wrong. She *will* answer for it."

The look Daisha gave her was too brief to interpret. "Turn onto that road."

On the other side of Rebekkah, Byron remained silent. He followed Daisha's directions, but he offered no comments on them—or any response to Rebekkah's remark.

The hilt of the knife Byron wore on his thigh bumped into her, and she glanced down at the holstered gun that he'd handed her when they slid into the truck. Holding it didn't make her uncomfortable. The idea of using it on her aunt, however, did.

It's not the first choice.

Byron pulled the truck off the road and into a cover of trees. Given the wooded area and the hour, they were fairly well hidden.

Byron got out of the truck and held out a hand. "I have a light."

"I can see fine," Daisha murmured from right beside him and Rebekkah.

Rebekkah hesitated before admitting, "I can, too, but if you . . ."

"No." Byron's voice was strained. "I didn't think about it when we were following Troy, but . . . I can see okay without a light."

Rebekkah glanced at him. To her, his eyes gleamed like an animal's when any light glanced off them. She turned to Daisha. "Do his eyes—"

"You glow from head to toe, and his eyes shine the same way." Daisha shook her head. "I don't know if . . . *live* people see it, though. At the graveyard, no one else seemed to notice the way you shine, so it could be just people like me."

Rebekkah nodded, and then began to walk the rest of the way to the house. She didn't feel that tendril guiding her toward the dead as she had previously. *Maybe there aren't any more.* She glanced at Daisha. *Or maybe she's so close I can't feel anyone else.*

As they walked, Byron stayed near enough that his mistrust for the dead girl was made quite clear. He didn't say anything, but he watched Daisha with the sort of studious attention reserved for the dangerous or foolish. Rebekkah couldn't blame him. Daisha was with them, but that didn't make her tame.

When we're done I need to convince her to go to the land of the dead—or take her there by force.

They arrived at the small one-story house. There were no lights on or vehicles in the drive. There was a garage, but the windows were blacked out.

A thick white line cut across the ground in front of the garage doors. Rebekkah bent down to touch it. Her finger brushed it, but didn't disturb the line.

"Don't!" Daisha grabbed Rebekkah's left arm and pulled her away from the white line. "Step away."

Rebekkah straightened and looked at the white powder on her fingertip. It wasn't chalk. It felt gritty. With her index finger still raised, she turned toward Daisha—who released her arm and stepped back.

"I think it's salt," Byron said. "Alicia mentioned that it's useful with *them*." He licked his finger, reached down, and dipped it into the powder. He tasted it and then nodded. "It is."

Rebekkah walked away to follow the line. It stretched unbroken in front of the garage and around both sides, stopping in a small pile that glittered in the sunlight.

Returning to Byron and Daisha, she said, "It extends all the way across the garage. To keep something in or out."

"I can't cross it, but"—Daisha smiled with such innocent glee that it was easy to forget that she was a monster—"if *someone* brushed it out of the way, I could go in."

Hoping that the barrier was intended to keep the dead out, Rebekkah stepped up to the door and brushed the white line away. If there were others inside, she'd need to stop them from leaving. *And take them home.* She frowned at the thought of the dead, the Hungry Dead who were supposed to seek the Graveminder, being trapped—and her inability to feel them because of the barrier Cissy had laid down.

"Let's go." Rebekkah touched Daisha's shoulder gently. It wasn't the hug she suddenly felt compelled to offer, but it was a touch.

Daisha gave Rebekkah a perplexed look and then shrugged.

"Sure. You able to open the door from this side or you need me to do it from the other side?"

"I can unlock the door." Byron walked past them. He pulled a thin black leather case from the inside pocket of his jacket, but instead of opening it, he glanced back at Rebekkah and Daisha. "Out of curiosity, how would *you* open it?"

Daisha vanished. The air where she'd stood was misty, as if a sudden fog bank had appeared there and only there.

"Daisha?" Rebekkah called.

The front door opened. Daisha leaned on the doorjamb. "Yeah?"

Byron furrowed his brow. "How did you—"

Daisha pointed to herself. "Dead girl." Then she pointed at the door. "No weather stripping." She fluttered her hand. "Whoosh. Like a breeze, I'm in."

"*Whoosh?*" Byron repeated.

Daisha dissipated into vaporous form and then resolidified. "Whoosh."

51

A T THE THRESHOLD, BYRON GLARED AT DAISHA. REBEKKAH STEPPED past them and went toward the garage.

She pulled open the door and stopped as five people turned their gazes on her in perfect sync. A man who looked to be Maylene's age sat with a wood-handled cane beside him on the bare cement floor; a woman and a man who looked to be in their twenties were beside the older man. Each of the three was encircled by a ring of salt. Against the opposite wall a boy who was barely old enough to be called a teenager paced the perimeter of his salt circle. The fifth circle held a still, lifeless body: Cissy's daughter Teresa.

"What has she done?"

Rebekkah walked into the room. As she looked at them, she re-alized that only Teresa, who was not yet awake, could be buried and given food, drink, and words. The others would need to be escorted to the land of the dead. *Like Troy. Like Daisha.* This wasn't how it was supposed to be. This was an abomination.

The young boy seemed to be the one who had been awake the longest: he clearly wanted out of his prison. The couple came to their feet as Rebekkah walked by. With arms outstretched over their heads as if they were reaching for handholds, they both leaned on the air that formed a boundary around them. The old man simply stared at her. He didn't move, but he tracked her.

"Bek?"

She turned. "She did this. This is what she did to Daisha, to Troy."

Tears were slipping down Rebekkah's cheeks; she felt them with the objective awareness that she was crying. In the presence of the dead she hadn't been able to protect, she was lost. They were *hers*, and she'd been unaware of their passing.

Because Cissy killed them.

"We won't let her do this to anyone else." Byron stood by her side, gazing at the dead, neither flinching from, nor oblivious to, their suffering.

"I need to get them out of here." Rebekkah couldn't touch or console them. *Not here.* She could take them to the land of the dead, however; she could break each salt circle, and one by one, she could lead them to where they would be themselves again. "I'm going to free them. I can take them . . . not Teresa. She needs to be buried. You can take her and—"

"And when Cissy comes back, she'll know she's been exposed. Think, Bek."

"I can't leave them like this." Rebekkah stepped toward the last circle, where her cousin Teresa lay. "Teresa's recently dead. I will mind her grave, and she'll never have to suffer, never *know*. The others . . . I need to take them home."

"Not yet." Behind her, Byron stood. He didn't touch her, but he was near enough to stop her if she tried to enter the salt circles.

Instead of looking at Byron, Rebekkah turned her attention to the old man. "He's recently awakened. It might still be possible to give him what he needs; he might not need to walk through the tunnel. I can take him to the house, give him food and drink."

Byron put a hand on her shoulder and spun her to face him. "And if we do that, Cissy will run. If you take Teresa's body, if you take Mr. Sheckly, Cissy will know. Do you want to tell me that you're willing to save these at the expense of those she'll kill next?"

"No." Rebekkah forced herself not to argue, but instinct vied with logic. The dead were trapped, and she *needed* to get them to their rightful places.

Byron's voice was firm as he said, "We can't free them yet."

She nodded and took his hand in hers as she looked at them. *My dead. Mine to protect.* The salt circles blocked the threads that should be calling her to them, and them to her, but she'd found them nonetheless. She whispered, "Tonight you'll go home. This is almost over for you."

Byron squeezed her hand, and together they went into the house.

Knowing the dead were here—*suffering*—and she couldn't help them yet made her feel physically ill. The threads that she should be feeling toward them were blocked by the salt, but seeing them and not being able to feel them hurt her in a way she couldn't express. She needed to get away, to step outside, where she couldn't see them, to put some distance between herself and them so she wouldn't ignore the logic in Byron's words.

She looked at Byron and asked, "Can you stay with Daisha? I'll be back inside, but I need a minute first."

"Do you want—"

"Stay with her, please." Rebekkah begged, and then she fled out the back door before she rushed forward and pushed away the salt that kept her from feeling her connection to the dead.

52

DAISHA HEARD THE VEHICLE IN THE DISTANCE. WITH HIS LIVING HUMAN hearing, the Undertaker had no idea that Cissy was approaching. Daisha, on the other hand, heard the engine stop, knew that the woman was getting closer. She was walking toward the house, presumably because she had seen their truck.

"Are you listening?" Byron asked.

"I am. Rebekkah needs a minute, so I stay with you," Daisha said. She considered and rejected the idea of telling him that she heard Cissy walking toward the house. *Give her a minute.* Rebekkah hadn't gone out to confront Cissy, but she had the right to do so. Like the dead inside the garage, like Daisha, like Troy, and like Maylene, Rebekkah had the right to confront the monster who had stolen so much from so many. *She is the Graveminder.* Daisha would give Rebekkah her chance to talk to the woman, and then she'd go outside and do what she'd come here to do.

Daisha tried to keep her features placid, not to reveal what she could hear outside, to let Cissy approach. *Buy the Graveminder some time.* The Undertaker wasn't a bad sort, not really. She couldn't blame him for his reaction to her. His job was to care for the grieving living and the truly dead. *Unlike Rebekkah.* The Graveminder cared for the truly dead and the Hungry Dead.

Byron narrowed his eyes and stared at her. "What gives?"

"Nothing. I wish Rebekkah hadn't seen that." Daisha motioned toward the garage. "The woman is cruel, and I wish Rebekkah hadn't been hurt."

Byron gave her a puzzled glance. "Why?"

"She cares for the dead. Like the last one. She would protect us from the woman. From you. From everything."

"I don't trust you," he said. "When this is over, you need to go to the land—"

"That, Undertaker, is not yours to decide."

53

ECKY." CISSY STILL HAD HER HAND INSIDE HER HANDBAG, BUT SHE lifted her gaze to Rebekkah. "What a lovely surprise. Did you come to tell me that you've decided to give me my inheritance? Leave the house and everything else to the rightful heirs?"

"No." Rebekkah stepped closer. "How could you do this? Your own daughter, your mother . . . You killed them."

Cissy pulled a black semiautomatic pistol out of her handbag. "Do you think you'll come back different? I've wondered what would happen if a *Graveminder* became one of the Hungry Dead."

For a moment, Rebekkah paused. She'd hoped that there was some explanation, some truth, to lessen the ugliness of the things that Cissy had done. "Why?"

"The Graveminder is supposed to be a *Barrow* woman. *You* are not." Cissy leveled the gun at her. "You're not a part of my family, yet here you are, the next Graveminder."

"You're going to kill me because I'm not Jimmy's biological daughter?" Rebekkah gaped at her. "Would you have killed Ella?"

"Ella took care of that herself." Cissy's arm didn't waver. "It should've been me. *She* decided I wasn't good enough, that I couldn't handle the dead. Look at them."

"You didn't handle them. You used them."

Cissy snorted. "They aren't people now. What difference does it make?"

Rebekkah knew she wasn't fast enough to outrun a bullet. She didn't know *how* to pick the next Graveminder. All she knew for certain was that Cissy shouldn't be it.

Is thinking it enough?

Rebekkah could imagine only one person she'd pick: Amity Blue. She whispered the name in case it had to be spoken. "Amity Blue. Amity Blue is the next Graveminder should I die here."

"What are you muttering?" Cissy took a step forward.

Amity Blue. I want Amity Blue to take this task.

"Becky? I asked you a question." Cissy aimed her gun at Rebekkah's leg.

"You won't ever be the Graveminder," Rebekkah vowed.

Cissy pulled the trigger.

There was no telltale sound as it happened, and it wasn't that Rebekkah saw the shot, even processed that it had happened. She simply crumpled. Her leg felt like it had been skewered by a hot poker. She put her hand on her thigh in a futile attempt to stop the bleeding. Blood slipped out around her fingers.

"I tried to talk to Mama, but"—Cissy crouched down beside Rebekkah—"all she could see was you. Rebekkah. Precious *Rebekkah*. After you and your mother ran away, I thought Mama would pick me or one of my girls . . . but do you know what she said?"

Rebekkah put her other hand on her leg, too, pinching the skin together. The pain of doing so made her vision blur. She swallowed twice before she could speak. "What?"

"That even if you died, she wouldn't lay the burden on my girls." Cissy stood up. She extended the hand with her gun in it again. The barrel brushed over Rebekkah's cheek. "I guess it was okay to burden you. Maybe she didn't love you after all, Becky."

Rebekkah reached up to grab the gun, but Cissy yanked it away.

"I'm not a murderer, Becky," she said. "I killed once, but now I just have them kill each other. I don't intend to go before my maker with those sorts of sins on my soul."

"Still on your soul," Rebekkah muttered, vaguely aware that Cissy was watching her. She struggled to get her shirt off. Every movement hurt, far worse than the shot that had grazed her in the land of the dead. *Shot twice in two days.* As she swallowed against the bitter taste in her mouth, she realized that she'd bitten her lip enough that the bitterness she was tasting was her own blood. *None to spare.* Blinking against the pain, she tied her shirt around her leg. It was a crude solution, but maybe it would stanch the blood.

"No. 'The sins of the dead rest on the Graveminder, for if she had done her duty, the dead would not be free to do harm.' I read the journals a long time ago, but when she died, I took them. Since you don't have Mama's journals, I wanted to let you know that part. These deaths? Every injury since Mama died, they are yours to carry. How fitting that you will go to your end with those stains."

Rebekkah looked up. Even in the haze of her pain, the tug in her chest told her that someone, that the Hungry Dead, stood nearby.

At the doorway, Daisha stood. She looked at the two women, but Rebekkah couldn't read her expression. She didn't want to call out, to alert Cissy. She glanced again at Daisha's expressionless face. *Is she attracted to blood? Will she kill me as she killed Maylene?*

Daisha vanished.

Cissy jerked to her feet and half pulled, half dragged Rebekkah toward the house. "I didn't intend to feed them yet, but plans change. Soon as you're dead, Liz will be the next Graveminder. She's the only one left. Teresa will become clearheaded and strong."

Cissy opened the door and shoved Rebekkah into the house.

"Why?" Rebekkah repeated. "You killed your daughter."

"Teresa understood. She'll be my warrior in this world, and Liz will be able to take me to the other." Cissy's smile was that of a zealot, of a woman whose beliefs were everything to her, and that sort of true believer was a terrifying thing. "The others weren't thinking. All these years, they worked for *him*—servants to Mr D . . . I read all about it when I was younger. I spent hours reading all those journals. We *serve* him, yet what do we get?"

Between the pain in her leg and her own doubts, Rebekkah had no answer to this question, but Cissy wasn't looking for one.

She continued. "All that power. *Two worlds*, Becky. Yet here we are trapped in a few miles of land. He has an entire world. Woman after woman is his servant. Barrow women. We've died because of his choices. No more. I'm not some dead man's servant."

"You aren't the Graveminder." Rebekkah forced the words out around the pain. She leaned against the wall and tried to stare at her aunt, but her eyes had lost their focus. The desire to close them warred with the fear that if she did so, she'd never be able to open them back up.

Behind them, Daisha reappeared and said, "Hello, Miz Barrow."

Cissy turned. "What are you doing here?"

Daisha sniffed. "I found the Graveminder. That's what I was supposed to do. I remember that . . . and now I have her."

"I don't want you in my house." Cissy didn't back away, but her posture was tense as she tried to surreptitiously look around the kitchen. "How did you get in?"

"There's no barrier around your house now. You pulled her over it." Daisha's voice was very matter-of-fact.

Rebekkah blinked. She wasn't sure whether her gun-waving aunt or the dead girl who'd murdered Maylene was the bigger threat. Given the choice, though, she'd put her faith in the dead. She took a step toward Daisha and stumbled. Her eyes drifted shut. "You . . ." she started.

In less time than it took Rebekkah to force herself to open her eyes, Daisha stepped forward and lifted Rebekkah in her arms. She held her aloft like she was a small child. "Is she for me?"

"I was going to give her to the others, but"—Cissy backed away—"you can have her. You seem alert. That's the consequence of eating. I'd rather they aren't alert yet."

The door to the garage opened then, and Byron stepped over the salt separating the house from the garage. He left the door open. The dead were no longer contained by salt circles. They stood waiting on the other side of the line of salt at the threshold. Byron was bloodied, but still standing.

Cissy's eyes widened. "What have you done?"

Byron didn't spare her a glance. He stepped up to Daisha. "Are you sure?"

"Take her out of here." Daisha handed Rebekkah to him. As soon as she released Rebekkah, she grabbed Cissy. The movements were so quick as to seem virtually simultaneous.

Byron walked into the living room and set Rebekkah on the sofa. He lifted a clear plastic container that looked like it should be filled with rice or cereal. Then he poured its contents on the threshold between the kitchen and the living room.

"Daisha!" Rebekkah struggled to her feet.

Byron walked over and stopped her. "No. She's staying a bit longer."

"You can't. She *helped* me." Rebekkah squirmed to get up.

"This is her choice. In a moment, I'll let her out. Trust me."

When she nodded, he stepped over the salt line and back into the kitchen. "We can do this another way," he said.

"This is the price of my help, Undertaker," Daisha said.

As Rebekkah watched, Daisha nodded toward the salt that kept the rest of the dead from entering the kitchen and directed, "Remove it."

"Montgomery! You can't listen to her." Cissy sounded terrified, but her present fear could do nothing to undo the horrible things she'd done.

"Byron?" Rebekkah called. He glanced at her, and she said softly, "Please do as Daisha asks."

For a moment, he hesitated. Then, without looking away from her, he scraped his foot over the line, removing the salt barrier, and letting four more Hungry Dead into the kitchen.

As he did so, Daisha shoved Cissy at the dead and put herself between them and Byron. "Go."

He didn't waste any time; he ran into the living room. He bent down to pick Rebekkah up off the couch, but she put out a hand to stop him and then glanced back into the kitchen.

"Not yet. I need to"—she made herself look at him—"bear witness."

"You don't." He tore his gaze from her eyes to the wound in her leg. "You were *shot*. Let me get you to the truck and then—"

"Not yet," she repeated. She looked past him to the kitchen, where the dead were consuming a pleading and screaming Cissy. "*This* is where I need to be."

If they were going to sentence someone to die, she'd not hide from that death. The sight of it, the shrieks as Cissy was pulled from one dead hand to another, wouldn't be anything she'd soon forget, but she watched nonetheless.

This was justice: the dead deserved recompense.

54

I T ONLY TOOK A FEW MINUTES. AFTERWARD, DAISHA CALLED OUT, "Un-dertaker?"

On the sofa, Rebekkah closed her eyes. Her wound needed tending, but Daisha didn't know how to help the Graveminder. All she knew was that she would do whatever she could so the Graveminder could get medical attention, get well, and survive.

"Let me out of here so we can get her to the doctor." Daisha pointed at the salt line.

Silently, Byron grabbed the container of salt that he'd carried into the living room. He held it poised. "On the count of three. One, two"—he brushed away a salt line—"three."

She ran forward, and he immediately replaced the line before the others could cross.

Byron stared into Daisha's eyes and said, "Rebekkah might forget that you're a monster, but I don't. You're still dead even if you aren't like them," he muttered, motioning toward the kitchen. "You're a killer."

"I am, but she needs to forgive us. It's who she is." Daisha lowered her voice. "And you . . . I don't think you are supposed to forgive."

"I don't really give a fuck about what we're *supposed* to do," he ground out.

She grinned. "Yeah? Me either . . . because I suspect I'm not *sup-posed* to want to help either of you, but I do."

His mouth opened, but he didn't say anything.

"Help her up, Undertaker. We have a few dead folk that need taken to that abyss under your home." Daisha frowned and then walked away. After a quick examination of the mostly barren bathroom, she grabbed a large towel, which she ripped into strips as she walked back to the sofa. She held the improvised bandage out to Byron. "Here."

He said nothing as he accepted it and gently bound Rebekkah's leg. Rebekkah, however, caught Daisha's hand. "Thank you," she said.

To that, Daisha had no words, so she nodded and watched the Undertaker. After a moment, she realized that she was still holding on to the Graveminder's hand and immediately dropped it.

"Will you help me for a few more minutes?" Rebekkah asked.

"Yeah."

"I need to get them to safety before I can do anything else." Rebekkah pointed to the kitchen, where the dead were waiting. They mostly watched Rebekkah the way lions in a zoo watch small children, as if she were a meal they would consume if only they had a chance. The old man was different. He hadn't participated in the attack on Cissy either.

"Bek, you *need* to get to the doctor."

The Graveminder turned her gaze back to her Undertaker. "And I will, after they are taken home."

The two live people stared at each other as if they could bend the other one by sheer will. Daisha opted to save some time. "I can bring one of them over to the salt line," she said.

"No." Byron sighed. "You can't go across the line, and I'm not going to keep opening the barrier. Let's get this over with so we can get you to help. I can go in and grab one."

"You go in, and they'll eat you alive." Daisha glanced at him for a moment, and then she looked at Rebekkah. "I trust you not to trap me if you tell me you won't."

"I won't," Rebekkah promised.

"So he"—Daisha looked at Byron—"can put me in and then I'll bring one over to the wall. There's enough salt to draw new lines. I trust you."

The Undertaker pursed his lips, but Daisha knew her plan made more sense. Byron removed the salt long enough for her to go in. Once she was in the kitchen, she grabbed the dead woman. Byron injected what seemed to be saline into her, and she went limp. While Daisha stood holding the dead woman, Byron walked over to the couch, lifted Rebekkah, and carried her to the doorway.

Cautiously, they removed the now-floating dead woman from the kitchen, and the four of them went to the truck.

Silently, they drove to the funeral home. Once he parked there, Byron carried Rebekkah into the building. The dead woman drifted alongside Rebekkah.

Daisha refused to even enter the place. She waited outside, watching for them to return.

When the Graveminder returned a short while later, she was limping, but she was walking on her own.

"What happened?" Daisha asked.

Byron said nothing, but Rebekkah said calmly, "It's healing."

At that, Daisha decided that it might be better to drop this line of questioning, so she simply nodded and climbed back into the truck. They repeated the process until each of the dead were escorted into the abyss. Each time, Rebekkah's injury seemed to have healed more.

When they returned to the funeral home with the last of the Hungry Dead, Byron went inside. Still holding the last dead man's hand, Rebekkah stayed outside. The Graveminder said nothing, and Daisha wasn't eager to hasten the inevitable moment of confrontation.

Together they stood in the quiet. The rest of the town slept, unaware. They had no idea that Daisha existed, that she'd been murdered by a dead man, that she had taken lives. As she'd been tearing flesh from living bodies, they had looked away.

It could stay that way. If she let me, I could stay here.

Daisha crossed her arms over her chest as if that would stop the shivers that threatened to overwhelm her. She didn't look at Rebekkah—but she didn't vanish either. Rebekkah was exhausted, alone, and trusting.

Like Maylene had been.

"You know you need to go, too," Rebekkah whispered.

Daisha said nothing. In some foolish part of her mind, she'd half hoped that Rebekkah would let her stay or that there would be some solution to her dilemma that the Graveminder knew. It didn't make much sense, but neither did being dead and still walking around.

"If you didn't know it was time, you would've left as I was taking the others. You could've; I know that, but"—Rebekkah gave her a thoroughly exhausted smile—"you waited."

Daisha looked away. "It's not fair. I wanted to *live* and now that I'm *me* . . . I don't want to kill people, but I don't want to die."

Gently, Rebekkah touched Daisha's shoulder. "It's a beautiful world there . . . I wish . . . if I were you, I'm not sure what I'd do, but I know that I want to go there. I want to *stay* there."

It wasn't the words but the hitch in Rebekkah's voice that made Daisha look at her.

Rebekkah offered her a small smile. "I can't stay there yet, but I would if I could. You *can*. There is no time there, no past or present. Every year exists all at once. No food here tastes as good. I don't know why, but I swear to you that what I saw there is not a world to run from."

"I'd be dead," Daisha said.

Rebekkah smiled gently. "You already are."

"I'm afraid." Daisha felt a lot less like a monster when Rebekkah looked at her, but she also didn't want to *end*. The idea of going to Heaven or Hell or wherever that abyss led wasn't comforting.

"I know." Rebekkah stepped up beside her and held out a hand. "I wish you were alive, but I can't do anything about that. I can take you to a world that feels like this world, but where you aren't condemned to eat flesh or blood."

Silently Daisha took Rebekkah's hand, and together they walked downstairs. In the storage room, Byron and the old man stood waiting. A cabinet had been slid back open, and a bright tunnel yawned open in front of them.

Daisha was terrified.

"How do we do this with two of them?" Byron asked.

"Lead us in," Rebekkah said. "I will hold them, and you will lead us."

Daisha's grip on Rebekkah's hand tightened. "If he's not sure, why should we go?"

The smile Rebekkah offered curbed Daisha's unease. "He worries over me. He usually holds my hand when we walk there, but it'll be fine. You are going where you need to go, and"—she glanced back at the Undertaker—"so am I."

She reached out to the old man and took his hand. The man looked confused, but he cooperated.

Rebekkah's gaze took in all three of them as she said, "Trust me."

"I do, but I think we need to trust your Undertaker, too." Daisha released Rebekkah's hand. Then she clasped the old man and the Graveminder's entwined hands, so both she and the dead man were holding on to Rebekkah's hand.

With a relieved sigh, the Undertaker stepped into the tunnel. He lifted a light from the wall, and then he reached back to take the Graveminder's free hand. "Come."

The Graveminder accepted his hand, and together they entered the tunnel.

55

THE VOICES OF THE DEAD WHISPERED COMFORTING WORDS TO REBEK-kah as she walked toward their land. The old man had extended his arm to the side, so Daisha was able to walk between and behind them.

Tomorrow she'll be on to her new . . . life. Is it a life when she's dead?

The words didn't matter, though. What mattered was that things were going to be set to rights. The Hungry Dead were being led to the place where they belonged, and then Rebekkah would look after the graves of the Claysville dead. She would give them words, drink, and food. She would see to their resting places so that they had no need to awaken. Her town was safe.

They stepped from the tunnel into the land of the dead. This time, Charles was there to greet them.

Not us—me.

Byron looked to the side, and Rebekkah surmised that Alicia was waiting as well.

Both the old man and Daisha released her hand. Frantically Rebekkah grasped at Daisha's hand, but the dead girl pulled away. She didn't vanish as Troy had.

"You met her after she was already dead," Charles said. "She's not *your* dead."

Daisha stepped protectively in front of Rebekkah. "Who's the old guy?"

"I am Mr. D, child, and I'll thank you not to call me old." Charles pointed at her with a dark wood cane.

The old man bowed to Rebekkah. "Your escort was appreciated, Miss Barrow." He walked off down the street with a jaunty poise that reminded Rebekkah of the gait of a much younger man.

"What about Daisha?" Rebekkah asked.

With a stern look at the girl standing between them, Charles said, "I suspect she'll be quite fine, but unless I misread the presence of the *elder* Miss Barrow"—he glanced to where, invisible to Rebekkah, Alicia apparently stood—"the girl will be offered a chance to be swept into the unsavory enterprises of those who enjoy frustrating me."

Daisha grinned at something Rebekkah couldn't hear. "Yeah?"

She hugged Rebekkah suddenly, and as she leaned in, she whispered, "Thank you."

Rebekkah didn't let go right away. "You'll be careful?"

"I'll be here when you come. You can check on me if you want," Daisha said.

"Alicia and I have some business to take care of," Byron started. "We can all walk Daisha over and—"

"I need to talk to Charles," Rebekkah interrupted. "He owes me some answers."

"Well then." Charles tucked Rebekkah's hand into the crook of his elbow. With his cane, he pointed to a small wooden building only steps from where they stood. "We'll be at the café."

Byron caught Charles' gaze. "Don't get her shot this time."

Charles didn't look away. "Those gentlemen have come to understand the error of their ways."

Byron looked at Rebekkah, and when she nodded, he walked off with Daisha—and presumably with Alicia, too.

Rebekkah followed Charles across a wood plank walkway, reminiscent of a frontier town. Her footsteps echoed as she walked. "No
swinging doors?"

He quirked a brow at her. "That would be overkill, wouldn't it?"

Without wanting to, she laughed. "You're never caught off
guard, are you?"

Instead of replying, Charles opened the rough planked door and
stepped to the side to let her enter. Inside, there were no people.
Plain tables were arranged haphazardly throughout the room. At
the far end was a small stage with a piano and bench. Thick but
worn deep blue velvet drapes were pulled to the sides in front of the
stage.

Charles pulled out a chair at the table where a very out-of-place
silver tea service waited. Next to it was a tray of sandwiches and
cakes. At either side of the table there were folded linen napkins. Despite the contrast with the surroundings, the tea and food seemed
perfectly right.

And what I need.

The comfort of hiding away in the darkened building was unexpected but undeniable. The urge to weep was less unexpected. Rebekkah couldn't say whether it was exhaustion or sorrow or relief,
but she simply couldn't help herself.

Charles didn't remark on the tears that flowed down her cheeks
as he poured their tea. "You asked about names. When my name
is known, it is soon forgotten. The word doesn't stay long in mortal minds." He leaned back and looked at her. "Not my name, not
the place's name. Knowing it, knowing me, is inevitable. Everyone
'dances with Mr. D,' but some mortals—like you—are already half
in love with death. It is who you are, and I'll not make it harder on
you by telling you things you don't need to know. Ask me again
when you die. Then I'll tell you everything, anything, nothing."

She wondered if it was worth the effort of denying that she was in love with death. Deciding it wasn't, she said only, "I'm not going to get your real name, then?"

"I'm fond of being called Charles." He took her hand.

She didn't pull away. "How much of this did you know? Daisha? Cissy? Maylene's murder? What about Alicia?"

"I know the dead when they slip out of my reach, and when they are in my reach. I knew of Daisha's death and her awakening."

"But Cissy—"

"Wasn't dead. Her actions weren't within my sight." He turned her hand over and peered into her palm as if he could read secrets in it. "I knew of Maylene's death before you did, but that was because I know of deaths, not because it was something I could stop. I loved her, as I love you and as I loved Alicia and the others who've been Graveminders. You're mine." His voice was gentle, but the fervent look in his eyes was unnerving. "You look after my children. You care for them, bring them home where they are safe."

"Your children eat people." She shuddered. Here, with him, her affection for the dead was lessened. Here, she could feel the horror of what they had done.

"Only when they aren't cared for," he pointed out. "You returned them here. Daisha could have gone beyond the town. She was strong enough, but you stopped her."

"So this means you're going to act like I'm some adopted mother to every dead person, like I'm den mommy to the dead?" She stood up and paced away from him.

"I've not had it phrased thus before, but"—he smiled beatifically—"yes, that works well enough as an answer. Graveminders are sacred. Both here and there, you are prized above all others to me, to our many children."

"So the bullets on my first visit were a Mother's Day gift? The lunging, let-me-eat-your-skin thing they do is a hug?" Rebekkah leveled a glare at him. "I don't think so."

"Some children can be unruly, I admit. You'll care for them, though, and I'll do all I can to care for you." He gave her a crooked smile and then held out a small plate with tiny sandwiches on it.

"This is all extremely fucked up," she muttered.

But she reclaimed her seat across from him all the same.

Charles looked content as he lifted a sandwich to his lips.

"What about Alicia?" she asked.

The hand holding the sandwich paused almost imperceptibly before Charles said, "The late Ms. Barrow is a never-ending headache."

"And?"

"And nothing. There's nothing else I'm inclined to say." He took a bite of his sandwich.

56

FOR A BRIEF MOMENT, CHARLES THOUGHT THAT REBEKKAH HAD AC-
cepted his answers, but then she scowled at him. "No."

"No?" he echoed.

"I just sentenced a woman to die because she wanted to be a
Graveminder, but not your 'servant.'" Rebekkah shook her head. "I
didn't sign a contract. I've been playing guess-the-rules, and you are
withholding information. I *deserve* some answers, Charles."

There was nothing that said he had to answer, no rule that he
must reveal his failings, but he hadn't lived for eternity without
learning how to judge people. His Graveminder would be more sympathetic if she knew the truth. For Charles, that was reason enough.

"Once, almost three hundred years ago, a woman, Abigail, came
here. Opened a gate and came to me. A living, vibrant woman had
entered my domain. She really was an incredible woman, my Abigail. Spirited like you." He gave Rebekkah a small smile. "There are
other lands of the dead, but this one was still new."

"Why?"

He waved his hand. "Space issues, mostly. They fill. New ones
appear. I took charge of this one, was honored to, really. I'm not the
only face of Death, my dear, but in some place before memory, I'd
been something else. I know that. Nothingness given shape."

"Oh."

"It makes a man"—he offered her a self-deprecating smile—"eager to prove himself, I suppose. I had my new space, new dead, and I was arrogant. I fell for her. I know it sounds silly, but from nothingness to being a *functionary* being can be dizzying. Abigail beguiled me, and so when she asked to visit the other world, I said yes."

He tried to gauge Rebekkah's response, but she was silent and hard to read, so he continued. "Once the path was opened, others went back, too. Unlike Abigail, they were dead. They ravaged people, nearly decimated the fledgling town—and Abigail began dragging them back here.

"I cannot go there, could not help her in any useful way, so I made an arrangement with the town." He took a deep breath, looked directly at Rebekkah. "I could not remove the gateway, but I could give the town other things, safeguards to help keep the world at large safe, protections so they would think that the change, the gateway, was *their* doing. If they'd known Abigail had been at fault for opening the door, they would've killed her, and then my dead would have overrun them. I had to protect her."

"So you lied," Rebekkah said softly.

"So I made a bargain," he corrected. "If she died, they would all have died. That world—Claysville—would've become an extension of this one eventually." He didn't flinch from Rebekkah's judgment. He simply waited.

"And Abigail?" Rebekkah prompted.

"She found a man, a living man, who protected her."

"The first Undertaker," Rebekkah murmured.

Charles nodded. "They helped make the contract with the town. The consequence of which is that there are new Graveminders and Undertakers who follow in their footsteps."

"Because you made a mistake," she said softly.

"Because I fell in love," he admitted.

57

Rebekkah knew without looking behind her that Byron had entered the room. Charles' pleading expression gave way to a wicked grin. "Being loved like that has an appeal, doesn't it?"

"You know I'll tell him, don't you?" she said.

"Of course." Charles smiled. "But when you're older than dirt, you do learn to take pleasure where pleasure is offered."

"No one's offering." Byron's voice was more exhausted than irritated, though. He pulled over a chair, spun it backward, and straddled it.

With a contented look at the two of them, Charles snapped his fingers. Ward appeared with a dusty bottle of Scotch in one hand and glasses in the other. "Drink?"

Byron nodded, and Ward poured.

"Rebekkah?" Byron asked.

"No thanks." She watched, bemused, as Charles and Byron assessed each other.

"I'll be back to read the contract," Byron said.

"Your sort always are," Charles answered with an odd cadence, as if the conversation were rote.

"I'm not just a sort." Byron picked up his glass.

Charles lifted his glass. "One always hopes."

They both emptied their glasses, and then Charles set his glass down, reached across the table, and took Rebekkah's hand in his. "Until next time, my dear. Please know you are ever welcome."

"I do know that."

"Good." Charles kissed her hand and then stood. He turned his attention to Byron then. "You are welcome to come peruse the contract at your leisure."

Byron tilted his head, but didn't rise. "I'm not ever going to like you, am I?"

With a small shrug, Charles said, "Such is the nature of our roles. I will remind Rebekkah of the world she could rule here, and you"— his expression was briefly pitying—"will do all you can to remind her that life is for the living." He looked then at her. "And we will both try to keep her safe from the dead as she forgets that they are dangerous."

Ward crossed the room and opened the door. Charles followed. "Unlike Alicia, I don't keep a ledger. The Scotch is a gift. No strings."

And then he was gone.

After a quiet moment, Byron stood up. He leaned down and pulled Rebekkah into his arms for a slow kiss, and then said, "Let's go home."

Despite everything she knew, Rebekkah still felt a twinge of loss as she left Charles and the land of the dead. Whether she liked it or not, she *did* belong to both worlds. She had no illusions that Charles was *entirely* trustworthy, but she believed him and she trusted him. *Mostly.*

Rebekkah didn't let go of Byron's hand as he replaced the torch in its wall mount and slid the cabinet across the tunnel. She held on to him as they walked across the storage room and into the hall. He released her hand only long enough to lock the door, and the moment that was done, she took his hand again.

With an easy silence that she'd never known, they ascended the stairs. She accepted his help with her jacket and helmet, and they sped into the night on the Triumph. There was no question as to where they would go—and it occurred to Rebekkah that she'd never seen his apartment, and probably wouldn't see it until he was leaving it. The funeral home was his home now. *Again.* Just as Maylene's house was her home now. *Again.* They were both where they needed to be, where they'd been headed for most of their lives.

Later, she'd tell him about Charles' story, but right now, she wanted to set it all aside. The peace she'd sought was hers. She'd felt it today when she rescued the dead, when she saw Daisha off to her new life, and when she'd seen Cissy go to her just end. This was her life, and Byron was meant to be in it.

He always was.

She enjoyed the connection to him, to her town, as they drove. When he stopped at the house, she got off the bike and took off her helmet. "I love you, you know."

"What?" He stood, holding his helmet.

"I love you," she repeated. "That doesn't mean I'm proposing or offering to have kids. I'm not, but I do love you."

He cupped her cheek with his free hand. His thumb stroked her skin. "Not sure I suggested marriage or kids."

"Good." She smiled. "I figured it's about time I admit the love thing. I'm not sure—"

He kissed her gently before telling her, "I'm not sure I'll ever be ready for kids. This . . . what we are . . . I don't want . . ."

"I know." She thought about the letter Maylene had written, about Cissy's envy, about Ella's death. "Me either."

She took his hand in hers and they went inside. Together they went upstairs and turned out the lights.

REBEKKAH AWOKE AS THE SUN WAS RISING AND MADE HER WAY TO THE FIRST cemetery on her list. She knelt before the stone and planted a small yellow rosebush. Then she brushed the soil from her hands and pulled a small bottle from her bag.

"I'm here now, Maylene," she whispered. She stroked the top of the stone. "Do you remember when we planted our first garden together? Peas, onions, and rhubarb." She paused at the memory, letting the sweetness she remembered fill her. "You, me, and Ella . . . I miss her. I still miss her. And Jimmy. And you . . ."

Rebekkah's tears rolled down her cheeks. There was no way to erase the ache inside of her, but she took comfort in knowing that Maylene had gone on to another life in another world, where she could be with the rest of her family.

She made the rest of her rounds through the cemetery, stopping to clear debris from stones, pour a bit of drink onto soil, and say her words. It was the first of the cemeteries on her daily agenda, but she didn't shortchange any of the residents on her list.

She glanced at the brightening sky and tucked her flask into her satchel when she saw him. His jeans were faded and frayed; the backpack he'd slung over his shoulder looked like it had seen better days; and the stubble on his face made it clear that he'd been in a hurry.

"You're up early," she said when he reached her side.

Byron kissed her, and then said, "Good morning."

"Hi." She wrapped her arms around him and enjoyed being held for a moment. "I figured I'd get to work so we could try going out or . . . I mean, I thought . . ."

He grinned. "So you wanted to free up your evening for me?"

"Yeah." She poked him in the chest. "Don't think that a few rides on the bike or trips to exotic locales with dead folk count as dates. I want the standard stuff, too. Cooking—"

"I planned to cook breakfast, but you weren't there." He didn't add that he panicked when he found her gone, but they'd been down this route enough times that she knew he had.

"I left a note on the table," she said.

He looked sheepish. "Sure. I know—"

"You didn't see it."

"I grabbed a few things and came to find you and . . ." His words faded and he took her hands. "You have a habit of running."

"I *had* a habit of running," she corrected.

"You sure?"

"I am," she admitted. "I love you, and you seem crazy enough to love me back, so . . . if you still want t—"

He silenced her with a kiss.

Being with Byron had always been right, so much so that she'd never been able to consider anyone else for more than a moment, but admitting the truth of this made her feel the familiar ease as well as a less familiar happiness.

"Okay, then"—she stepped back—"let me get back to work."

He frowned. "Is there anything that says I can't come along? Help?"

"No." She stared at him. "You want to spend the day wandering graveyards?"

"Is that where you'll be?"

"Well, yes."

"Unless I get a call, I don't see why I'd need—or *want*—to be anywhere else." He laced his fingers with hers. "I'm not going to go to work with you every day, Bek, but once in a while . . ." He shrugged.

For a moment, Rebekkah paused, bracing herself for the fear of being trapped, the anxiety of too many threads of entanglement, but the usual panic was absent. For the first time since she'd left Claysville, she knew where she belonged.

Here. With Byron. Minding the dead.

EPILOGUE

REBEKKAH OPENED ANOTHER OF THE JOUR-
nals that she'd recovered from Cissy's
house and began to read.

> William tells me he saw Alicia
> again. It's foolish of me to feel envy,
> but I do. Graveminders cannot see
> their own, and I've accepted that.
> As I've come to terms with Charles'
> games, I've realized that some of the
> rules are for our own protection—
> not just his. That doesn't mean I
> like them. Sometimes I weary of
> secrets. I grow weary of feeling so
> alone. It's tempting to go there, to
> stay and let myself slip into that
> world, to let myself see if the vi-
> brancy of the dead remains when I
> too am one of them.
>
> I can't.
>
> Yet I stay here knowing that
> my family has been devastated

by the burden that Alicia passed on to my mother. I stay here knowing that she will not answer my questions if I have William carry them to her. I tried sending a letter. It vanished when she touched the envelope.

Does it get easier? Does knowing that you will pass this one to one you love ever not hurt? I have questions. I do what I do. I'm lived my life for this town, and I do so knowing what I do is for the love of my town and my family—even as I know that it will also destroy them. The child I love best, the one I find strongest, will also be the one I contract.

Sometimes I loathe Charles. I loathe Alicia. I loathe my own mother. Yet I will do as I must, and I will hope that my granddaughter will forgive me.

Rebekkah understood that she could've written that entry, that she could've written so many of the entries in the journals that her grandmother had kept for her. These were the answers that she had been seeking. She was not alone. Even as those who had written these words were gone, they were still here for her in their absence.

Instead of continuing reading the next entry, she turned to the end of the most recent journal and began to write: "Daisha was the first dead girl I met . . ."